PENGUIN

I'm a Gay Wizard

I'm a
Gay
Wizard

V. S. SANTONI

PENGUIN BOOKS

PENGUIN BOOKS

UK | USA | Canada | Ireland | Australia
India | New Zealand | South Africa

Penguin Books is part of the Penguin Random House group of companies
whose addresses can be found at global.penguinrandomhouse.com.

www.penguin.co.uk   www.puffin.co.uk   www.ladybird.co.uk

Published in Great Britain by Penguin Books in association
with Wattpad Books, a division of Wattpad Corp., 2019

001

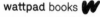

www.wattpad.com

Printed and bound in Great Britain by Clays Ltd, Elcograf S.p.A.

A CIP catalogue record for this book is available from the British Library

ISBN: 978-0-241-43891-6

All correspondence to:
Penguin Books, Penguin Random House Children's
80 Strand, London WC2R 0RL

To Zak,

For always pushing me to make my dreams come true.

For never giving up on me, no matter what.

Excerpt from the Diary of an Unknown Wizard

There's an old story wizards tell around the Institute. Some say they first heard it in the Night Market, that place where all the dream creatures slither around. It goes something like this:

In the beginning, there was the Void. Darkness. But not nothing. No. Nothing is the absence of something, but this darkness wasn't the absence of something. In fact, it had a lot of something in it. The darkness was alive. Maybe the Void was one consciousness, or maybe there's no such thing as oneness in the Void—either way, some of the Void split away and became the immortal Asuras.

Some Asuras were content to exist in the endless nothing, but others longed for more than the Void's cold embrace. They longed to feel love. Even though they'd never known such a feeling, they dreamt of it. Some say their dreams took life, became Everywhen—the dreamworld. Those Asuras fled into Everywhen and, with the Void's influence gone, they changed; they became Devas.

The Void grew jealous, sending its loyal Asuras to destroy the world the Devas had created, but the Devas had planned for such treachery and built another world: this one. Using clockwork they'd forged in Everywhen, they built this world and gave it meaning, purpose. And so, before the Asuras could wipe them out, the Devas fled into this world, continuing on their quest to build a place of infinite love.

But the Void's loyal servants wouldn't let the Devas go in peace—no, they chased them, fought them, hunted them down, even in this world. The war lasted for eons. Some say the Asuras eventually succeeded in their tireless quest to annihilate the Devas, but in doing so, they lost their way back to the Void, and the maze of Everywhen trapped them between our world and the dreamworld. As the story goes, the Asuras came to know our world, their new prison, as Samsara, a cursed land that damned their bodies to an endless cycle of death and rebirth.

Still others in the Night Market insist that a shadow war continues between the Devas and the Asuras, and that wizards are their descendants.

Wild story, huh?

Chapter 1

1 HOUR AFTER EXTRACTION

Rumbling under my head. A stink like rotten raspberries. I cracked open my eyes. The rumbling grew. Was I dreaming? Last thing I remembered, a couple of men in black suits threw me into the back of a van. I wobbled up to my feet. Built into the sides of the van were two metal benches across from each other, with grab handles suspended over them.

My head cleared. My home. My dad. I had to get out of this van. Behind me was a pair of doors. I rushed over, grabbed the handles, and pulled, pulled, pulled. *Oh my god, oh my god, oh my god.* They weren't opening. I battered my fists against them. "Help me! Let me out! What the hell's going on?"

I turned away from the doors. This couldn't be happening. This had to be a dream. I looked down at my knuckles. Bruised. Skinned from battering the door. *Clunk.* The van shook and sent me teetering, wobbling, almost falling. Steadying myself, I searched the van's interior for an escape. Metal floor. Metal walls. Metal roof. Everything completely sealed. I was trapped. Really trapped. This was actually happening, and I couldn't do anything about it. I was going to end up the prisoner in someone's sex dungeon or maybe—maybe they were selling me off to rich cannibals. *What am I going to do?*

I prayed: *Please, please, please make this stop. I'll stop thinking about boys—in fact, I'll do anything, just please, please, please make this stop. I swear, I swear, I'll be good.*

I waited. . . . No miracles for me today. Defeated, I slumped onto a bench and imagined the horrible things that might happen to me. Escape was impossible . . . for now. So, instead, I recalled the events leading up to that moment.

Chapter 2

Alison's basement was so hot and dusty it was like being trapped inside an overheating vacuum cleaner. Twice as smelly too. I wondered whether anyone had worked on the air conditioning system since the house had been built, which was probably sometime in the late nineteenth century. Summer heat waves hit like firestorms, turning the old Victorian's insides into a sauna. It didn't help that Alison's mom and grandma refused to hire a gardener to chop down all the ivy overtaking the spooky-looking thing. I felt like I was being baked inside one of her grandma's greasy cabbage rolls.

I sneezed once. Twice. When my nose stopped tickling, I looked down at the magic book staring up at me. We'd snatched it up in our most recent Candle Creations haul, Alison's favorite witchcraft store. Our trips to Candle Creations consisted of Alison buzzing around like a witchy bee gathering occult nectar and me ogling the hot store clerk.

Smelly incense? Check.

Oddly named candles? Check.

Crystals that promised to absorb evil spirits? Check.

The instructions in the book read, "To cleanse your chakras, imagine the negative energy clogging them as little bits of string and pull them out." A diagram showed where all the chakras were. The little naked man in the drawing had two chakras on his palms, so I tried pulling invisible strings of bad mojo out of my hand.

"This isn't working," I said. "I don't feel anything."

I was getting on Alison's nerves. Nothing bugged her more than when I tried to shake her faith in magic. When she was ten, her mother had bought her a toy magic kit, and Alison made me sit and watch her learn how to pull stuff out of a collapsible hat. I told her magic wasn't real, so she made my shoes "disappear," forcing me to walk home barefoot across the sizzling sidewalk.

"Johnny, the book's legit. Maybe you're doing it wrong."

My name's Juan, but everyone just calls me Johnny. Juan "Johnny" Diaz.

"I've been sitting here literally all day trying to 'cleanse' my chakras."

"Figuratively."

I flipped my black hair to the side. "What?"

"That's not what *literally* means." Alison tossed her long brown hair behind her shoulders. "You mean figuratively."

"Okay, I've"—I air quoted—"'figuratively' been sitting here all day cleaning out my chakras, and I don't feel any better."

She batted her green eyes at me. "Maybe if you paid attention at the store instead of checking out the clerk's ass, you'd know what you were doing."

She was right. The only reason I went to Candle Creations was because I hoped the hot clerk would one day devirginize me. "Shut up!"

"You should just ask him out the next time we go."

"He's, like, twenty-three. Plus . . . he'd just think I'm weird."

She laughed and blocked her face with a big fat grimoire we'd found in the bargain bin. "You're going to be a virgin forever if you don't do something about that pathological awkwardness."

You could say Alison was goth or emo or whatever. She wore way too much black, watched way too many vampire movies, and kept a My Chemical Romance poster enshrined in her locker. Sometimes, she'd twist her Hot Topic rosary around her fingers, slap her hands together, and hail Gerard before planting a big red lipstick smear right on his lips. She had everyone at school convinced she was a Satanist because she wore a *Hail Seitan* pin on her vegan leather jacket. Alison's sense of humor had always been a little more sophisticated than most high school students'. She said it came from being hopelessly trans in a hopelessly cis world.

I guess she rubbed off on me. After my parents got divorced, I stretched my earlobes, put little tunnels in them, and filled my closet with black T-shirts. She even got me listening to a bunch of old punk bands like Against Me! and AFI.

Alison slammed down the book on the floor next to her, keeping it open on the page she'd been reading. With a piece of chalk, she copied a pentacle from the book onto the cement. Then she set down a piece of paper in the middle of the symbol.

"Okay, Johnny," Alison said, "get across from me." I stood up and walked around the chalk image, knowing if I stepped on it, Alison would gouge out my eyes. Reaching the side opposite her, I knelt. "We're going to do this levitation spell by chanting something. The book says what we chant isn't important, so long as it helps us focus on what we're trying to accomplish. The chanting and the pentacle—they're just there to help us imagine the spell. Now, put your hands down around the ring and chant something."

"Like what?"

"I don't know, just something that makes you think about float-ing . . . stuff."

"*Floating stuff?*"

"Johnny."

"Okay, okay . . . floating stuff."

I placed my hands around the ring and closed my eyes. She started chanting in Latin—it sounded like Latin, but it could've been anything, I guess—so I muttered something in pig latin: "Oatflay, aperpay." I focused on making the paper float; imagined it hovering up into the air like a feather and dangling there.

We chanted until my stomach growled. Alison shushed me. I tried focusing on the spell, but little floating hamburgers kept spin-ning around my head. Alison would've killed me if she'd known I was daydreaming about fast food while we were trying to cast a spell, but I didn't believe in magic. Whenever she forced me to sit through Harry Potter movies or Criss Angel videos on YouTube, I'd stare at my phone the whole time, looking at guitar tabs or brows-ing cute guys on Instagram.

Alison gasped. I cracked open an eye. Then I gasped too. The piece of paper was floating in the air right in front us, dangling like it was being held up by an invisible fishing line. Awestruck, we smiled at each other, then slowly turned our gaze back to the paper. We didn't even have to keep chanting. So long as we imagined it floating, it stayed.

"Alison!" her grandma called from upstairs. The piece of paper fell, and Alison threw a tarp over the chalked pentacle so her very

Christian grandma wouldn't see it and ban us from using the basement. She already suspected we were down here worshipping Satan, anyway.

"Coming!" Alison said. She motioned with her head for me to follow. Before I did, I shot one last glance at the tarp, not quite believing what I'd seen.

Chapter 3

48 HOURS UNTIL EXTRACTION

This isn't happening again.

I'm just going to walk in there, tell them all to go to hell, and hope they leave me alone.

Maybe if I pretend I'm someone different, they'll treat me better.

Or, could I just maybe disappear?

Okay, Johnny, let's just get this over with.

That was me suffering through the five stages of grief every morning before school. No, no one died, just my soul. I went to Lincoln Park High School in Chicago.

High school was like a petting zoo, and all the other kids were cute little frolicking goats. Me? I was Black Phillip from that movie, *The Witch*. I had a reputation for being the weird gay kid. It didn't help that my best friend had been burning sage at her locker every morning since the start of sophomore year. That is, until Principal

Welder told her it was against the rules. Alison declared it was against her religious freedom, threatened to go to the ACLU and make it into a big deal, but she never followed through. She lost interest and moved on to using a dowsing crystal to search campus for hidden gravesites.

I was sliding up the handle of my dingy red locker when Spencer Pruitt slammed his hand on the door. "Hey!" he said, putting his face right in mine. Spencer was a tower with a neck like a honey ham. He took out his phone and scrolled through it. "I saw this movie about you on Netflix last night." He chuckled and showed me the screen: *Gayby*. "Is that what they call baby fags when they're born?"

Spencer had started tormenting me in the ninth grade. I didn't even know why. Back in middle school, Spencer was a quiet D&D nerd. Then puberty hit, and he turned into a six-foot-tall gorilla-human hybrid with a thirst for blood.

I tuned him out, fidgeting with my locker until he slammed his hand against it again. "Hey, gayby, I'm talking to you."

"Hey, Spencer!" Alison called from down the hallway. Wedging herself between two sour-faced cheerleaders, she headed for my locker. Once she was beside me, she gave Spencer a curt smile. "You know, for someone with a micropenis, you sure do produce a lot of testosterone. Have you ever thought of submitting yourself to a scientific study?"

"You're both freaks. I should ruin you right here."

Alison flipped him off as he walked away. "That guy is such a troglodyte." She leaned on the locker next to mine. "You see, J, if guys bottle up their gayness for too long, they become Spencer Pruitt."

"What?" I said, finally getting my locker open.

"He's got a huge crush on you. Duh. The only thing he wants to ruin is your—" She looked pointedly down at my butt.

"Gross. What're you even talking about?" I looked over at Spencer, still glaring at me from his group of equally boneheaded friends. "That guy hates my guts."

"Look at how he's staring at you. That's repressed longing. You remind him of what he can't have because of heteronormativity or whatever."

I closed my locker and we headed for homeroom. "Sure, *that's* what it is."

"What, you don't believe me? He's a wrestler, J. It's scientifically proven that's the most homoerotic sport in the world."

During English, Alison texted me memes while I watched the clock *ticktock, ticktock, ticktock*. My neck going slack, I laid my head on the desk and counted every tick. One. Two. Three. When I got bored, I turned my face to the side and stared at the classroom door, imagining a black mist filling the hallways. Some unknown force was invading, so while my classmates cowered, I darted to my feet, the only one fit to stand against the impending evil. The mist seeped in under the door and materialized into a giant talking troll, who then pointed a mechanical claw at me and said, "Johnny, you must be destroyed!" I threw back, "No, *you* must be destroyed!" as a magical sword appeared in my hands, then I charged the fiend, leaping into the air and bringing my blade crashing down on it. My classmates gasped as I—the weird, quiet, and probably gay kid— wowed them with my swordsmanship.

One perilous swing after another, I forced the beast out into the hallway. Students hurried out of their classrooms to investigate the clatter, raising hands to their gaping mouths as I kicked off walls and lockers, smacking my blade against the monster's mechanical arm. Then the bell rang, snapping me out of my daydream. I really needed to stop watching *Scott Pilgrim vs. the World* so much.

My torture continued in P.E. I always wore gym clothes under my regular clothes because I was too embarrassed to get undressed in front of the other guys. I wasn't fat, but I certainly wasn't fit. Just awkward.

Spencer caught me sitting on the bench tying my shoes and clomped over, holding a jockstrap. "Hey, freak," he said, dangling it in front of my face. "You perverts like this stuff, right? You sniff them or something, don't you?" I continued tying my shoes. "C'mon," he insisted. "Don't you want to sniff it, pervert?" He snatched the back of my head and shoved my face into the jockstrap. Surprisingly, it didn't smell like Spencer's balls—close call.

The coach passed by and caught Spencer holding me in a head-lock. "Pruitt!"

Spencer whisked the jockstrap behind his back. I popped up onto my feet and furrowed my eyebrows at him.

"Just messing around with him, Coach," Spencer said.

"Move it along, Pruitt."

Spencer snarled at me and walked away.

The rest of the day passed in more or less the same way, a metaphorical jockstrap-to-the-face kind of day. Because Alison didn't live far away, after school she could walk home, but me—I had to take the bus. Slumping into a squeaky vinyl seat, I hoped the springs poking through would stab me to death. Kids screamed and shot spitballs and slung wads of paper at each other, their whining and screeching—like a swarm of doomsday locusts—a perfect reminder of why I hated my life.

Thirty painful minutes later, the bus dropped me off not far from my house. Our neighborhood used to be middle class, but the crabgrass growing through the cracked sidewalks told the story

of white flight into trendier subdivisions since then. My neighborhood was like a ghost wandering in an urban wasteland.

My dad and I lived alone on a cul-de-sac among a bunch of
other squat little houses whose residents were being shaken down
by the landlord for exorbitant rental fees. I walked in the front
door and found Dad slumped on the couch in front of the television. He leaned forward a little bit and grunted. "Hey there,
kiddo."

"Hey." I slipped my shoes off and stored them on a rack near
the door.

"How'd your day go?"

"Same as always. Yours?"

"I got a gig writing a freelance article for some up-and-coming
music blog."

"Is this like that last up-and-coming music blog that refused to
pay you?"

"Come on, Juanito. You can't be so cynical. You need to have
some faith in people."

"Consider my faith officially spent."

Today's mail was on the entryway table. One of the letters was
from Dad's divorce lawyer. He hadn't even opened it yet.

"Have you talked to Mom?" I asked.

Dad got quiet. He settled back in the recliner, TV images dancing in his lifeless eyes. "No."

"Isn't Mom supposed to come see me this weekend?"

"I don't know. I think she has something to do with that
Michael."

I wasn't surprised. "Have you bought groceries?"

"No."

"Dad, there's nothing to eat in there."

"We'll go get pizza or something."

"Dad, the last time we spent the budget eating out, we had to eat rice and fried eggs for three days."

My dad sat up. "Juanito! Let me be the adult, okay? I've got this. Do you want to go get pizza or not?"

"No. I'm not hungry." I started for the stairway.

"You just going to lock yourself up in that room, Count Dracula?"

"Yes." I hurried upstairs before he could make any more conversation. Once in my room, I shut the door with my back and snatched my headphones off the desk. I slipped them on, scrolled through my phone for my "I Hate Myself" playlist, and crashed face first onto my bed, zoning out as music filled my ears. The late afternoon sunlight came in through the window, orange at first, then, as I lay there, going red, purple, black.

Rolling onto my back, I looked up at the little stars glued to my ceiling. They'd used to glow, but over time, had grown dim. After a while, boredom struck, so I grabbed my phone, Googled some random porn, and slipped my hand into my boxers. I didn't get far before my phone dinged with a text from Alison:

> Hey, loser. Stop playing with your wiener and come to the mall. I'm at the arcade.

Busted.

•

On my way into the arcade, I accidentally crashed into a man wearing a crisp white suit. He grabbed my shoulders to keep me from hitting the floor, then flashed me a big fox-like smile that put me at

ease. The air around him smelled like the pages of an old book—
earthy, warm.

"Sorry," I stammered.

"It's fine," he said. "Sometimes I get caught up in daydreams
too."

I flashed a shaky smile and kept on my way, braving the
sour-smelling underarm stink of the arcade, looking for Alison.
Briefly, I looked back: the smiling man in white was gone, almost
like he'd never been there at all.

Beyond a gaggle of sweaty fighting-game fanatics, I found
Alison playing her favorite zombie shooter. She called it training for
the zombie apocalypse. One eye shut, she lined up the sight of the
plastic gun with a zombie's head.

Boom. The head exploded.

"Another one bites the dust," she said, blowing the plastic barrel
as though it were smoking, then holstering the gun on the cabinet.
"Come on. Kurt and Chloë are waiting for us."

In the food court, we met up with Kurt, a shaggy-haired pot-
head who carried his skateboard everywhere, and his girlfriend,
Chloë, a cybergoth girl with a neon-pink dreadfall. They didn't go
to Lincoln with us—I actually had no idea which school they went
to. As far as I was concerned, they were Alison's mall friends who
didn't like me much. Kurt used to call me a "soft-boy faggot" until
I pierced my ears and started wearing all black. Then he said I was
a poser until he got messed up at a party one time and kissed me.
After that, he never bothered me again because he was scared I'd
tell Chloë.

Gross mall-Chinese food in hand, we sat down at a round table.
Alison and I were sharing a plate. While I prodded a slimy piece of
broccoli with a spork, Alison kept glancing behind her.

"What're you looking at?" Chloë asked.

Alison spun around in her seat. "Nothing."

"She's looking at that table of jocks over there," Kurt said, grinning. He pointed at a table on the other side of the food court, where Spencer and his goons were sitting. Alison was probably looking at Todd Pilkerton, one of Spencer's good friends, a dark-haired guy who also had a neck like a Christmas ham and not much in the brain department. They were accompanied by Matt Bowler and Nick Price, two other jocks who went to our school. Ali had had a crush on Todd back in middle school. They used to be friends—he even came to her twelfth birthday party and spent the night with us—but after she transitioned, things went south. He wasn't really Ali's type, but I think she remembered how he used to be, and she was stuck on that. I chuckled and went back to stabbing the broccoli, pretending it was Spencer's head.

Chloë turned her sights on me. "What's so funny? Who's she looking at?"

"I don't know," I said. Chloë raised an eyebrow at me.

"Come on, Johnny," Kurt said, kicking me under the table.

"Yeah, tell us who it is."

"You guys, quit it," Alison said.

Kurt grabbed my shoulders and shook me. "Dude, come on, who's she looking at?"

Chloë got up on her knees on her seat and leaned across the table toward me. "Tell. Us."

"Come on. Tell us."

Tell us tell us tell us tell us tell us tell us tell us tell us—dammit.

"Todd Pilkerton! Leave me alone!" I said so loud the people at the table next to us gave us dirty looks.

Alison stabbed the toe of her boot into my leg. "Johnny!"

"Ow!" I shrank in my chair and mouthed *Sorry*.

Kurt adjusted his cap and laughed. "What's the big deal? It's just some dumb jock."

"He goes to our school," Alison said, teeth gritted.

"So? Tell him you like him," Chloë said.

Alison shook her head. "No. Oh my god, no."

"Then I'll do it for you!" Chloë rose to her feet and headed to Spencer's table.

"No!" Alison reached for Chloë's arm, but her fingers fell short of catching her sleeve. Alison recoiled like she was watching a nuclear explosion in slow motion.

We held our breath as Chloë walked up to Spencer's table. Her big fuzzy boots and neon-pink hair had Spencer's crew gaping at her like a freshly landed space alien. Chloë hunched over close to Todd and pointed at our table, drawing his attention to us. Alison curled her fingers back, balling her hand into a fist. I shouldn't have opened my big mouth. This was all my fault. When Chloë finished talking, Spencer said something we couldn't hear, and Todd's face went red. Then Spencer, Matt, and Nick exploded into knee-slapping laughter. Todd shot his goons a nasty glare and shut them up, then he scowled at Chloë and said something back to her.

Chloë puffed up like a blowfish, snatched a soda cup off the table, and emptied it on Todd's head. Then we burst into laughter as Chloë launched into invective: "What's wrong with you cis-white-hetero dirtbags! Are you for real, right now? You ought to check yourselves and deconstruct your patriarchal notions of gender."

Everyone in the food court turned to stare as Chloë roared like a neon-maned lion. I watched Alison's body tighten, stiff as a poker, her usually pale skin going two shades lighter. Todd and his friends gaped at Chloë as she swung her neck around and unloaded every bit of social justice vocabulary the internet had taught her. They didn't entertain her tirade long before shooting to their feet.

"We've got to go, Kurt. Tell Chloë we left, okay?" Alison grabbed my arm and yanked me off the seat. We rushed outside and headed around the mall for the bus stop near the Sears entrance. Darkness caped the parking lot on that side of the mall because the ancient lampposts barely worked. People never parked there, so it was kind of sketchy, but it was the closest bus stop. "I'm sorry, Ali," I said.

My words missed her. "I can't believe Chloë did that!" she said, loud enough for the squirrels hiding in the landscaped buffers to hear. "She's so weird. All she ever does is sit online and call everything problematic, like she's supposed to parade me around and fight for me all the time. I can't stand it. I'm, like, this isn't Tumblr, Chloë, no one cares. And she's like blah, blah, blah, social justice—"

"Isn't that good, though? That she stands up for you?"

Alison stopped walking. "Why are you still in the closet, J?"

"I—I don't know," I said, looking at my feet.

"I do. It's because you're scared. Because we don't live in a stupid teen movie where everyone does a musical number when you come out. The world is full of jerks who don't like us for no good reason. Sometimes, you don't want to be the center of attention in a room full of strangers. People like Chloë don't get that. To them, it's all about looking more 'woke' than everybody else."

I tried lightening the mood. "People *should* do musical numbers when you come out."

A red Miata screeched by, power-sliding to a stop in front of us. Todd, Spencer, Matt, and Nick piled out through a pair of suicide doors. Todd slammed his door shut and cracked his knuckles. I grabbed Alison's hand so we could run away, but before we could move, they circled us like a pack of Lacoste-wearing jackals.

"Did you think that shit was funny?" Todd said. "You think trying to embarrass us was a good idea, freak?"

"Chloë was just being a jerk, Todd," Alison said. "We didn't do anything to you."

Todd walked over and sized me up, towering over me. He pressed his hands against my chest, deep and hard, and pushed me down. Pain shot up my back as I slammed onto the ground. When I saw him snatch Alison's shirt collar, I scrambled to my feet, but Nick drove his fist into my stomach, and I fell to my knees, gasping.

Alison's eyebrows shot up when she saw Todd hit me. "Todd, we didn't have anything to do with Chloë being weird. Leave us alone."

"So you like me?" Todd said. "You think I'm cute?"

Alison's body went rigid. She looked away, too embarrassed to keep her eyes on him. Hyena-like, Todd chuckled and gave his friends a quick nod. Then his face soured, and he kicked Alison in the stomach. She screamed and dropped to the ground, her arms wrapped around her midsection, covering the sooty boot print on her shirt.

"Leave her alone!" I yelled, struggling to my feet. I flung myself at Spencer and Nick, but they grabbed me and held me back. "Leave her alone!" I shouted again.

Todd and Matt loomed over Alison, their shadows swallowing her in darkness. "You know, the world would be better off if freaks like you just died!" Todd kicked her in the back. She yelped, twisting her arms around her body and reaching her trembling fingers toward the injury.

I reeled back my arm and slugged Spencer in the mouth. Shoving past Nick, I charged for Alison, but Todd socked me right in the jaw, throwing me off balance. Then Nick wrenched the scruff of my shirt and jerked me back. I thrashed around, trying to free myself from his grip, my shirt tearing. Matt walked up and punched me in the face.

Todd was distracted watching Matt and Nick torture me, so Alison searched the ground frantically until she found her purse spilled over nearby. She reached inside, yanked out her keys, and balled her fist around them so the blades poked out between her fingers. When Todd turned his attention back to her, she stood up and punched him, slicing his cheek. He staggered away with a hand over his cheek as blood dripped onto the concrete. Spencer grabbed Alison's wrist and twisted it until she dropped the keys, then he slung her back to the ground.

Backing away, Spencer glanced from side to side, checking to see if anyone was watching them. Matt and Nick stood over Alison, kicking her as she lay limp on the ground. I choked on phlegm and tears, fighting to get away from Nick. Finally, my shirt ripped, slackening Nick's grasp, so I spun around, dug my nails into his hairy arm, and clamped my teeth down until I tasted blood. He screamed and shoved me off, tossing me like a rag doll against the side of their car and knocking the breath out of me. My knees buckled and gave way.

As I hit the ground, my burning eyes glimpsed monstrous shadows swarming around Alison like vultures circling a carcass, their bloody beaks begging for another bite. I reached a quavering hand toward them, gritted my teeth and closed my hate-filled fingers around them—crushing them—fighting to form words to convey that I hated them, that I wanted them to stop. All that came out was a pitiful grunt.

"You guys, quit it!" Spencer said, his face riddled with fear. When they turned to him, his mouth hung open for a second. "We need to get out of here!"

"Freak!" Todd said before spitting on Alison. "Maybe now you'll start acting like a man."

They hurried back into Todd's car and squealed away, leaving skid marks on the pavement, leaving our blood on the pavement. Lying there, staring up into the lightless void, defeated, I wondered if they'd killed her, and begged god to kill me if they had. If only I could've conjured up a magical sword right then. But I'd only ever been a hero in my dreams. People like us never had power. In the real world, the monsters always won.

I staggered to my feet and limped to Alison's side. Dropping to my knees, I helped her into my arms, wiped a smear of blood off her chin, hugged her—she was breathing, alive. I was grateful. She held me for a minute, not saying anything, just clutching my arms and trembling like a frightened child. Then, she cried.

Chapter 4

We hobbled to the bus stop just as the bus was pulling up. The driver raised an eyebrow when I shouldered Alison onto the bus. I paid our fare and we hurried to the back. Groaning, Alison slumped in the plastic seat near the window, and I eased myself down next to her, pain searing my nerves like a blowtorch. The bus was empty, so the concerned driver kept eyeing us in the rearview mirror.

"Something happen to you kids?" he asked.

Alison cradled her ribs with one arm and sat up. "No."

"Do you need to go to the police or the hospital?"

"No, we'll be fine," she said, ire bubbling up in her voice like groundwater.

"Alison," I whispered, "they almost killed us. We need to go to the cops."

"I don't want to, J!"

I didn't push it.

Luckily, Alison's nosy grandma was already asleep when we crept into her house. I shouldered her all the way up to her room. She collapsed onto her bed. I went into her bathroom and rolled some tissue around my hand, then I sat on the bed next to her, dabbing blood off my nose.

I looked down at the wad of bloody tissue in my hand. "I need to get home."

She grabbed my arm. "Stay."

Limping back into her bathroom, I flipped on the light and gave myself a scan in the mirror. My hair was matted with blood, my lips swollen. The pain in my head was already dying down, though. Maybe it was that extra vitamin C Alison had been telling me to take every morning. I turned on the faucet, splashed my face, then pressed a towel to my skin, hoping to wipe off the dried blood, but the coarse cotton stung. Leaving the bathroom, I texted my dad, told him I was staying over at Ali's, and slumped into bed next to her.

•

I found myself in a darkened hallway in my school. Time moved like molasses, and I heard something ticking. Swaying from side to side, I waded forward and spotted a black cat sitting atop a locker. It hopped down, scratched itself with a hind leg, and sauntered away. Following the cat, I slogged through the syrupy air. It turned its head and looked at me with shining yellow eyes, then behind me, I heard a slimy noise, like churning clay. Spinning around, I saw shadowy pools forming on lockers, floors, ceilings. Black tentacles sprang from the inky blots and reached for whatever they could snatch. Abyssal pools opened up everywhere, closer and closer to me. I ran, but I couldn't escape the shadowy masses. They swallowed everything around me, and when fear conquered my senses, the dark wriggling masses caught my legs, yanked me to the ground and dragged me—my nails scraping across the floor—into the darkness.

•

Alison's phone vibrated on the nightstand next to me. I looked at the time: six o'clock in the morning. She hadn't even stirred. Not feeling like walking into school looking all beat up, I fell back asleep.

A few hours later, I woke up alone. Standing up, I noticed my body wasn't sore anymore. Weird. I walked into the bathroom and studied my face in the mirror. Most of my injuries were gone, except for the cut on my lower lip. How was that even possible? Had I imagined all those bruises and cuts last night?

I headed downstairs and found Alison in the basement, kneeling on the dusty cement, drawing a weird-looking circle on the floor with red chalk. She still had some bruises, but overall, her injuries looked much better today too. Weird.

"Where is everyone?" I asked.

"Mom's been in bed all day, and my grandma's probably at the grocery store."

"What're you going to say when they see you all beat-up?"

"I'll say you knocked over the shelf with all the paint cans onto me because you've always been secretly jealous of me."

"Seriously, Ali?"

"J, could we not talk about this?"

"I'm sorry. About not coming quicker when . . . they were beating us up."

"I'm not some delicate flower, Johnny."

I put my hands on my hips and examined the diagram she was drawing. "What's this thing?"

"I'm copying out a picture from this," Alison said, pointing at a thin book on the floor next to her.

I studied the featureless vellum cover, the parchment pages covered in scribbly handwriting, and imagined some guy in a tricorn hat and frock slashing through pages with his quill in an ink-splattering frenzy.

"Look at the dog-eared page," she said.

On the page, the words *weaver* and *cintamani* next to a complex diagram leaped out at me. Smirking, I asked Alison, "What's a cinta . . . cintamini?"

"*Cintamani*. It's an ancient jewel that grants wishes."

"Seriously?"

"Yes, seriously," she said, sitting back on her heels.

I flipped the book around and scanned the back. "Where'd you even find this thing? Candle Creations?"

"So, this is totally weird: I go out to get some Tylenol, and on my way back from the store, I see this pale lady standing in the middle of road on North Oketo Avenue. Morticia vibes. Anyway, so she motions for me to come over, and I'm like, 'Whoa, creepy, no way,' but I walk up to her anyway, because, you know, what the hell. When I get close, I notice she has—no joke—cat's eyes. Freaking cat's eyes."

"Cat's eyes?"

"Like, big yellow cat's eyes, with slits for pupils."

"Shut up."

"I'm not kidding! When I'm close enough she says, 'This world is full of monsters constantly rewriting the rules for the rest of us.

Why don't you rewrite the rules for a change?' And then she hands me that book and tells me I'll find what I've been looking for inside. I take it from her and start looking at it, and when I look up again, the lady's gone. Like she just disappeared."

I shook my head. "Ali."

"I'm not messing around, J! I have the book, don't I?"

"So what exactly are you looking for?"

"Revenge."

"*Revenge?*"

"Yeah. Did I stutter?"

"Hey, calm down. I'm on your side, remember?"

"This is exactly what I wanted, J. I begged for it all night, and then, *boom*, here it is. We can get revenge on Todd and Spencer and the others. You can help me perform the ritual."

"Ritual?"

"To conjure the cintamani."

"Ali, this sounds so dumb. Okay, you ran into some random crazy woman with special-effects contacts who gave you a book— but magic? Real magic?"

"We made that paper float, didn't we?"

"That was just a weird draft or something."

"If you don't believe it'll work, then why not just help me?"

I kept giving her a funny look, so she rolled her eyes, stood up, snatched the book from me, and continued drawing the diagram.

"Fine," I said. "I'll help you cast the stupid spell. What do I have to do?"

She snatched a knife off the floor, grabbed my wrist, and nicked my palm with the tip of the knife. I gasped and jerked my hand away.

"Alison! What the fu—"

"We need blood to perform the ritual," she said, dripping my blood off the knife and into the circle. Alison knelt again. "Come on, put your hands around the ring." I glared at her, wiped my palm off on my shirt, and knelt across from her. "There's actually an incantation for this spell," Alison said.

"Agnew lee Trev, eonism et hum. Bron mein tug egret thines whi, cintamani. Eggo fifo hum troths, bili sumps tier, beech hes I tee. Mat tenere to: cintamani. Cintamani, cintamani, cintamani."

"I can't say any of that."

"Fine. We'll practice it a few times."

We practiced the incantation until I could almost repeat it. Then we chanted the whole long-winded verse three times with our hands on the floor around the circle.

Though I didn't expect it, I waited for something to happen. Outside, a bird, probably a nightingale, chirped. Alison's white cat, Chairman Meow, scuttled downstairs, rubbed himself against a wooden beam, yawned, and started to clean himself. Her grandmother's footsteps echoed over us. *Clomp, clomp, clomp, clomp.*

"Did it work?" I asked.

"Shh! Concentrate on the spell."

I was about to close my eyes again when black tentacles sprang forth from the circle and whipped around in the air. They whirled faster and faster, spinning into a gloomy tornado, a funnel of darkness that groaned and climbed higher and higher until it exploded into a million shadowy wisps flying in all directions. They swirled over us, then plunged into the ground. Then, everything started shaking . . . a great, horrible shaking, like the earth was yawning open. A roar echoed through the room as the circle glowed crimson. We shot to our feet.

"What the—"

"Hold on to something!" Alison said as dust from the rafters trickled down on top of us. Bracing ourselves against the walls, we glued our eyes to the ceiling, wondering if the main floor would cave in on us. The circle's red light filled the room, and the strange characters Alison had drawn on it danced like strips of paper in the wind, floating above the circle, whisking through the air, then slamming back down, burrowing deep into the earth, disappearing. My blood seeped into the earth, too, the last thing to vanish along with the circle.

The tremor stopped. Silence. Then car alarms. Above us, we heard Alison's grandma issue a great, "Oh my goodness!" so we dashed upstairs to investigate.

Emerging from the basement, we found her grandma braced under the archway leading into the kitchen. "Alison?" she said, turning toward us. She was probably wondering why we weren't at school.

Alison's mom, Cecilia, was hurrying downstairs in her bathrobe and the headwrap she wore to hide the baldness caused by chemotherapy. She looked over the banister at us. "Was that an earthquake?" she asked over the blaring car alarms.

"Sure was," Alison said, bolting out the front door. I followed close behind, finally catching up to her on the sidewalk in front of her house. Panting, I grabbed my knees and leaned over.

Alison's nosy neighbor on her right, Mr. Feffer, was wearing knee socks and short shorts, his belly paunch sticking out like a boil as he ambled about on his phone, eyes fixed toward downtown. He'd parked his push mower in the middle of his lawn and was standing by the white picket fence between Alison's yard and his. To

the left of Alison's house, Mrs. Traynor was walking up her driveway
to the curb, her son half a pace behind her, still holding a brown
paper bag filled with groceries. They, too, were looking in the same
direction as Mr. Feffer, their faces pinched and confused. The wail
of distant sirens joined the ruckus of car alarms.

Nothing looked damaged. Alison's street had always been
pocked from disrepair; there was no sign the earthquake had disturbed it any further.

"Does this mean the spell worked?" Alison said.

I took in a deep breath. "There's no way we—"

Before I could finish, she rushed back inside, and I trailed after
her, catching up just as she turned on the living room TV. Her
mom and grandma inched up behind her. Cecilia wrapped her fingers around Alison's shoulders as they stared at television.

"A state of emergency has been declared for the city of Chicago.
All public transit lines are suspended until further notice," the news
anchor said. "Chicago hasn't experienced any seismic activity since
February 10, 2010, when a quake of magnitude 4.3 rattled north-
ern Illinois." There was no mention of anything strange about the
earthquake. A geologist came on and said the earthquake had been
of low magnitude and that the epicenter was downtown.

Alison pointed at the screen. "That's where the spell went off, J!
Downtown! We've got to go!"

"What on earth are you talking about?" Cecilia said. "Why
aren't you two at school?"

"I'm going home, Ali," I said.

"J, if we conjured that cintamani thing, then it's clearly downtown somewhere."

"We didn't conjure anything. It was just a coincidence. I'm
going to check on my dad."

Cecilia raised her voice. "Alison! What are you doing at home? And how did you get all those bruises?"

Alison got hung up lying about the night before, so I slipped out before she could badger me any further. The buses weren't running, so I had to leg it a few blocks home. Winded from the walk, I found Dad on his phone, pacing in the living room.

"Oh my god, Juanito!" he said, throwing his arms around my neck. He pulled away and put his big hands on my shoulders. His face tightened when he saw my scrapes from the fight with Todd and his goons. "What happened to your face?"

Good thing it didn't look nearly as bad as it had the night before. "I don't feel like talking about it right now, Dad."

"Who did this?"

"Dad."

He hesitated. "You were over at Alison's? Did you skip school today?" When I didn't say anything back, he changed the subject. "How's Cecilia? Is everyone okay over there?"

"Yeah, Dad. Everyone's fine."

He paused and stared at me a minute, then slipped his hands off my shoulders. "I'm glad you're safe."

"Same."

•

That night after I'd gone to sleep, a shiver tiptoed up my back and woke me up. I sat up in bed and searched my room. No one there. After sliding my feet onto the cold floor, I made my way over to the light switch and flipped it. Nothing happened. I flipped it a few more times. *Click. Click.* It wouldn't turn on. Rubbing the sleep from my eyes, I walked out into the hallway and puffed out a cloud of vapor. I hugged myself to stave off the bizarre chill and called for my dad, but when my voice just bounced off the walls and died in the darkness, I headed out to look for him. I peeked inside his bedroom. His patchwork eiderdown was still folded at the foot of the bed. He hadn't slept in his room in months. He was probably downstairs in the recliner, as usual.

As I headed downstairs, dread haunted my every step. Sweat rolled down the back of my neck, followed by a symphony of pinpricks stabbing me all over. Something was wrong. I couldn't put my finger on it, but things were off. Reaching the bottom of the stairs, I looked through the arch into the living room. There, bathed in the pale moonlight shining in through the bay window, a figure in holey jeans and a hoodie loomed over my dad's recliner. "Dad?"

Enveloped in a black halo that flickered like beating moth's wings, the stranger turned, his shoulders quivering, slouching his entire body toward me. A hiss like shifting sand sliced through the air. My feet were glued to the floor, my eyes fixed on the shape's hypnotic movements like a rat caught in a king cobra's trance.

When the figure turned around enough that I could finally make out his face, a gasp slipped from my lips.

Inside the hood, where a person's face should've been, poured a cascade of hissing sand. No eyes. No mouth. Nothing but a falling sheet of dust. At the figure's sides, sandy stumps vaguely shaped like hands seeped into a swirling cloud around its feet. It raised a dis-integrating digit at me, then took a shambling step forward. Then another. And another.

"Dad?" I squeaked. "Dad?" I groped around on the wall behind me until I snagged my finger across the light switch and flipped it on, but the shower of light didn't change anything. The monster was still there, and its twitching, shuddering body was heading right for me. This had to be a dream.

Stumbling back, I hurried to the front door, grabbed the handle, and turned it—locked. The Sandman staggered toward me. I spun the locks, turned the knob again—still, nothing. Fussing with the door was pointless. Turning to flee, I bumped the entryway table and knocked off the planter. It tumbled through the syrupy air and shattered on the floor as I bolted up the stairs, around the banister at the top, and rushed into my room, slamming the door behind me. Every muscle in my body tensed, I eased away and watched the frame. This had to be a dream. I clenched my eyes shut, shook my head, fought to wake up. *Wake up, wake up, wake up*. I cracked open an eye. No change. This wasn't a dream.

Hoping for a way out, I ran over to the window, unlatched it, tried pulling it up. Stuck. It never got stuck. What the hell was going on? I jerked it upward a few more times, but it wouldn't move.

Sand blew into my room through the crack under the door. It flowed and flowed and formed into a satiny pillar that shapeshifted into the Sandman. Then the creature reached out its hands and staggered toward me.

Clawing through the muddy air, I sank to my knees on the bed, and as the world around me rocked like an unsteady boat, I waded into the corner between my bed and the two walls, pressing my back against it and shrinking. Hands raised in front of my face, through my trembling fingers, I watched the monster crawl onto the bed, its sandy limbs casting crooked shadows over me. It stretched out its gritty hands, reaching for me. I pushed back deeper into the corner, clenching my teeth. *Please, please, please, this is a nightmare, let me wake up please, please, please.* The monster broke past my hands and clutched my neck, so I dug my fingers into its wrists and reeled back, pushing away and kicking up the bedsheets with my feet. Then it drove its sandy thumbs into my larynx, bearing down until I couldn't breathe. But the monster wasn't done pressing. It pushed down even harder. Breaking skin. Trying to rip off my head. I wheezed and kicked, the covers bunched in my hands. My skin turned purple and blood trickled under the monster's fingers. I was going to die.

Chapter 5

I heard a crash and woke up from the nightmare. Bolting up, I scanned the room. Through bleary, sleep-worn vision, I saw two large shapes heading toward me. My post-sleep haze delayed my instinct to scream, so I kicked my legs and scooted back against the wall. When my vision cleared, a brown-haired man in a black suit was crawling onto my bed and reaching for me.

"What the hell?" I yelled. "Get away from me! Who are you? What do you want?" He grabbed me and yanked me off the bed, spilling me onto the floor as I kicked and screamed. "Get off me!" Nearby, a second man in a black suit with bright blue eyes waited, ready to back up his friend.

"Dad!" I cried, praying he'd hear my pleas, "Dad! Dad!" He didn't come. Writhing on the floor, I struggled against the brown-haired man's heavy hands. "Let go of me, shit bag!"

He crossed my arms over my chest and drove his fingers into my wrists, pressing down so hard it left bruises. I kicked and kicked, so he put a knee over top one of mine and pushed down. Searing pain shot up and down my leg. Everything hurt so bad that I screamed and screamed.

The picture frames on my floating shelves rumbled in place, then launched themselves at my attackers, their glass frames shattering on impact. Books flew off my shelves, my desk drawers popped open and notebooks and pencils jumped out; everything in my room sprang to life and attacked the two men. Unfortunately, it wasn't enough to stop them. They merely swatted the flying junk away. The blue-eyed man joined the other in pinning me down, scooting down to hold my legs.

"Help! Somebody, help me!" Tears filling my eyes, I wriggled helplessly under their hands. Again, my voice cracked, "Help me, Dad!" I couldn't free myself. Nobody was coming to help me. "What're you doing? Get off me!" With one hand, the man pinning my arms reached into his jacket and drew out a metal canister. After giving the can a quick shake, he sprayed me in the face with something that smelled like rotten raspberries. I sneezed.

My eyes burned, throat went dry, limbs went dead. My body was paralyzed but my mind was racing. The men got off of me, and I tried hurling curses at them, but I couldn't speak. My frightened eyes darted around, finally settling on my fingertips. Homing in on them, I focused hard, tried wriggling them. Nothing. I fought to move my toes. Nothing.

The brown-haired man scooped me up, flung my body over his shoulder, and marched out of my room. As he carried me downstairs, I hovered in and out of consciousness, my arms swinging side to side like dangling cables. When we passed the living room, I saw

Dad sitting in his recliner, eyes fixed to his laptop, perfectly still—
frozen. My dad had always defended me, but now, he couldn't do
anything. We were both powerless.

After lugging me outside, the brown-haired man headed for a
black van. It was daylight. They were kidnapping me in *broad daylight*. Mrs. Areson, our next-door neighbor, was standing behind
her garden fence, frozen as she watered her begonias. Even the
shimmering water droplets spraying out of the hose hung in the air
like someone had paused life.

When the brown-haired man tossed me into the van, everything
went black.

•

The van ground to a halt. Getting up off the bench, I trained my
eyes on the doors, forgetting the pain in my throat, the fear in my
heart. Once those doors were opened, I would run until I couldn't
run anymore. It didn't matter where I went, so long as I got the hell
away.

Swwwwfffffffffff!

A hiss filled the air. Rotten raspberries. They were pumping gas
into the van. My vision grew blurry, my knees wobbly. I fell to the
floor. Then the dark sea of unconsciousness carried me away in its
undertow.

•

I was falling—no, not quite falling. Floating. Like a feather. I was
floating down a well with walls made of ticking clocks—cuckoo
clocks, grandfather clocks, alarm clocks, mantel clocks, too many

clocks to name—all stuck together in big ticking clumps. I tried
to swim over to inspect them, but no matter how hard I stroked
through the air, I didn't move any closer. Before I could reach the
bottom of the shaft, I woke up.

My eyes fluttered open. My head lurched from side to side,
but everything was shrouded in a milky fog. My quick movements
sent shards of pain hurtling through my body. I stopped moving. Focused on my breathing. Waited for the white haze to clear.
Eventually, blurry forms took shape all around me.

I was sitting in a cold metal chair in a plain white room, rows
of glaring lights humming over me. A white door marked one end
of the room, and an observation window spanned the length of
the opposite wall. Springing off the chair, I charged for the door,
slamming against it with a clang. I wrapped my hands around the
door handle and tugged, tugged, tugged—but it wouldn't move, so
I rammed my shoulder against it, but still it didn't budge. Defeated,
I battered the door with my skinned knuckles.

"Let me out of here! Let me out of here!" I screamed until my
throat felt like sandpaper.

"That's enough," said a man's voice behind me. I spun around.
Standing behind the observation window was a man in a gray lab
coat, with tan skin and long white hair. He folded his hands behind
his back.

"What's going on? Who are you? What do you want from me?"
Without answering, the man straightened his back, his piercing
gray eyes sharp as an owl's. "Please, let me out! What'd you do to
my dad?" I said.

"Unfortunately, we can't let you go. I have a lot to explain, so
you'll need to calm down, Juan." He spoke in a slow, measured
tone, his every word precise and deliberate, as if read from a script.

My stomach was twisted like a conch shell, and my heart was pounding in my throat. I wanted to vomit, but I held it down. I took a deep breath. Maybe if I complied, he'd let me go. "Everyone calls me Johnny."

"Very well, Johnny. What I'm about to tell you is going to sound rather fantastic at first. You may not be able to accept it now, but in time, you will come to embrace it. My name is Melchior, and this is the Marduk Institute, a top-secret facility developed almost one hundred years ago. Its sole purpose? To cultivate and train those known as *wizards*."

Wizards? What was he talking about? Any minute now, a white-faced doll with red spirals on its cheeks was going to roll out on a tricycle, ask me if I wanted to play a game, and then lock my head in a death cage. I inched closer to the window, studying Melchior's pristine skin. He was probably in his early thirties, but something about his well-preserved, almost angelic looks made him look even younger.

"What is a wizard?" he continued rhetorically. "All humans are born with latent psychic potential. But few ever develop this potential into abilities such as clairvoyance, telekinesis, psychometry, and so forth. Even fewer ever cultivate these abilities into what we call 'magic.' Less than one percent of the total human population, to be exact. Wizards.

"For those who have newly manifested their powers, the world is fraught with danger. It is also riddled with temptation to use those powers in ways that could harm the natural order of things. For these reasons, we built the Marduk Institute."

"It's a . . . prison for wizards?"

"An elite training facility. You have been given great power, but your new abilities need to be focused, and you need protection during this volatile time. The Institute will help you learn your place in the world."

I didn't know whether my skin was clammy because I was covered in a cold sweat, or because of all the baffling things he was saying. "What about my dad? My mom? My friend Alison?"

"Alison is here."

"And everyone else?"

"To you? Gone. Forever. Any record of your existence will be terminated, and you will be assigned a new identity. Everyone you once knew will forget about you. Any contradictions in memory will be dismissed as irreconcilable cognitive dissonance."

"Irreconcilable what?"

"They'll dismiss it as complete impossibility. Our agents will thoroughly scrub any proof of your existence from the mundane world. Your room in your father's house, your locker at school, your birth records."

The lump in my throat turned into a big, heavy rock. Mom. Dad. My whole life had been ripped away like a Band-Aid. Even more frightening, this was happening because I was a wizard. I had a flood of harrowing realizations: the floating feather, how quickly my wounds had healed after that fight with Todd and his goons, all that stuff floating around my room and hitting my kidnappers. Had that all been magic? Had it been . . . *my* magic?

"Why are you doing this?"

"I've already explained, Johnny. You're special. More special than you fully realize. And that puts not only you at risk, but also those around you." I looked back at the door, considered trying to force it open. "It won't open," Melchior said, like he'd read my mind. "It would be best for you to ask your questions now. I can provide you with the most clarity during this orientation."

"What happens to me now?"

His razor-sharp features were unmoving, like a statue. Just as cold too. "The Marduk Institute is a fully realized micro-community equipped with housing units and various educational buildings. Once you become a legal adult, you'll be thoroughly evaluated, then released on your own recognizance. However, should you choose to take advantage—and we strongly advise that you do—the Institute offers adults a special training program and continued housing."

"So you kidnap people and don't let them go until they're eighteen?"

"Your *extraction* may have seemed severe, but nascent wizards can be quite unpredictable."

"What happens if I try to escape?"

"You are welcome to try, but the Institute is surrounded by miles of wilderness, and the nearest town, Misthaven, is under our control. Furthermore, your miniscule chance of escape would be curtailed by the fact that we could simply follow your aura."

"My *aura?*"

"Consider it your magical signature, the imprint you leave on the living world. Every wizard has one. All around you is the machinery of the *vivit apparatus*, the magical clockwork that governs the laws of this reality. People such as yourself can freely move the machinery, bending the world to your whims. But you leave behind traces of your presence, like fingerprints at a crime scene."

"Vivit apparatus?"

"Close your eyes." Suspiciously, I narrowed my eyes. He raised his hand, his movements fluid, easy. "What I'm about to show you will tap into just a fraction of your true power. Now, close your eyes."

I hesitated. His unflinching gaze was trained on me, so I slowly lowered my eyelids, shutting out Melchior behind the blackness of my closed eyes.

"Imagine the world around you as the inside of a ticking clock, every constituent piece operating in tandem. You can see the pieces that make the clock run. For you, they are as real as the room you are sitting in. When you've visualized the world as it truly is, with the pieces in your mind's eye, open your worldly eyes and look."

I remembered an old cuckoo clock Alison's grandma had hung near the door leading to the basement. We'd accidentally knocked it down one day and found it lying busted at the top of the stairs, its springs spilled everywhere. After gathering up the pieces, we tried hiding it, so her grandma wouldn't find out. But it was impossible to hide anything from her. Once she'd found it, she tore into us for hours.

A golden-orange radiance slipped in through the slits of my eyes. My eyelids slid open, then popped wide. Shock and awe overcame me. With my back against the door, I slid down and hit the ground. All around me, ghostly cogs and wheels danced like the inner workings of a phantasmal clock. The glowing machinery shimmered like chiffon spun from late-noon sunlight. Runes swirled around the pieces, occasionally pulsing a deeper orange.

I worked my way back up to my feet and propped myself against the door so my shaky knees wouldn't give way. As I reached out to touch one of the parts, Melchior said, "I wouldn't do that if I were you."

I stopped my hand. "Why?"

"Because there's no telling what you might change by moving that one piece. You see how everything around you has its own machinery? The floors, the ceiling, the lights? Once you move it, you might change that thing forever."

"You're going to . . . teach me how to use this?"

"No. It's far too dangerous. I am showing you this to make you understand the enormity of your situation."

Pulling back my hand, I dragged a smudge of golden light through the air like paint. Then the light smear broke into flecks, wafted up into the air, and disappeared, so I swished my hand in front of my eyes, dragging the glowing paint everywhere. My every move left streaks in the air that cracked away and disappeared moments later. "What is this stuff?"

"The visual traces of your aura. Everywhere you go, it follows. When you interact with the machinery, your aura leaves behind its stain. The auras of non-magic-users do not leave behind the same markings. When you wish to stop seeing the vivit apparatus, merely blink, and all shall be as it was."

I closed my eyes, and when I opened them again, all the glowing machinery was gone. "Can I do that any time?"

"Yes. Your resident assistant in Veles Hall will give you a more well-rounded introduction. Now, if you don't mind, one of our agents will reenter the room. Please do not fight him. I think you know our recourse will be swift."

The door opened behind me, and one of my kidnappers entered the room. I wanted to lunge at him, gouge out his eyes, and make a run for it, but Melchior's threat kept me from taking any drastic action.

"Come on, Mr. Juan 149," the agent said.

"My name's Johnny Diaz."

"Not anymore, snowflake. You're now officially the 149th Juan we've had at the Institute."

"Call me Johnny."

"Whatever, kid." He stood at the door, waiting for me to exit.

Melchior was already gone; a metal shutter was sliding down soundlessly behind the observation window. I stepped through the door into a white hallway. The agent closed the door behind us. "Stay close, kid. You don't want to get lost down here. Trust me on that one."

Chapter 6

3 HOURS AFTER EXTRACTION

With one hand on my back, the agent led me through a series of white hallways that smelled like antiseptic. Both sides of the metal corridors were lined with closed doors, each with a numbered plaque and a sealed hatch. *Are there people in those cells*, I wondered, *screaming and demanding to be let free, their cries muffled by the oppressively thick metal doors?*

"Where's Alison?" I asked the agent. He didn't respond.

One hallway bled into the next, part of a labyrinthine network of lifeless, sterile corridors. Down one such passage, another agent passed us, ushering a pale boy with white hair in a blue jumpsuit. The pale boy's gray eyes were fixed on the floor as he walked quietly by. His right pinkie finger twitched intermittently. Where had he come from? Why had his hair gone white? And where was the agent taking him? I glanced at my guide, still as stiff and cold as our surroundings. There was no use asking him anything.

He led me to a steel elevator at the end of one hallway. The doors slid open and I went inside. The agent followed suit, turned his back to me, and placed his hand on a biometric scanner. The device flashed green and beeped, then the doors slid shut. I didn't even feel the elevator start moving. Like everywhere else in this place, it was quiet as a crypt. The agent knotted his hands behind himself and tilted his head back, watching the numbers on the digital display climb.

"Who are you?" I asked him.

He kept his back to me. "No one to you."

"Where are we? What's this building?"

"It's called the Heka Building, kid. Now, stop asking so many annoying questions."

My ears popped on our way up. How deep underground had we been? The doors slid open, and I followed the agent into an equally sterile office space full of people working in rows of white cubicles. Looking up, I saw crisscrossing metal beams that narrowed as they rose upward to form a triangular atrium.

Hundreds of fingers stopped their skittering across computer keyboards. Paranoid-looking guys boxed up in suits and ties craned their heads around the sides of their cubicles to get a look at us. Some others were gathered around a water cooler, covering their mouths and whispering as their eyes followed us. What did they do here? I guessed that kidnapping people must involve a lot of paperwork.

We exited through revolving doors. Outside, the sun fired up the paved walkway like a griddle, burning my feet like bacon. My guide didn't seem too concerned with my agony, so I ignored the pain and kept walking. I looked behind at the building we'd just left: a giant black pyramid piercing the blue sky, its shiny glass surface swallowing light, reflecting nothing. Beautiful. Terrifying. Tall pillars lined both sides of the walkway leading away from the building, and perched high atop their capitals, stony geometric faces scowled down through eyes as wary as those of the personnel inside.

"Come on, kid," the agent said, yanking me along.

The walkway eventually fed into a crosswalk. On the other side of the street stood a great lawn that ran the length of several football fields. Buildings lined the field on its western, southern, and eastern sides. When I was twelve, Dad had taken me on a business trip to DC. Every minute he wasn't working we spent walking up and down the National Mall, visiting different Smithsonian museums. We stayed the night at the Hilton near Capitol Hill, an ugly cement block compared to all the beautiful neoclassical architecture surrounding it. That was what the Institute reminded me of: DC, all fancy old buildings next to crude cement blocks.

I'd half expected to see kids casting spells, zooming around on brooms, or talking to elves, but the Institute was nothing like that. The one thing you couldn't miss was the towering thirty-foot wall surrounding the Institute, keeping everything caged in. We crossed the street onto a walking path that ran in front of the great lawn and headed northeast. The street running parallel to the path circled behind every building on campus. We passed through a sparsely filled parking lot and made our way to a three-story rectangular building. A plaque near the entrance read *Veles Hall*.

Across the street from the building stood a traffic gate. Two lanes with boom barriers ran on either side of a security booth. Inside, an agent sat scrolling through his phone. Turnstiles to the right of the gate allowed pedestrians passage onto and off of campus.

My guide jogged up some steps and stopped in front of the building. With one hand on the glass door's handle, he looked over his shoulder at me. "You aren't part of a Lineage, so you'll be staying in the non-Legacy housing."

"Lineage?"

He opened the door. "Some people are born for greatness, kid. The rest of us are just born."

"What's that supposed to mean?" I asked, following him inside. In the checker-tiled entryway was a mounted map of the campus. The key listed the every building in the Institute.

> Allanon Hall: Housing for Students (7–14)
> Ansalom Hall: Library
> Apollo Hall: Housing for the Legacy of the Spires
> Ares Hall: Housing for the Legacy of the Thorns
> Aumar Hall: Care Center for Children (1–6)
> Dedi Hall: Adult Apartments
> Elric Building: Medical Building
> Gwydion Hall: Adult Training Facility
> Heka Building: Research Facility
> Majere Hall: Main Administrative Building
> Odin Hall: High School
> Plutus Hall: Housing for the Legacy of the Coins
> Shipton Hall: Elementary School
> Sparrowhawk Hall: Middle School
> Veles Hall: Housing for Students (15–17)
> Zeus Hall: Housing for the Legacy of the Crowns

Feet propped up, a boy with a short red mohawk and a septum ring sat behind a desk in the entryway. He was so busy flipping through pages in a skating magazine he didn't even notice us walk in. Staring at him with my wizard sight, I startled when I saw the golden halo enveloping him.

"Hey, Blake," the agent said. "Got you a new playmate." Then he turned and left without a parting word.

Blake slid his shoes off the table, sat up straight, and finally looked at me. My eyes followed his hand, watching as his aura painted a gold line through the air. He set aside the magazine—leaving golden fingerprints on the cover—stood up, tall as the Sears Tower, and walked around the desk, his movements lithe. He flashed me a playful smile that shone against his bronze skin and reached for my hand. "Hey, buddy," he said. His grip was gentle. None of that macho stuff. So many guys used handshakes to demonstrate strength. Not Blake. He didn't have anything to prove. "Let me show you your room."

He started down a hallway behind the desk, so I hurried after him. "Veles Hall works on an honor system," he said, "so there's next to no adult supervision. No house parents or anything. Me and the other RAs are expected to keep you guys in line, but we're not going to jam ourselves up your butt or anything." We reached a halfpace staircase. He vaulted up the first few steps, and I followed. "What do you do for fun?" he asked, slowing down so I could catch up.

I'd just been kidnapped, found out I was a wizard, and been told I'd never see my family again, and he wanted to talk about what I did for fun? Pausing midstep, I considered what to say. "I . . . I write poetry," I muttered. "Play guitar. Kind of."

"Sick. We should start a band." Blake resumed walking up the stairs. Start a band? Was he serious? Maybe he was just making small talk. I shook my head and kept following.

He led me down a hallway to my room. He'd just opened the door when a familiar voice called out behind me.

"Johnny!" I spun around and saw Alison in her *Nightmare Before Christmas* pajamas charging for me. She threw her arms around my neck, and I squeezed her tight. "Oh my gosh, J, I was so scared." She clasped my hand and walked into the room with me, shoving Blake out of the way.

He raised a hand. "That's not allowed."

Alison gave Blake a look that could've sunk a battleship. "We're not going to make babies in here." Then she flung the door shut so hard it shook the frame.

My room was the most depressing white box I'd ever seen. More like a cell than a dorm room. It held a metal bed frame with a cheap mattress, and right behind the stiff bed, a half dresser. A single window over a writing desk peered out into the quad. At the other end of the room, an upright closet stood against the wall next to a tiny bathroom. Another door along the same wall led into a walk-in closet.

Alison put her hands on her hips and nodded. "I know, fancy, right?" The open space amplified every sound we made. "They could've at least let us change before they kidnapped us." She checked the bottoms of her feet. "I got dirt all over my feet from walking through the quad." I opened the half dresser by the bed. Inside, a few stacks of black uniforms were lined up in three rows. Inside the closet, I pulled a dangling cord to switch on the light and looked around. On either side of the closet was a rod hanging below a wooden shelf. A polyester backpack sat on one of the shelves. A wire shoe rack was fixed to the wall on the left-hand side. Dress shoes. White gym shoes. Slippers. Sandals. All the bases were covered.

"You think we're really never going to see our families again?" Alison asked me.

I went to the window and stared out between the blinds' plastic slats. My room was toward the back of the building, so I had a view of the great lawn. Directly behind Veles Hall, a trio of neoclassical buildings sat lined up. The road that circled the Institute ran just behind them. People were walking around outside, their bodies enveloped in glowing auras. Squeezing my eyes shut, I willed away the awkward wizard sight. When I opened them again, no one was glowing. I turned back to Alison. "I don't know."

"I'm so glad you're here. I mean, not glad you're going through all this, but—"

"I know what you mean. Same."

"Whatever's going on, you and I have this, okay? If we could survive Lincoln High, we can survive this too."

A knock drew our attention to the door. Alison glared, stomped over, and threw it open. She took a few steps back and crossed her arms as Blake walked in. He was accompanied by a girl with a tousled, raven-black bob and freckles on her nose. She smiled and flung a handful of confetti into the air. "Welcoming committee!"

Alison stared at the girl like she'd grown a second head. I didn't know whether to laugh or scream. Maybe both.

"Hey, you two. This is my friend. She's the other RA. She'll help you get used to things around here too."

She waved and gave us a big, cheery smile. "Hi, I'm Linh Kim Tuyến—I mean, Linh 2. Nice to meet you."

"Are you seriously that happy to be here?" Alison said, wrinkling her face. "Can't you just leave us alone?"

Blake tightened his shoulders. "We're not the ones who extracted you."

"Extracted us? You mean kidnapped?"

"They prefer the term *extracted*," Linh said.

"Yeah? Well, I prefer not being kidnapped," Alison came back at her.

"Look, I'm required to give you guys the rundown of this place," Blake said, his jaw tense.

Alison looked back at me for a reaction. Mind blank, I shrugged. I probably would've had the same reaction if he'd told us to go bounce a ball on I-90. I didn't want a tour. I wanted to go home.

Alison fixed her cobra-like gaze on him. "You're not going to leave us alone until we go along on your prison tour, are you?"

Linh shot us another uneasy smile and slipped away. "If you need me, I'll be in the dining area," she said before heading out the door.

Once Alison and I had put on some slippers, Blake led us downstairs, out a back door, and down a special access ramp onto the great lawn. Not too far off to our right, the menacing Heka Building loomed. As we crunched over the neatly trimmed grass, he said, "You two don't know how lucky you are. I've never heard of two people being extracted from the same city before." So we were outliers. Even in this weird place, we stuck out like two cats in a pack of dogs.

Blake walked us to a stone water fountain with a sculpture of Pan playing his syrinx while a bunch of kids held hands and danced around him. From that position, there was a view of several different buildings. Blake sat at the fountain's edge, Alison sat down next to him, and I sat beside her. "All of the buildings are named after famous wizards," Blake said. "Allanon Hall is the dorm for middle school kids. Aumar Hall's the child care facility for really little kids. Majere Hall's the main administrative building. You can find all the important offices in there. Dedi Hall's the apartment for adults, Ansalom Hall's the library," and he went on and on until I couldn't keep track of all the halls anymore.

"You might have noticed that everything on campus is arranged a certain way," Blake continued. "Buildings are lined up perfectly, most are the same height, everything's equidistant . . . it's called sacred geometry. Those big walls are part of it too." He pointed at the thirty-foot wall surrounding the Institute. "Everything here is part of an array, like a big circle. They use it to detect magic outside the barrier—at least, that's what they tell us—although it's only good for detecting really big magical outbursts, like when someone becomes a wizard. A lot of people can get away with little spells. But when someone becomes a wizard, the circle picks it up as a big blip on their magic radar. Then the agents go out and extract them. Magic is banned on campus—so if you do it, don't get caught—and highly discouraged off campus. If the Institute discovers a wizard using magic off campus, they send out their agents—"

"Those guys remind me of the Smiths from *The Matrix*," Alison said.

"Yeah, they do all kind of look the same, don't they? Anyway, the agents sanction people who use magic off campus. Repeat offenders get hunted down and brought back to the Institute, then they're taken underneath the Heka Building."

"What happens to them?" I asked.

"I don't know. But I don't imagine it's anything good. The north and south gates control all the traffic going in and out of the Institute. Agents with knockout spray are positioned at both, and the turnstiles have metal detectors, so you can't sneak anything into or out of campus."

"Exactly who is in charge here?" Alison asked.

"The Administrators—everyone just calls them Admin—are the highest ruling body, but no one's ever seen them."

"How does anyone know they exist, then?"

"Whispers, mainly. The agents talk among themselves and sometimes we hear them, and word gets around." So the Smiths were the gap in the armor. Eavesdropping on them could reveal all sorts of secrets. I stored that away in the back of my head. "Supposedly, the Admins sometimes come to the Institute, but nobody knows when, not even the agents."

Blake pointed out Elric, the medical building, and four big houses barely visible just behind it. Each of them stood three stories tall, with a red-brick face and gabled dormers along its shingled roof. Pediments above their front entrances depicted different legends: Eirene with baby Plutus on her hip; Zeus reclining and raising a cornucopia; Apollo charging through the sky in his chariot; and Ares poised to attack with a spear in hand. "Those are the Legacy houses, where the Lineage kids stay. Zeus Hall houses the Legacy of the Crowns, Ares Hall houses the Legacy of the Thorns, Plutus Hall houses the Legacy of the Coins, and Apollo Hall houses the Legacy of the Spires."

"You mean Zeus and Ares and Apollo and Plutus were wizards?" Alison asked.

"According to the Institute, yeah. Some of the earliest and most powerful wizards, in fact. That's why they were canonized as gods in the normal world. You'd be surprised how many cultures apotheosized wizards into gods."

"And what're Lineage kids?" I asked.

"Wizards whose parents are also wizards. They get all kinds of special treatment, like getting to stay in those fancy dorms.

"None of the rules really apply to Lineage kids," Blake continued.

"If one of them uses magic on campus, no one really does anything about it. They can come and go as they please, and since they didn't get extracted, they get to keep their last names and stay in touch with their families. They don't go to the same classes we do, and they don't even have to eat lunch with us—they have a special VIP area in Majere Hall. Some of them are really entitled, so just try and ignore them."

Even the magical world was full of bullies.

"Lineage kids are broken up into four groups, called Legacies. The Crowns are the kids of politicians, the Thorns are the kids of military personnel, the Coins are the kids of bankers and Wall Street tycoons, and the Spires are the kids of academic elites. Technically, a non-Lineage kid can try to join a Legacy by rushing it, but most of the time, they don't let anyone in. I think they only do rush week to embarrass people. Legacies are only for high school students, anyway. After graduation, Lineage kids have access to the best colleges in the world, so they don't stick around for the Institute's adult training program."

"What's the adult training program for?" Alison asked.

"Just training more Institute personnel. That's what a lot of non-Lineage wizards end up doing after they graduate: get a job working here in the cafeteria or in one of the offices. A lot become teachers."

How magical.

"So they keep us here as prisoners until we're adults, then find a sneaky way to indenture us afterward," Alison grumbled. Encouraging wizards to work here must make it so much easier for them to keep track of us.

"Curfew's eight o'clock," Blake said. "Students must report to their dorms by eight, and are forbidden from spending the night in each other's dorms."

"Trying to keep the magical teen pregnancies down?" Alison said.

"Something like that. Tomorrow you two need to go to Majere Hall, the main admin building, for your placement test. It's Room 216. The test determines what grade you're in. On your first day of class, they'll give you a box with your books, a laptop, and a phone."

Free housing, food, computers, and phones. The Institute seemed like a dream. Except dreams didn't come with thirty-foot walls. It was like they were trying to placate us so we wouldn't try to escape.

"You can't really use the internet on campus, unfortunately," Blake continued. "Instead, we have the forum—it's a Facebook knockoff that's heavily monitored."

Well, so much for porn.

"Wait," Alison said. "You mean we can't get on YouTube or Twitter or anything?"

He shook his head. "You can join one of the clubs on the forum."

"What if we don't go to the placement test tomorrow? What if we skip the whole thing?"

"I *encourage* you to go. If you don't, they'll come and get you. When you turn eighteen, you can leave. Supposedly the Institute monitors you for the rest of your life."

"What if you shake them off?"

"They'll label you a Defector and hunt you down."

"A Defector?" I asked.

"They're like an anti-Institute terrorist group."

"This place kidnaps people," Alison said. "An anti-this-place group doesn't sound so bad."

"The Institute protects regular people from dangerous wizards.

It also protects us from . . . all kinds of things. Watch what you say, by the way." Blake tapped on his phone. Of course the phones were free—they were bugged. It was pretty clever of the Institute to use phones to spy on us, actually. Who wouldn't jump at the chance to have a new phone?

Alison's outrage boiled over. She stood up in front of Blake. "So this is basically a cushy prison we're trapped in for the rest of our lives? And even if we graduate and leave this hellhole, our options are being watched for the rest of our lives or becoming fugitive Defectors?"

"What do you want me to say? That you've been kidnapped by a top-secret international organization, and from now on, any hope of the freedom you once had is gone?" Blake said.

"A little honesty would be refreshing, yes."

He stood up and met her eyes. "You were kidnapped and brought here because your powers scare a lot of people. You can mope around all you want, or there's the second option: deal with it."

"You think what they're doing to us is okay?"

"This place isn't perfect, but it's better than what's out there. You haven't seen what I've seen. It's really dangerous."

"Oh, great, another knight in shining armor."

"I'm not trying to be a knight in shining anything. I'm just being realistic."

The two of them continued to argue about the Institute and the idea of freedom as though they were standing at invisible lecterns in the middle of a vigorous debate. Blake called the Institute a necessary evil while Alison ranted about the unlawful detention of US citizens, just like in Guantanamo. I tuned them both out. I didn't have the energy to argue. I couldn't decide which was worse:

almost being killed by Todd and his goons or being dragged off to this place.

> *We're lost, adrift on a black lake. Using our oars, we comb the silty lake bottom for hope, but in the sloshing water, we find only bones. Our bones. Our family's bones. Everyone's bones.*

Chapter 7

Things had gone from zero to *Hellraiser* fast, leaving me disoriented and nauseated. I changed into a black shirt and shorts that I found in the nightstand drawer and fought back waves of nausea. When I couldn't stave it off any longer, I lurched into the bathroom and threw up in the toilet until I was red-eyed and snot-faced. Wobbling back into the room, I fell onto the bed and groaned. Eventually, my stomach settled down, but the dread, the fear of this reality becoming the rest of my life, didn't go away.

The Marduk Institute was a secretive micro-community walled off from the outside world. A place where nascent wizards were kept safe from the myriad magical dangers lurking outside its walls. At least, that was what they wanted us to think. You didn't have to dig too deep to realize we were being detained in a magic school that wasn't really a magic school. The whole world had turned its back on us, declared us too dangerous. This was the only place fit for us now.

I considered doing some writing. Back home, I'd throw open my lyrics notebook and jot down everything I was feeling. Alison said I had the heart of a poet. I wasn't really a poet—I just found it easier to talk about things if I wrote them down like a poem or the lyrics of a song. I felt powerless without my notebook. Inside me, new sentences were brewing, new poems. In my heart, a small city was rising from the ground up, its foundations words like *pain*, *alienation*, *loss*, *confusion*, and *fear*.

The top drawer of my half dresser was filled with school supplies, so I snatched a composition notebook and a pen, sat at the desk under the window, and tried writing something. After sitting with my pen poised over the paper for an entire minute, I gave up. Using an unfamiliar notebook felt awkward. Ordinarily, the words would just pour out of me. Now, they were stuck like water in a clogged faucet. Utterly defeated, I fell back on the crunchy plastic encasing my new bed and wished for my old one. My old room. My old life.

Rubbing my face against the coarse sheets, I remembered the one-thousand thread count linens Dad had bought me for my sixteenth birthday. He'd said he couldn't let me invite a boy over unless I had a nice-looking bed. He was always saying awkward crap like that, trying to prove how progressive he was. Sometimes he'd try to fill my room with junk. One day, I caught him suspending paper model airplanes from hooks he'd hammered into the ceiling. Furious, I asked, "What the hell are you doing, Dad?"

"I thought they'd look good in here, Juanito."

"Stop calling me Juanito. And since when have I given a crap about airplanes?"

"You went wild at the National Air and Space Museum."

"I was twelve!"

Right now, I would've given anything to hear my dad call me Juanito, to catch him hanging little planes from my ceiling. I rolled my head to the side and stared at the digital clock on top of the half dresser. It was turned off, so I slumped out of bed and lumbered over to it. Digital clock in hand, I found a wound-up power cord and some instructions taped to the bottom. After unraveling the cord, I slid the dresser a few inches away from the wall so I could plug it in. The clock beeped on, and *00:00* flashed on its display in red numerals. Not knowing the time, I couldn't set it.

I peeped out the door to see if any other students were in the hallway, then stepped outside. Snooping around a bit before heading to Alison's room across the hall seemed like a good idea. For the year before Mom and Dad's marriage fell apart like a lemon sold off a crooked car lot, they'd sent me to Marian Catholic High, a boarding school in Chicago. In some ways, the Institute reminded me of Marian. At least single rooms were an upgrade from the double occupancy rooms back at Marian.

For a building full of teenagers, the hallways were weirdly quiet. The stairwell running through the entire building didn't end at the first floor; a little sign with the words *Laundry Room* pointed down to a sublevel. I didn't bother exploring that. Instead, I headed into a hallway that branched off the entryway and led into the dining area. The room had a smattering of round tables, walls lined with vending machines that sold everything from pies to sandwiches, and a sign on the wall that warned students not to eat in their rooms.

My stomach growled as I walked up to a sandwich machine and rested my forehead on the glass, pining for the rubbery-looking sandwiches inside. At that moment, I could've eaten anything. Unfortunately, I had no way of getting the food out of the machine. A card reader along the side had a yellow strip that read *Slide Student ID*, but I didn't have one yet.

I dragged my fingers down the glass, smudging it. Turning to leave, I bumped into green-eyed boy with short chestnut hair and a golden tan. He dropped a plastic container of cheesecake onto the floor, but luckily it landed flat, sparing the dessert. Embarrassed, I looked up at him. His spoon was dangling from his lips. He gave me a surprised look before breaking into a cute, squinty-eyed smile. It was a perfect semicircle, his smile, like an orange slice.

"Sorry," I mumbled.

"No problem." His voice carried the faint lilt of a Southern accent. He knelt down, the leather arms of his letterman's jacket squeaking as he grabbed the container and stood back up. "You new?" he asked, plunging his spoon back into the cheesecake.

"Yeah. Um, where is everyone?"

"Probably at the caf in Majere Hall. A lot of kids go to dinner about now." My stomach rumbled on cue. I hadn't eaten in hours.

"Oh. What time is it?"

He reached into his pocket, pulled out his phone, and slid his thumb over the screen. "Seven-thirty." He shifted his attention back to me. I could feel my face starting to flush, so I whipped around before he noticed, and just as he asked, "What's your name?" I was already headed back upstairs. Damn it. I'd only just arrived and already I'd embarrassed myself.

Back in my room, I set the digital clock. Out the window, I spotted Linh creeping out into the quad. She looked around nervously before skating off into the darkness. Maybe she was off to Majere for dinner too. I worried a zit on my forehead as I thought of Dad sitting at home, his vacant eyes pasted to his laptop. Had he really forgotten I'd ever existed? What lies had the Institute put in his head? How could they just *erase* us?

From the bed, I stared up at the ceiling, focusing on one of the holes in the ceiling tile, sinking into that void staring back at me. In that cold, wet darkness, dread lurked, slithering around in the inky blackness, waiting for me to close my eyes so it could snap me down, choke me out.

"You'll lose yourself in there if you aren't careful," said a voice beside me.

I bolted up and looked around. No one was there. "Hello?"

Something squeaked from the half dresser. The digital clock. "That was me."

The digital clock was talking to me.

"What the hell? How . . ."

"You're hallucinating from hunger."

My stomach growled again. The weird thing must be right. Studying the clock, I wondered how long it'd been here, what it'd seen. "Who stayed in here before me?"

"Another boy, just like you."

"What happened to him?" I asked, wondering if he was still here at the Institute, working.

"He went mad and bit off his own tongue."

"What?"

A knock at the door startled me. I shook my head and went to open it. Alison slipped in with a few plastic containers filled with sandwiches. I almost kissed her, I was so happy to see food. "Were you talking to someone?" she asked, handing me a sandwich and plopping onto my bed.

Popping open the plastic container, I glanced at the alarm clock. "No. How'd you get these?"

"There's a temporary ID in your top drawer. I used mine to get some food and brought you one just in case."

"Just in case what?"

"Just in case you were so busy pacing up here you forgot to eat."

Annoyed that I'd triggered her big-sister instinct, I changed the subject. "What've you been up to?"

"Just trying to get used to everything."

"What did you think about all that stuff Blake said?"

"Who cares what he thinks. He couldn't be more in love with this creepy place."

"Do you think they really have the ability to erase us?"

"I don't know. Maybe. Or maybe it's just a lie so we won't try to escape. Maybe the whole thing is a cover story."

"What do you mean?"

"I watched this old documentary on Netflix one time about reptilian aliens, and how some humans are genetically linked to them, so the lizard aliens kidnap them."

"You watch way too many dumb conspiracy movies."

"Look, either way, we can't just stay here. My mom's sick."

"Yeah. And my dad's alone and depressed."

"We can't just bust out, though. Those guys in the suits aren't messing around. And that Melchior guy gave me bad vibes. We'll start snooping around once we're settled. Maybe we'll find some Defectors who can help us or something."

"I saw this kid with white hair and a blue jumpsuit under the Heka Building. One of the Smiths was guiding him around like he was a prisoner. He had this weird look on his face, like he was hypnotized or something."

"This place is supercreepy, lizard people or not."

A scream pierced the air. We set down our food, hurried to the door, and cracked it open just in time to glimpse two Smiths wrestling a boy out of his room.

"No!" the boy screamed, legs kicking and arms flailing. "I'm not a Defector! I swear! Please don't take me to the Heka Building!"

A Smith with curly hair had the boy's arms locked in a nelson hold while the other, who had a short ponytail, was struggling to grab his legs. The boy kicked the ponytailed Smith in the mouth and managed to wriggle free of the curly-haired one. He bolted down the hallway away from them, but the curly-haired Smith vanished and reappeared in front of him. The boy's fear-stricken face went white, his jaw dropping. The Smith drew a canister out of his jacket and sprayed the kid in the face. With a wild gasp, he clutched his throat and spun around, hacking and wheezing until he was unconscious. Then the Smiths picked him up and carried him away.

Chapter 8

1 DAY AFTER EXTRACTION

A hissing sound shook me awake. Sitting up, I looked around. The sound was coming from outside my room, so I crept out of bed and inched to the door, the hissing growing with every step. When I reached for the doorknob, sand started seeping in under the sill and pouring in around the sides and the top of the door. Backing away, I watched the sand spread across the floor, flooding the room. First, it gathered around my feet, then to my ankles, piling up. The window shattered, sand surged in through it, and amid the chaos, the word *cintamani* whipped through the air.

Heart pounding in my throat, I jumped awake and scanned the room. No sand on the floor. No sand coming in through the window. It'd all been a dream. Once my fear subsided, I stood up and took a few breaths before opening the drawer of my nightstand and staring down at the uniforms tucked inside. White shirt. Black tie.

Black blazer. Black trousers. At least it was mostly black. I hurried to get dressed.

There was a knock at my door. I answered it and found Alison standing there, adjusting her tie. "You ready?"

We left for the administrative building, Majere Hall, another stark cement block with rows of blacked-out windows facing the quad, watching us, studying us. All the buildings had their eyes on us, especially that big black pyramid at the other end of campus, the Heka Building.

"Did you have any weird dreams, Ali?" I asked.

"I had a nightmare last night that I was kidnapped . . ." She paused for drama. "Oh, wait." I didn't press it. Nightmares were probably common for freshly extracted people.

Majere Hall was northwest of the Pan fountain, squeezed between Veles Hall and Allanon Hall. The building stood at three stories, as tall as Veles Hall, but nowhere near as big. Outside its revolving doors, a brass plaque read *Administrative Offices of the Bureau of Marduk Institute Affairs*. Majere was split into three wings: to the left of the entryway was a commissary where students could use their ID to buy different things, to the right was the office of student affairs, and directly in front of us was a towering reception desk with a finnicky-looking woman sticking different-colored Post-its onto a bulletin board in her work area. I glanced at one of the Post-its as we approached the desk.

> ~~Water the ficus~~
> Don't water the ficus, it's not real
> Google ficus
> Ficus is a fig tree
> Buy Fig Newtons

"Hey," Alison said.

The receptionist jumped, then smiled at us. "Hey there, kids. Are you new?"

"We need to take our placement test."

The receptionist perked up like talking to us was a welcome reprieve from the boredom. Newcomers must be rare around here.

"Okay, so you're going to want to go to the second floor. You can take the elevator there, the glass one. Once you're on the second floor, you're going to take a right past Room 208—it's closed for renovation—and you're going to head past the conference room—it's marked 212 right outside the door. Go down the hallway, past the bathrooms—not the bathrooms near the student lounge, but the bathrooms near Room 218. That room's closed up now too—bug problem. Then take a left past the big potted plant—not the palm-tree-looking one, but the one that looks like a big bush, the one with spiky leaves, not round ones—and it should be right there on your right: Room 220."

Her directions were as confusing as a snowstorm in July. When she was done talking, we smiled at her and left without saying anything else. Alison gave me a *what the hell was that* look, and I shrugged. We walked into a hallway to the left of the reception desk and called down one of the elevators.

We rode up to the second floor. All the floors above the first circled the perimeter of a cafeteria on the ground level. Looking down, I could see counters serving everything from burgers to sushi skirting the room. Students were gathered in lines at the different counters and sitting at round tables in the middle of the cafeteria.

"You think the food is any good?"

Alison leaned over the railing, staring at the sushi counter. "I'll reserve my judgment until I've tried the prison food, but I don't have very high hopes."

We got lost and had to stop a bunch of janitors, students, and personnel for help before we found Room 220. It looked nothing like what I'd have imagined a magic school's classrooms to look like; it was nothing special, all gray terrazzo floors and red plastic chairs with the attached desks. The proctor, a balding, middle-aged man in a brown cardigan, sat behind a pedestal desk reading *Through the Looking-Glass*. We were the only students there.

I trembled my pencil over the bubbles on the answer sheet, swallowing big gulps of fear.

Which word is derived from the name of a German physician who used hypnotism on patients in the late eighteenth century?

- ○ Chauvinism
- ○ Mesmerism
- ○ Dadaism
- ○ Humanism

I wanted to write in *screw you* and leave. Enough was enough. Gripping my pencil, I stood up and charged to the front of the room, yanked the proctor out of his seat, got behind him, and held the point of my pencil to his throat. This was it. This was my chance. I didn't care how long I'd have to hold that teacher hostage; I was getting out of this place. "What're you doing?" he said fearfully as I twisted his arms behind his back.

"Shut up!" I pressed the pencil tip to his throat.

Alison got to her feet slowly. "Johnny?"

"We're taking him hostage, Alison. They wouldn't let one of their teachers die, would they?"

"Actually," Melchior said, materializing at the far end of the room, "we really don't care what happens to individual teachers."

"Melchior!" the proctor yelped, sweat beads crawling down his forehead.

"Please," Melchior continued, gesturing to the teacher with his hand, "go ahead."

"You don't believe me?" I gritted my teeth. "I'll stab him!" Melchior gave me a blank look. He wasn't buying it. Soon, the Smiths would pop up, spray me, and drag my ass under the Heka Building.

Alison cleared her throat, ejecting me from my daydream. Of course they wouldn't give a crap if a teacher were held hostage. Things would play out exactly as I imagined.

Alison was handing in her test already. She glanced at me as she walked out. She always finished tests before me.

Rushing through it, I filled in random circles, hoping I wouldn't end up in a kindergarten class, and when I was done, I handed my test to the proctor. He told me I'd have my results and school schedule by the end of the day.

Outside the classroom, I found Alison sitting on a bench. She stood up when she saw me. "Let's get our IDs. Then I've got to go to the medical building. I don't have any of my medications here."

"Were they weird about it?"

"No. One of those Smiths just came by my room and said I had to go to the medical center for my 'special situation.'"

"Being the victim of a top-secret wizard kidnapping scheme?"

She smirked in response.

In the office of student affairs, a sort of toad-like receptionist was scanning a *Southern Living* magazine. Alison rested her arms on the counter. "We need student IDs."

The lady set aside her magazine, adjusted her little glasses, and studied us with beady eyes. In a melancholy voice she said, "Can I have your temporary IDs, please?" She typed the information on our temporary IDs into her computer, took our pictures, printed off our new ID cards, and slipped them into a couple of holders on lanyards. "Keep these on you at all times, and the agents won't bother you," she said, handing them over. "Most kids just hang them around their belts. The card has an annual limit of two-hundred-and-fifty dollars per student that can be used in the commissary to purchase supplies. If you get a job with the Institute, your payments will be loaded onto your ID, and the card will double as a debit card."

Slipping the lanyards around our necks, we left the office. We headed over to the commissary before leaving Majere. The store was filled with the kind of junk you'd find at any school commissary: books, stationery, cards, a wall full of refrigerated name-brand drinks and candy. I scanned the toiletries and snatched up some cologne and hair gel. Alison had formed a makeshift basket with the bottom half of her shirt to hold her candy and soft drinks. She emptied everything out onto the counter. The employee behind the counter gave her flat look. "Will that be all?"

"Two-hundred-fifty bucks is hardly anything," Alison remarked. "If they're going to kidnap us, they could at least up the yearly spending limit." The employee didn't respond. She rang in the items, asked Alison to scan her card, then repeated the process with me. Our mini haul in tow, we headed for the medical building.

•

The Elric Building towered at nine stories high, the tallest building on the grounds. Like a giant gnomon, its massive shadow followed the sun's movements, sweeping over everything on campus.

After whirling through a pair of revolving doors, we spoke to another overly talkative receptionist and ended up in a waiting room, sitting in uncomfortable vinyl-backed chairs. Cold air blew through vents perched high on the walls, circulating a stomach-turning antiseptic stench. Alison reclined in her chair and browsed a *Teen Vogue* magazine. After a while, feeling thirsty, I went in search of a water fountain and found one in a hallway outside.

Before heading back, I spotted a couple of Smiths standing around the corner talking, so I decided to eavesdrop on them. I crept behind a wall and listened.

"The Institute's on high alert," said a tall Smith with brown hair. "Heard the higher-ups say Defectors may have infiltrated the campus."

The other Smith, shorter with a square jaw, said, "That's nothing new."

"It's different this time. They found some kid using the forum to send messages to a Defector in Misthaven."

"Dumb kid. Did they find the Defector the kid was talking to?"

"Nope. I also heard old man Bal say that a couple of kids they just extracted have something to do with it. Apparently they cast some weird spell, got the Defectors in Chicago scuttling around. Bal says the kids are under observation while we try to figure out what they did."

"Lineage kids?" the shorter one said.

He shook his head. "The old man and Melchior don't even talk anymore, not since Gaspar left. They don't trust each other or something, so who knows what's really going on."

"Yeah. A couple of our guys went missing looking for Gaspar a while back."

"You think he joined up with the Defectors?"

"Maybe. But why?"

"I don't know. It's not like they tell *us* anything about this place. I thought it'd be different if I was working here. Thought things would get less mysterious. But that's not the case."

Who was old man Bal? Gaspar? And why were they at odds with Melchior?

Alison stepped into the hallway then, drawing the attention of the Smiths. They spotted me lurking behind the corner, narrowed their eyes, and left.

Alison shook her prescription bag at me. "Got 'em. We can go."

We headed out of the medical building.

"Ali," I whispered, "those Smiths were talking about us. They said Defectors have infiltrated the Institute, and it's got something to do with that spell we cast."

"The cintamani spell?"

I nodded. "And apparently we're under observation until they learn more about what we did."

"Under observation? Why not just ask us?"

"I don't know. I couldn't understand a lot of it. They said that kid they dragged out last night was talking to a Defector in Misthaven."

"So there *are* Defectors on campus."

"And in that town too. They also mentioned some guy named old man Bal, and another guy called Gaspar. Supposedly, Melchior doesn't trust them or something. And one of them may have even joined the Defectors."

"We need to find these Defectors on campus."

"I don't know. You saw what they did to that one kid, Ali."

"We're not getting caught, J."

Chapter 9

1 DAY AFTER EXTRACTION

Alison paced around her room, tossing around more conspiracy theories while I sat back on her bed. Eventually she'd moderate and we could figure out some more practical explanations; then again, being locked up in a top-secret wizard prison eschewed practical explanation. Around eight that night, Blake knocked on the door with our placement test results and schedules. He handed them over to Alison.

Before she could slam the door in his face, he rested his hand on the doorframe. "Hey, can I come in for a minute?"

She eyeballed him like a pit bull in a dog fight before stepping aside and letting him in, then she folded her arms over her chest and stared. "What?"

"I just wondered if you might want to hang out sometime. There's a coffee shop in Majere Hall. We could go get a drink, and you could read me some poetry or whatever," Blake said.

Alison was eyeing him warily. She hadn't much trusted guys even before Todd and his goons beat the crap out of us. She'd once met a guy online who went ballistic when he found out she was trans. The guy had accused her of trying to "trick" him, left her crying for almost a week over the whole thing.

She shrugged, acting cool. "Whatever. Okay."

"Sounds good," Blake said with a smile. He started for the door, but Alison stopped him.

"Hey, Blake, can I ask you something?"

He looked glad she was holding him up. "Sure, I mean, of course. What?"

"Who're old man Bal and Gaspar?"

"Old man Bal's the nickname the agents use for Balthasar. He and Melchior are the head scientists. I've heard there used to be a third one, but no one knows what happened to him. I don't know who Gaspar is."

"Scientists?" I interjected. "What do they research?"

"Stuff to do with magic. There's a rumor they experiment on wizards here. Why're you asking?"

Alison played him off with a cute smile. "No reason."

Blake swaggered back to the door and flashed her another of his effortlessly charming grins. "You two have a good night."

Alison watched the doorway for a moment after he left, like she was imagining him still standing there.

"Ali," I said, drawing her attention. "What's up with you?"

"Nothing." She crawled onto the bed next to me and set our schedules down side by side:

Student Schedule Card			
Marduk Institute			
Name 149, Juan		Homeroom 126	
		Locker No. 248	

Class	Time	Teacher	Room Number
Homeroom	7:05 a.m.-7:20 a.m.	Sharma	126
Math	7.30 a.m.-8:20 a.m.	Happ	103
P.E.	8:30 a.m.-9:20 a.m.	Masterson	120
Parapsychological Investigations	9:30 a.m.-10:20 a.m.	Bigsby	205
Chemistry	10:30 a.m.-11:20 a.m.	Schmendrick	210
Lunch Break			
Occult History	12:30 p.m.-1:20 p.m.	Trude	310
English	1:30 p.m.-2:20 p.m.	Gray	212
French	2:30 p.m.-3:20 p.m.	Brown	109

It was just regular school with some weird electives. Alison and I didn't even have any classes together. Alison set aside the schedules, grabbed a pillow, and rolled onto her stomach. "Do you think he just wants to hang out with me because he's a spy?"

"You think he's a spy?"

"Of course I do."

"Why're you asking me, then?"

Her face went red, maybe from anger, maybe from embarrassment. "I don't know." She thought Blake was cute, I could tell. But after what Todd had done, I could also tell she was feeling really confused. Trusting Blake would mean possibly putting herself in harm's way again, and understandably, Alison didn't feel like unpacking any of that right now. "Look, let's just focus on getting out of here, okay?"

Chapter 10

Sand. Hissing. Nearer. Nearer. My eyes popped open. The perforated ceiling loomed over me, each hole staring down like a menacing eye. I was still trapped in the Institute. A knock at my door had me up and out of bed. Outside, I found a package sitting on the floor, so I brought it into my room and set it on the desk. Sliding a fingernail along the taped sides of the box, I opened the lid. It was full of sand. A giant mound of sand. Again, the hiss of falling sand sounded in my ears. I looked up and all around me, searching for the noise's source, but as quick as it came, the sound vanished. The sand inside the box disappeared too. I rubbed the remaining sleep out of my eyes. This place was messing with me.

Looking inside the box again, I found six books, a laptop, a phone, a locker ticket. I spread the books out on my desk and scanned their covers. *The Hidden History of Will Working. Everywhen and Other Mysteries.* I shook my head.

Alison showed up half an hour later. We were both quiet for a minute, trying to come up with an appropriate comment for our situation.

"This is weird," Alison said.

"Maybe it'll seem more normal once we're in class."

"Doubt it." We started down the steps to the lobby, our voices echoing in the stairwell. "Do you think it'll be like our old school?" she asked me.

"You mean do I think people are going to be jerks? Yes."

She sighed. "Hell is other people." My stomach growled. Alison glanced at me. "Have you eaten?"

"No."

"Let's go to that dining area downstairs and grab something before class."

The dining area was full of students sipping coffee and nibbling on donuts. Curious eyes followed Alison and me as we walked in. They were probably waiting to barrage us with questions. We hurried to one of the vending machines, swiped our cards, and withdrew a couple of plastic boxes with bagels in them. Alison locked her arm around mine and pulled me out of there. I bit into my bagel as we walked out of Veles Hall and into the quad.

"Gross," I said, mouth filled with styrofoamy bread.

Alison popped open her box, tore off a corner of the bagel, and tasted it. "It's like one of those memory foam pillows."

"I think a pillow would taste better. I had another weird dream last night. Then this morning, I opened that school package and I swear it was full of sand."

"I've had a few nightmares too. We'll probably have weird dreams for a while," she said.

I thought about bringing up the nightmare I'd had the night before I was extracted, but I didn't want to bother Alison with my dreams. They'd probably go away eventually.

It took us forever to get across the quad. When we finally did, we stopped to gape at the exterior of Odin Hall. It was a towering three-story structure built on a platform of steps leading up to a portico with Corinthian columns. On the pediment was a relief sculpture of Odin riding his eight-legged horse, Sleipnir.

We hurried up the steps into the front hallway. There were several rows of metal detectors, each manned by an agent waving students through.

Alison and I got in line and waited.

"It's not nearly as fancy inside as it is outside," Alison said. "It looks like our old school." I nodded. "You're your usual talkative self, I see," she said.

Beyond the metal detectors, the main hall branched off in two directions that circled and weaved through the building like vines. We walked straight ahead, then right, then left, then around and around, passing all manner of jabbering students standing at cheaply painted lockers, and then we found ourselves back at the entrance.

"This place is a maze. Let's go the other way this time."

We took the right branching path and again found ourselves tunneling through a warren of bustling students, going round and round like a carousel. We traveled through the building for almost thirty minutes in the quest for our lockers. We eventually found Alison's locker near some science labs. "My homeroom's in one of those labs," she said.

"I've got to go, Ali," I said. "I haven't found my homeroom yet, or even my locker." I hurried to the other side of the building, found Room 126 across from a pair of bathrooms and a water fountain, and dropped into my seat, exhausted, just as the bell rang.

Our homeroom teacher came in looking flustered, like she'd been rushing to get here too. She had big, curly hair and a sizeable pair of Coke-bottle glasses that made her look like a scuba diver. She pushed back her hair with her pinkies and took a deep breath. Some of the students giggled at her, so she smiled at them to play down how winded she was.

"Well, hello there," she said when she spotted me, her face one big grin. Everyone turned and gawked. I melted into my chair. "New students are rare. Please, go ahead and introduce yourself. I'm Professor Sharma."

"My name's Johnny," I mumbled.

"What's that? Please, stand up and introduce yourself."

I stood up, looking away from the sea of curious eyes, and said, "My name's Johnny."

"Welcome to your first day of classes, Johnny. Please, everyone, say hello to Johnny."

A chorus of unenthusiastic hellos murmured through the room. After the teacher took attendance, we sat through some girl robotically reading announcements: "All students participating in the sports program in Misthaven are to be dressed and at the bus stop no later than two-thirty p.m. A message board has been posted on the forum listing the various fun and educational Legacy and non-Legacy programs offered to students at the Marduk Institute . . ."

The hissing sound of pouring sand swept past my ears. I quickly scanned the room. Kids chattering. Teacher checking her teeth in a compact. The bell rang, and everyone started leaving. Heading for the door, I gave the room one last careful glance. I must've been imagining things.

When I finally found the lecture hall for my first class, I hurried in, but before I could reach an empty seat, the gods decided on a bit of mischief. The bottom of my backpack gave out, releasing my books onto the floor behind me. I knew what had happened without even looking back; the commotion was self-explanatory. My head fell to my chest like there was a loose hinge in my neck. I spun around and looked down. My eyes swam at the sight of my scattered things—a metaphor for my life, really, one big mess. Sighing, I threw up my hands and knelt down to gather everything back up.

"You need some help?" came a familiar voice from above.

Looking up, I saw the green-eyed jock I'd met two nights ago. He swept his chestnut hair aside and smiled at me, waiting for a response, but I just gawped at him like a bird.

"Here, I'll help you anyway" he said, taking a knee beside me. He grabbed a book off the floor and handed it to me. "Hey, haven't we met? The other night, in Veles Hall." Unable to think of anything to say, I stacked my books in an awkward teetering pile. He checked out my busted bag. "Guess you'll need to carry them until you get a new backpack."

"I couldn't find my locker."

"You want me to help you find it after class?"

I looked away from my book pile long enough to dive into his emerald-lake eyes. "Yeah, okay." *What the hell did I just say?*

He smiled at me again, stood up, and walked away. I held tight to my books and fell into the nearest desk, hoping no one had seen my flashy display of awkwardness.

In my seat, I glanced around. A walkway split the room down the middle, each side with twenty-five desks, enough seating to accommodate fifty students. The teacher, Professor Happ, was a six-foot-tall behemoth with a paunch and a hearty belly laugh. He gave us a lecture about how magic couldn't exist without math, and how even though we were wizards, the world still operated according to set laws. Part of being a good wizard was learning how those laws worked. According to Happ, the best wizards were also great mathematicians.

Much of what he said melted into nonsense once it hit my ears. My thoughts trailed off. I missed Dad so much. The thought that I'd never see him again felt like someone was digging out my guts with an ice-cream scoop. Occasionally, the feeling would briefly pass, and I'd have a moment of denial instead. I told myself, *I'll get out of here. I'll see Dad again. My life will go back to normal, somehow.*

At some point, I made the mistake of looking up at the guy I'd crashed into earlier. He'd slung his blazer over the back of his chair to show off his built arms. *Pfft.* He was trying too hard. I craned my neck and studied them. Well, they *were* nice. He leaned back until his chair was balanced on its hind legs. One arm dangling behind the backrest, he flipped through his textbook. He cracked his neck from side to side. He reminded me of Spencer and his meathead friends.

With my book propped up like a battlement, I spied on him from behind it. He yawned and stretched his arms over his head, sending a pencil rolling off his desk. Reaching down for it, he caught me staring like an ostrich spotting a wildlife photographer. He threw me a *you're a little weird* smile and waved. I shot back down behind my book. After a few seconds of self-loathing, I stole another look over the top of my book and confirmed he'd gone back to fidgeting with his pencil, flicking it back and forth and jiggling his knee. I felt like such a creeper. I had to get out of there as soon as I could.

When Happ dismissed us, I bolted for the door, but the cute

guy cut me off. "Hey, you still want help finding your locker?" he asked.

I opened my mouth, but lost the ability to use words, so rather than make myself look even weirder, I smacked my lips together and nodded. He perked up an eyebrow, grinned, and walked away, shaking his head and chuckling, making me feel like I had the word *dumbass* tattooed on my forehead.

"You never told me your name," he said as I walked up beside him in the busy hallway.

My tongue flopped around in my mouth until I garbled out, "Johnny."

"Mine's Hunter. Am I making you nervous?"

Pfft. Me? Nervous? I shook my head so hard it must've looked like a blur on my shoulders. "No, nah, I'm not nervous," I said, tripping over my own foot and stumbling forward. I dragged my eyes back over to him and shrank under his smirk. "I'm not awkward. Do you think I'm awkward? I'm not being awkward, am I?"

"A little."

I reigned in all my anxiety. "Look, I'm sorry. I'm new here, and everything's been really . . . *weird*."

"Because of your extraction? It's cool, I get it. I was messed up for a while when I first got here. Hey, show me your locker ticket. It has the number on it." I slipped it out of my pocket and handed it to him. "It's on the second floor. Come on."

He grabbed his backpack straps and jogged up a flight of stairs to the second floor, then led me to a quiet alcove near some tall windows. "Here it is, 248." I focused on my locker combination, expecting him to leave, but he didn't. "What's your next class?"

"P.E."

"Me too. I'll walk you there."

While I spun in my combination, Hunter leaned against the locker next to mine. Refusing to look at him, I fixed my eyes on the little white numbers etched on the lock. He was making me feel funny, and it was pissing me off.

"What was your extraction like?" Hunter asked.

I glanced at him, then kept turning the dial. "They pulled me out of my bed."

"Oh, wow. That must've been awful." Hunter squinted at an announcement board behind me. "Nice!" he said, approaching it. "I didn't hear this in announcements this morning. They must've just posted it. Check this out." He waved me over.

I stopped fiddling with my locker and joined him at the announcement board, squinting as I scanned each of the colorful flyers pinned on it. "What am I looking at?"

"This," he said, placing his finger on a flyer with golden scroll-work around the heading,

RUSH THE LEGACY OF THE CROWNS

I shrugged at the unnecessarily fancy flyer. "So what?"

"*So what?* Don't you want to be in a Legacy?"

I hadn't given it much thought, but the Legacy kids *did* seem like the only people who got fair treatment at the Institute.

"It says they're meeting in front of the Keep after classes let out," Hunter continued.

"The Keep?"

"That's the nickname for Zeus Hall. The Legacy of the Crowns' house. Listen, I know you just got here, but . . . do you want to rush them together?"

Maybe if I joined a Legacy, I could find a way out of this place. "Okay," I said, against my better judgment.

I put my books in my locker and tossed the busted backpack into a nearby trash can. Then, it dawned on me I'd forgotten to bring my gym clothes this morning. I didn't dwell on it, though. It wasn't like I was going to change anyway.

"Those hurt?" Hunter asked, pointing at one of my stretched earlobes as we started off for gym.

"For a little while."

"You going to go any bigger?"

"I don't know."

"Where you from?"

"Chicago. Where are we, anyway?"

"From what I've heard, somewhere in the Ozarks."

Missouri. Almost nine hours away from Chicago. "What about you? Where're you from?"

"Tennessee." He paused. "I lived on a farm there." I laughed, so he asked, "What's so funny?"

"No, it's just, that's such a stereotype. Being from the country and living on a farm."

"I hate to be ster-e-o-typical, but that's where I lived."

"With cows and stuff?"

"And horses and pigs too. Pigs're fast, let me tell you, and when they're covered in mud, *zoom*"—he swept his hand through the air—"they'll go right on past you, slick as cat crap on linoleum, leave you wallowing in the mud just like one of their cousins. But not me." He punched his hand. "I'm a pro pig catcher. Best in the game. They rush right on past me and *boom*"—he skipped up into the air—"I got 'em."

I grinned at him. "Just like that, huh?"

He smiled back. "Just like that." We stopped talking and each gave our shoes an awkward glance. Then he said, "What about you? What do you do?"

I paused. "I can burp on command." I burped to prove myself. "No, seriously."

"I can kind of play guitar."

"I'm trying to learn guitar too. But I'm slow as an ox when it comes to picking things up. Maybe you could teach me sometime."

"Sure, probably." We smiled again. I looked at his eyes, at the glints of sunlight dancing in their lustrous green. Another timid silence. I watched the tips of my shoes moving, thinking of something to say. *I could talk about the weather . . . no, who actually talks about the weather? Boring people who have nothing to say. But, then again, why do I care if he thinks I'm boring? I don't even know him. Why am I worrying so hard about this?*

"You're pretty laid back," he said.

No. No, I'm not. "Thanks."

We made our way to the boy's locker room at the other end of Odin Hall. Between the musty smell and the aisles and aisles of lockers with chipped paint, like the rest of Odin Hall, the dressing room was a distinctly non-magical affair. For a second, though, the pervasive stink had me nostalgic for my old P.E. class. I followed Hunter to a vented locker, where he stashed his backpack and pulled out a gym bag. He eased onto a creaky bench and rustled through the bag for his gym clothes.

I peeked around some lockers and saw the more athletic boys taking off their shirts, flexing their wannabe abs. Hunter noticed me squirming. "What's wrong?" He cast aside his blazer and unbuttoned his shirt, revealing his chest. "Why aren't you changing?" he said, pulling on a black tank top.

Hunter was one of the cutest guys I'd ever seen. He had a perfectly pointed nose and big sweet lips that curved into a movie-star smile so flawless you'd swear he'd spent hours in the mirror practicing it. My eyes went up like an elevator, starting at his chest and dinging at his heavy-lidded eyes. "I didn't know my schedule so well this morning—you know, first day—so I didn't bring any gym clothes."

"I got some extra clothes in my bag. You want to borrow them?" He reached in and tossed me a pair of shorts and a shirt. I held them in front of me and stared around them at Hunter, who was kicking off his pants and slipping on some basketball shorts. After adjusting his waistband, he looked up at me. "Aren't you going to change?"

I lowered the clothes. "I don't feel like it."

"Come on, bro. It's basically a free A."

I looked at my feet, too ashamed to articulate my insecurities. He laughed and pulled on the edge of my shirt. "Dude, what's wrong with you? Just change."

"No!" I yanked my shirt away and bunched the edge between my fingers. "I can't . . . I'm not fit or anything. . . . It's embarrassing."

"Embarrassing?" He laughed. "You think these guys're checking you out?"

I must've looked like a freshly plucked beet right then. "N-No!"

"I'm just messing with you. No one cares if you're fit or not."

Feeling awkward, I went ahead and wormed out of my shirt. Hunter cocked his head to the side and checked out my stomach. "You don't look too bad to me." Then he grinned like he was messing with me.

•

Odin Hall's gym was nothing special either. Red bleachers lined the walls on opposite sides of a basketball court. An outline painted around the basketball court marked out a walking track. I got the usual line of curious stares from the other kids. Not surprising, considering how rare newcomers apparently were. I felt like I was standing in the middle of a room with a fresh coat of purple paint all over me. The coach didn't even bother acknowledging me, though. He just arranged us in rows and had us pair off for warm-ups.

"Warm up with me?" Hunter asked.

I nodded, surprised. We barely knew each other, so it was cool he was watching out for me, but I wasn't used to someone randomly being so nice. Our first exercise was sit-ups. He got down on the floor and lay on his back. "Kneel on my feet."

I joined him on the floor, resting my knees on his feet. Unsettled by the feeling of curious eyes swimming all over me, I tried focusing on the workout. Hunter did a few reps and his tank top rolled up, revealing his sweaty stomach. My mind turned into a dumpster. I looked away so I wouldn't pop a boner, but his grunting between reps made it hard to fight dirty thoughts. A few guys started chuckling, making me feel even more self-conscious. Hunter furrowed his brow at them and they shut up.

"Hey," he said at the top of a sit-up. "Imagine a wall so people don't go looking around inside your head."

So people don't go looking around inside my head? What did that mean? A cold sweat broke on my brow. Were the guys reading my thoughts? Did they know I'd been having all these pervy thoughts about Hunter? I quickly imagined a wall.

When the coach blew the whistle for us to switch up, I sucked in a deep breath, proud I hadn't sprung one, and rolled onto my back while Hunter grabbed my ankles and held me down. He encouraged me as I struggled through a few shaky sit-ups, laughing about how out of shape I was. I didn't bother explaining my favorite exercise was lying in bed, sad.

After warm-ups, I walked around the track while everyone else played basketball. Every now and then, I looked up and watched Hunter playing with his friends. He flagged them down, yelling for them to pass him the ball, and when he got hold of it, he jumped through the air like a frog, dunked the ball in the basket, and dangled off the rim with his tongue hanging out. After dropping down, he chest bumped one of his teammates and grunted. He was ridiculous, but for some reason, I thought it was cute.

I needed to get my head on right. Why was I checking out some random guy when I was trapped in a wizard prison? Refocusing, I ran scenarios through my head, plotting an escape plan.

Hunter floated around the edge of the court, waving his arms around like an aircraft marshal, signaling for his buddies to toss him the ball. One of them threw it to him, and he squeaked across the floor trying to catch it. He pivoted on his heel in pursuit, but the ball slipped through his hands, and he tripped. I looked up just in time to see him careering toward me. I froze and pinched my eyes shut as he crashed into me and sent us both slamming onto the floor.

The tumble left me a little shaken. When I opened my eyes, he was on top of me, his green eyes gazing into mine, his heart pounding against mine. A sweat bead dripped off the tip of his nose and hit mine. *Crap.* I was going to spring a boner. *Calm down, Johnny.* I searched my thoughts for boner-killing material: Alison's grandma, wrinkly, old, and mildly sinister, wearing a nightie and leering at me as she crawled around on a bearskin rug. It didn't help. A cute boy was lying right on top of me, his feathery hair tickling my face, his sweaty body pressed up against mine. All my blood started redirecting to below my waist.

A drumbeat tickled my ears. Somewhere in the distance, "The Lion Sleeps Tonight" started playing: *A-weema-weh, a-weema-weh, a-weema-weh, a-weema-weh*. Then everyone in P.E. started snapping and swaying their heads from side to side. *Snap. Snap. Snap. Snap.* All the lights went out except for a single spotlight shining just on us. The minute Hunter felt how excited I was to have him on top of me, the rest of my high school career at the Institute would be doomed.

Hunter lowered his face until his lips were only a minty breath away from mine, then he pushed himself off me, grabbed my hand, and yanked me back up. "Sorry about that," he said before running back to his friends. The coach blew the whistle a second later.

Chapter 11

After P.E., Hunter walked me to parapsychological investigations, so I wouldn't get lost.

"You've got to be careful what you think around here," Hunter said. "Most folks can read your surface thoughts. Just remember, if you feel eyes on your back, that means someone's looking into your head. Usually, if you focus, you can figure out who it is. Going into someone's head is a two-way street. Don't worry about anyone finding out your deepest secrets, though. Only really strong wizards can go that deep. Most people won't try it because it's against the rules, but sometimes you get folks who're feeling brave. This girl tried it on me one time."

"Did she see anything?' I asked.

He grinned. "No. Good thing, too, or she would've found out what a huge perv I am."

As if this place weren't bad enough, now I had to worry about people snooping around in my thoughts.

Before I went in to class, Hunter and I compared schedules. "We don't have any more classes together," he said. "That sucks. What's your name on the forum?"

"I haven't made an account or anything yet."

"They make one for you. Until you change it, it's just the name and number they gave you."

I reached in my breast pocket and pulled out my lanyard. "Juan 149."

"Cool. I'll look you up on there and we can talk. See you this afternoon at the Keep," he said, before walking away. What a relief. I just couldn't talk to him anymore. He was the nicest guy I'd ever met, but he was making my brain short circuit. I needed some time away from him to gather myself.

Inside the classroom, I spotted an empty stool near the back. I sat down, laid my textbook on the table, and rifled through its pages, seeing all manner of weird pictures and diagrams.

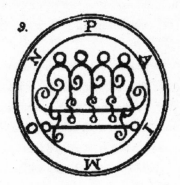

The teacher, a fussy, balding man with a thick moustache, waddled in just before the bell rang. "Good day, students," he said, his moustache quirking upward as he smiled. He unpacked his satchel while everyone murmured greetings, then returned to gawping at their phones, popping their gum, or chatting. Finally, he picked up a clipboard, adjusted his glasses, and squinted around the room, eventually homing in on me. "I see we have a new student. Why don't you go ahead and introduce yourself?"

Every chair in the room squeaked as the other students turned to stare at me, grins stretched across their curious faces. Staggering up off my stool, I slid my hand across the tabletop and knocked my pencil onto the floor. I was about to duck down and grab it when I remembered I was on the spot. "My name's Johnny." Flashing a gawky smile, I felt for the stool with my foot, but screeched it across the floor and almost fell when I tried sitting back down. Luckily, I braced my forearms on the tabletop and caught myself.

"Freak," someone muttered. A wave of snickering followed. Man. Even at the Institute I was a total weirdo.

"Welcome to Parapsychological Investigations. I'm Professor Hamden Bigsby," the teacher said with a smile. "Lucky for you, we're starting a new unit today, so you needn't worry about being confused. Will everyone please turn to chapter seven in your textbook."

I flipped to the chapter. The heading across the top read *Everywhen*. "Are we all somewhat familiar with the concept of Everywhen?" Bigsby asked, surveying the bored faces and yawning mouths around me. "All right, let's talk about our dreams and the collective unconscious. When we sleep, we dream—but our dreams don't exist in some bubble, secluded deep within our own minds. On the contrary. Our dreams exist as part of a continuum." Bigsby drew a circle on the whiteboard. "That continuum is Everywhen"— he scribbled the word in the middle of the circle—"the place where the boundaries between dreams disappear, and all dreams come together.

"For example, some oneironauts—those are dream explorers—have come across a place that is essentially every city that ever was and ever will be, created by the sleeping minds of the entire world, the collective unconscious. They've taken to calling it 'the city at the end of the world.'"

I didn't have a clue what he was talking about, but I wasn't going to interrupt for clarification. "The Chinese philosopher Zhuangzi said he could not tell whether he was a man dreaming of being a butterfly, or a butterfly dreaming of being a man. Nowhere are these contradictions more evident than in Everywhen. There are just two states outside of our own material reality that we've identified: Everywhen, the dreamworld; and another phenomenon called the Void, death. A popular theory among wizardkind is that True Tongue, the language of dreams, may be mankind's first-ever language. This has led some wizards to hypothesize that this world may, in fact, be a transitory point between the world of dreams and death."

Turning the page to the section on True Tongue, I was struck by what I saw there. Staring up at me was an incomprehensible mishmash of words very much like the ones Alison and I had used to conjure the cintamani. Then, it hit me: we must've used True Tongue to cast the spell. I had to tell Alison when I saw her again.

"One central truth remains," Bigsby said. "Only wizards have the power to interact with Everywhen."

•

Next: a boring chemistry class. The professor had an aquiline nose and wore all blue. He walked in and took stock of the classroom, his eyes flickering on me. "Good afternoon, everyone. For those of you who are new, I'm Professor Schmendrick."

Like Happ, Schmendrick insisted that understanding science was central to understanding magic. Tuning him out, I stared out the window. I didn't care about the intersection of science and magic. All the magic in the world hadn't put us in bubble colonies on Mars. All it'd done was rip my world apart.

After chemistry, it was lunchtime. Students filed out into the quad, some heading to Majere Hall and others back to their dorms. I scoured every inch of Odin Hall before I found Alison. We headed for my locker first, so I could put my books away. "That language for the incantation we used to summon the cintamani? I think it's called True Tongue"—I opened my parapsychological investigations textbook and showed her while we walked—"see?"

"I can't believe that nonsense was actually a language," she said, studying the words.

I closed the book. "It's not, really. It's the way things communicate in dreams. That's why it looks and sounds like nonsense in this world."

"Weird. So how's your first day going?"

We reached my locker. "Meh. Have you seen Blake?"

"No. I have a class with Linh, though. I sat with her," she told me as I stowed my things.

"What was that like?"

"She just talked about Hayley Kiyoko the whole time, called her 'lesbian Jesus.' Did you meet anyone?"

I thought about Hunter. "Kind of."

"No way, you actually talked to someone? Tea, *por favor*."

"It was just this random Southern guy. He was really sweet for some reason."

We left Odin Hall, climbed down the front steps, and walked into the quad. A cool breeze held fast to the autumn air, the drone of students' laughter and conversation flowing through it like birdsong. People were sitting on the steps, chattering away like nothing was happening. Like this whole situation was normal.

Alison noticed me staring, my mind wandering. "Should we try that cafeteria?"

"Sure," I said, snapping back to the present.

We made our way across campus to Majere Hall, which took us a good ten minutes, then headed down to the cafeteria on the bottom floor. Alison dragged me over to the sushi counter, and we each got a Philadelphia roll. We managed to find a secluded table and sat down.

Alison took a bite of her sushi and made a sour face. "Blech. It's totally bland."

"Hey, guys," Blake said as he sat down beside me, uninvited.

Alison gave him a dirty look. "Wouldn't it be easier for the Institute to just mail us a survey?"

"I just want to make sure you two are okay." He peeled the cellophane off his sandwich. Blake could've sat down anywhere he wanted, but the smile he shot Alison told me everything. Too bad the look she gave him back wasn't nearly as nice.

"This is pretty fancy for prison food." Alison stabbed a piece of sushi with her chopsticks.

"The Institute isn't punishing you for being a wizard."

"Have you had the sushi?" Alison said.

"The sushi's busted," he said. "I stick to the sandwiches."

"Blake," I asked, "did you have any . . . weird dreams when you first got here?"

"Sure. A lot of people do. Extraction can be pretty rough.

There's a psychiatrist in Elric, if you need one. Some people have nightmares about their extraction for a long time, and it helps to talk about it."

That had to be it. Aside from getting my ass kicked by Todd and his goons, being extracted had been one of the most horrifying experiences of my life. Maybe a psychiatrist was exactly what I needed.

"How did you get here?" Alison asked him. "What was your extraction like?"

"They just came and took me."

Alison rolled her piece of sushi around like a wheel. "From your parents' house?"

"No, I'm an orphan. I was staying in a group home with a bunch of other kids when they extracted me."

"How long have you been here?" I asked.

"Almost two years."

"Ever tried escaping?"

"The one-month rule . . ." he said.

Alison's sushi wheel fell on its side. "What's the one-month rule?" she asked.

"All extracted kids try to break out after a month."

I clacked my chopsticks against the plate. "Did you?"

"No. So, what classes do you guys have next?" he asked, quickly changing the topic.

"Occult history," I said.

Alison sighed and perched her cheek on her fist. "English."

"Cool. I've got occult history, too, Johnny. I'll walk you there if you want."

As the three of us returned to Odin Hall, I struggled to find anything meaningful to say to Blake. If Alison was right and he was a spy, it was best I keep quiet, anyway. Once Alison left for English, Blake broke the silence. "Alison's cool. I mean, you're cool too."

"Okay . . . ?"

"She's sassy. I like that." I wanted to laugh at his awkwardness. "What kind of guys is she into?"

I was starting to doubt Blake really was a spy. "I don't know. Guys who aren't massive jerks."

"So she likes nice dudes?"

"Most people do."

We walked into a classroom with a bunch of chair-desks. Blake sat on the left side of the room near the front, and I sat right behind him. "This class is a funeral," he said as I settled into my desk. "The teacher's old as Moses, and she rambles on forever about random stuff."

The class was indeed very boring. Professor Trude, a stuffy Englishwoman who used big words like *historiographical* and *pedagogy*, chattered on about Merlin, whom I half believed she'd known in real life. She wore a suit with a cinched pencil skirt, and her hair was piled in a bouffant that practically reached the ceiling, elevating her already severe look. I imagined her as a character in an old-fashioned English drama. It made the class more bearable. Most of the other students just slept through it.

While Trude prattled on about Merlin's genealogy, something through the window caught my eye. In the quad stood a strangely familiar man in a white suit with a dapper haircut and a fox-like smile. Enveloped in a pale-white glow, he stood staring at me. Squinting, I tried getting a better look at him. He raised one hand and gestured for me to join him. I looked back at Trude, who was still drawing genealogical diagrams on the whiteboard, then I remembered where I'd seen the man before: the mall. I'd bumped into him at the arcade the day Alison and I got beaten up. When I looked back into the quad, the smiling man in white was gone.

"What's wrong?" Blake whispered. He must've noticed my piqued expression.

"Nothing. Just thought I saw something." I glanced between him and the quad. The strange vision had left me unnerved, but I settled down before the end of class.

Afterward, we shuffled out to the hallway.

"What're you doing after classes let out?" Blake asked.

"I'm going to that rush thing for the Legacy of the Crowns."

"You're what?" Blake asked in a high-pitched tone. "You can't—"

"I'll see you around." I rushed to my locker, swapped my books out, and went to English. Boring. *Ticktock, ticktock.* Then French. *Ticktock, ticktock.* After the last class was dismissed, I ran to my locker, put away my books, and sped outside to meet Hunter. He came out wearing his letterman's jacket.

"You ready?" he said.

Nope. "Yeah."

"Let's go."

Now was my chance. If I could get into a Legacy, maybe it would help me find a way out of this place.

Chapter 12

2 DAYS AFTER EXTRACTION

A noisy crowd had gathered at the base of the Keep's steps, blocking access to the portico. Perched atop the stone steps, a pale, scruffy blond guy with a smile like a gameshow host scoured the crowd with his blue eyes. Desperate students waved at him, yelling, "Aiden!" in an attempt to capture his fickle attention. The lack of girls in the crowd told me Legacies were primarily a guy thing, which, I guess, meant the elites of wizard society were mostly men. I could just hear Alison scoffing and saying, *Typical.*

Hunter yanked my arm and squeezed us between two other boys, a chubby redhead and a tall skinny one with freckles who kept yammering "Aiden" in a frog-like voice. Hunter raised my hand along with his. "What're you doing?" I asked, jerking my hand away.

"We've got to get Aiden's attention. Don't you want to rush the Crowns?"

Part of me knew I had to do this to find a way out of the Institute, but the other part of me—the rational part—thought this was the dumbest idea I'd ever had. Either way, there I was. No turning back now. "Yes." I raised my shaky hand.

Aiden wrinkled his nose like he was picking through a pile of dog crap for a diamond. "You," he said, pointing vaguely at a group of boys. A tall, skinny boy standing among them lit up. "No, not you," Aiden said. "Him." He pointed to a more athletic-looking boy next to the first one. "No one wants you in their Legacy," he said to the skinny one. "You smell like Fritos. Go back to your dorm and put some more lipstick on your body pillow, you loser."

Yikes.

Stroking his chin, Aiden narrowed his eyes and kept sorting through the crowd, peering across the sea of swaying hands. "You," he said, looking toward me.

The chubby redhead next to me pumped his fists. "Yes!"

Aiden scowled at him. "No, not you!" The redhead's mouth fell open, his cheeks sagging. "How many times have you tried rushing us, Brian? Get real. I've never even seen you finish a sit-up. Hop on a treadmill and come back when you've lost that twin you swallowed in utero." Aiden fixed his searing gaze back on me. "Never seen you before."

All the kids around us eased away, their eyes trained on Hunter and me.

"Come up here," Aiden said, waving for me.

Knees buckling, I turned into a statue. Me? Of all the people he could've chosen? I gave Hunter a panicked stare, so he nudged me forward with his shoulder. "Go," he said.

Enduring all manner of nasty looks from the other kids, I edged up to the portico steps and climbed them. Aiden, on closer inspection, had ruddy cheeks pocked by a few acne scars. His dusting of stubble was auburn, a different color from the hair on his head. It was obvious he was trying to grow a beard, possibly to mask his bad skin. Aiden gave me the once-over. "How long have you been here?"

"This is my second day."

"Perfect." He flashed another big game-show-host smile and ushered me over to the group standing behind him.

The other rushees were a band of gawping mouths waiting for flies to land in them. That these guys were being considered for future wizard royalty made the whole thing seem like a cruel joke. Like Blake had said, though, Aiden and his buddies probably picked these guys for a good laugh. Of course, that was why I was up there, too, then.

Aiden looked back into the crowd and noticed Hunter. "You get up here too." Hunter flashed a smile and bounded up the stairs. I struggled to hide my discomfort. Whatever we were in for, there was no way I was ready for it.

A few kids shouted and whined as Blake tunneled his way through the crowd and up onto the portico. Two Legacy boys whose big arms stretched the sleeves of their polo shirts flanked him. Tall and lean, they stiffened their jaws and squeezed their hands into fists, but Blake stood unmoved by their threatening looks.

"Whoa, Blake. I didn't choose you," Aiden said, coming down between the two behemoths.

"I'm not here to rush, Aiden. I'm here to get him out of here." Blake cast his eyes toward me.

"Blakey, Blakey, if the boy wants to rush, let him rush." Aiden's lips curled into a smile.

"He's new!"

"It's his choice, Blake," Hunter said.

"Fine. Then I'm rushing too," Blake said. He tried joining us, but the two hulks blocked him again. Blake squared his shoulders, his eyes burning through them like he was ready for a fight.

"Let him through, guys." Aiden waved for Blake to join us then looked back at the crowd. "All right, everybody, we've got our rushees." The crowd erupted into groaning and murmuring as it dispersed.

"What are you doing here?" Blake said, clearly pissed.

Hunter stepped between us. "He's rushing, Blake. What's the problem?"

"The problem is—"

"Ladies," Aiden said, snaking an arm around Blake's shoulder. "Is something wrong?"

Even if their goal was to humiliate us, the Legacy of the Crowns was still my best shot at finding a way out of here. "Just let me do this, Blake."

"See there, Blake? Discussion closed. Let's go in, fellas."

We followed Aiden through a pair of heavy wooden doors into the Keep's shimmering foyer. Inside, the grand staircase wound up to a mezzanine that circled over the entrance. Aiden climbed onto the bottom step and surveyed us while we gazed at the sparkling chandelier hanging over us. With shiny gold paint covering almost every surface, the circular room had sandy marble floors and fancy crown molding with egg-and-dart motifs. Beyond the steps leading up to the mezzanine, an archway next to a red door led to other parts of the house. Hunter and the other rushees were awestricken, but Blake scowled, unimpressed by the flashy display.

Like a murder of crows, a number of Crowns skulked in the overhang, some leaning over the balustrade with their arms folded under them, others standing upright, following us with their menacing eyes.

Aiden clapped his hands. "Details time, people. There's an Asura in Darkwood Forest known as the Bandersnatch. Heard it's been giving the locals quite the time. Now, I don't care how you deal with it—capture it, kill it, marry it—but whatever you do, we need proof you found it. The first person to bring us proof gets the prize: the status of Legacy pledge."

"What's a Bandersnatch?" one of the kids asked.

What the hell was an Asura? What the hell was a Bandersnatch? What the hell had I gotten myself into?

"You'll know it when you see it. Magical creatures have weird auras." He scanned us for objections or questions. There were none. "Now, if you guys don't mind, we'll head downstairs and seal the deal." Aiden stepped off the stair and walked to the red door next to the arch.

Blake tugged on my sleeve. "Let's get out of here before they bind us."

"What?" I tried to shrug off his grasp.

"They're going to bind us to the task with magic, so they can make sure we stay until it's done."

"What's that mean?"

"It means there's no way out until that Bandersnatch thing is dead or captured. We'll be stuck looking for it until the binding expires or the creature's dealt with. If this thing is dangerous—"

"There's no way to get out of it?"

"We don't know what could happen if we break the bond. We

could end up cursed. Some binding spells can even kill if they're broken."

"Gentlemen?" Aiden said, standing in the doorway.

I had to take my chances. Swallowing my fear and ignoring Blake, I followed Hunter and the other rushees through the door and down a winding stairwell. Blake hesitated then followed too. Inch by inch, the walls in the stairwell transformed from brick to rock, the leveled cement stairs melting into lumpy, crude steps, as though the architect had abandoned the project halfway through. I braced myself against the walls to keep from tumbling down the uneven stairs. Finally, we arrived at a dimly lit cave beneath Zeus Hall. Candles burned in recesses cut into the rock face. A gust of wind blew in, causing the candle flames to flicker before returning to their twisting dance. The cave ceiling reached only five feet over our heads, low enough to be claustrophobic.

In the middle of the chamber, two magic circles drawn in red paint covered most of the floor. The one farthest away from the staircase had a series of smaller interlocking rings inside it with strange-looking symbols around them, but the circle closest to us had only one ring, with a triangle inside it. Aiden stood in the triangle of the smaller circle and waved for us to stand in the larger array.

"Gentlemen, each of you take a spot in one of those rings, and we'll begin the binding ritual." When everyone was in position, Aiden cleared his throat. "This is an oath sworn to the Legacy of the Crowns to fulfill the task of obtaining the Bandersnatch." He surveyed us for protest, but no one said anything.

He closed his eyes, chanted in True Tongue, then opened his eyes again—they flashed yellow. The rings started glowing red. A hot wind swept through the room, knotting my stomach with dread. The candles guttered, but didn't go out. In a burst, the light from the circles expanded and swallowed everything in the chamber in crimson.

Ritual completed, we headed off to Darkwood Forest to find the Bandersnatch.

Chapter 13

2 DAYS AFTER EXTRACTION

Black sap bled from the trees in Darkwood, staining their bark and giving the forest its name. Were it not for this one natural barrier, students would probably be able to flee the Institute without problem, but the imposing black-treed maze kept students quiet behind the Institute's forbidding walls.

A swift wind rushed through the trees, knocking dead leaves off their gnarled limbs and sending them spiraling to the forest floor. The other rushees had gone their own ways, but Blake, Hunter, and I stayed together. We walked along an embankment skirting a bronzy lake, crunching through a rug of browns, reds, and yellows, walking deeper and deeper into an ancient place whose mysteries had their own mysteries. "How are we supposed to find this Bandersnatch thing, anyway?" I asked.

Blake looked over his shoulder at me. "Just feel for it with your wizard sight."

"Like, the vivit apparatus?"

"No, just close your eyes and feel everything around you. Everything has an aura. You can see it in the vivit apparatus, but you can feel it too. It's like a spider sense or something—I don't know how else to explain it." Blake led us away from the embankment into a gully.

I stopped walking and closed my eyes. "I don't feel anything."

Blake scowled at Hunter, probably blaming him for getting my magically clueless ass into this situation. "Look, just close your eyes and imagine what the trees feel like—emotionally," Hunter said. "Like, imagine what the trees are thinking."

Imagine what the trees are thinking? Rather than roll my eyes like I wanted to, I closed them and did what Hunter said. First, I imagined the trees must've felt a little cold because it was chilly out-side. Then I imagined them reveling in the sun's last rays—no. Not reveling. Worrying. They were worrying because the sun was going down, and they were afraid of the dark creeping in; the trees had to watch out for one other. When the fog off Lake Misty wound its pale fingers around them, nighttime smothered the ground in its ghostly blanket. That was why the trees clutched each other's hands—because they were afraid. All this time I'd looked at their twisted fingers with fear, but they weren't trying to trap me. They were asking me to free them. Somehow. They were trapped here too. Everything was trapped in this place.

In a rush, a tingle spread through my body, starting in my toes and fingertips and spreading to my legs and arms. It worked its way into my core, where it pulsed in my chest. I could *feel* the trees worrying as night approached, their anxiety rising as the sun's caressing rays abandoned them to the chill night's touch. I could relate to them. It reminded me of the last time I'd hugged Alison before being sent away to boarding school. The mounting dread. The discomfort, the sadness. Loneliness and fear.

Eyes opened, I looked at Hunter and Blake. Not only could I see their auras transposed against all the world's magical machinery, I could feel them too. Blake's aura felt like hot summer days spent practicing kick turns on half-pipes, *Street Fighter* tournaments and Bruce Lee movies and *Dragon Ball Z* marathons. Hunter's aura sounded like wild horses running free, like crowds cheering at small-town football games.

Then, I sensed something else, something creeping along my emotional periphery: an otherworldly presence. "What's that . . . creepy feeling?"

"That's the Bandersnatch," Blake said. "Sometimes magical creatures leave behind aura trails just like ours. It feels superweird because it's not from this world. Look, if we split up, we'll find this thing quicker."

"What do we do if we find it?"

I heard Blake's voice in my head. *Tell me with your mind.*

"Whoa!" I stumbled back, almost falling down. "What was that?"

Blake laughed. "I'm talking to you with my mind."

"I was imagining a wall, though. How did you do that?"

"I wasn't trying to read your thoughts I was just shooting you, like, a psychic DM. Say something back. Just imagine you're talking to me in your head."

I closed my eyes, and in my mind, I said, *Hey.*

Hey, Blake's voice replied. I opened my eyes again. "Pretty cool, huh?" he said.

"How far can it reach?" I asked.

"Depends on how well you know the person. We know each other now, so as long as you're thinking of me when you do that, I'll more than likely hear it, no matter where I am." Blake climbed a small slope, dead leaves crackling under his feet. "I'm heading out. Good luck, you two." Blake jogged away, northward.

"I can't believe he's going after that thing alone." Hunter shook his head and shoved his hands into his pockets. In an exaggerated motion, he lifted one leg high in the air, pivoted on the other ankle, and took a big step westward. We walked to a thicket, where Hunter started snapping and bending branches as he plowed his way through. Going ahead a bit, he held tree limbs aside for me so I could follow. We travailed the thicket and found a grassy clearing on the other side. On the horizon, the sky was turning a sherbet swirl of pinks and oranges.

"What the hell even is an Asura?" I asked.

Hunter turned around, crossed his arms behind his head, and walked backward as he talked to me. "That's what the Institute calls them, but no one really knows what they are. Some're like ghosts, some're big as houses, others the size of caterpillars, some're really dangerous, and some don't do anything at all. Some folks even think they're aliens."

He spun back around and kept walking.

I examined the Misthaven High logo emblazoned on the back of his letterman's jacket. "What's the jacket for?"

"I wrestle and play football at Misthaven," he said over his shoulder. "A lot of us play sports in Misthaven because the Institute doesn't have a sports program."

"So the town isn't just some big cover-up? Normal people with kids live there too?" The path cleared a bit, so I moved up to walk beside him. "And the Institute lets wizards play sports at their high school?"

"If your grades are good enough. I'm supposed to be at practice today, but I'm skipping to rush. I'll get crap for it tomorrow."

"Wait. How do you get to practice?"

"You've got a million questions, don't you?" He gave me a smirk, so I clammed up, but he answered anyway. "The Institute buses us to all the practices and games."

Curiosity stoked, I kept asking him questions. "Has anyone ever tried getting help while they were in Misthaven?"

"Yeah, right. 'Please, help me. I'm trapped at the magic school right over the hill.'?"

"Don't the Misthaven kids ask questions about the Institute?"

"Sometimes, but, like I say, they'd laugh at the truth. We tell them we're a gifted school."

"Have you ever tried escaping?"

"Once. There's this delivery truck that drops things off at Majere Hall every week. I hopped on it and tried to get away. But the agents caught me in Misthaven and dragged me back."

"You know anyone else who's tried?"

"You know the other RA, Linh? She used to date this girl, Maleeka. She tried escaping. No one knows what happened to her, though. Maybe she got away, or maybe she's under the Heka Building."

The day's last pinks and oranges now lay along the horizon, a starry purple blanket inching over them. Soon, the violet would go black, and only the stars would light the sky. Fireflies hovered about, flashing their abdomens and filling the air with glittering light.

"Do you know anything about the Defectors?"

"Not really. The Institute says they're terrorists, but I've never seen one. You should be careful who you talk to about this. Kids like to get brownie points for ratting people out." I recalled watching

that student get taken out by Smiths the other night and decided to
follow his advice. I should stop asking so many suspicious questions.

"What kind of music do you like?" he asked. "You look like you
listen to skater music."

I laughed. "That's not the worst guess." Past the clearing, we
came to a fallen log over a gully. Water trickled gently over the pebbles resting in the silt. Hunter spread his arms, balanced himself,
and started across the log. "What kind of music do you like?" I
asked, wobbling after him.

He spun around and faced me. "I guess I listen to a lot of sad
music."

A fragment of rotting wood gave way under my foot, but Hunter
grabbed my arm before I fell. Steadying myself, I said, "That sounds
emo."

"I am emo," he said, hopping off the end of the log and smiling
back at me. "Country emo."

I laughed again and finally reached the other side myself. It was
so easy to talk to him. I could say anything, and he'd know exactly
what to say back. "What's your favorite food?"

"Pizza," he said, sliding his hands into his pockets as we continued deeper into the forest.

"That's a generic answer."

"What do you mean?"

"Nobody hates pizza, and if they do, it's because they secretly
hate happiness."

"Fine, then. What's your favorite food?"

I looked up into the gloom. "Probably teppanyaki."

"Tep-what?"

"Teppanyaki. You know, where they cook the food on that char-
coal grill?"

"I've never had that. Do you always use big words?"

"Like teppanyaki?"

"No, like generic."

I chuckled. "Is that big word?"

"It is to me."

I smiled at him. He smiled at me. His emerald eyes twinkled like freshly unearthed gems in the creeping darkness. They hushed all the harsh notes in the world, woke the strings of a quiet symphony in my chest. A few minutes later, we found a well-trodden path tunneling deep into the forest. Soon, our steps were filled with a growing alien dread—the feeling Blake had told us followed the Asura. The closer we got to the monster, the stronger the feeling grew.

"What're your folks like?" Hunter asked, distracting us from the creepy feeling.

I thought of how much I hated them, how much I missed them. "Messed up."

He laughed. "Yeah? Same. Mine were always going at it like cats and dogs."

"Mine too. My mom cheated on my dad with her assistant. Then they got divorced. Now, my dad just lies around all day, depressed."

"Got any other family?"

"My best friend, Alison. She's here at the Institute too. I bet she's freaking out, wondering where I am right now. What about you?"

"Nope. Just me." Before the inky pall of night swallowed us, Hunter held out his hand, and rays of light collected over his palm and burst into a glowing ball.

"Whoa!" I said.

"You think that's neat?" I nodded, with a big grin on my face. "It's a pretty simple spell. I learned it from one of my friends in a Legacy. Even though non-Legacy kids aren't supposed to learn magic, spells get around the Institute like memes, and we just sort of pick them up."

He spun the orb on his finger like a basketball before letting it go. The orb climbed a few inches into the air, sweeping away the shadows.

"Do you remember when your powers came in?"

"Sure do," he said. "I was running away from home, got my foot caught in a train track not far from my house. Then I heard this train coming down the tracks toward me, so I started praying to god and everything. Before the train hit me, I closed my eyes, and when I opened them again, I was at the other end of the yard. Later that night, I found this old abandoned church and decided to sleep in it. When I woke up, I was in the white room with Melchior."

He stopped and looked around. "I wonder where all the other rushees are? We've been walking forever. I hope this isn't some dumb Legacy trick to get us to walk around the forest all night." Without warning, he tripped over a branch and hit the ground. He rolled onto his back, gritting his teeth and tucking his knee against his chest. "Ow, crap! My leg."

I knelt to help him back up, and the branch he'd tripped on rustled in the leaves, moving like it was alive. My dread spiked as the shuddering limb rose off the ground and bent like a joint. Instantly, other bits of fallen timber danced alive, shifting and pivoting, buglike. Inch by horrifying inch, a giant stick bug emerged from underneath the leaves strewn all over the forest floor. The monster shook them off its back and lurched one of its massive stalks forward, rumbling the ground where it landed. It snapped its jaws and spun its head 180 degrees, watching us through its dome-shaped compound eyes.

Hunter and I looked at each other and screamed. Certain we

were about to become the giant bug's dinner, I quickly searched the ground for something to distract it. I spotted a soggy tree branch nearby, grabbed it, stood up, and started swinging it side to side, teetering after every labored swipe. The creature's head started following the branch.

"Just get out of here, Johnny! Now!" Hunter shouted. I ignored him and kept waving the stick. The beast followed a few more passes, then I hurled the branch away from us. The giant bug looked to where I'd thrown the stick, and when it heard the branch crashing down somewhere, it stomped off toward the commotion. My eyes still trained on the creature, I slapped around for Hunter until I felt the arm of his jacket. I clamped my hands around his arm and pulled him up. He wobbled to his feet, groaning the entire way. Once he was standing, I shouldered him.

We didn't have long. The monster would soon lose interest in the branch and come back for us, so I scanned the forest for an escape. Hunter's light ball shone over a nearby ditch.

"Come on," I said, "we're going to hide in that ditch."

Dragging Hunter with me, I steered us toward the crevice. At the bottom of its steep sides was a muddy ravine. Creeping along down the embankment, foot by foot, I sought to inch us into the opening, but I miscalculated how slick the slope was and sent us both tumbling down into the ditch, splashing into the mud at the bottom.

Covered in mud, I got up on my elbows and looked around. Hunter was kneeling beside me, his light orb floating a few inches above us. Hunter waved his hand and dimmed it so the Bandersnatch couldn't follow it to us. Then he stuck his finger in the mud and started drawing a magic circle.

"What's that?" I whispered.

"It's a healing spell. I've got to fix up my leg or we're screwed."

While Hunter etched the symbol in the mud, I eased my way up until I was half-standing. With my back against the side of the ditch, I closed my eyes and listened for the massive bug. Not too far from us, it skittered through the forest, leaves crunching under its quick feet.

"Do you think it ate the other rushees?" I asked.

"I don't know. Call for Blake with your mind!" he said.

I clenched my eyes shut. *Blake, we found the Bandersnatch. We're trapped in a ditch west of where we split up. Hunter's hurt. Please help us!*

Blake's voice rang out in my head. *I'm coming. Hang in there.*

Hunter finished his magic circle, then thrust his foot into it. Briefly, little embers wafted up from the glowing ring, its soft blue light surrounding Hunter's foot—then he popped back up on it like he'd never been hurt. Looking around the ditch for a makeshift weapon, he settled on a branch he found sticking out of the mud.

"Can't you, like, shoot a fireball or something at it?" I asked.

He tightened his fingers around the branch. "Sorry, no fireballs."

From inside the ditch, we had no way of knowing where the monster was or what it was doing. "We've got to get out of here," I said.

Hunter motioned with his head for me to climb the hill ahead of him. Planting my fingers into the mud, I started trying to climb out, but I hadn't even anchored my foot into the earth before the giant bug appeared, straddling the trench with us beneath it. I staggered away from the wall, gaping up at it.

Hunter lifted the branch and swung it at the Bandersnatch. "Johnny, get out of here!"

The monster snapped at him and clamped its jaws down onto

the branch. Digging his heels into the mud, Hunter tugged back, but the creature shattered the limb between its teeth and sent Hunter plopping backward into the muck. Before Hunter realized what had happened, the Bandersnatch reared back its neck and thrust its head into the gap. Hunter's face went pale as the monster's dripping teeth came for him, but I snatched the back of his jacket and pulled him out of the way and kept pulling until he was up on his feet and running alongside me.

We barreled down the trench, shielding our faces with our hands as wiry roots growing through the sides whipped us. An icy muck caked my jeans and sploshed inside my shoes, turning my socks into little ice bags, but the adrenaline pumping through my body burned away the chill and launched me forward like I had rocket boosters strapped to my back. The longer we ran, the higher the ditch's sides grew, but we didn't get far before the ravine dead-ended, steep dirt walls rising all around us.

Hunter stabbed his foot into the moist dirt, wriggled it in place until it was secured, then squished his hand into the dirt wall and hoisted himself up.

"Help me, Johnny. If I get out, I can pull you out," he said between grunts.

I got under him and boosted him upward, but the dirt clumps he was holding on to gave way, sending us both splashing into the mud.

We scrambled back to our feet, fear in our eyes as the monster positioned itself directly above us.

"Get behind me," Hunter said, scooting me over.

"What're you going to do, wrestle it?"

"Not the best time for jokes, Johnny."

We turned our heads away as the monster reared back, ready to strike. This was it. I was going to be eaten by a giant magical stick bug. As my brief and unsatisfying life flashed before my eyes, Blake leaped out of the gloom and landed on top of the beast. He had a glowing light sword in his hands. He drove the sword into the monster's back, and green blood spurted out of the wound as the beast thrashed around.

With the monster distracted, Hunter got on his hands and knees and started climbing up the muddy slope again. "Come on," he said, reaching out. I gave him my hand, and he hoisted me up as I dug my feet into the slippery soil. We clawed our way up slowly. When he saw I was almost out, he abandoned his own mad dash, put his hands under my shoes, and pushed me so I wouldn't slide back down. Once I was out of the ditch, I lay on my stomach and extended my hand to him. He grabbed it, and I gritted my teeth and pulled. He planted his filthy shoes in the dirt and launched himself upward, nearly jumping out of the ditch.

Lying on the ground, I watched Blake hop off the Bandersnatch and land on a patch of dirt a few feet away from the ditch. Enraged, the Bandersnatch stomped over to Blake and snapped at him with its giant mouth. He rolled out of the way, got up, circled the monster, and swung his sword clean through one of its legs. Green blood spewed from the severed stump. The creature roared so loudly the waning moon must've heard it.

Once we were on our feet, Hunter grabbed a rock and yelled, "We've got to help Blake!" He tossed the rock and hit the monster, but the attack barely registered.

"You two get out of here!" Blake yelled. "I can't fight this thing and protect you at the same time!"

Blake ran under the Bandersnatch, jabbed his light sword up into its abdomen, and dragged the blade across. Green blood spewed from the gash, covering him. Then he climbed onto the screeching monster's back and plunged the glowing sword down into it. The monster thrashed around, spewing more blood everywhere.

We hurried behind a tree and watched Blake finish off the monster, then—covered in slimy green blood—he climbed on top of its corpse and raised its severed leg into the air. With the creature dead, a strange sensation filled my body.

"I'm tingling all over. What's going on?" I asked Hunter.

"I'm tingling too. That just means the binding spell is done. Now all the other rushees know it's over and they can head back to the Institute."

I ran up to Blake. "That was amazing!"

He scratched the back of his head and gave me a cute smile. "It was just a big bug."

"I guess we should head back to the Keep," Hunter said.

Blake tossed the leg into the air and caught it as it fell back down. "Let's go."

Chapter 14

2 DAYS AFTER EXTRACTION

Caked in green blood, Blake burst through the Keep's front doors, looking for Aiden. He stormed through the arch in the foyer and found Aiden and his buddies in the parlor, sitting around a card table, absorbed in a game of Poker. Hunter and I walked behind Blake, following the oozy trail he'd left all over the pristine floors.

He tossed the monster's severed leg onto the card table, splattering the Crowns with green goo and scattering their cards to the floor. They hopped to their feet, backing away from the table and swatting at the monster blood on their shirts. Hunter and I hovered at the entrance to the parlor, just outside of view.

Aiden raised an eyebrow at the leg, now dripping a stretchy glob of blood onto the rug, and crooked up the corners of his lips.

"You sent them out there to die!" Blake said.

"Come on, Blakey—"

"You knew what that thing was, didn't you?"

"Don't you think I would've warned the rushees if I had known they were after a"—he examined the leg as one of his buddies warily picked it up—"giant bug?"

Blake kept his heated gaze trained on Aiden as he walked over and slid his arm around Blake's shoulder. "We should celebrate. You've now earned the status of Legacy pledge."

Blake cast off Aiden's arm. "Keep it."

"What do you mean *keep it*?"

"I don't give a damn about your stupid Legacy."

Aiden's cronies surrounded Blake. "Excuse me?" Aiden said.

"I said"—Blake stepped forward, nose to nose with Aiden—"you can take your Legacy and that leg and shove them up your—"

"Enough!" A voice boomed from behind me and Hunter. We moved aside as two Smiths and an older man with a mane of white curls stepped past us into the parlor. With his long, twisting beard and his elegant movements, he was like a lion, regal and intense. He scanned the room through a pair of spectacles, his steely gray eyes freezing everyone in their place.

"Balthasar," Aiden muttered, his dirty look melting. So that was old man Bal. The other scientist in charge of the Institute. He didn't seem anything like Melchior. For one, he was much older. His aura felt like warm sun rays through an attic window drenching time-worn floorboards. It was soft as a feather floating onto a still lake, not a ripple in sight. But you could sense the fury of crashing waves, a lightning storm brewing in gray summer clouds.

"There seems to have been a series of violations of Institute policy this evening." Balthasar said, his rolling voice gentle and firm, like how I imagined a lion would sound if it could talk. "Aiden, was this rush event cleared by the committee?"

"Not all the way . . ." Aiden said.

"Was it cleared?" Balthasar said, his tone pointed.

"No, sir. It was still under review."

"I take it you knew the committee wouldn't approve such a proposal? Asuras can be deadly."

"Not just anyone can become part of our Legacy. We only want the strongest—"

"That's funny coming from some spoiled brat who can't fight his own battles," Blake said, his eyes punching holes through Aiden.

Blake and Aiden looked ready to fight, until Balthasar held up a hand and silenced everyone. "What would you have done if a student had died?" Aiden looked around like he was hoping to cobble together a lie, but nothing came out of his mouth. "Nothing to say?" Balthasar continued. "That's no surprise. Your Legacy is prohibited from holding further rush events for the rest of the semester."

"You can't do that!" Aiden said.

"I can, and I am. As for you, Aiden, the committee shall review your record, as well as the records of your housemates, and sanction you." Next, Balthasar turned his attention to Blake. "Blake, you will be temporarily suspended from your position as a resident assistant at Veles Hall. I assume you know the first thing you should've done was to contact someone, an agent or teacher?"

Blake lowered his head. "Yes, sir."

"Why didn't you?"

"I don't know."

"Was there, perhaps, a need to prove something to members of this Legacy?"

Blake might've wanted to say something, but he thought better of it and stayed quiet. The silence grew uncomfortable before

Balthasar slid his attention to me. "You are newly extracted. What's your name?"

Following Blake's lead, I lowered my eyes to the floor. "Johnny."

"How much do you know of the Legacy system? Did you truly want to join the Legacy of the Crowns?"

"Yes, sir!" I said emphatically, hiding my true intentions. No one could know I was really hoping to escape.

Balthasar stared at me, no doubt perusing my thoughts. I quickly erected a wall in my mind, shutting him right out. "And you, Hunter? Is this your first time rushing for a Legacy?"

"Yes, sir," Hunter, unlike me, was more committed, and he locked eyes with Balthasar.

"And what did you think of the task Aiden set?"

"He's right: if the Crowns are the most powerful Legacy, they need to find the most powerful students."

"Even if that costs lives?"

Hunter looked down, his fingers wiggling at his sides. "Y-Yes, sir." A note of uncertainty had crept in.

"Are you hoping to impress Aiden with that answer?"

"No, sir!" Hunter said.

"What if your new friend here had died? What if the beast had killed him?"

Balthasar loomed over him, his chest rising and falling as he took heavy breaths through his nose and waited to see whether Hunter dared show any more impudence.

"I'm really sorry I put you in danger, Johnny," Hunter said.

Balthasar scanned the room, wiggled his thick mustache, and looked back at us. "The three of you, return to your rooms."

●

As we marched back to Veles Hall, Hunter stared at the ground, his fists balled, fuming. Every now and then he threw Blake a sidelong glance. "Why'd you do that?" he said, finally. "Why did you turn down their offer to join? You earned a spot. And you know how hard it is to—"

"Why would I join the Crowns?" Blake stopped walking and faced Hunter.

"Because they're, like, the *chosen ones*. They're the most powerful Legacy at the Institute."

"*Chosen ones?*" Blake scoffed. "There are no chosen ones. Anyone who believes in that kind of stuff doesn't know how to think for themselves."

"Don't you think joining them would give you more freedom?"

"Freedom? In this place?"

"Yes! They can do whatever they want. I bet Aiden won't even get punished for what he did."

"You think that's freedom?"

"It's a hell of a lot more than we have now, isn't it?"

"I became an RA because I wanted more freedom. It didn't take long to realize no one's free here, not the RAs, not the Legacy kids, not the Smiths, not even the head scientists. This place is like a machine, and everyone inside just does what they're supposed to. Those Legacy kids are just as much a part of it as anyone else. The Institute convinces them they're better than us, and in return, they keep us in line. But nobody's free in this place. Everyone's shackles just look different."

"Their shackles are still better than ours."

"Maybe. Maybe one of these days that psycho who thought it'd be fun to get us all killed, who sees us as expendable pawns in his little game, is going to become a powerful leader—not because he deserves it, but because he was born into it. That's what the Crowns are, okay? A bunch of weak, spoiled jerks who have everything handed to them. Then they tell us *we* don't work hard enough to succeed. I don't want to be one of them. They can keep their golden shackles. And people need to stop worshipping them just because they have money and power. We need leaders who know how to lead."

"You're just being dense," Hunter said. Unphased, Blake shook his head and walked away. "Hey! We're not done talking!" called Hunter.

Blake didn't even look back.

I pressed my lips together and drove the tip of my shoe into a crack in the sidewalk. Hunter seethed, breathing hard as he watched Blake disappear into the shadows. After a moment, he calmed down and turned to me. "Guess I should've thanked him for saving us before I started arguing with him. Guess I should thank you too. For saving me, I mean."

My ears burned like someone had put a lighter to them. "No problem."

We talked all the way back to Veles Hall, then we headed up to the third floor. Halfway back to my room, I found Alison hovering outside my door.

"J! Where the hell were you?" she said when she spotted me.

"Long story. This is Hunter," I said, pointing my thumb at him.

Alison raised an eyebrow at him. He wasn't the kind of guy I usually hung out with.

"Hunter Brantley. Well, Hunter 158," he said, extending his hand. She smirked at what she doubtless thought was a *quaint gesture*, so he pulled back his hand. "Hey, Johnny, today was wild—I'm pretty wasted. I'm going to go to my room. Let's hang out tomorrow, okay?"

"Sure, 'night," I said.

I watched his butt as he walked away.

"Are you checking him out?" she whispered.

"No way!"

"I saw you." Alison grinned.

"Why would I check out some jock?"

"I don't know, J . . . you tell me."

"It's not like that."

"Oh yeah? What's it like?"

"He doesn't even like guys."

"*Brokeback Mountain* over there? Ha, yeah, right."

"What're you talking about?"

"Nothing, J. So where the heck were you?"

I told Alison the whole story in my room, wowing her with the details, going on and on about how brave Hunter was, how kind and unlike other jocks. I talked about Blake, too, but not nearly as much. After she left, I realized something terrible: I liked Hunter.

Chapter 15

Almost getting killed by a giant bug was scary, but nothing was scarier than the thought of seeing Hunter in class every morning. I tried talking myself out of it. *He's a jock, you guys have nothing in common. He'd hate half the bands you listen to, make fun of the rest, and force you to listen to country music.* No matter what I told myself, though, I couldn't stop thinking about his eyes, his smile—his perfect, *perfect* smile.

What was I even thinking? Not only was he the opposite of what I normally liked in a guy, he wasn't even gay. We were like *bros*. Nothing else. Morning breath, body odor, dirty clothes—he wouldn't have noticed any of that on me. Regardless, I still stood in front of the mirror for almost an hour, primping and preening, hoping I might awaken Hunter's inner gayness.

First, I played with my black hair. I usually kept it short, but it had grown. Slapping some commissary hair gel on it, I sculpted it into a fauxhawk. Then I looked in the mirror. Awful. I looked like a puffer fish. Forget the fauxhawk. I shoved my head under the faucet, washed out the gel, and swept my hair to the side.

Second, I opened my mouth and scanned my teeth. Those were good. They needed a quick brush before I moved on to the next problem area. After scrubbing my mouth clean, I pulled out a bottle of cologne called "Deer Hoof." Another commissary purchase. I popped it open, and a sharp, musky scent hit my nose. I scrunched my face and jerked it away from the bottle. *Why the hell did I get this damn thing?* It smelled more like deer balls. I closed one eye and studied the bottle once more before spraying myself with it. Maybe it wouldn't smell so weird after it settled.

Third: a shave. Touching my face, I felt for hair, stubble, anything. Nothing. My face was smooth. Even though I didn't have any facial hair, I found shaving awfully refined, so I had to do it. I dabbed some shaving cream onto my face, brought a shaky razor to my cheek, and pressed down, but when I dragged the shaving cream off, I cut myself.

"Dammit," I muttered. A little blood dripped into the sink. I splashed my face, washed off the rest of the shaving cream, and stuck a Band-Aid over the cut.

I looked in the mirror: My hair was blah, I smelled like deer balls, and I looked like a sixteen-year-old Tony Montana. Even if Hunter weren't completely straight, there was no way in hell he'd go for me now. I gave up and left for class. Alison made fun of my smelling like a cheap motel all the way to Odin Hall.

In class, I stood at my desk, sorting through my books. I still hadn't gone by the commissary for a new backpack. Hunter came up to me. "I'm going to switch seats so we can sit closer, okay?" he said. Great. Today of all days. When I smelled like I'd been tea-bagged by a reindeer.

He grabbed his backpack and sat down next to me. I sat there imagining the smell climbing into the air like a ballerina twirling across a stage, pirouetting and tiptoeing over to Hunter's face, then kicking him on the nose. His nostrils flared. He sniffed the air. He could smell the weird cologne. I sank in my chair, hoping he wouldn't say anything. He looked over at me and grinned. I rubbed my face and hid my flushed cheeks. "Is that you?" he asked.

Little men in my brain screamed, *Damage control! Play it off.* "What do you mean?"

"That smell. Is that you?"

I swung my head from side to side, but he kept smiling, so my head shake melted into a sheepish nod. Next tactic: own it. "Oh, yeah. That's me."

"What is that?"

"It's called Deer Hoof. I got it at the commissary."

"Yikes, you can tell. Smells more like deer *balls*."

I let out a breathy giggle. Luckily, the smell was dying down.

During class, I had a hard time concentrating. Since Blake and Hunter had shown me how to sense auras with my wizard sight, I was eager to try the trick on everyone. Hunter's aura smelled like pasture and grass clippings, and it sounded like shoes squeaking on a gym floor. But there was sadness there too. Secrets. Pain. He caught me staring at him with a worried look on my face, smiled, and whispered, "What?" I shook my head and stopped looking at him. I felt guilty for reading too deep.

Sweeping the room with my wizard sight, I took in everyone's auras. I smelled cotton candy and popcorn and heard laughter and video games buzzing and book pages turning and voices gabbing, and music blaring, drawers opening and closing, credit cards swiping, perfume spraying, car engines revving. Then I heard crying and yelling and arguing and vans squealing out of driveways and desperate prayers made to god and wishes for death. Overwhelmed, I stopped. People were far too complex. And I felt bad for using my wizard sight on them. At that moment, I decided I wouldn't read people's auras anymore.

Class let out, and we left for gym. On our way there, Hunter kept grinning at me.

"What?" I said.

"What's his name?"

"Whose name?"

"The deer."

"What deer?"

"The one you blew before class."

I narrowed my eyes at him. "Ha, ha."

He pointed at my bandage. "Did your boyfriend do that to your cheek too?"

I rolled my eyes. He nudged my arm. I pushed him back. He laughed, and we smiled at each other. He rubbed his tongue over his lips, trapping me in his verdant gaze: I ran through the forest in his eyes, danced laughing in the glimmering flecks of sunlight raining down through the rich canopy. My lips parted. I wanted to say, "I like you, but I don't know why." Then his lips parted, like he might say the same thing. Instead, he broke the stare and chuckled. "Let's get to P.E."

As we were changing in the locker room, Hunter took off his shirt and flexed one of his biceps, curling his arm and watching the little muscle bulge up. I looked up from tying my shoes and almost laughed.

Hunter tensed his stomach. "Do you think my abs look good?"

Glancing up at him, my mouth fell open. I scrolled through the database in my brain for a response. The best thing I came up with: "Yup." I looked back down to see I'd knotted the shoelace around my finger.

Hunter smiled, checking himself out with his phone camera. "Do you think I'm cute?" My temperature hit absolute zero. "Come on, you can tell me if you think I'm cute. No homo."

Sweat beaded up on the back of my neck. Maybe I'd huffed too much of that nasty cologne, or maybe *he* was the one who was high. Either way, I didn't know how to answer that question without coming off at least a little gay—so I didn't. I kept very still, like I was hiding from a T. rex. One that sniffed out gay kids.

He grinned over his shoulder at me. "I'm just messing with you, bro. You get so weird about stuff." Then he turned to face me. "*Are* you gay?"

The lockers, floor, and ceiling all slid away, and I was transported to the set of *Jeopardy!* A lectern bearing my name—scrawled in my illegible handwriting—rose from the floor right in front of me. I looked to my right and saw Hunter standing like Alex Trebek, cue cards in hand, waiting for me to play the Final Jeopardy round up on the board: *Johnny's sexual orientation.*

The Final Jeopardy music ticked in my ears. I considered writing *What is a horse?* No reason why. Then I remembered the question.

I looked up. Behind Hunter, tentacles slithered across the floor from backstage. More tentacles inching their way around the board. The screens turned red. The music took on a discordant, menacing tone. *Tick. Tick. Tick.* Blood started pouring from my lectern. What the hell? I felt something sliding up my leg and looked down to see a tentacle wrapping itself around my calf.

"Bro," said Hunter, yanking me back into reality, "it's cool if you are. You don't have to answer if it's weird."

I swallowed. "I . . . I am. I'm gay." I'd finally come out to someone besides Alison and my parents. This was huge. I wanted to do cartwheels. Or maybe something less strenuous.

He nodded. "Cool." Then he slipped on his gym shirt. That was it? No bells? No cheering? I wanted a studio audience up and clapping. "So?" he grinned at me again. "You think I'm cute?"

I got up and headed upstairs without responding. I couldn't deal with Hunter's straight-boy ego right then. Plus, he must already have known the answer. "Johnny!" he called to me. "Wait up!"

We started with warm-ups again. Hunter rapped his knuckle against my arm. "Work out with me." He lay on the polished gym floor, so I joined him, placing my knees on his feet, grabbing his ankles, and holding him down. On his first rep, he sat up and snarled at me with his tongue sticking out the side of his mouth. I raised an eyebrow. The next time he sat up, he crossed his eyes and puffed up his cheeks like a blowfish. I smirked. Then he puckered his lips and waggled his eyebrows like he was flirting. He kept making funny faces until I finally giggled. "Dork," he said with a chuckle.

After warm-ups, I was ready to take my place as resident track fixture, but Hunter had other plans. He snatched my arm. "You're playing basketball with me today."

I stumbled a few steps as he dragged me along. "I don't know how."

He walked up to his basketball friends with me in tow. "Hey guys, this is Johnny. He's cool." He grabbed the basketball off the floor and spun it on his finger.

One of his friends studied me, cocked his head to the side, and looked at my ears. "Why do your ears look like that?"

"I stretched them."

"Cool." He rolled his shoulders. "My name's Doug."

Another one of the friends nodded at me. "Brandon." The rest of the crew murmured a welcome.

Throwing one arm around my shoulder, Hunter dribbled the ball with his free hand. "I'm going teach him how to play basketball, so don't mess with him." His friends emitted another wave of consenting groans, then we started playing.

Hunter dribbled the ball between his legs, spinning around and alternating his feet, pounding against the floor to the beat of my heart. "One day I'm going to be a baller," he said, flashing me a cocky smile. My eyes followed him like a pair of heat-seeking missiles. He slipped the ball behind his back and passed it to me. I held my hands up, but it just bounced off my palms and fell to the floor. I watched it roll a few inches away and hung my head, defeated.

Hunter picked up the ball and dribbled it again. "Come on, bro. Just catch it when I pass it to you."

I was about as coordinated as a drunk moose stumbling in front of oncoming traffic. I held up my hands again and prayed I'd have at least enough sense to clasp my fingers around the ball when he passed it to me again. Again, he passed the ball between his legs a few times before spinning around and tossing it to me. I closed my eyes, and soon as I felt the leathery thing hit my palms, I closed my fingers around it. Then I opened one eye and looked down. It was in my hands. Somehow, I'd managed enough coordination to grab the ball.

"Hey!" he said. "See, it's not that hard." We threw the ball back and forth a few times until I got the hang of it. "Okay, now dribble it."

I stared at the ball. In my head, I heard it say, *Come on, queen.*

Bounce me on the floor." Queen? Who the hell did this ball think it was? And why did it sound like it'd been smoking since the day it was first inflated? I tried popping it against the floor, but when it bounced back up, it swerved right out of my grasp. As it rolled away, it said, *Ha, give it up, princess! Basketball's a man's sport, and you're just a little boy.*

"Shut up, asshole!" I said out loud.

"Who're you talking to?" Hunter asked.

Crap. "No one."

I walked over to the ball and looked down at it. *Hey there, queenie,*" it said.

"I'll show you who's queenie," I muttered. I gritted my teeth, snatched it up, and with new focus, pushed it down to the floor. When it bounced back up, I slapped it down again. And again. And again. Brandon and Doug were watching me, whispering to each other and snickering. But I was on fire.

"All right, pass me the ball," Hunter said, opening his palms. I bounced it off the floor to him. He dribbled over to the basket, hopped up, and bounced the ball against the backboard, sending it through the hoop. Then he grabbed the ball and stepped back behind the blue box painted on the floor. He lined up his shot and flicked his wrist, sending the ball flying. It went through the basket again. He picked it up on a bounce and walked over to me. "You want to try and shoot it like I just did? Or do you want to try a layup?"

I didn't know what a layup was. Must've been that first thing he did. I took the ball from him, walked over to the spot behind the blue box, and considered whether to try shooting it or doing that layup thing. Layup. I jogged up to the basket, leaped up, and bounced the ball off the backboard—and right into my face. I fell on the floor, holding my nose. Hunter's friends fell out laughing. As I lay there, I heard the ball snicker as it rolled away. Hunter walked over and stood over me, hands on his hips, smiling down.

•

After that psychotic basketball made me its bitch in front of Hunter, I couldn't look him in the eye, so I hurried away to my next class. At lunch, I fled to the quad, looking for Alison, and found her sitting on the grass, eating yogurt and playing around with her new laptop. I sat down next to her. "Hey."

"This forum thing is awful."

I looked at her screen. She was using her usual internet handle, AlisonAffliction, on the forum. She'd even managed a cute selfie for her profile pic, and with a laptop camera, no less. We'd been here a week now, but I still hadn't visited the forum. I slipped out my new phone and considered setting up my account. "What's wrong with it?"

"It's so basic. The main page forces everyone to be friends, and you can't post anything privately unless you DM someone. The only good thing is watching people argue and post completely random things. Look at this." She pointed at the screen.

KevThaKiller

Hey guys it's your boy Kev. Everyone knows me & SophiE have been going out for a while. She asked me about sex last week but I didn't feel very confident about my size. I mentioned it to her and she told me to cast a spell to make it bigger. I didn't figure a regular spell would work, so I used the vivit apparatus and

started moving things around. Now I have a third nut.
Does anyone know how to fix this?

456 people liked this, 1.1k comments, posted 6 hours ago

JakeDresden

What the hell are you thinking posting this on the
forum Kev? Take this crap down. You're making the
Legacy look bad!

127 people liked this, posted 5 hours ago

KevThaKiller

I need help bro! I got three nuts!

354 people liked this, posted 5 hours ago

JakeDresden

I don't care if you're a tri-nut, IDIOT! Take this crap
down or Mark's going to kick you out.

621 people liked this, posted 5 hours ago

Thornmallow

Tri-nut!!! SKSKSKSKSK!!!

599 people liked this, posted 5 hours ago

InstitutePersonnel443

Kevin Magus, use of magic on Institute grounds is an
infraction with a penalty of up to 3 days detention
within your quarters. Your case is under review. You
will receive further notice by the end of the day. This
thread has been locked.

600 people liked this, posted 2 hours ago

Alison swept some hair behind her ear and kept browsing the forum. I looked up at the cirrus clouds stretched across the blue sky. From the corner of my eye, I could see her staring blankly at the screen. "Are you worried about your mom?"

"Of course. I can't stop thinking about her."

"I know what you mean."

"Where's the gay cowboy?" she asked.

"Hunter?"

"Do you know any other gay cowboys?"

"I don't know. He's probably having lunch with his friends or something."

"Did you rush the other day because of him?"

I jerked my head back and made a funny face at her. "Are you serious? Hell, no! Why would I do that?"

"Because you want to have a million of his babies like an alien queen or something."

"Gross. I don't like jocks, Ali. I thought joining a Legacy might make it easier to escape."

"Why're you being so defensive?"

"I'm not being defensive."

"Yes, you are."

"Quit it."

"Quit what?"

"You're trying to trick me."

"Trick you into what?"

"Into telling you I like him."

"A-ha! I knew it!"

"I didn't say I liked him! Quit it!"

Something blocked our light. We looked up to see Blake standing over us. Alison shaded her eyes with her hand. "Can we help you?"

"What are you guys doing?"

"Basking in the suffering of stupid teenagers," Alison said.

"Can I sit next to you?"

She waved her hand at the grass next to her. He plopped down and nodded at me. "Hey, Johnny." He looked over her shoulder at her screen and grinned. "'AlisonAffliction'? No one ever accuses you of being predictable, do they, Ms. Black Eyeliner?"

"Pfft, whatever. How many different colors have you dyed your mohawk, Mr. Originality?"

Blake ran his fingers through his hair. "Umm, green, red . . . purple, orange . . . like four, maybe five?"

"Where do you buy that stuff, anyway?"

"I get it at the commissary. You owe me a date," he said. A change of subject as smooth as pumice.

"Are you always so cheesy?"

"Like Kraft Dinner. You guys want to get lunch at Majere Hall?"

"You could have lunch with, like, a million other people. Everyone around here likes you."

"But I want to have lunch with you."

Alison smiled and glanced at me questioningly. Before I could say anything, my stomach growled loudly. "I think you have your answer," she said, grinning back at Blake. She shoved her laptop into her satchel and got up. I trailed behind her and Blake.

"Thanks for saving Johnny's ass," Alison said.

"Yeah, he's already said it, like, five million times." Honestly, he probably saved me just to impress Alison.

"Where'd you learn to fight like that, anyway?" Alison said. "Johnny said it was like watching a *Star Wars* movie."

"Black belt in karate . . . and I watch a lot of kung fu movies."

"What other kinds of movies do you like?"

"Romantic comedies." He took one look at Alison's face and said, "What? They make me feel good."

"So does digging too deep in your ear with a Q-tip. Doesn't mean it's good for you. Romantic comedies are like brain cancer for saps with unrealistic relationship goals."

"Ouch," he said with a chuckle. "You always this mean?"

"You think I mastered this level of bitchiness to let it go to waste?"

Our walk to Majere Hall was cut short when we crossed paths with Aiden and two of his goons. "Isn't this cute," Aiden said, smirking. "I was on my way to class, but I guess I have time to take a peek at the freakshow." He checked out Alison. "I heard the agents saying they extracted a—"

"Leo on the cusp of Virgo?" Alison said, fluttering her eyelashes. "I've also got a charming personality."

"Why don't you go back to your circle jerk at the Keep?" Blake said.

"I would, but you and I have some unfinished business, dear ol' Blake. You see, I've been stewing on it all week, and I've decided you owe me a wizard duel," Aiden said.

Alison checked her nails. "I swear, guys are always trying to measure their wands."

"Wizard duels are banned on campus, Aiden," Blake said.

A sinister smile crept across Aiden's face. "Oh, come on, I'm sure your little *girlfriend* wouldn't mind."

"Let's just go, Blake," Alison said, looking askance at Aiden. "This guy's parents obviously don't give him enough attention."

"Listen to uh, *her*, Blakey."

Blake stomped up to Aiden, snatched his shirt collar, and reeled back his fist, but when he swung, Aiden vanished, popping up a moment later behind Alison. Leaning forward, he whispered, "Isn't he cute when he gets mad?" into her ear. Alison spun around and punched Aiden so hard it staggered him. He took a few steps back, coddling the big red spot she left on his cheek. He clenched his fists like he was going to hit her, so I pushed him from behind and drew his attention to me.

Aiden's goons looked ready to jump in when Blake said, "Okay, Aiden! You want me to make you look bad again? Let's do it." He'd probably just stopped the situation from turning into a full-out brawl.

Aiden extended his hands, and his goons placed a salt carton in each palm. He tossed one to Blake. "You know how to stage a wizard duel, don't you, Blakey?"

"Just pour the salt, Aiden."

They walked in opposite directions, pouring salt on the ground and using it to draw a big circle. When each of them reached where the other had started, they cast aside the salt cartons and stepped into the circle across from one another. "You ready?" Aiden said.

Blake looked to the sky. "Ares! I invoke thee—"

"You don't really have to do the corny invocation, Blake."

"It helps me cast the circle, Aiden." Blake continued. "Ares, I invoke thee: bless this circle with the spirit of war!" The clouds darkened, spinning as whips of electricity lashed around inside them. Then they parted, and a lightning bolt struck the middle of the circle. The salt ring melted into sizzling black tar. Alison ran to pull Blake out of the circle but crashed into an invisible barrier around the ring.

"Sorry, honey," Aiden said. "This is couples' skate only."

Attracted by the lightning, rubbernecking students gathered around the ring. Blake smacked his hands together and drew a glowing sword from one of his palms. It was the same weapon he'd wielded in Darkwood Forest against the Bandersnatch. Aiden spread his arms and looked up to the clouds. Lightning bolts burst from the heavens and crashed down around him, buzzing and snapping. "Let's make this quick," he said.

He balled his fists, dropped his head, and yelled. A wave of force shot out from his body, tearing up the ground and throwing up shards of cement as it flew toward Blake. Eyes closed, Blake formed an unseen barrier and held fast as the torrential force exploded on contact with his shield, rippling the air around him and sending a powerful gust sweeping through his clothes. The nosy onlookers gawked at Blake's raw power.

"There's no way some non-Lineage trash could've blocked that spell!" Aiden swept his hand through the air and produced a light sword of his own, then he and Blake leaped at each other, clanging their glowing weapons together and sending sparks flying. "I've been trained in magic since I was a child," Aiden grunted.

Blake shoved him back, breaking the lock, and swung his sword at Aiden's face. "Brats like you have everything handed to you—that's why you're so mediocre."

Aiden deflected the attack and backed away. Hands held in front of his waist, Blake pointed the tip of his sword at Aiden. His insult had cracked Aiden's fragile ego. Enraged, Aiden pulled back and thrust clumsily, but Blake sidestepped the attack, spun around to Aiden's flank, and sliced his cheek. Aiden staggered back, pressed his hand to the wound, then held his bloody fingers before his unbelieving eyes, rage warping his face.

"Stop!" a voice yelled from outside the ring. A burst of wind swept through the quad, turning the black ring back into piles of salt and blowing it apart. In a fit of murmurs, the crowd dispersed.

When Blake and Aiden spotted Balthasar stomping toward them with two Smiths at his sides, they disappeared their weapons. Aiden ran a finger along his cheek and vanished the cut.

Balthasar's wrinkled face was twisted with anger. "How dare you take part in a wizard's duel on Institute grounds. The two of you are under house arrest, effective immediately."

●

News of the fight spread quick. After classes let out for the day, Hunter found Alison and me at my locker. "Did you hear about that fight in the quad?" he asked.

Alison scoffed. "Hear about it? We were there."

"We're going to check on Blake," I said, closing my locker.

"I'll come with you."

Alison sure was preoccupied with Blake's well being, considering she thought he was a spy. She raved all the way through the quad. "I don't know why he even did that. I didn't need him to take it up for me. What was he going to do if he got killed? *Oops, sorry about the whole dying thing.*"

Walking into Veles Hall, we found Linh behind the entryway desk, no doubt filling in for Blake while he was in trouble. "Hey, guys."

"Where's Blake?" Alison asked.

"He's upstairs in his room, but I wouldn't go up there if I were you. There's a bunch of Thorns in there right now. I think they're trying to recruit him."

"A bunch of what?"

"The Legacy of the Thorns," Hunter said. "Some of them are on the football team with me in Misthaven."

"'Legacy of the Thorns' sounds like a CW show," Alison said.

"Their Lineage is descended from magical warriors," Hunter said. "A lot of their parents are military elites. They're nothing like the Crowns."

"They can be kind of mean," Linh said.

"Mean?" Alison scoffed. "Wait until they meet me." She started up the stairs.

Linh waited for Alison to climb the first flight before turning back to us. "How badly did Blake beat him?"

"He cut Aiden's face pretty bad," Johnny said.

"It was probably an improvement. You'd better go after her. I've got to stay down here."

We hurried after Alison. Upstairs, a crowd of tall, athletic kids skulked outside Blake's door. They all turned as Alison walked right up to them. Out of the group of hulking boys emerged a smaller girl in a leather motorcycle jacket. She had red hair that curled up like wood shavings, and she fixed her fierce blue eyes on Alison. The other Thorns followed her lead, forming a wall around the door and keeping their stern eyes on Alison.

"Excuse me," Alison said.

"You're going to have to wait," the blue-eyed girl said.

"Blake's our friend," I said, walking up beside Alison.

The red-haired girl scowled at me. "And right now, he's busy."

The door opened. Blake was standing there next to a short boy with spiky hair and a weight lifter's brawny arms. "I'm not pledging to your Legacy, Anthony."

"That's the leader of the Thorns, Anthony Velásquez," Hunter muttered to me.

"The Thorns are a good fit for you, Blake," Anthony said. "Please, consider my offer."

Blake spotted Alison behind the wall of Thorns. "Hey," he said with a smile, obviously pleased to see her. He turned back to Anthony. "Get out."

"Just think about it, okay?" Anthony jerked his chin at the other Thorns. "Let's go, guys."

I was surprised he'd taken Blake's rejection so well. The Legacy kids I'd encountered so far were jerks. But Anthony seemed grounded, elegant. Hunter and I moved out of their way, pressing back against the wall as they marched past us. We watched until the last of them disappeared down the stairs. "What was that all about?" Alison asked.

Blake leaned against his doorframe. "Anthony wanted to recruit me because I kicked the crap out of Aiden, but I'm not interested."

"They did seem a little pushy, but not nearly as messed up as the Crowns," I said.

"Thorns hate Crowns. Crowns hate Thorns. Legacy politics are weird. Anyway, what's up?"

"We're checking up on you, considering you almost got killed."

"Yeah, right," Blake scoffed. "You think Aiden could take me?" He pushed himself off the frame. "I thought you had more faith in me than that."

"You could've gotten really hurt."

"Well, I'm banned from leaving Veles Hall for a while. You want to come down to the dining area to scrounge up some food?"

"You guys go on," I said. "I've had enough excitement for one day. I'm going to my room."

"Can I come?" Hunter said.

"Okay."

Alison gave me a knowing smirk. "All right, Blake," Alison said, "our frozen burrito quest will be less two explorers."

"Let's hope we don't freeze to death on our expedition through the fridge," he said.

Alison patted my shoulder and grinned as she passed.

Hunter and I headed to my room. I flopped face first onto the crackly bed. Hunter scanned the room for somewhere to crash and decided on the dingy carpet. He grabbed a notebook from under my bed, ripped out a piece of paper and balled it up, and started tossing it in the air and catching it. "Can't believe how weird Blake is about the Legacies."

"He's right, though. They're a bunch of brats."

"So what? Don't you want to be a brat, too, and get your way all the time, never answer for anything? Isn't that why you rushed with me?"

"I rushed because I thought becoming a Legacy would get me out of here faster."

He looked over at me and laughed. He must've thought I was joking. "I'd give anything to be part of a Legacy," he said, his eyes following the paper ball. "Get out of here when I turn eighteen. Be rich."

"You're not going to stay for the training program?"

"Nope. I've been in this place long enough. I'm getting out soon as I can." He sat up and turned to me. "Hey, you want to go to Misthaven on Saturday?"

"I can leave campus?"

"Long as you're accompanied by a second year or higher."

I wasn't going to say no to those dewy eyes. "Okay!"

For the rest of the night, Hunter lay on the floor telling me wild stories, like how his redneck uncles had once used a radiator as a still for making moonshine. For a minute, I forgot the Institute had kidnapped me. When I was with Hunter, all the suffering melted away, and all I could hear was his voice, sweet as a nectarine, or better yet, a peach. Hunter made me feel strong—strong enough to make it through all this. Maybe I made him feel that way too.

Chapter 16

1 WEEK AFTER EXTRACTION

Hunter had only been gone an hour when I heard a knock at my door. I opened it, and Hunter walked in, his tender eyes fixed on my lips. "Hey," I said awkwardly.

"I couldn't stop thinking about you," he whispered. My heart fluttered in my chest. He grabbed the front of my shirt and tugged it, pulling me in close. He brought his face an inch away from mine. Just an inch. His eyes danced over me. I couldn't look back; I looked away, too embarrassed to meet his eyes. "Look at me," he said. I sucked in a breath, turned to him. Our faces were so close, I could feel his breath on my skin, could feel his nose barely touching my cheek. His eyes were boring into me. He studied my lips, stared into my eyes. Then he closed the space between us. His hands went around my sides and brought us closer, so close our hearts entangled in a rumbling dance.

And then he kissed me. His kiss was rich and sweet, like a honey-comb. I closed my eyes and let those lips lift me out of this place, away from this nightmare. When I opened them, he was gone.

Out in the hallway. Hissing. Like sand. It was there. Watching me. Waiting for me. I stepped outside in search of Hunter, looked to my left, looked to my right. My eyes widened when I spotted a sand trail leading into one of the other rooms. Slowly placing one foot in front of the other, I followed the trail, inched toward the room it led to. The hissing noise grew. I placed a shaky hand on the doorframe, creaked the door open, and looked inside. A shape stood in the darkness. Its features were impossible to make out because its back was turned. A swirling darkness enveloped its body. A shadow aura.

I heard the word *cintamani* lap at the air like a viper's tongue.

•

Then, I woke up. *Another day in this prison.* I was still hoping the nightmares would eventually let up. It was no coincidence they'd started after Alison and I did that spell. I was still in bed when she knocked. She was early.

"We're skipping," she said, soon as I answered.

"They could drag us under the Heka Building."

"Blake got into a straight-up magic fight, and all they did was ground him."

"Okay, so what're we doing instead?"

"Come by my room. There's something I want to show you."

In Alison's room, she shoved me onto her bed, then sat down next to me. She lay back. "Lie down and close your eyes." I complied. "Okay, now imagine something really nice. When it starts to get kind of lucid, you'll see what I'm talking about."

I tried thinking of home, but instead, the first thing I pictured was Hunter hovering over me in my bed, bathed in sunlight, his hands planted on the sides of my face. I fought the image away. The next thing I imagined was Dad eating spaghetti with me at our favorite pizza place, laughing and making legs out of forks and walking them around. I felt heat from the lamp hanging over the table; felt the cracked leather of the seat underneath me; smelled the oven's earthy scent and the oregano, garlic, and cheese of the pie baking in it—so amazing; I even heard the cooks yelling orders at each other as the phone rang off the hook.

Then the memory grew layers. It was raining outside. I could hear the cars swashing through puddles on the street, heard thunder gurgling in the clouds like an empty stomach.

"Hey, kid, you got a boyfriend yet?" my dad said.

I groaned. "Dad."

"What? You know, one of these days, you're going to meet some lucky guy, Juanito, and he's going to fall in love with you." His eyes grew glassy as tears misted them. "And maybe . . . maybe you two'll get married, you know? And you'll get a house, and you'll have kids, and then I can come over and spoil the kid, and your mom"—he stopped and looked outside, pressed his fist to his lips, watched the storm through the window. Some people were running across the street, covering their heads with their hands, umbrellas, newspapers—anything to shield themselves from the rain.

I looked down at my plate. The pizza lay there, a lifeless pile of cheese and bread that, when my father was sad like this, seemed flavorless.

"*Okay, J,*" said Alison's voice in my head, "*could you not be so depressing for like five minutes?*"

The world spun around me; everything melted into a paint-like blur like I was whirling on a carousel through time and space. My eyelids swung shut from the force. When the spinning stopped, I found myself standing in front of the Bean in Millennium Park. I stared up at its shiny surface, reached my fingers out, touched it. Solid. Real as anything. I startled, pulling my fingers away. I hadn't expected it to feel so real. Then, reflected on its shiny surface, shapes of light swirled together. Alison emerged out of the light blob as though the Bean were made of quicksilver, then landed on the ground next to me.

"I haven't been to see the Bean since I was four," I said.

She took a few steps back and stared at it with me. "Isn't this amazing?"

"What's going on?"

"We're in Everywhen."

That was the dreamworld Bigsby had rambled about, the place nestled between our world and death where the dreams of the entire sleeping population united. I hadn't bothered exploring it since coming to the Institute, but it didn't surprise me that Alison had.

She grabbed my hand and squeezed. Staring up at the Bean, we grew quiet. Like globs of wax inside a lava lamp, our reflected shapes melted and distorted in the Bean's shiny surface. They danced like two comets spiraling through the sky, leaving behind a glimmering trail of white stardust. "What did you and Blake do last night?" I asked.

"He got a sandwich from the vending machine, and we sat down and talked while he ate."

"And?"

She clicked her tongue. "And he came by my room and showed me how to do this."

"So you two were asleep next to each other?"

"No one was weirder about the whole thing than me, J. Trust me."

"Do you like him?"

"Get real, Johnny. I don't trust any guys. Except for you, of course."

"Because of what Todd did?" She looked down, got quiet. Paint flecks of anger burned like embers in her big brown eyes. Todd had put those there. Our wounds had healed, but she still felt the sting in her heart. It had made her timid. She'd never been timid before. I hated Todd for doing that to her.

I changed the subject. "I'm still having weird dreams. I always hear hissing sand and stuff."

"Hissing sand?"

"I had a dream like that the night before they kidnapped us too. There was this monster made of sand that was trying to kill me."

An uneasy feeling came over me. It was like someone was watching me. Ali must've felt it too; she looked around like she was searching for something, then shuddered. "We should get back. There's other stuff I want to get done today."

When we woke up, we were still lying in Alison's bed. "What was that creepy feeling?" I asked.

She sat up. "I don't know. That didn't happen when I went with Blake."

"There's something weird going on, Ali. What if the dreams are connected to the cintamani?"

"We're going to look into this cintamani thing, okay? We're going to the library to read everything we can about it."

We trekked across campus to Ansalom Hall, a four-story rotunda with a coffered dome next to Odin Hall. Just beyond the vestibule, a circular marble floor rested under the watchful oculus in the center of the dome. Classes hadn't started yet; students were wandering around doing last-minute homework research. I walked a few steps behind Alison, taking in our surroundings. "So what're we looking for?"

"A library catalogue." She spotted a computer sitting on a desk at the end of an aisle. "There we go." The screen read, PLEASE SCAN MARDUK INSTITUTE ID TO CONTINUE. She passed her ID under a mounted scanner, and the screen switched to the forum home page. As she accessed the catalogue, I glanced at the time on my phone. With ten minutes left before the first bell, students were already filing out of the library.

Alison turned to me. "All right, all the Institute stuff is on the second floor." We climbed the staircase, found the aisle full of books about the Institute, and fanned them out on the floor around us. Outside, the bell rang, but it didn't register as much more than a dull ring where we were, deep in the library.

We pored over the books for almost an hour before we turned up some interesting facts. The Institute had been built sometime in the early twentieth century, its construction financed by a group of like-minded wizards, including—

"Harry Houdini!" Alison said.

"Shh! We don't want to get caught," I whispered.

Alison looked around, then showed me what she was reading. Indeed, Harry Houdini had helped to build the Marduk Institute. There wasn't much information about the Institute itself, though, besides its being a training facility for wizards. "Something tells me we're not getting the full picture," Alison said. "All this just reads like propaganda."

I closed a book. "Why would they leave"—I stopped when I looked up and saw the smiling man in white at the end of the aisle. He stood perfectly still for a long moment, then walked off to the left. Alison was watching me in confusion over my sudden silence. I rose, hopped over our books, and hurried after the man.

"Johnny?" Alison said. "Where the hell are you going?"

Peeking around the corner, I spotted the smiling man in white step between two stacks. I bolted into the aisle after him, but he was gone. I did find a single book sitting open on the floor. Curious, I crouched down to look at it.

The page was covered in scribbly handwriting, just like the handwriting in the book Alison and I used for the cintamani ritual. Wedged in the spine was a black-and-white photo of three people. My blood ran cold when I examined it closer: it was Melchior, a younger Balthasar, and the man in white, also much younger. They were all smiling, and they were standing in front of the Heka Building. I looked for a note on the back, anything that might tell me where the photo had come from. Nothing. I turned the book over and studied the blank spine. Again, nothing.

Alison walked into the aisle. "Hey, why did you just leave like that?" I looked at her, doubtless as pale as a death row inmate on his final day. Her brows tightened. "J, what's up?"

"Look at this." I handed her the book and the photo.

She gave both them a brief scan. "What is this? How'd you find it?"

I pointed at the smiling man in white in the picture. "This guy led me to it."

Alison looked around. "Where'd he go?"

"I don't know. I saw him go down this aisle, then he disappeared."

"Do you know him?"

"No. But I've seen him a couple of times, in random places. I thought it was my imagination at first. He's older than this, but still the same guy. The Smiths in the Elric Building mentioned a man named Gaspar who joined the Defectors, and Blake mentioned a third head scientist who disappeared. You think they're the same person?"

"Maybe." Alison looked back at the photo. "Melchior, Balthasar, and Gaspar. All three wisemen, lined up."

"But one of them is gone, and those Smiths said that Balthasar and Melchior don't trust each other anymore."

"I wonder why. And that Melchior guy . . . he's the only one in the picture who hasn't aged." She studied the handwriting in the book. "This almost looks like—"

"Like the book with the cintamani spell."

"Yeah." She slipped the book into her satchel. "I'm sure they won't notice this is gone."

"Did you find anything about that cintamani thing in the catalogue?"

"Only one book reference, in a book on the third floor."

We found the book, *Secrets and Mysteries of the Invisible World*, brought it to a table, and hovered over it, scanning the pages. Alison groaned. "All this says is that it's supposedly cursed."

"We conjured something cursed?"

"Possibly?" Alison smiled awkwardly.

"Do you think that has anything to do with my nightmares?"

"I don't know. It doesn't say anything about dreams."

Great. We'd summoned something cursed, which was possibly the reason for my strange dreams. But I couldn't just run to the head scientists and beg them to fix whatever was wrong with me. They'd probably just drag me under the Heka Building for experimentation.

"What's the plan now?"

"Blake said Dedi Hall is where all adults stay and have training, right? There's got to be someone there who's been here a while and knows stuff other people don't."

Dedi Hall was another ruthlessly cold cinderblock on the grounds. At seven stories, it was one of the tallest buildings on campus, only two stories shorter than the medical building. Luckily, it was also right next door to Ansalom Hall, lined up with all the other buildings along the southern perimeter of the Institute, so we didn't have to creep around too much. The building sat a few yards south of Aumar Hall and only a walkway's breadth west of the Elric Building. It also faced the largest gate and parking lot of the Institute. If visitors and teachers were going to park anywhere, it would likely be across from Dedi Hall.

What Dedi Hall lacked in height it more than made up for in size; its exterior was as wide as many of the other buildings' added together. Inside, halls branched off to the left and the right, and in front of us, a short flight of steps led down to an arcade around a courtyard with a recreational pool. Heading off to the right, we followed the building's white hallways in a loop around the courtyard. Along the way, we encountered little robot vacuums that buzzed around, keeping everything pristine. More than a couple of the robots, however, were on the fritz, smacking into walls over and over again.

Alison's bright idea was to start asking random people questions like, "Who's the oldest person in the building?" But since there weren't any people just hanging out in the hallways, she decided we should go door to door.

My shyness had me cringing at the idea. "Alison," I said, just as she was poised to knock on a door. "Don't you think this is a little ⸫ . . awkward?"

She shook her head at me then knocked. A few moments later,

a violet-haired woman with piercings who couldn't have been any older than twenty answered the door. "Hey, nice hair," Alison said. "We're new here."

"I'd say welcome, but I think sorry is more appropriate."

"We've been getting that vibe."

"Did the old guy give you the spiel on how privileged you are to be here?"

"Sort of. Can you help us? We're looking for the oldest person in the building."

"Mrs. Newman is ninety-one. Why're you looking for old people?"

"Sorry, that's not what I meant. Who's been here the longest?"

"There's a lady on the seventh floor, Suhaila—I think she's been here fifteen years."

Fifteen years? That was it? The Institute had been around since the beginning of the twentieth century, and its longest staying resident had been here only fifteen years?

"No one's been here longer than that?" Alison asked.

"Not that I know of, but Suhaila might. She's in apartment 7C."

We left in search of an elevator. "No one's been here longer than fifteen years? That's kind of spooky," I said, trailing behind Alison.

"You might be overthinking it, J. Everyone else probably just left."

I calmed down. Alison was the conspiracy nut. Working myself up over something so vague didn't seem worthwhile. We rode up to the seventh floor and found Suhaila's door. A woman in a red cardigan answered our knock. She was holding a cup of coffee in one hand and a cigarette in the other. She puffed on it as she watched us behind her horn-rimmed cat's-eye glasses. "Yes?"

Alison smiled uncomfortably under the woman's heavy gaze. "We're looking for Suhaila?"

"That's me."

"Hi, we're new here, and we were just wondering if you could answer some questions?"

Suhaila studied us, then stepped aside and let us in. Her little apartment stunk of cigarettes; there were several glass ashtrays filled with butts. Where there weren't ashtrays, there were ceramic figurines of praying hands and children crossing bridges while watched by guardian angels, as well as self-help books opened to highlighted inspirational quotes. She walked us into her living room. An old, boxy TV was blaring a soccer game. She turned the volume dial down, then she took a seat in a floral armchair. Knitting needles and a skein of purple yarn sat on a TV tray beside her. She had been knitting a scarf.

Suhaila couldn't have been any older than forty-five. She had piercing green eyes and a tangled nest of brown curls that fell around her face. "Make it quick? I haven't got all day." She lit a new cigarette with the butt of her last, then snuffed out the nub in an ashtray.

"Are you allowed to smoke in here?"

She laughed. "What're they going to do?"

"I don't know. Kill you?"

"That'd be a mercy."

"Someone told us that you've been at the Institute longer than anyone else," Alison started.

"No, Dr. Shelton has been here the longest: twenty-nine years."

"Do you know anything about the third scientist who went missing, or a man named Gaspar?" I asked.

Suhaila rubbed her lower lip, squinted, and smiled. "I've only ever heard whispers of a third scientist. I've never heard of anyone named Gaspar, though."

"Do you know anything about the Administrators?" Alison asked.

"No one knows anything about the Institute besides what they tell us. And no one knows anything about the Administrators either. I looked into all of it for years and turned up nothing. It's all very hush hush."

"Have you ever been under the Heka Building?"

"No. And I'm thankful for that. I've seen people go in there and never come back. They say the scientists experiment on wizards down there."

"I saw a white-haired kid down there. Do you know anything about that?" I asked.

"Somnambulists—sleepwalkers. They live half inside this world and half inside Everywhen. They're said to be quite powerful, so the Institute tucks them away, extra safe." She flicked her cigarette.

"Ever heard of the cintamani?" I chewed my lower lip.

"No."

"What about the Defectors?"

She grew quiet, studying us like a snake winding around a mouse. "We don't talk about the Defectors."

"What do you know about them?"

"Not a damn thing. Now, I need you to leave." She got out of her chair and led us to the door, slamming it shut behind us.

Alison looked at me, wide eyed. "Well, that wasn't very useful."

"You two!" We turned and spotted a Smith down the hallway speed walking toward us. Alison grabbed my arm and yanked me in the opposite direction. "Hey!" the Smith yelled.

Turning a corner, we found an unattended cleaning cart standing outside a utility closet. A janitor was inside, on his knees and showing some serious plumber's crack as he reached under a wire rack full of cleaning supplies. "Come here, you little rat," he muttered.

Alison grabbed the cart, rolled it around the corner, and sent it barreling toward the Smith. He couldn't react quick enough; the cart crashed into him, and both toppled onto the floor. A bucket that had been hanging on the side of the cart fell off and plunked the Smith on the head, covering him in gray, sudsy water.

Hearing the commotion, the janitor rushed out just as we resumed our flight down the hallway. Finding his cart overturned and seeing our guilty expressions, he raised a fist and yelled, "You little runts!"

We hurried into an elevator, laughing. "So, the building has rats," Alison said.

"All this magic and they're too cheap to hire a pest control service."

The elevator door slid open to reveal the soaked Smith standing there, his face bunched up like he'd eaten some sour candies, his hand resting on the spray canister inside his jacket. He must've used magic to route our escape.

Alison and I raised our hands. "White flag," she said.

The Smith walked us back to Odin Hall and made us go to the principal's chilly office. Luckily, they didn't check Alison's bag and find the book we'd stolen from the library. We sat in stiff wooden chairs, waiting for him to spin around in his high-back office chair. When he did, we shuddered. He was spookier than a door-to-door noose salesman, with a gaunt pale face like a starving horse and scraggly white hair on the sides of his head like moth-eaten curtains in a haunted house. His eyes were a sickly green color, with little red veins spidering through the whites. He clasped his hands in front of his face, leaned forward, and, in a voice like razors scraping glass, said, "Children, is there anything you'd like to say?"

"Yeah," Alison said. "I got this skin cream from the commissary—you know, you should check it out sometime. It could really help that graying, zombie-like complexion of yours."

His monstrous face turned a shade more hideous, wrinkling and twisting like knobby tree limbs. "I don't think you're funny, young lady."

"Really? The Rotten Tomatoes score for my stand-up special is a hundred percent."

I almost thought I saw his shadow strangling Alison's. "You and I will come to like each other after a while," he managed.

"Will that be before or after you help Frankenstein raise his monster?"

"I'm letting you two off with a warning this time. Next time, two weeks' detention."

"Oh, goodie. Will we have it with you?"

He slid his slimy tongue across his chapped lips. "You certainly will."

We shrank in our seats.

Chapter 17

1 WEEK AFTER EXTRACTION

Storm clouds groaned overhead like creaky joists in a crumbling house. It was going to rain. I'd already felt the sky's leaky plumbing drip onto my nose.

To leave the Institute, you had to pass through one of its four checkpoints, so I headed for the north gate right across the street from Veles Hall. Before I could pass through the arch, I had to stand still and spread my arms while a tall, bald-headed Smith scanned me with a security wand. After I was cleared, I went through the turnstile. Hunter was waiting at a bus stop right outside the gate, his arms crossed behind his head, squinting at the cloudy sky. I smiled, and when he saw me coming, he lowered his arms and smiled too.

"Hey," Hunter said.

"How're we the only ones here? Why isn't everyone lined up to get the hell out of this place?"

"Because no one wants to get up early on Saturday." He kicked at the dirt, then looked up at me. "Where were you yesterday?"

"Alison and I skipped class."

"What'd you guys go do?"

"Went to the library."

Hunter laughed. "You skipped school to go to the library?"

"We wanted to do some research on this place."

"Find anything interesting?"

"We found this weird book that looked like someone's journal. Inside, there was a photo of Melchior, Balthasar, and a third guy we think might have been the third head scientist. And get this, everyone in the picture looked younger—except Melchior. He looked the same as he does now. We also went to Dedi Hall and talked to this lady there. She told us no one's been here longer than about thirty years."

"But the Institute's, like, a hundred years old."

"Exactly."

"I guess people just move on."

I shrugged. "Yeah, maybe. Anyway, we asked her about the Defectors, and she lost it and kicked us out."

"Some people are paranoid. They worry the agents'll come snatch 'em up." He pulled down his shirt collar and showed me his neck. "Hey, smell me." He grinned. "Come on, here, smell my neck."

I raised my eyebrows at him. "You want me to smell you?"

"What?" he said. "It's nothing weird. I've got good cologne on. Maybe you can borrow it sometime so you don't go around smelling like a bunch of reindeer ran a train on you."

"Gross." I liked Hunter's dirty jokes, though. "Fine." I leaned forward and sniffed him. His cologne smelled fresh and clean, somehow athletic. I closed my eyes and filled my lungs, inching my nose forward until I accidentally touched it to his neck.

He flinched and snickered. "You trying to give me a hickey, bro?"

"I'm sorry . . . I didn't mean to—"

"Sure."

A small bus joggled up to the stop, its gears churning as it stopped. We boarded, and as he went down the aisle, Hunter slapped each of the seats. He threw himself into the last bench in the back, making the cracked vinyl hiss, then he smacked the seat next to him, so I joined him. The familiar bus smell—vinyl, burnt rubber, engine oil—reminded me of home. For a moment, I missed riding the awful school bus, missed how normal it was to get on it, go to school, and be miserable all day.

Hunter snapped his finger in front of my face, pulling me out of my thoughts. "Hey," he said, "we can get on the regular internet out here." I checked my phone. Twitter. YouTube. Instagram. We were delivered from the Institute's internet tyranny. "Just don't bother making new accounts anywhere—they'll find them and delete them."

On the way to Misthaven, I Googled "Marduk Institute" on my phone and checked out the official website. There were pictures of students walking in the quad, talking and laughing; Majere Hall's busy cafeteria; even a student helping an older adult carry their groceries into a Dedi Hall apartment. Wholesome. But a complete mirage. They'd completely fooled the outside world. The website even had an application for people who wanted to attend. No doubt any applications from non-wizards were rejected.

I opened the Faculty and Staff page. All the teachers and administrative personnel were listed, with little pictures over their names.

I tapped on their faces to read their About pages. They all lived in Misthaven.

Hunter looked at my phone. "What're you looking at?"

"Just reading about the teachers. You ever try talking to one of them outside of class?"

He shook his head. "I don't think they'd be much different from how they are at the Institute."

I stared back down at their pictures. The fake smiles. Uncomfortable. Pinched. They were probably as afraid as we were. Prisoners just as much as us. Whether in Misthaven or back at the Institute.

I put away my phone and watched Darkwood Forest blur past, sunlight flashing in indistinct patches through its naked branches. A map pinned to a board behind the driver's seat showed that the road leading from the Institute to Misthaven looped around Lake Misty. Darkwood Forest surrounded everything, just as the wall surrounded the Institute. Misthaven was one big circle cradled deep in a valley. Maybe if you looked down at it from above, it looked like a big eye.

Eventually, the trees thinned, and I could see a factory perched on Lake Misty's shores. Big red pipes plunged into the water.

"What's that?" I said.

"Pura. The water bottling company. Pretty much everyone in Misthaven works there."

A whole town built around a lake, but the lake was controlled by a private company outside of town. How unfair was it for the people living there to have no say over their livelihood?

"Hey, look at this." I took my eyes off the factory and looked down at a meme on Hunter's phone. As he scrolled through a web-site Alison's friend Chloë would've found "problematic," I nestled close to him. When my arm brushed against his, he glanced over at me. For a moment, our eyes danced. I studied his lips, wondered what kissing them would feel like, wondered if the teensy hairs on his face would tickle me. "What?" he said.

My cheeks grew hot, so I turned away. "Nothing. Tell me about Misthaven. Melchior said the Institute controls it."

"I reckon he isn't lying. There're tons of agents working in town, making sure the Institute blends in. Cute little town with an elite private micro-community just around the corner."

Little buildings rose up in the distance. The bus drove down Pine Street, past the entrance of a trailer park full of aluminum-sided, double-wide trailers, all next to an old fairground that clearly hadn't been used in years. A weathered wooden sign, splintered and discolored by the elements, read *Darkwood Housing Community*.

"Misthaven's only got one post office, one fire department, and one police station," Hunter said. The town was small. Small and weird.

A ways down the road from the trailer park, the town sprang up around us. We passed the library and the high school, and near the end of Pine Street, the bus drove through a more idyllic neighborhood, a subdivision with a sign reading *The Pines* sitting in a land-scaped traffic island. Strands of sunlight barely pierced the elm tree canopy shrouding the neighborhood, casting a shadowy kalei-doscope over everything. On either side of the road were white aluminum-sided colonials, one after the other, each with red doors and its own miniature American flag holstered in a bracket. Through a crack in the bus window, I could smell barbecue, and when the bus slowed to a halt at a stop sign, I could hear children playing and people laughing.

At the end of the Pines, we turned left onto Smithsprings Road.

We rode by the elementary school, crossed George Street, then Maple Road, and took another left onto Main Street, finally stopping in front of a weather-worn bus shelter near a traffic circle. Hunter hopped off the bus and spun around with his arms wide open. "Welcome to Misthaven."

I stepped onto the curb and looked around. Beyond the tops of several small buildings, forested hills were painted across the mountains, a plume of mist floating over them. I wasn't impressed. "Wow."

"What do you mean? This place is awesome!" He was beaming like a Christmas tree.

Sure, all this country stuff was cute, but it gave me the creeps. We crossed the street onto a sidewalk along Misthaven's only thoroughfare. The people seemed friendly—runners smiled at us in their Nike-checkmarked everything, store owners waved at us as they swept dead leaves off the sidewalk, dog walkers being pulled along by their dogs said hello—but I couldn't shake the feeling they were all spying on us. It was in the way they cut their eyes just after we passed by, and in the figures standing behind dusty shop windows, watching us. "This place is weird," I said.

"Yeah it is. Kids at school call it the Witch's Cauldron because late at night, the mist from the lake swallows everything in the valley. Weird thing about the mist is it never comes over the Institute's walls. Supposedly, if you look real hard, you can see giant shadows roaming in the mist. Like Asuras the Institute's forced into servitude. I've never seen no giant shadows, but then again, I never looked real hard either. Some kids say the mist is a spell, but no one knows what it's for. Others say it's alive and it eats people. No Institute kid I know's ever been in it, though, so what do they know. It's just fog."

Hunter's words left a chill in my soul. I shuddered.

"You scared?"

I rolled my eyes, and he laughed. We walked toward the more populated part of Main Street. A bronze signpost in the traffic circle read *Explorer Park*. In the middle of the park stood a statue that was little more than a featureless blob of stone pointing to the sky. "That's supposed to be the town's founder," Hunter said, nodding at the misshapen rock. He pointed out all the fixtures surrounding the park: "That's the largest church in town—it's called Holy Cross. That old colonial mansion to the northeast is Doc Smither's B and B. South of here, that's Bayard House—it just serves overpriced breakfast food all day."

He squinted and pointed northeast toward Ashford Street, off Main. "Honestly, though, everyone'd rather eat at Amhert Diner. It's been amazing, few times I've been. The lady that owns it is real nice too. Her name's Claudette."

After passing the traffic circle, we ventured onto Main Street proper. Weathered brick storefronts lined the main road on both sides. Main Street was a mélange of worn brick buildings with striped awnings and their business names painted on their windows in blocky 1950s fonts. It was ramshackle wooden structures with paint flaking off walls in sheets, leaving the exteriors mottled. Even the newer-looking businesses had retro-style signage to match the older ones.

We stopped in front of a store called Frontier Supplies. Hunter nudged my arm. "Let's go in here. I love this store."

Inside, rusting display shelves were packed with kitschy, old junk: World War II–themed greeting cards, dusty cans of Spam, toy firetrucks, a cowbell. Hunter grabbed it off the dusty shelf and dangled it at me, drawing a nasty look from the mummy-like store owner lurking behind the front counter. He had so many wrinkles that he looked like a big, hairless mole rat. I couldn't even tell if his eyes were open, his eyebrows were so bushy.

"Isn't this place neat?" Hunter said. "It's like a theme park: 'Old World.'"

"More like *Westworld*," I said.

A few ropes tied across some barrels blocked off the very back of the store. Sitting atop one of the barrels was a folded, pitched paper sign that read *Under Renovation*. "I hate that they're changing it," Hunter said, flicking over the paper sign. "I like that it's old, you know? Gives it character."

I looked at the exposed wooden rafters, heard the musty old beams groaning. They were as tired of holding up this old place as the mummy falling asleep on the front counter was. "You like the feeling that the roof's about to cave in on us?"

Hunter dropped his shoulders. Then his eyes brightened again. "Hey, there's something I want to show you."

We left Frontier Supplies and headed north. We broke off from the vein leading out of town and took a road beside an old split-rail fence. I'd never seen such a banged-up road before, full of potholes and cracks.

I closed my eyes for a moment and sniffed the crisp summer air. Being cooped up in the Institute, with its stale, recycled air and stale, recycled people withered your soul and bones. Hunter kicked a rock and sent it *clack, clack*, clacking down the road. He kicked another one, and I tried to join in. I swung my foot— *swoosh*—and completely missed. Hunter looked at me like I'd somehow managed to spill a sealed can of Coke all over myself. They were just rocks; they weren't moving or anything. I tried again. *Swoosh*. Missed. Hunter laughed at me.

We chanced upon a frog hopping its way to the creek across the road. "Hey," Hunter said, "you ever caught a frog?" I wrinkled my face in disgust. "What? Never?"

"No. Gross."

"Gross? It's just a frog."

"Alison would kill me if she found out I was kidnapping frogs."

"It's not like you're taking them the Institute to become frog wizards or something."

"We should. We could have our own little army. Be kings of the frog wizards."

He laughed. "You're already king of the frog wizards."

Normally, my defensiveness made me feel like every joke was a deeply wounding personal attack. Not with Hunter, though. No matter how much he made fun of me, it never felt mean. He was teasing me because we were friends, because he liked me. That felt nice. "What'll you do if you catch it?"

"Help it get across the road." He ran ahead of me and hunched over. The frog hopped a few more times. Hunter snatched it up with both hands, then ran back to flash it in my face. I recoiled, so he pulled it back, jumped the split-rail fence, jogged to the creek on the other side, and set the frog down in the babbling water. He watched as the frog hopped around on the rocks. When he was satisfied, he legged it back over the fence to join me again.

"You're such a Boy Scout," I said.

"Eagle Scout, actually."

"Do you have a Captain America costume in your dorm room?"

"Maybe. Do you want to see me in a Captain America costume?" My face tensed. Was he flirting with me again? "I'm just messing with you, Johnny," he said. I needed to stop writing fan fiction in my head every time he made a funny comment.

We kept walking until we reached a gravel driveway branching off to a farmhouse built on a mile-long stretch of prairie. Cows grazed in a field of switchgrass behind a wooden fence to our right, and in the distance, a cacophony of chicken clucks and rooster crows filled the air alongside the smell of cow crap. I wrinkled my nose. "Don't like that smell?" Hunter asked. I shook my head. He smiled and said, "Smells like home to me."

"You lived in a pile of cow crap?"

"Close enough."

Maybe long ago the house had been white, but years of wear and tear had left the crumbling wood a patchwork of browns and grays. A bench swing with rusty chains hung in the creaky storm porch in front, and the sweet smell of cinnamon seeping through the front of the house was a welcome relief. Hunter rapped his knuckles against a ratty screen door, and the clatter of moving furniture and clanking pots echoed from inside.

An old woman slogged open the heavy wooden door behind the screen. "Hunter?" she said, her shaky voice as high as the whine on a tuning fork. She unlatched the screen door and opened it. "Get your skinny ass in here!"

"Hey Ms. Alwina, I brought a friend," he said.

I smiled awkwardly as she adjusted the spectacles sitting at the tip of her pointy nose. "Well, you get in here too."

We left our shoes in the mudroom before entering her house. Alwina's home, if you could call it that, was more like a dusty old tourist trap, one of those log cabin museums you see off the side of the road that promises wonders, but has only taxidermied jackalopes. Photographs, newspapers, and books were piled up to the vaulted ceilings next to old-fashioned stuff like wood-burning stoves, Victorian dressers, and all manner of brass lamps. A preponderance of junk nevertheless arranged meticulously. Floating shelves high up, near the cornices, were lined with old pictures trapped in ancient wooden frames. I tried to make out what they showed, but the shelves were too high up and the pictures too old.

Standing guard outside her living room, a mounted moose head hung on a hat rack, quietly judging all passersby. Alwina took a seat in a rocking chair in front of a cold fireplace. "Sit anywhere," she told us. Hunter stayed standing, so I didn't sit down either. "I was hoping to show my friend the horses," Hunter said.

"You're here to see Amalthea again, huh? She loves when you come see her. Where have you been lately?"

"Busy. School stuff . . ."

"Well, you know where she is. I'd love for you to come back sometime, Hunter. I've got plenty of work for you."

"Will do, Ms. Alwina." Hunter nudged my arm, so I followed him. We squeezed back through the cluttered hallways to the mudroom. Shoes back on, we sent the screen door swinging as we hopped outside. Hunter led me to a paddock round the back of the farmhouse.

Excited, he got a little ahead of me. I jogged up beside him. "How do you know her?"

"I clean the stables here sometimes. When I first came to the Institute, on my first trip to Misthaven, I saw this flyer for a stable cleaner—said it paid. I missed doing stuff like that on my folks' farm."

Hunter darted ahead and flung himself against the paddock's wooden rails. "Hey, Amalthea!" he called, waving to a beautiful white mare trotting around inside the pen. She snorted and approached him, stretching her neck over the rail. He hugged her neck and ran a hand through her mane, the white strands shimmering like strings of sunlight between his fingers.

"You like horses, huh?" I said.

"You think she's just another horse?" A grin crept across his face. "Why don't you use that trick me and Blake showed you, feel everything around you with your mind?"

I closed my eyes and focused on the emotional energy thrumming all around me. The soft breeze carried the smell of rain, exciting everything: busy ants gathering food for the long winter dreaded that the impending storm would ruin their progress; exhausted, drooping willows were ready for a fall bath; and gossipy blades of grass whispered rumors only they knew and giggled as the sunlight's wispy rays tickled them. Then I felt something else, like Dad's gentle fingers guiding me along Lane Beach's shores for the first time. He'd crouched and wrapped his big arms around my tiny body, pointed to the sky as the sun tucked itself in, told me to reach for the stars and never stop. I opened my eyes and gasped. A single, glowing horn crowned Amalthea's head. "Is this for real?"

"Yup."

"She's a—"

"Unicorn."

Amalthea peered into my soul with eyes as blue as a cloudless summer sky, and just as warm too. Her aura was as different from the Bandersnatch's as you could imagine. It welcomed you to approach, to hand her all your trust, with no exception. I inched toward her, my trembling fingers reaching for her shining mane, a powerful feeling of tranquility filling my every step. She glowed; sunlight shimmered in soft patches on her gossamer hair and bloomed around her like a halo. I sifted my fingertips through her hair, fine as freshly spun silk. Then I closed my eyes, let her gentle aura carry me off to a sparkling ocean whose lazy waters danced with floating daisies. When I had basked in her all-encompassing light for some time, I opened my eyes and turned back to Hunter. It took me a minute to gather enough air to speak. "Her aura is s-strong. Is she like, an Asura or something?"

"I don't know."

"Does Ms. Alwina—"

"Ms. Alwina's a wizard, too, so I'm pretty sure she knows about Amalthea."

"Did Alwina go to the Institute?"

"I asked her about it before. She said she did, but didn't get too specific. Just said she went, and when she was done, she moved out here."

"You think the Institute knows about Amalthea?"

"Nope. And Amalthea wouldn't let you see her horn if she didn't trust you, so keep it between us. I don't want her to end up in the basement of the Heka Building." He nudged me with his elbow. "You want to go for a ride on her?"

"Seriously?"

"Yeah, come on," he said, grinning. He walked around to the gate and entered the paddock. He steadied himself against Amalthea, then vaulted onto her back like he'd done it a million times before. He leaned forward and whispered into her ear, and she trotted out of the pen and approached me. He stretched his hand toward me. "Come on." I grabbed it, and he reeled me up behind him. He wrapped his arms around her neck and looked back at me. "You better hold on tight." I grabbed his hips. Then he patted her neck. "Take us somewhere, Amalthea."

She gaited off the farm, first at a canter, then quickening her step until she was galloping through the flaxen countryside. Her stride was gentle, like a whisper, like a dream. I watched the tall grass glide under us like a golden carpet. Laughing, Hunter sat up and spread his arms. The wind rustled up his jacket, so I scooted in closer, rested my face against his back, and pressed it down. His cologne filled my nose, and his heartbeat filled my ears, thumping in rhythm with Amalthea's gallop like they were synchronized.

My fingers slid up over his waist, not intentionally, but because I was holding him so tight. He looked back and made me self-conscious, so I slackened my grip. "What're you doing?" he said. "You could fall off." I answered his warning by replacing my hands around his stomach. This time, tighter.

Just two guys riding a unicorn. Nothing gay about that.

We rode for a while until Amalthea stopped to drink from a creek. Hunter hopped off and slapped my knee. "Race me to that tree up there." He pointed at an old oak tree sitting on top of a hill. We ran, while a crisp breeze pushed back the swaying, tall grass like fingers through golden hair. Halfway up, I caught up to Hunter, so he wrinkled his nose and shoved me; I pushed him back with my shoulder. We laughed, and he closed the space between us. Wrapping his arms around my waist, he tackled me, sending us rolling through ryegrass and baby's breath. He held me tight as we tumbled down the hill. At the bottom, I lay on my back, head spinning. I gathered my bearings and looked up. Hunter was on top of me, his arms on either side of my head.

He hovered over me, his head blocking the glaring sunlight. The wind sifted its jealous fingers through his chestnut hair. His breath carried the sweet scent of mint, tickling my nose. I saw myself floating in his shining green eyes, felt his chest so close to mine I could feel his heart racing. He reared back his neck, smiled at me, brushed hair out of his face. Then he leaned down until his nose was only an inch from mine. Only an inch. I froze, my eyes fixed in his gaze. He tickled my nose with his. Then . . . he kissed me.

For a minute, I thought I was having one of my wild daydreams, but when he bore his soft lips down against mine, deepening the kiss, I closed my eyes and kissed back. And my heart swelled, threatening to burst. And a million strings crescendoed, a symphony playing in my chest. And we unraveled, ribbons twisting in the wind. And the whole universe stopped. Just so the stars and the moons could smile down on us.

Feeling him pressed against me, our hearts dancing in lockstep, I was changing, losing fear, losing anger. For years, I'd been lost, wandering in a long, cold night, winter's icy bite like spears lancing me, bleeding me all over the snow. Hunter brought me out of that long, cold night, into sunlight so bright and so warm it blasted away the frost crystals around my heart.

If not for the surge of thunder crackling through the sky, who knows how long we would've lain there. Probably until the end of time, until the galaxy froze and the sun exploded and everything died but us.

Hunter set his eyes on the tumultuous sky. Another lightning crackle called down the rain, drenching us. He jumped to his feet and reached down for me. I grabbed his hand, and he whisked us away under the old oak tree at the top of the hill.

After taking off his shirt, Hunter twisted the water out of it and slung the sopping bundle over his shoulder. Then he cupped his hands around his mouth. "Amalthea!" he called. When she didn't come, he muttered, "Dammit," then grabbed his shirt again and wrung it out some more.

"What was that?" I asked him.

Hunter kept his back to me. "What?"

"You kissed me."

"Oh"—he tittered—"yeah, I don't know what I was doing."

"What do you mean?"

He turned around, sliding his shirt back on. "It wasn't anything, okay?"

"Seriously?"

"Come on, don't be mad."

"Then why did you kiss me?"

"I don't know, okay? All I know is that when I'm around you, I can't take my eyes off you. And when you laugh, I laugh. And it's weird and confusing."

"Why?"

"Because I'm not"—he stopped himself, flicked his tongue—"because I'm not gay. It was a dumb mistake, okay? I'm sorry, let's not make a big deal out of it."

Hunter could've said so many more things to me, but he didn't. He just gave up and turned around, called for Amalthea. But she still didn't come. Hands on his hips, he scoured the countryside for the unicorn, never turning back to acknowledge me. I leaned back and looked up, watched raindrops nestle on acorns, shining on their brown skin, then drop and hit my nose, hit my forehead, hit my cheeks. I agonized over the kiss until I wanted to lie out in the grass, catch pneumonia, and die. Eventually, the storm passed, and Amalthea trotted up, her pristine coat untouched by even the smallest pearl of water. Hunter put his hand on her neck and started back to Alwina's farm. I followed behind them, hiding in his shadow like a secret.

"We should probably head back to the Institute," he said, leading Amalthea back into the paddock.

We walked back to town quietly, waited at the bus stop quietly, rode back to the Institute quietly. He wouldn't even look at me. I wanted him to say something, anything. He didn't. I wanted to say something, anything. I couldn't.

When we arrived back at the Institute, he said, "I'm sorry . . . about what happened out there. I didn't mean to do that."

I hoped he'd snap out of it and realize he liked me, according to what he'd said. He stared down at his reflection in the bronzy puddle under his feet. Thunder rumbled in the clouds, threatening more storms. "We'd better get back to Veles. It's probably going to rain for the rest of the day."

So we headed back to the dorms. As we walked into the front lobby, he said, "I'm supertired, Johnny. I'm going up to my room. I'll see you in class." With that, he vanished up the stairs, behind his door, behind a wall higher than the one around the Institute.

I went back to my room, my heart in tangles. For a brief, fleeting moment, I'd thought I might be able to get through this, get through my time at the Institute. With Hunter by my side, I'd thought maybe I could shore up enough courage to face being trapped here. Tears bloomed in the corners of my eyes, wilting petals that dripped down my cheeks and into the sink.

I fell on my bed, crying for my old life, for my new one. Crying because it was the only thing that made sense.

Chapter 18

1 WEEK AFTER EXTRACTION

Alison barged into my room around nine on Sunday morning. "You know what this thing is?" she said, waving the book we'd found in the library.

Getting back into bed, I rubbed my face against the coarse sheets, muffling my voice. "No."

"Look at this, J."

I stared at the words on the page. "Remove the wire by opening the diameter of the lower wire holes the lifting wires attach to. This gives an opening for the lifting wire to slip out and be removed . . ." I rolled onto my back. "It's instructions for fixing a clock."

"Exactly. Don't you want to go investigate this?"

I rolled over again and groaned. "No."

"Why not? What's wrong with you?"

I covered my head with a pillow and ignored her, so she crawled on top of me, yanked the pillow away, and threw it on the floor. Then she flipped me over and pinned me to the bed by the wrists.

"Ali, just leave me alone. I don't feel good."

"Seriously, you weren't this upset after we almost got killed."

"I wish Todd and them *had* just killed me."

She tightened her grip on my wrists. "Look, drama queen, you're going to tell me what's going on, or I'm going to tell Hunter you suck your thumb to fall asleep sometimes."

"Go ahead. He wouldn't care, anyway."

She slackened her hold. "Is this about Hunter?" I didn't reply. "Johnny, you're not allowed to be this weird over someone whose wardrobe consists of fifty shades of gingham."

"Just get out. I want to be alone."

"I can't believe we're trapped in a creepy magic school, and you're sitting in here worrying about some dumb boy," she said, finally getting off me.

I turned back over and covered my head with the blanket. Alison slammed the door behind her.

With the room quiet again, I rolled over and found she'd left the book behind. Sitting up, I gave it another look. It really was just a journal on building, setting, and fixing old clocks. If a book on horology was all we had, we were never getting out of here. I pushed the book away until it fell into the space between my bed and the wall.

It briefly crossed my mind to look for Hunter and talk to him again, but that would've been too awkward, so I stayed in my room all day.

Come Monday, lack of sleep coupled with heartbreak had left me looking haggard, with dark rings drooping under my eyes like brimming grocery bags. When Alison saw me looking like a waterlogged zombie, she knew to skip the usual spiel about why men aren't worth it. She handed me a backpack. "Here. Got you a new one." I packed my books up and we left for school.

Outside, the clouds sputtered with thunder. They had been doing it all weekend. We splished through a few shallow puddles on our way to Odin Hall. "You feel like talking yet?" she asked.

"I guess."

"What happened? I mean, obviously this place sucks, but you're, like, a lot sadder than last week—"

"Hunter kissed me."

"Wait, Gay Texas kissed you? That's bad?"

"He said it was a mistake."

"Ouch. Maybe he's just confused."

By some terrible irony, almost as soon as we walked into Odin Hall, we saw Hunter . . . kissing a girl. He pulled back and smiled at her—that everything smile, that golden smile, that *wake me up in the morning just so I can see it* smile—and I felt like someone had shoved a hot coal down my throat. He was acting all macho, making jokes and acting cool. The girl smiled coyly, so he leaned in close and kissed her again. I watched like a damsel tied to train tracks, witnessing her impending doom come speeding down the rails right for her head.

"Yeah, he looks real confused." I turned and left for my locker. Alison chased after me, rambling a billion miles per hour, but I wasn't listening. I opened my locker, gathered my books, slammed the door shut, and walked past Alison, the image of Hunter kissing that girl looping through my head like an animated GIF.

In class, I tapped my foot until Hunter showed up and sat next to me, tapped my finger on the desk until he glanced at it, flashed me his galling smile, and said, "Hey."

What was he even thinking? On Saturday he'd kissed me, and here he was on Monday, sitting next me like nothing had happened, like nothing *was* happening. I drew my lips into a big fake smile, returned his casual *hey*, and fidgeted with my pencil, swinging it back and forth like a metronome, fighting the urge to scream.

Hunter opened his textbook. Then, an arrow flew into my chest. I scanned the room for the sniper, but couldn't find them. Professor Happ took roll, then segued into his lecture. Hunter chewed on his pen, tearing up the little plastic cap between his teeth, then another arrow flew into my heart. Blood was running down my chest, down my leg. The sniper—I had to find them before I bled to death. Hunter scrawled some notes in his composition book, and like clockwork, another arrow sank into my chest.

Dizzy from blood loss, I stood up, dragging my feet across the floor. Everyone watched as I staggered into the aisle, my uniform drenched in blood. I collapsed, and the other students huddled around me. Hunter pushed through, his face pale with horror, then he picked me up and cradled me in his arms. "Johnny!"

"Come closer," I muttered. He leaned in. "Closer." He leaned even closer. "Closer." When he was close enough for me to whisper into his ear, I said, "I'm sorry for bleeding all over your shirt." Then I died.

At least, that was what played out in my head as I scribbled black rings in my notebook.

Hunter looked over, saw the black rings, and gave me a funny look, so I stopped drawing and pressed my lips into another artificial smile. When he was done staring at me like I was a serial killer, I balled up the paper.

After class, he followed me into the hallway. "Hey, you're being kind of quiet today. You all right?"

"I'm okay, thanks for asking," I said and kept walking. He

must've heard the bubbling acid in my tone because he kept quiet the whole way to P.E. and in the dressing room.

As usual, Hunter paired up with me for warm-ups. I rested my knees on his feet and held him down for sit-ups. Hunter did a few reps, then smiled at me like everything was all right. The cauldron of anger roiling in my heart boiled over. I mashed my knees down onto his feet. "Ow!" he said, sitting up and scowling at me. "Johnny, you're killing my feet. Take it easy." I eased up, inching back and squishing his toes instead. "Johnny!" he said, sitting back up. "What gives?"

"Sorry."

When it came time to play basketball, Hunter picked me for his team. While playing, Hunter was dribbling the ball to the basket when I ran up beside him and stole it. A few of his friends stopped and chuckled, then I made a three-point shot and missed. Confused, Hunter pinched his face at me. "Johnny, we're on the same team."

Later on, I was on my way to the net, and Hunter ran up beside me to assist me, but I didn't want him there, so I shoved him aside with my shoulder and took the shot. Missed again. Hunter stormed up to me and put his nose in my face. "What's your problem, Johnny!"

"You! You're my problem!"

The coach blew the whistle and broke us up. "Okay, that's enough, boys. Everyone, head back to the locker room."

●

While I was changing back out in the locker room, Hunter stomped up to me. "What's going on, Johnny?"

I cast off my gym shirt and reached into my locker for my uniform, pretending not to hear him. He slammed my locker door shut and glared at me. "What?" I snapped.

"Is this about Saturday?"

"Of course this is about Saturday!" I flung back open my locker and stuffed my gym shirt into it, then I pulled on my white shirt and started buttoning it.

"We're just going to stop being friends because of something stupid?" he said. *It wasn't stupid to me*. I ignored him and kept buttoning my shirt. "Hey, talk to me."

I put on my blazer, threw the door shut, and slung my backpack over my shoulder. "About what?"

"Are you seriously that mad at me?"

"You kissed me on Saturday, and two days later you're kissing some random girl?"

"Belinda isn't random. She's in my homeroom. We've been talking since before Saturday."

"Does she know you randomly kiss boys while you're talking to girls?"

"I told you I wasn't gay, and now you're mad at me because I'm not gay? That doesn't make any sense." Hunter bounced his fingers off his head.

"Then why'd you kiss me?"

"Because, I"—he shook his head and exhaled through his nose—"I told you it was a mistake!" He said it so loud a few guys walking by gave us funny looks.

Tears were welling in the corners of his eyes. Asshole. He was lying. But I was on the verge of tears myself, so I clamped my lips and walked away, fleeing to my room to skip the rest of my classes. I didn't care if they gave me detention. Hell, they could lock me up under the Heka Building for all I cared. I just wanted to lie in bed and sleep and sleep and sleep.

Later that evening, a fit of hunger woke me up. I walked downstairs to the dining area, swiped my card, got a sandwich, and headed back upstairs. On my way back to the room, I froze when I saw the smiling man in white standing in front of my door. With half the sandwich in my mouth, I watched him step through the door like a ghost, so I hurried into my room and found him standing in front of the windows, pointing into the quad. Following his finger, I saw Linh sneaking out of Veles Hall again. When I looked back up, he was gone.

What was Linh up to? Why had the smiling man pointed her out? There was no time to fetch Alison. Alone, I raced after Linh before she vanished. She was headed for Ansalom Hall, directly south of Veles, across the great lawn.

There weren't any lampposts on the lawn, so I dimmed my phone and used the light to see in the darkness. The lack of lighting also meant no Smiths patroled the lawn late at night, but the grounds around Ansalom were crawling with them. To make things even harder, the only way in was through the front—the side of the building facing the southern gate.

I crept into some shrubbery that wrapped around the building, hiding from a couple of Smiths who were sharing a cigarette near the emergency exit behind the building. Easing my way through the shrubs, my foot landed on a branch and snapped it.

One of the Smiths, tall and sallow, perked up. "Did you hear something?"

Handing off the cigarette, the shorter, beady-eyed one said, "Let me check it out." She clicked on her flashlight and started combing through the shrubs. Pressing my back against the wall, I bent my knees and ducked just as her beam whisked over my head. Pointing the beam into the shrubbery, she squinted against the dark. The light skirted toward me, inch by inch, coming closer, so I hurried forward on hands and knees, my movements shaking the shrubs and drawing her attention. Quickly, I lay on my stomach, and flat to the ground, I tried sinking into the earth. It didn't work.

On the walking path, she came to stand only a few feet away from me, still searching with her flashlight. The beam shone right into my eyes, so I pinched them shut and froze. Crap. How could she *not* see me? My heart was beating so hard I was sure she could hear it. She leaned forward like she noticed something, then she reached into the bushes and parted a few branches. A nightingale flew out of the shrubs, startling her. Putting her hand to her chest, she chuckled and sighed. "It was just some bird." She walked away.

Once I was certain I was in the clear, I crawled the rest of the way around the building and spotted Linh slipping in through the front door. Odd. The Institute wasn't the kind of place to leave buildings unlocked past curfew. I hurried out of the bushes and crept in after her. Once inside, I weaved through the shadows on the ground floor, peeping around bookcases and sneaking around study carrels. Flashing lights on the second floor caught my attention. I turned off my phone and went upstairs. Passing aisle after aisle, I strained my ears, listening for anything. Eventually I picked up a couple of hushed voices down an aisle, so I glided into the one next to it, knelt down, and peered between the rows of books. Linh was standing in front of a Smith who had long, crinkly hair and a tawny face with deep-set eyes. She looked to be in her midtwenties.

Linh gave the Smith a dirty look. "No, Aquila. I'm not feeding you any more info, okay? You said you could help me get out of here."

"Linh," Aquila said, "mapping this place out will make it easier for the Defectors to sneak people out."

"I'm not going anywhere near the Heka Building. You promised that if I helped, you'd get me out."

So this Smith was a Defector, and Linh had been talking to her—to them. No wonder she'd been sneaking around. Now it was obvious how Linh had been able to walk in through the front door: Aquila had unlocked it. And if another Smith came to investigate, Aquila could cover for Linh.

"I don't have the authority to make a decision like that. You'll have to go to Misthaven and talk to Luther."

Linh looked like she knew who Aquila was talking about. I hurried back outside and rushed back to Veles, intent on confronting Linh.

Chapter 19

1 WEEK AFTER EXTRACTION

Back at Veles Hall, I watched Linh reach the top of the stairs. She spotted me, gave me an uneasy smile. "Hey, Johnny . . . you're up late. And . . . in front of my door."

With my mind, I said, *You're working with the Defectors.* She winced. It looked like she was about to storm past me, so I continued quickly, *You've got to help us escape. Alison's mom is sick. She's got to go back and see her.*

Linh narrowed her eyes. *Did you follow me?*

Of course I did. It wasn't exactly hard to find out what you were up to.

So sue me. I'm new to this supersecret spy thing.

We heard footsteps tromping upstairs. Linh wasn't on duty, so the Smiths must be enforcing curfew tonight. *Into my room.* She shut the door quietly behind her just as a flashlight beam struck the floor. We waited until the footsteps passed by. When all was quiet again, she walked over to her desk and rummaged around in the top drawer.

You can't tell anyone.

What about Ali?

She stared up at me sternly. *No, not even Ali.*

I didn't like keeping secrets from Ali, but I didn't want to ruin our chances of getting out of here. *Fine.*

I've got to go talk to Luther Dorian, the leader of the Defector faction working inside Misthaven. He's the only one who can help us find a way out of the Institute. I'll tell you when I'm going to Misthaven, and you can come with me. She grabbed a ruler out of her drawer and shoved it against my chest. *If anyone sees you leaving, you came to borrow this.* She yanked me to the door.

Wait, what do you know about the smiling man in the white suit? Is that Gaspar? Is he the third head scientist?

I don't know what you're talking about. She opened the door, peeked outside, then shoved me out of her room before I could question her any further.

I hurried back to my room and tossed the ruler on the floor. Finally, we had a way out. We were getting out of this awful place. But who was the smiling man in white, and was he trying to help me escape?

●

The excitement of the night before left me pale and tired the next day. At lunch, sitting in the cafeteria with Alison and Blake, I yawned and perched my chin in one palm while struggling to lift a forkful of salad.

"Well, you're glowing this morning. Where were you yesterday afternoon?" Alison asked.

"I skipped classes after P.E."

"They're going to lock you up," she said. "In case you were wondering where I was after class, I was in Everywhen again."

"You need to be careful with that," Blake said, eyes on his phone. "A lot of people fall in love with Everywhen and spend so much time in it they end up losing their minds there. Like, literally, lose them; their minds get lost. It's called a dream trance. Sometimes someone can go in and find you—otherwise, it just leaves you messed up. You could become a somnambulist. Once the Institute finds out you're in a dream trance, they stick you under the Heka Building."

"I get it," Alison said, annoyed. "Thanks for the warning, champ." Being a wizard was learning one creepy thing after another and then trying to keep a straight face about it. She didn't want to hear Blake's warnings. She didn't want to hear anyone's warnings.

After lunch, Alison and I walked back to Odin Hall together.

"So why're you going into Everywhen so much?" I asked her.

"Because I see Mom there."

"But it isn't your real Mom—it's a dream mom. Isn't that a little weird?"

"What, are you telling me you wouldn't go into Everywhen to make out with dream Hunter?" I got quiet. I'd done *plenty* of things with dream Hunter. "Blake says if you dream about someone who's a wizard, they'll know. They'll also know what you dreamt about them." I almost swallowed my tongue. Sweat broke out all over my neck. Alison watched me for a moment, then said, "Just kidding."

Jesus. Playing it off, I said, "Anyway, I don't dream about Hunter."

Thunder rolled in with the clouds overhead. Alison looked up at the sky. "It's going to rain forever."

"You should listen to Blake. He saved my life. You could end up a somna-somna—a sleepwalker."

"Johnny, I'm fine."

"Have you forgotten why we're here in the first place?"

"What're you talking about?"

"This is all your fault—"

"My fault?"

"We're here because of that stupid spell of yours. You're the one who got the spell book and forced me to cast the spell."

"You were totally onboard."

"No, I wasn't. I just didn't want to say no and get into a big fight with you about it."

"Fine! You want to have a big fight now? Let's do it."

"Maybe if Blake says not to do something, you should listen. He's been here longer than us. And he's obviously looking out for you, because he likes you."

"He doesn't know what he likes."

"What?"

"Never mind. So how else do I see my mom? Don't you want to see your dad?"

"The people in Everywhen aren't real, Alison. Everything about that place is make-believe."

"It's real enough for me."

She wasn't going to listen to me. She never listened to me. So I just stopped arguing with her.

•

After classes let out, I went to Alison's room and knocked, but she didn't answer. My forehead pressed against the door, I sighed. I'd pissed her off. Alison was all I had here, and now she was mad at me. Or maybe she hadn't heard me knock because she was in Everywhen. Maybe she'd already given up hope that we'd ever escape. It was no wonder she preferred to spend her days in a dreamworld.

I went to my room, crashed face first onto my bed, and pinched my eyes shut. In the darkness behind my eyelids, I saw Hunter. I wanted so badly to hate him. I'd ball up my hands and clench my teeth so hard I thought they'd break. Then I'd remember his perfect smile and turn back into a wounded marshmallow. I hated that I couldn't hate him.

Above me, the intercom screeched on. I stared up at the crackling and fizzing speaker until a man's voice sounded. "Institute personnel will be conducting a search of Veles Hall. All students are requested to wait outside their rooms until the end of the search."

A search? Were they sniffing out Defectors? I slumped out of bed and went outside where everyone else was gathering outside their doors too. Alison wouldn't even look at me. I guess she *was* pissed. A couple of Smiths, one with slate-colored eyes and the other with curly hair, surveyed the students as they lined up. A few doors down to my right, Linh eyed me like a cat dangling from a tree limb over a pack of snarling dogs. If they found out she was working with the Defectors, who knew what they'd do to her? And I'd be in just as much crap as she was.

The gray-eyed Smith walked into the first dorm off the landing, and the curly-haired one paced to the far end of the hall, turned, and started coming back this way.

Hands clasped behind his back, he studied each bored, nervous, or apathetic face as he passed. If he was searching our thoughts, Linh and I were screwed. Down the hall, I saw Hunter staring up at the ceiling. Hunter'd told me only strong wizards could dig deep into our minds, but I didn't know how strong these Smiths were. Maybe if I cleared my thoughts, he wouldn't see anything. I blocked up my mind, tensed my body.

The Smith's shiny boots inched closer. *Clomp. Clomp.* I balled up my sweaty hands and looked straight ahead. Swallowed. Alison noticed me squirming and looked at me curiously. The Smith stopped in front of Hunter, and Hunter's lips quirked into an awkward smile, like he was trying not to laugh.

"Something funny?" the Smith said, leaning down to look in Hunter's face.

Hunter fought back a snicker. "No, sir. I just get like this when I'm nervous."

"What're you nervous about?"

"Nothing, sir. Just nervous."

The curly-haired Smith hovered in front of Hunter's face like he was analyzing him, then a knowing smile curled across his face. When Hunter saw the Smith's leer, his features tightened, and the humor melted clean off his face. What had the Smith seen in his mind? The Smith straightened up, turned, and looked over at me. I trained my eyes straight ahead, like everything was normal. Still smiling, he looked between me and Hunter, then headed straight for me. What had Hunter been thinking about? Was he thinking about me? That kiss in the field? *Clomp. Clomp.* My heart was fixing to explode and sweat was pouring down my forehead like a tiny waterfall. *Clomp. Clomp.*

The Smith came to stand right in front of me, so I swallowed hard and tried focusing beyond him, but I knew he could see the sweat on my brow, on my upper lip. I rubbed my fingers against my palms. "Why do you have your mind locked up?" he whispered. I didn't answer. I probably should've, but I didn't. I just kept staring ahead. "Are you hiding something?"

He leaned back and looked from me to Hunter. Then he placed a big, calloused hand on my shoulder. Squeezed. If I'd had worse bladder control, I would've pissed myself. Shutting my eyes, I tried calming down, breathing slowly, but I knew the Smith could see me trembling.

"Hey, Pierce, check this out."

I opened my eyes. The gray-eyed Smith was poking his head out of the first room.

Pierce relaxed his hold on my shoulder and watched the other Smith carry out a crate full of dirty magazines. He dropped the box onto the floor next to the freckly boy whose room it was. Everyone snickered. The gray-eyed Smith crouched down and picked up one of the nudie mags—the centerfold flipped open. "Don't kids get all their porn on the internet these days?" he said, grinning at his partner. The freckly boy turned white as chalk.

Pierce looked back at me, then put his lips down beside my ear. "Don't worry. Your little romp in the grass with your boyfriend is safe with me." Then he walked over to investigate the porn crate.

Hunter's face was pinched in anger, eyes downcast. It looked like he was on the verge of bursting into tears. The Smith, Pierce, had invaded his thoughts, leaving him so embarrassed and ashamed he couldn't even look up. It was disgusting, prying into someone's thoughts like that. I hated the Institute. Hated that they could do these horrible things to us.

The two Smiths laughed loudly, still browsing through the freckly kid's porn stash. Standing up, Pierce tucked the crate under his arm. "Sorry, kid, we'll be confiscating this. All right, the rest of you can get back to your rooms." But nobody moved until the chuckling Smiths had gone down the stairwell. Linh sighed and shook her head.

Alison walked up to me as the hallway emptied out. "What'd he whisper to you?" she asked. Hunter gave me an uneasy look as he went back into his room.

"Nothing," I said. I wouldn't tell, no matter how much Hunter had pissed me off.

Chapter 20

Linh dragged me out of my room Saturday to the bus stop outside the north gate. We left our phones behind so the Institute couldn't spy on us. On the bus, we sat quiet as a couple of monks. Now that I knew she'd been working with the Defectors, her keeping mostly to herself made sense.

"I nearly crapped myself during the room check yesterday," I said finally.

She smiled. "Tell me about it. They hadn't done one of those since I started working with the Defectors."

"I was wondering about that."

"What did that one agent whisper to you?"

"It was nothing." With Hunter fresh on my mind, I said, "Hunter said you had a girlfriend named Maleeka . . . who disappeared?" Why had I brought that up? It wasn't exactly small talk.

She looked out the window at the whirl of moving trees. "Maleeka, Blake, and I, we were all extracted around the same time, so we became really good friends. Maleeka was wild, always picking fights with the agents. Blake and I were constantly trying to settle her down. When she talked about trying to escape, we both tried to stop her, but she went anyway. I haven't talked much to Blake since then. I think he blames me because I was her girlfriend. Maybe he thinks I should've been more forceful about her staying."

"What do you think happened to her?"

"I don't know. Maybe she escaped, or maybe they locked her up under the Heka Building."

The familiar markings of Misthaven rose up around us. We got off at a stop in front of the library, a squat rectangular building. We climbed a short flight of steps to a covered entryway and passed through the automatic doors into the gallery. Left of the entrance, another pair of automatic doors led to the largest portion of the library, containing books and periodicals, study carrels, and computers. To our right was a round conference room partitioned off with glass walls, and directly in front were the librarian's office and a children's area, also walled in with glass.

Aside from our own footfalls, it was totally quiet. I hadn't expected Misthaven Library to be a bustling place, but for it to be so empty seemed odd.

"This is weird," Linh said, walking into the main room on the left. Following her, I scanned the room. The vaulted ceiling rose twenty feet over our heads, and art-deco light fixtures cascaded soft light over everything. Behind a few magazine shelves to the left of the entrance was a line of leather armchairs and study nooks, and a series of tall windows admitted the early morning sun. To our right, a round help desk connected to the librarian's office sat unattended.

Leaning over the help desk, Linh called into the librarian's office. "Luther?" There was no reply. She backed away and muttered, "Luther's always here."

We were heading for the book stacks when someone ran toward us out of nowhere. It was Hunter. "You guys, get down!" he yelled, grabbing my arm and hurrying us under a table.

"Hunter?" I said, confused.

He put a finger to his lips. Then he pointed up. From our crouching position, we looked upward.

Skittering along the ceiling was a shimmering mechanical centipede, at least twelve feet long and almost as wide. It stilled and fixed its glowing yellow eyes on us. The creature's body looked like it was built from the clockwork pieces of the vivit apparatus. "What the hell is that thing?" Linh asked. The creature's eyes turned red, then its entire body blended into the background, completely camouflaged.

When we heard the creature crash onto the floor, we bolted from under the table and fled between two bookstacks. "Any ideas, you guys?" Hunter asked.

Air rippling around its camouflaged body, the centipede charged through the library, sending tables and chairs and magazine racks flying in all directions before it launched itself into the air and landed on a nearby bookshelf, wobbling it. Like dominos, the bookshelves fell, one after the other, forcing us to retreat before we were crushed between them. "That room with all the kids' books!" Linh said as we ran past an old-fashioned card catalogue.

We darted into the children's area, then Hunter slammed the door behind us. Hands on my knees, I gathered my breath. "What the hell was that thing?" Linh asked, panting.

Before Hunter could answer, a bookshelf near the door shook, then came crashing to the floor as the centipede shattered through the wall. We rushed into a storage closet in the corner of the children's area, and once the door was shut, darkness swallowed us. The dank smell of dirty rags and the sharp stench of chemicals had my stomach doing backflips. There was a click, and a single lightbulb hanging overhead lit up. Linh had found a pull cord and switched it on. The space was little more than five by two feet big. I was crammed up against Hunter, and Linh was pressed up against the cinderblock wall next to a wire rack full of cleaning supplies and a mop bucket.

"Shhh," Hunter said.

Outside, the sounds of skittering mechanical feet rang in the distance, coming from outside the children's area. The monster must've left after we fled into the closet. Eventually, the scuttling noises stopped.

"Hunter," Linh said, "what're you doing here, and for the third time: What. Was. That. Thing?"

Hunter, his chest rising and falling, kept his eyes on the door like he was waiting for that thing to break through any second. "Ms. Alwina's friends with the librarian. She told me to come check on him because she hasn't heard from him in a while."

"Ms. Alwina?" Linh asked.

"She's this old lady I do stable work for sometimes," Hunter said.

Linh shifted, accidentally kicking over the empty bucket and sending Hunter and me into each other's arms in a panic. She steadied a couple of mops before they fell over, and Hunter and I realized we were clamped onto each other, so we quickly let go and squeezed into opposite corners of the tiny closet. Linh narrowed her eyes curiously at us.

"And that thing?" she asked.

"It's a magical construct. It's made of pieces of the vivit apparatus. It looks like it's mostly air. Wizards make them for all sorts of reasons, but they're really hard to control."

"Great," I said. "Now we're stuck. We can't stay in this closet forever." *Actually, Hunter probably could,* I thought.

"The Institute'll come looking for us after curfew," Hunter said. "They can deal with that thing."

I searched Linh's face for a response. Her pale expression told me everything. Hunter could wait around for the Institute to send help, but if the Smiths found out why Linh and I were here, and if anyone found out what she knew about the Defectors, it'd ruin our plans and put a lot of people at risk.

"What're you guys doing here?" Hunter asked, his eyes on me.

"Book report!" Linh blurted out.

"We have a library back at the Institute."

She crossed her arms and tried leaning against the wall, but miscalculated its stability and almost fell over. She gave Hunter an awkward smile. "This is a special book report, and we could only find the books here."

He wrinkled his forehead at Linh, then stared at me again. I was still mad at him, so I dug my hands into my pockets and looked away. We all lapsed into silence for several minutes.

"Come on, Johnny, you can't stay mad at me," Hunter said finally. I shot him a glare like a wound-up rattlesnake, so he pressed his lips together and went quiet.

"What's with you two?" Linh asked.

We both turned and said, "Nothing!" at the same time.

After about fifteen minutes, Linh started clearing her throat and making *what are we going to do?* faces at me. It was obvious Hunter had no intention of going anywhere until the Institute came. But it was barely ten in the morning, and curfew wasn't until eight at night. "We can't stay in here all day," I said.

"Why not?" Hunter asked.

"Because"—Linh stammered, trying to think of something—"what if we have to pee?" Hunter pointed to the bucket. "Ew!" Linh said. "It'd be easy for you guys, but how am I supposed to use that!"

"How exactly do you plan on dealing with that thing outside?" Hunter said.

Linh's scowled. "I don't know! God, the universe could've trapped me in a closet with Hayley Kiyoko, but *no*, here I am, stuck with you two."

We stood around fidgeting, each of us searching for something to occupy our minds while we were trapped in the closet. Another fifteen minutes passed.

"Linh, can I ask you a question?" Hunter said. "When did you know you were gay?"

"Weird timing for a heart to heart, but whatever. I had this boyfriend who used to come over to 'study' with me in my room—which was weird because my parents are superuptight Vietnamese Catholics, but they let us study with the door closed and everything. Anyway, he'd start trying to make out with me, sticking his big slimy tongue down my throat, and I remember I had this poster of Elle Fanning on the wall, and I'd just stare at it and pretend I was kissing her, then it wasn't so bad anymore. After a while, I figured I liked girls. I think my parents knew before I did, though."

Hunter was quiet. I looked over, saw a storm raging in his tender eyes.

"Where I grew up," he said, "my dad was the pastor at our

church, real hellfire and brimstone type, the kind you see holding up mean signs on TV. Mom was different, though—she wasn't that religious, not after Papa died. Anyway, I had this friend, his name was Joe. We hung out all the time, and one summer, we started liking each other. Then we started . . . fooling around. . . . One day we went up to my bedroom to fool around, and my dad walked in and caught us. My dad beat the crap out of me and said he'd kill me if he ever saw that again. Then Mom found out he beat me up and started fighting with him all the time. She said he was being an asshole, and he said her babying me was turning me into a . . . a pervert. They just kept fighting about me. You know? Because they thought . . . because I'm . . . you know . . ."

"Gay?" I muttered.

"Because I'm gay."

"You think it's your fault your parents were fighting?" I asked.

"They *were* fighting about me. I heard them."

"Is that why you were running away from home when the Institute took you?"

"Part of the reason."

For a long moment after that, Hunter didn't say anything else. It was like the air had been sucked out of him, and now he was thrashing around like a fish on dry land. He'd just come out to us, and I didn't know how to react, given our situation.

Linh pressed her lips together awkwardly. "That was random and kind of intense."

"We have to get out of here," I said.

"How?" Hunter asked.

Linh's face lit up. "I've got an idea. That thing is made of pieces from the vivit apparatus. If we rearrange the pieces, maybe we can break it down."

"It's not that easy," Hunter said. "If you don't know how the pieces all work together, you can't get them to do anything. Like, you couldn't make a heart stop by just screwing around with its clockwork randomly."

I was hit with an a-ha moment. "Whoever made it probably based it on a real centipede. It's like Professor Happ always says: science and magic are inseparable. If you know the science behind how something works, it's easier to control it with magic. If we know the anatomy of a centipede, how it all works, we could probably stop that construct."

Hunter caught on to what I was saying. "We need to go out there, find a biology book, something with a diagram of a centipede, and that'll help us break it down. Like, if we know how a centipede's heart's works, we can rewire this one so it stops working."

"And which one of you brave lads is going to do the rewiring?" Hunter and I exchanged a nervous look. "Never mind, I'll do it," Linh said. "One girl's as good as two guys. You two had better not let me get killed."

We crept out of the closet and snuck under a table in the children's area. Linh scanned the shelves in the children's science section. The sounds of scuttling mechanical feet drew our attention, so Hunter darted out from under the table. "What're you doing?" I said, grabbing for his jacket but narrowly missing it as he ran out into the larger room.

"Hey!" he yelled, waving his arms. "Over here!" I crept out from under the table and inched over to the door.

Still camouflaged, the centipede dropped from the ceiling, smashed a row of carrel desks, and charged. Hunter leaped out of the way as the centipede rushed past him and smashed into a bookcase.

Linh traced her finger over book spines in a mad dash to find the right title. "Hurry," I said to her.

"Why don't you get over here and help me?" she asked. I waffled between helping her and watching Hunter. "Johnny," Linh said, "the quicker I get this book, the safer he'll be." Maybe she'd read my mind, or maybe it was just that easy to pick up that I was worried about Hunter. Either way, I ducked down, crawled next to her, and searched the shelves too.

"How is it literally no one else has walked into the library during any of this?" Linh said, her eyes still skimming over book titles. We were lucky the commotion hadn't carried outside, but our luck was running out; the centipede was turning the building into rubble. Another crash outside. I flinched. Not knowing how Hunter was doing was nerve-racking, but at least he wasn't screaming. That gave me some assurance he wasn't hurt.

"*Amazing Sea Creatures. Time and How It Works. Zero, the Loneliest Digitaria.* Here we go!" Linh pulled out a book called *Insectopedia* and threw it open on the floor. I scampered over and watched as she flipped through the pages, finally landing on an anatomical diagram. "Here! Here it is," she said, shoving the book into my hands.

We rushed out of the children's area. Hunter was standing beside some book carousels and a planter. Carefully watching for the rippling of the air, he leaped out of the way as the centipede charged again. The creature barreled through the planter, covering itself in soil. Now it was partially visible to us.

"We've got it, Hunter," I called. "Get away from that thing!" Linh ran out into the main library area, waving her hands as Hunter had done earlier, while he ran past her and slid over to me. Its attention drawn, the centipede changed course toward Linh. Hunter and I held our breaths as it zoomed right at her. Just before the beast trampled her, she sidestepped it and grabbed onto the machinery of its back.

Wedging her fingers into the spaces between the machinery, she held tight as the construct climbed up a wall. For some reason, having Linh on its back interfered with the centipede's camouflage; the cloaking fell, and it became fully visible once again.

"Okay," Linh yelled down to me, her voice echoing through the vast room, "now would be a good time to start telling me about centipedes."

I opened the book on a nearby table and stared at the diagram of the centipede's vascular system.

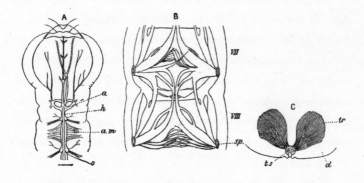

My eyes caught on the diagrams, the letters, the random numbers. Too many things going on. I fumbled my words reading the page: "The heart . . . ligaments . . . muscles . . . hemo-hemo-coel?"

"Let me see it," Hunter said trying to snatch the book from me.

"Hunter, I got this," I said, pulling it back.

The centipede crawled onto the ceiling, turning Linh upside down. She clamped on, wedging her arms and legs between pieces of machinery, and yelled, "Guys!" just as the centipede sideswiped a small chandelier and sent it crashing to the floor.

"Okay, the heart is a muscular tube that runs under the back!"

"Got it!"

From where I was, I could see a tube running under all the machinery on the construct's back. Linh reached down for it, but it was too big to manipulate. "Johnny, I can't do anything with this big old pipe."

"Not the first time a lesbian's said that, I bet," Hunter joked.

I glared at him and went back to the book. "Along the heart runs a series of valves that allow blood to enter the heart." I looked up as the centipede skittered down the wall again. The valves in question were pulsing with glowing energy. "Can you shut off those valves?"

The centipede got back on the floor and started for Hunter and me. "There you are," Linh said, reaching for one of the valves. I tucked the book under my arm, and Hunter and I hurried back to the children's area as the centipede smashed through the table we'd been standing at. Linh reached between the machinery and spun the handwheel on one of the valves. Once she'd sealed it, the golden light flowing through it went black, dimming part of the construct's body. The creature hurried up a wall and climbed back onto the ceiling again.

Following the construct with my eyes, I realized if it fell from there, it could horribly injure Linh. "Hunter, we've got to catch Linh if she falls." Hunter nodded, and we ran back out to the main area and circled below the beast, ready to catch Linh. She inched toward another valve, but lost one of her footholds and slipped. Dangling from one arm, she swerved with every one of the monster's jerky motions. She swung her other arm up and wrapped it around some machinery, then gritted her teeth and pulled herself up, kicking her legs and swinging like a pendulum until she regained a foothold and wriggled back into place on the centipede.

Steadier this time, she grabbed another handwheel and spun the valve shut. The centipede came to a halt and shuddered, the light in its body flickering like a dying firefly. Then it fell, sending Linh plummeting to the ground.

Hunter and I ran around with our arms wide open, but because our eyes were fixed on Linh, we weren't watching where we were going, so we crashed into each other. First, Hunter hit the floor, then I landed between his legs, and Linh landed on top of me. The construct crashed to the floor a few feet from us, its body glimmering a few more times before completely disappearing. Still on my back, Linh sat up, pushing me and Hunter closer together. I met his eyes—between us an expanse of unspoken words—then went red and jumped up, flinging Linh off me. She got up, brushed herself off, and gave me a dirty look.

Standing up, Hunter looked around. "So, did that thing kill the librarian?"

"Fortunately not," came a man's voice from behind the help desk. A little old man emerged from the librarian's office. Bald with huge glasses that enlarged his blue eyes, he was neatly dressed in a green vest and khaki trousers.

"Luther!" Linh said, running over to him. Hunter and I exchanged a glance—held for just a bit too long—then followed. "I thought you were dead," she said.

"No—at least, not yet," he said. His voice rose up from his wrinkly throat like a high-pitched croak. "Just hiding under the desk in my office, trying to figure out a way to deal with that beast. Of course, by the looks of it, I won't have to worry about that anymore."

"Couldn't you have just used magic?" I asked.

His magnified eyes fell on me. "You'd be surprised how ineffectual magic is against something that's made of magic." He scanned us. Hunter didn't know Linh was working with the Defectors, and I had no intention of letting him in on our secret. "Aren't you Ms. Alwina's stable hand?" he asked Hunter.

Hunter nodded. "She asked me to come check on you."

"And you?" Luther said, his eyes narrowing on me.

"He's with me," Linh said, giving Luther a knowing look.

Luther turned back to Hunter. "Why don't you go back to Alwina and tell her I'm fine."

"O-Okay. I'll see you guys back at the Institute." Hunter side-stepped the bisected tables and shattered planters on his way out.

Luther walked over to inspect a row of smashed carrels. With one hand on his chin, he surveyed the destruction throughout the library. His aura felt warm, like candlelight, but if you closed your eyes, you could hear whispers, unintelligible secrets passed between suspicious parties, knives unveiled in the dark of night. In case you didn't know Luther traded in secrets, his aura left little doubt.

"I built the construct to help me with tracking something down. A research assistant I conjured up in Everywhen."

I glanced at Linh and saw my uncertainty reflected on her face. Luther noticed our confusion and continued. "I've been conducting deep research into the Institute's operations in Everywhen. I'd overheard some Maras talking about creatures they conjured up to help them with day-to-day chores in the Night Market. They called them Nobodies. I thought it might be useful to have one around, so I summoned a Nobody to help me keep track of all my research. But somehow, the thing found a way out of Everywhen and into the real world."

"Everywhen things can just do that?" I asked.

"Not everything has the power to step from dreams into the real world, but yes, some things do. That Nobody I called forth surely did."

"This is Johnny," Linh said. Luther studied me, his fingers still wrapped around his chin. "He knows about us. He saw me the other night meeting with Aquila . . . about escaping the Institute."

"Escaping the Institute?"

"I've helped the Defectors long enough. There's a crackdown going on now; the Institute's getting nervous, and they're taking kids left and right. I have to get out of there before they catch me," Linh said.

"I understand, but I can't risk contacting our allies until that Nobody is dealt with. If the Institute discovers it and tracks it back to me, they'll unearth our entire operation and throw every one of us in the cells under that big pyramid. Perhaps if the two of you were to help me track down that Nobody, I could then safely contact my allies and find you a way out of here."

"Fine, we'll help you. Do you have any idea where the Nobody went?" Linh asked.

"Not at all." Luther reminded me of a jittery old toy that was barely held together, a jumbled pile of screws and bolts. The bumbling geezer probably had no business using magic.

"We'll see what we can do." Linh tapped my arm and started for the door, but I didn't move yet.

"Mr. Dorian," I asked, "have you ever heard of something called a cintamani?"

"Yes, it's an old myth that goes by many names: the philosopher's stone, divine quintessence, melancholia, chaos. Essentially, it's a magic stone that grants wishes. Pretty silly to believe in such foolishness, if you ask me."

"How does it work?"

"Sadly, that's about all I know."

"What about the Institute? Do you know anything about the

head scientists? Ever heard of someone called Gaspar?"

"That's a nut we're still trying to crack." Useless. He didn't know any more than we did.

On our way out of the library, we passed a couple of local kids walking in. They froze, eyes wide and mouths agape, stunned by the state of the library. Linh shot them a smile. "The library's under renovation." As we headed out the door, a light fixture fell from the ceiling and crashed to the floor behind us.

•

After all that excitement, Linh and I were dying for a snack, so when we got back to Veles Hall, we headed to the dining area. I got two steps in before I spotted Hunter and Belinda talking near a soda machine. Hunter took a sip of soda and caught sight of me. My stomach twisted like a corkscrew, so I turned and left without saying anything to Linh.

Hunter called after me, but I was already up the stairs, rushing to my room. I slammed the door shut and took a few steps in before my stomach grumbled. Seeing Hunter with Belinda, after everything that had happened in Misthaven, hit me like a bag of bricks. Falling back on my mattress, I closed my eyes and collected myself, but the insides of my eyelids were like a projector screen, and the projector was stuck on the image of Hunter gawking at me in the dining area. I changed the reel to play the clip of him kissing Belinda, telling me our kiss was a mistake, and I ended up enraging myself. Then I heard a knock at the door. Expecting Alison, who'd no doubt want to know where I'd been all day, I opened up and found Hunter standing there.

His eyes pleaded with me better than any lawyer. I looked at his lips. I wanted to kiss him—I always wanted to kiss him—but when the surge of hormones subsided, anger roiled in me. "What do you want?" I said, lying back down on my bed.

He approached the bed. "Can we talk?" Hearing no resistance from me, he eased onto his back next to me. "Running out of the dining area like that was kind of weird."

"Did you come here to make fun of me?" I said, turning my back to him and resting my head in the crook of my arm.

"I made a mistake the other day," he said quietly. As he turned to me, the mattress sank under his weight, pulling me toward him. He was the Earth. I was the moon. I couldn't escape his orbit. His cologne struck first, then the warmth of his body so close to mine.

I squeezed my eyes shut, trying to block him out. "I know. Don't remind me."

"I don't mean kissing you. Kissing Belinda."

I waited for his words to germinate in my mind, spread their roots, and take hold. When I realized what he was saying, I rolled over to face him. "What do you mean?"

"That stuff I said after I kissed you—I was lying." He reached for my hand and looped his pinky around mine. "I'm sorry."

"Everything you said today . . ."

"It was true. It felt good to finally get it all off my chest."

"What about Belinda?"

"We just broke up." He rested a hand on my cheek. "I want to be *your* boyfriend, Johnny."

I smiled until my eyes were little slits, so he laughed and scooted in closer to me. His forehead pressed to mine, he bore his soft green eyes into my soul, his gentle hand still cupping my face. He glided his hand to the base of my neck, his silky fingertips like wisps of smoke sailing over my skin, leaving trails of goosebumps in their wake. Nuzzling me, Hunter tickled my lips with his before he kissed me. His lips were honey, his lips were chocolate, his lips were the first drop of water in the middle of a desert, the first sweet dream in a void of nightmares. If heaven had a taste, it'd be Hunter's lips, all mint and boy spit and just the slightest hint of Coca-Cola.

Chapter 21

I'd never had a boyfriend before. Weird that it took me getting locked up in a wizard prison to finally get one. Hunter spent the whole weekend in my room, kissing me, telling me how much he liked me. He was the ultimate distraction; with Hunter around, the whole world could've caught on fire, and I still would've lain there kissing him, waiting for the flames to engulf us. Before he left, he told me to meet him at his locker before class on Monday (so he could boggle my mind with more of his weird country stories).

But first, I'd have to get past Alison. "Where were you all weekend?" she demanded as we walked through the quad.

"In my room."

"Just in your room, huh?"

"What's that supposed to mean?"

"I went by your room last night and saw Hunter coming out of there. I thought you guys weren't even friends?"

"We are now."

"Just friends?"

"Just friends, Ali." I wouldn't out Hunter to anyone, not even Ali.

•

We met up at Hunter's locker. He barely disguised his flirting, flashing me a cocky smile and muttering, "I wish we were lying in your bed right now." On our way to class, I kept seeing other kids staring at us and whispering. Being bullied had made me hypersensitive to other people talking about me, but Hunter—normal, well-adjusted Hunter—was oblivious, rambling about some mechanical bull that busted his nuts at a state fair one time.

Sitting in math, I couldn't shake the feeling the other kids were watching us—and not just one or two, but everyone in class. Hunter knitted his eyebrows at me and rubbed the back of his neck uneasily. He must've felt it too. Then, we realized what was happening: everyone in class was trying to get in our heads. I was lucky Hunter had taught me to block my thoughts the first day of school. You really couldn't let your guard down in this place. He pushed back his chair and stood up. Happ stopped his lecture on a matrix. "Is there a problem, Mr. Hunter?"

Hunter swept the room with his eyes, taking stock of every snickering face shooting him knowing looks. "Why're you all trying so hard to get in my head?"

I closed my eyes, and every thought floating around the room hit me at once: "Can't believe that dumb jock is gay." "That's so cute! I knew he was gay." "Look at that guy trying to be tough. Bet he's the bottom. The macho ones always are."

Someone had outed Hunter.

"I'd suggest you all keep your thoughts to yourselves, unless you want to end up in the principal's office," Happ said, his usually jovial voice now hard as stone. "Mr. Hunter, take a seat, please."

"Nah. Come on, Johnny," Hunter said, grabbing his things. He stormed out of the room and I followed, Happ's voice calling after us. We walked into the nearest bathroom. Hunter was fuming. "I can't believe all those jerks were in there trying to read our minds."

"Maybe they heard something and were trying to find out if it was true?" I said, leaning against a sink.

"I don't think Linh would say anything. I'll ask Belinda."

"Are you embarrassed?"

"Why would I be embarrassed?"

I stared at the blue floor tiles. "Because . . . everything."

He grabbed my hand and rubbed his thumb against my palm. "I'm tired of being scared, Johnny. I like you, and I want to be with you." He put his arms around me, so I reached around his waist, and we hugged, our heads nestled close on each other's shoulders. His warmth eased me, but his racing heart told me he was scared.

The bell rang. Hunter slung his backpack over his shoulder, grabbed my hand, and left the bathroom. We marched up to Belinda's locker as she was putting away her books. She closed the door and startled when she saw Hunter standing right behind it.

"Did you tell anyone about me?" Hunter asked.

"I didn't tell anyone," Belinda said. "But my friend Katie asked me why we broke up, and when I wouldn't tell her, she read my mind."

So Belinda's nosy friend had gleaned her thoughts, then spread rumors about Hunter. Being in the closet at a school full of mind readers meant if even one person knew, soon everyone would. "I'm really sorry, Hunter." She looked at me. "You, too, Johnny."

Hunter sighed. "It's not your fault, Belinda. Thanks for telling me what happened. Let's go, Johnny."

In the locker room, Hunter sat on the bench, quietly tying his shoes. Knotting my own shoelaces next to him, I tried guessing where his mind was. From his tense expression, he may have been reliving the moment his father had caught him with Joe, but this time, in his mind, Hunter was reacting the way he'd wanted to, not the way fear had dictated.

We stood up, and he put his hands on my hips. "You coming to my game Friday?"

"Do you want me to?"

"For sure."

I grabbed his shirt and twisted it in my fingers. "What about your teammates?"

"They're going to find out about us, anyway. So?"

"I don't know. It's not really my thing."

"What? You have to come."

"Why?"

"Because it's Boyfriend Commandment Number . . . Five, or something."

"Boyfriend Commandment?"

"Thou shalt support . . . thy boyfriend in his . . . sports."

I laughed. "Sounds serious."

He touched his nose to mine and whispered, "It is."

I didn't speak until we both cracked a smile. He kissed me. "Okay," I said.

"Yessssss."

Doug and Brandon walked by, and when they saw Hunter touching me, they started chuckling. Hunter scowled, balling his fists. The sight of Hunter so mad shook them, so they hurried away. I touched Hunter's shoulder. "Hunt, we need to go."

His chest rose and fell for a few breaths before he calmed down. "Yeah, I know. Come on." He flashed me a smile, but I knew he was a sleeping volcano; any more prodding and he'd burst.

Holding Hunter's ankles down during warm-ups, I overheard someone say, "Bet he's down there a lot." A chorus of snickers followed. I frowned and searched for the comedian.

At the top of his sit-up, Hunter noticed my expression. "What's wrong?"

I shook my head. "Nothing."

I was leery of playing basketball with Doug and Brandon after what had happened in the locker room, but I didn't think Hunter cared as much. We lined up so Doug and Brandon could pick teams. They picked Hunter and me last, which left Hunter seething.

The game got underway, and things played out as I'd expected: Doug and Brandon ignored Hunter every chance they got. When Hunter ran up behind Brandon to block him, Brandon, probably feeling insecure—or just being a dick—spun around and pushed him. "Ease up, faggot!"

Uh-oh.

Hunter got in Brandon's face. "What'd you call me?"

"You heard me"—Brandon shoved Hunter back again—"faggot."

Mount Hunter finally erupted. He headbutted Brandon in the face, and Brandon went down like a bloody-nosed Hindenburg. Raising his fist, Hunter looked ready to pound Brandon like he was playing Whac-A-Mole, but Doug and the other guys formed a wall around Brandon. I ran up beside Hunter as a few other guys surrounded us. Hunter clenched my hand, then he lowered his head, ready to charge like a rhino on one of those *National Geographic* shows. They all backed off. "He's my boyfriend," Hunter said, "and if you don't like it, I don't fucking care!"

Hunter turned to me, grabbed my face, and kissed me in front of everyone. When he pulled away, I looked at him dumbstruck, so he kissed me again.

●

At lunch, Hunter sat next to me, straddling the bench. "How many chips do you think I can fit in my mouth?" he asked. I smiled and shrugged. "Come on, stick 'em in my mouth. Let's see how many we can fit." He opened his mouth wide. I set the first chip on his tongue.

Blake and Alison sat down at our table with trays of food. "Has something . . . changed since this morning?" she asked.

"What's up, guys," Hunter said, crunching on the chip. He chuckled. "I messed up, Johnny. Let's start over."

Alison locked eyes with me. "Is there a reason you're feeding Hunter chips, Johnny?"

"We're trying to see how many we can fit in there," I said, stacking three chips in his mouth.

Anthony, the muscly leader of the Thorns, showed up with a few friends and surrounded our table. Blake rolled his eyes, set down his sandwich, and turned to face them.

"Can we sit?" Anthony said. His taut facial features never betrayed what he was thinking. I wondered if Blake had, like Aiden, offended Anthony when he rejected his offer to join the Thorns. If so, was Anthony here to challenge Blake to a wizard duel too? Blake shrugged, so Anthony and his friends sat down around us.

"Have you given my offer any thought?"

"What do you want me to say, Anthony?" Blake responded, exasperated.

"Well—yes."

"What'll you do if I say no?"

"We're not going to push you into anything, Blake, but the Thorns need guys like you."

"What, who're strong?"

"No. Who stand up for people. That's what we want. The other Legacies go around bullying non-Lineage kids. You've seen it. I've seen it. But we want the non-Legacy kids to feel safe. You beat the leader of the Crowns in a wizard duel, you made the non-Legacy kids feel safe, and everyone likes you. You're exactly the kind of guy I want in the Thorns, by my side."

Anthony was appealing to Blake's sense of justice. Smart. Blake couldn't easily dismiss Anthony's appeal; he looked torn. Hunter finally swallowed all the crunched-up chips in his mouth.

"Fine," Blake said. "I'll come by Thorn Hall later and we can talk about it some more."

Anthony's usually stony demeanor softened. He smiled at Blake, stood up, and left the cafeteria, the other Thorns trailing behind him.

•

I met with Linh that night at Ansalom Hall. She'd walked past me in the hallway that afternoon and given me the details, mind to mind. Luckily, Hunter was at practice, and Alison was at the cafeteria with Blake.

"We need to figure out how to find this Nobody thing if we ever want to get out of here," she said as we walked between two bookshelves to the right of the entrance.

"Can you explain to me exactly what a Nobody is?"

"Let's find out." Halfway down the aisle, she crouched to peruse the books on the bottom shelf. "We need a bestiary."

"Like for D&D?"

"Same idea, I guess." She grabbed a heavy grimoire and took it to a table at the far end of the aisle. Flipping through the stiff, yellowed pages, she came across a diagram of what looked like a shadow. The text under it was scrawled in German.

"How are we supposed to read this?" I asked.

"Duh. Look at it and imagine that you can."

Looking down at the page, I imagined what the words might say in English. As though I'd just slipped a pair of glasses over my near-sighted eyes, the words unfogged and became legible. They didn't turn into English—rather, I now understood what they meant. At the top of the page were the words *Niemand, oder Schattengänger*, which meant "Nobody, or Shadow-Goer." The entry read:

> *The shadow-goer is a cannibal by nature. Once it has found a bridge—usually a mirror—the shadow-goer takes on the form of the nearest person and enters the real world. There, the shadow-goer—a doppelgänger—must continually imitate other human forms, as it has no body of its own, despite being humanlike in shape.*
>
> *Because of this limitation, the shadow-goer prefers to hunt in large crowds. It can go several days without food, but after too long without succor, it will lack the strength it needs to imitate a human form and will revert into a shadow. In its*

shadow form, the creature exists only as a contrast to light. In other words, in its shadow form, the creature cannot exist anywhere that a shadow could not.

I looked up from the book at Linh. "Hunter's got a football game on Friday."

"Can we maybe just focus on the man-eating shapeshifter thing?"

"This says they prefer to hunt in large crowds. Hunter said football games are the biggest things in Misthaven."

"God, you're right. That thing's going to have a buffet at your boyfriend's football game. How do we stop it?"

We both looked back at the book.

The best way to stop a shadow-goer is to banish it back to Everywhen using a bridge. If a shadow-goer is struck by light reflected off a mirror while in its shadow form, it will be forced back into Everywhen.

"All right, so, first we make sure it stays in its shadow form, and then we . . . hit it with reflected light?"

"So we bring a mirror . . . like, a big mirror or a little mirror?"

"A smaller mirror would be easier to get out of the Institute. But how do we track down something that could look like anyone?"

I chewed my thumb for a minute, remembered the Bandersnatch. "Its aura. It should feel weird or something, right?"

"It's a shapeshifter, though. Can shapeshifters copy auras?"

"I don't know."

Linh leaned back in her chair. "Maybe we could lure it out with some carrots or something."

"Carrots?"

"I don't know. Do you have any better ideas?"

"Yeah." I stood up. "We hope this Nobody thing has a weird aura and follow that right to it."

"I hope we don't get eaten."

Chapter 22

1 MONTH AFTER EXTRACTION

On Friday, before the football game, I met up with Linh behind Veles Hall. "There's Institute agents all over the stadium, so if you see anything strange, remember to act normal, otherwise they'll notice you creeping around," Linh said. "If one of us does get caught by an agent, we'll send each other a psychic message: *The night's especially dark.*"

"That's pretty dramatic."

"I know." She smiled. "I'm really into all this spy stuff."

"What happens if we see the Nobody?"

"Then the message is *Nobody's here.* Once we're ready to move in"—she opened a compact—"we use this to send it back to Everywhen."

Above us, the moon was hidden behind a screen of black clouds. It *was* an especially dark night. If Misthaven High's football stadium wasn't well lit, our chances of success were slim to none. "If we fail—"

"We'll never get out of here. So, don't fail."

I hurried to the north gate, passed through the turnstile, and met up with Alison and Blake on the curb, where all the other students attending the game had gathered to board the buses the Institute hired to take students to sporting events at Misthaven. We could only attend home games, but anything was better than nothing.

"Where were you?" Alison asked as I walked up.

"I . . . had to go to the bathroom."

Luckily, they bought my excuse and we filed onto the bus. I sat next to the window, Alison beside me, and Blake across the aisle from her. "Did you join the Thorns, then?" Alison asked Blake.

He nodded. "Seems like the right thing to do."

"So, are you leaving Veles Hall?"

"Yeah, I have to move into Ares Hall. My schedule won't change this semester, but next semester I'll be in Legacy classes."

Briefly, Alison's eyes cut to the side. Maybe she wanted to tell Blake she'd miss him. Maybe she wanted to ask if we'd ever see him at lunch again. But she didn't say anything.

•

As we pulled into Misthaven High's parking lot, the rattle of distant drumlines greeted us. The stadium's giant floodlights thankfully provided all the light we'd need to send the Nobody back to Everywhen.

Towering over us, the home bleachers faced away from the parking lot. A two-story press box sat at the top of the stands, painted with a red-and-black dragon and the words *Misthaven Drakes*. The guest bleachers across the way were smaller, but equally packed. My nose perked up at the smell of fried food—corn dogs sopping with grease, extra-charred hamburgers, potato strings fried into husks of their former selves—emanating from a concession stand under the home bleachers.

These were strange conditions for my first football game. Even though I was on the lookout for a cannibal shadow monster, the chance to see Hunter play had my heart running exercise drills.

"I'm going to grab some grub," Blake said. "I'll come find you guys." He headed toward the concession stand, and we headed up the bleachers until we found somewhere to sit. I searched the field for Hunter, but the Drakes hadn't come out yet. Blake found us about ten minutes later, his hands full with paper trays of cheesy nachos, cheesy fries, and cheesy hot dogs.

Alison wrinkled her nose at the goopy pile of unnaturally orange cheese. "Wow."

"What?" Blake grabbed a dripping french fry. "I'm a growing boy."

"Ten bucks says you'll grow an extra limb if you eat all of that crap."

I caught a glimpse of the Drakes and jumped to my feet. "Look, they're about to come onto the field!" The Misthaven fans rose along with me, clapping and cheering as the Drakes tore through a badly drawn dragon banner and rumbled onto the field. Once my eyes landed on Hunter in his red-and-black uniform emblazoned with the number forty-six, I lost it. "That's my boyfriend, look"—I yanked on Alison's sleeve—"that's my boyfriend!"

Alison rolled her eyes at me and laughed. "Okay, Johnny!" She spun her finger. "Go, team."

"What position is Hunter, anyway?" Blake said, munching on a hot dog.

I sat back down. "He's the backup quarterback."

"We probably won't even see him play," Blake said.

Eyes trained on the field, I imagined the home team's quarterback fumbling the snap, and the away team's defense turning him into lawn mulch. The sooner he was out of the picture, the sooner Hunter could get in there and show everyone how awesome he was.

"Does anything prevent them from using magic?" Alison asked Blake.

"Well, standard Institute rules," Blake replied. "But they suck so bad even magic couldn't help them." He laughed.

"Why don't you play any sports?" Alison asked him.

"I'm in a band. I play instruments."

"No, you don't."

"Yes, I do: air guitar and air drums."

"You're so corny."

"I find your lack of faith disturbing."

"Okay, Darth, I'll bite. What's your band's name?"

"Air B&B."

"B&B?"

"Blake and Badassery."

Alison laughed. I knew she'd never admit it, but she liked how corny Blake was.

Once the game was underway, I knew I couldn't just sit there and wait for Hunter to play. Using my wizard sight, I combed the stands, searching for any unusual auras. In Darkwood Forest, the Bandersnatch's aura had been hard to miss, but out here, nothing stood out. No unsettling dread creeping around the corner. Nothing. This was going to be a lot harder than I'd thought.

"I've got to go to the bathroom," I said, standing up. Alison was so busy asking Blake questions about football, neither of them noticed me starting down the bleachers. Sweeping the stands with my eyes, I didn't turn up any strange auras, so I headed for concession. If the Nobody hunted in large crowds, the gathering around concession would be a buffet table.

On my way over, I got stuck in a sea of chattering townsfolk. *The Nobody could be anywhere in this forest of faces*, I thought, so I narrowed my eyes and tried parsing through all the auras. Distracted, I crashed into a handsome Smith with hazel eyes. "Watch where you're going, kid," he said, shooting me a quick glare. I feebly apologized as he walked away.

Down near the concession, I blended into the line so the Smith guarding the entrance wouldn't notice me snooping around. On my tiptoes, I scanned the crowd around the gate and the concession stand for any unusual auras, but still, nothing hit me. How was I supposed to find something I couldn't sense? Then a thought struck me: what if the Nobody didn't have an aura? Everyone had an aura, whether it was the confluence of sounds, smells, and feelings around them or the golden halo that only appeared around wizards. But was it possible the Nobody didn't?

The line inched forward. Looking between heads and shoulders, I noticed something strange in an anti-theft mirror hanging in the concession stand: a blurry face amid a sea of ordinary reflections, not like a smudge obscuring the glass, but like someone with no reflection at all. Turning around, I searched for the non-reflection's owner and, not far behind, spotted a man in a red cap with no aura. His eyes combed through the crowd like he was looking for something. A brown-haired girl walked past him toward the gate—then the man's shadow took on a life of its own, stretching its long fingers, elongating its thin body, looming over her shadow, menacing, hungry. The man followed her. Quickly, I got out of line, pushing between people and eliciting all manner of funny looks. With the Nobody trailing close behind, the girl passed the Smith guarding the gate and headed into the parking lot. There was no way I was getting past him so easily, so I stopped giving chase.

I sent Linh our message. *Nobody is here.*

Where did it go? she responded, almost immediately.

Into the parking lot.

Where are you?

Inside the gate. I'll try to find a way out.

Spinning around, I searched for another way to the parking lot and found a narrow passage between the chain-link fence around the football field and the home bleachers. The Smith at the gate yawned so widely his eyes shut, so I hurried into the alley while he wasn't looking. I speed walked about fifteen feet, looking over my shoulder the whole time to make sure the Smith hadn't seen me. When I was clear of him, I looped my fingers around the chain and gave the fence a light shake. It was sturdy, so I could probably climb it without making too much noise, but I'd have to find a point where no one would notice me scaling it. The Misthaven fans burst into cheers, and the bleachers above me shuddered, their beams groaning unsettlingly.

Looking down, I found a hole in the bottom of the fence, leading directly into the parking lot. Abandoning my plan to climb the fence, I studied the opening. It'd be a tight squeeze, but I could make it. I was about to crawl through when someone said, "Hey, kid." I froze. A Smith came up behind me, so I turned my back to the fence and covered the hole. "What're you doing back here?" he asked me.

What am I doing back here, what am I doing back here, what am I doing back here. "I got . . . lost . . . looking for a friend."

"Why don't you just come along with me—" Another fit of cheering cut his words short. The stands shook furiously, distracting the Smith, who nervously watched the wobbling beams under the bleachers like they were about to collapse. Now was my chance. I squeezed through the small opening to the parking lot. The Smith turned back around. "Hey, kid!" he yelled as I ran off.

Darting behind a red minivan, I watched as the Smith tried crawling through the hole after me. First, he weaseled his shoulders through the opening, then tried pulling the rest of his body along, but the wires caught onto his jacket and trapped him. He pulled back, trying to escape, rattling the whole fence and cussing like someone with a freshly stubbed toe.

I thought, *Linh, I'm in the parking lot, where are you?*

Near the buses.

At the other end of the parking lot, the Institute's buses sat parked in a row. I kept my body low to the ground and snuck between cars until I found Linh creeping along the side of a bus. She had her back to me.

"Hey," I whispered.

She almost jumped out of her shoes. "Johnny! We're after a cannibal—could you not sneak up on me right now?"

"Sorry. Have you found it?"

"I don't even know what I'm looking for. Show me with your mind." I stared at Linh, perplexed. "Close your eyes, and instead of sending me words, send me pictures, specifically a picture of what that monster looks like." I closed my eyes and sent her an image of the man in the red cap. "Okay, let's go find this thing before it eats someone."

We set about searching the parking lot, but didn't get far before we spotted three Smiths combing the lot with flashlights. We ducked behind a gray sedan and watched the Smiths shine their lights into a Mustang. Two teens popped up, embarrassing the Smiths, who apologized and kept searching. "We really don't have time for all this," Linh said.

"They'll follow our auras right to us."

"We can gloss our auras. Here, watch me do it."

With my wizard sight, I saw the machinery spinning all around me. Linh dragged a hand through the air, leaving a golden trail. Then she rubbed her hand over the trail like she was wiping off a stain. After a few passes, it was gone. I closed my eyes and tried sensing Linh's aura, but couldn't. She'd erased the entire thing and gone completely invisible to the sight. "How did you do that?"

"Like we do everything. Just imagine your aura doesn't exist, and it goes away. If you do any magic while you're glossed, though, you have to erase the imprint it leaves behind. Just imagine yourself wiping it away, like with a rag or something. There's no guarantee it'll be perfect—a really strong wizard could still find traces of your aura, theoretically—but it's the best way to hide from agents and stuff. Hurry, let's get under this car." We slithered on our bellies under the car and watched the Smiths' feet come nearer and nearer.

It all seemed so easy, but then again, Linh had been working with the Defectors for a while. If anyone knew how to avoid agents, it had to be them. I closed my eyes and pretended my aura was gone, that all the little markings my aura left were gone too.

Footsteps came into earshot. I clenched my teeth, shrank down, and imagined I wasn't even there. To my right, leather shoes clomped. I could almost feel the Smith's body heat as he stopped right where I was hiding. *Please, please, please, go away, go away, go away.*

He lowered one knee, like he was about to search under the car. I balled my fists. "Anything, George?" another Smith asked, from farther away.

George stood back up, pivoted on his heel, and tapped his toe against the pavement. "No. Maybe he went back inside."

"Let's go look. If this kid makes a break for it, we're dead."

At the sound of retreating footsteps, I finally relaxed. We crawled out from under the car. "Did the Defectors teach you to do that?" I asked.

Linh brushed the dirt off her clothes and nodded. "Maleeka taught it to me. It's the trick the Defectors use to escape the Institute and stay hidden."

A woman's scream cut through the air like a siren. The Nobody had found its quarry. We followed the shrieking and found the brown-haired girl with her back up against a car, grappling with the man in the red cap.

We charged at him, shoved him off the girl, and sent him sprawling. The girl put her hand to her mouth and stared in horror as the man rose to his feet. His gaunt, elongated face was white as alabaster, with millions of spidery blue veins underneath. His eyes flashed yellow like a caution light, then he opened his unnaturally long mouth and revealed rows and rows of sharp teeth, slimy gobs of drool dripping off them. The brown-haired girl screamed and ran away.

"You know any good magic?" I asked Linh.

"Just the glossing trick."

The Nobody lowered its back, arched its arms. Claws sprang out like razors. A low growl rumbled out of its lips and sent us racing in the opposite direction, but the creature's inhumanly long legs gave it a wide stride that was impossible to outrun. We hurried between a pair of cars, but the monster leaped and landed on top of one of them, the vehicle teetering under its weight. The Nobody leaned forward and snarled at us, so we grabbed each other and screamed, then Linh yanked me the other way. As we sprinted from aisle to aisle, the Nobody leaped from car to car like a giant grasshopper, pursuing us. We kept running until we glanced back and saw the monster had vanished.

"Where'd it go?" I asked.

"I don't know. Let's get under that car." She pointed to a gray sedan.

I was tired of Linh's tactic of scuttling under cars and hiding, but I wasn't going to argue, so we crawled under the car and waited . . . and waited . . . and waited. Nothing. No feet traipsing across the parking lot. No cars awkwardly wobbling like something heavy and monstrous had jumped on top of them. I kept watch on the parking lot, searching for anything strange. Linh dug into her pocket for the compact.

Just then, something clanged on top the roof of the car we were hiding under; the undercarriage sank down toward us. We exchanged a horrified glance, then the Nobody popped its head down on my side and reached for us. We screamed, Linh fumbling for the compact while I kicked at the creature's hand.

The Nobody snatched my collar and pulled me toward it, so Linh grabbed my arm and dragged me with her out from under the vehicle, tearing my shirt a little but freeing me from the monster's grasp. I scrambled to my feet and chased after Linh, who was already running ahead of me. Before I caught up to her, the Nobody landed in the lane ahead of us. Linh fell backward, dropping her compact on the floor and shattering the mirror inside. I yanked her up beside me just as a car came crashing into the monster and sent it flying.

"Talk about good timing," Linh said.

I quickly thanked every deity I could think of. The car screeched to a halt. In the driver's seat, the brown-haired girl we'd saved earlier gave us a horrified look, then peeled out of the parking lot, her tires squealing. A few feet behind the car, the Nobody lay motionless on the ground, as if every bone in its body had been smashed. We stared at it.

"What happens now?" I asked. Linh looked back at me and shrugged. Then the monster lifted an arm, placing a wobbly hand against the ground and pushing itself up. Linh and I grabbed each other in terror. It took a shaky stance, feet pigeon-toed, legs unsteady, and fixed its wild and hungry yellow eyes on us. But when it took a step forward, its knees gave way—it landed face-first on the pavement and burst into a shadow.

"The compact!" Linh said. Realizing mirror fragments were scattered all over the asphalt, we fell to our knees and searched for the largest shard. The shadow warped and swayed like a blob of oil coming to life, fighting for a fixed form.

I grabbed a piece of glass—it cut me. "Ow!" I dropped the shard. The shadow was spreading, almost ready to take shape and flee. We didn't have much time, but all the fragments I'd found were too small. Just then, I spotted a larger piece under a Hummer. On my hands and knees, I scampered over like a tarantula, snatched up the shard, and knelt, holding it up in the air, hoping to catch a ray from the floodlights. The Nobody finally took shape, but as it scurried to hide under a car, a light beam bounced off the fragment and struck it. With a strange groan, the shadow bulged and distorted like an ink blot on a Rorschach test, then it disappeared. Inside the glass shard, the angry shadow zipped around, trapped.

"Got it!" I said with a big smile. I could hardly believe we weren't rumbling around in that thing's stomach.

Linh's face lit up, but we didn't have time to celebrate. "Let's get back to the game, quick."

After tossing the glass shard into a trash can, we snuck back in through the hole in the fence. The third quarter hadn't ended yet. Linh hurried off to join some Institute kids walking around the track and chatting, and I climbed the stands back to Alison and Blake. They raised their eyebrows at me when I finally joined them again.

"Where were you?" Alison asked.

I struggled for a response. "I got lost."

"For three quarters of the game?"

"Really, really lost. You wouldn't believe how confusing this place is."

They gave me funny looks, but resumed watching the game. In the last quarter, the primary quarterback injured his ankle. The coach knotted his fingers around Hunter's helmet, said something to him, then sent him out onto the field.

Hunter was only about two inches shorter than me, but compared to all the mastodons roaming the field, he looked like an ant. I chewed on my nails, watching the two teams assemble on the line of scrimmage. Standing behind the center with his hands on his hips, Hunter scanned the field.

They're going to squish him, I thought to myself.

The center snapped the ball into Hunter's hands. He took a few steps back, his eyes trained on the wide receiver, but before he could launch the ball, the away team's entire defensive line pounced him. Blood drained from my cheeks. The crowd issued a collective groan, confirming my worst fears: Hunter had been killed playing this stupid blood sport. When the away team finally vacated the murder scene, they left Hunter splattered on the field, his arms and legs stretched out, a bug on a windshield.

"Ouch," Alison said.

Hunter sucked in a quick breath, then sprang back up on his feet like a ninja. He huddled with his teammates, unphased, as they planned their next move. I started to relax. Hunter was a lot tougher than he looked. In fact, nothing could keep him down long. He'd be getting trampled one second, and the next, he'd be bobbing and weaving through the field with the grace of a dancer, sending the tacklers crashing into each other's arms.

I had no idea why Hunter was only a backup. He single-handedly carried the whole game until he scored the last touchdown and won it for Misthaven. The crowd cheered and stormed the field. Hunter's teammates hoisted him onto their shoulders, then carried him around, whooping and grunting.

"Do you want to go down there?" Alison said, surveying the post-game chaos.

"Should I?"

"He told you to, didn't he?" I nodded. "Then we should."

"What're you so scared about?" Blake said. "Let's just go down there."

Eventually, Hunter's teammates set him down. He took off his helmet and searched through a sea of laughing and smiling faces until his eyes landed on me. Hunter smiled, big and wide, like I was all he'd been looking for. Plenty of people were showering him with adulation, and the only thing he cared about was me, the awkward boy with the clueless look on his face.

He ran up to me and grabbed my hands. "Hey!"

"Hey." I lit up like a streetlamp at dusk.

"Did you see me out there?"

"Yeah."

"What'd you think?"

"You're awesome, Hunt. You're always awesome."

He reeled me in and hugged me, his sweat-soaked hair sprinkling my face. I rested my face on one of his shoulder pads. He stank of sweat and grass. It was kind of gross, but I guess I kind of liked it too. He pulled away, still smiling, and kissed me. No one was paying attention I didn't think, and even if they were, they weren't about to say anything to the guy who'd just scored Misthaven the win.

When he pulled away, I saw something over his shoulder, through the crowd: the black shape from my dreams. Every sound around me went dull, like someone had put my head in a fishing bowl. Then I heard the same familiar hiss of sand. Nothing but hissing sand. Louder and louder. The dark shape didn't move at all. It just stood in the crowd, its void-like face fixed on me. It raised its arm and pointed one sandy digit at me. The word *cintamani* sliced through the air on a sibilant whisper.

"Johnny," Hunter said, bringing me back to reality. "What's wrong?"

When I looked back, the monster was gone. Shaken, I looked at him and forced myself to smile. "Nothing."

Chapter 23

The next day, Linh and I visited Luther at the Misthaven Library. We found him up a ladder, stacking books on a high shelf. "Two weeks," Luther said, balancing his wobbly legs on the ladder rungs. Since our run-in with the centipede, he'd already managed to fix up the library, but he was still sorting through all the books that had been scattered everywhere in the fight. Linh and I held the ladder steady for him. "That's how long it'll take me to get a hold of the only person I know who can ferry you to Sanctuary, the Defectors' hideout."

"Two weeks?" Linh said. "Luther, if the Institute does another room search and looks through our minds, we're going to be in big trouble."

Luther eased down the steps like a shaky old cat and shelved another pair of books. "That would be quite unfortunate. But there's no guarantee that I'll be able to make contact even in that length of time."

"So it could take longer." I sighed.

"Longer, shorter"—Luther made his way down to the floor—"you never can tell with these kinds of things."

We felt no more assured leaving the library than we'd felt going in. "I guess we're just going to have to pray they don't do another inspection," I said as we waited in the bus shelter.

"Well, at least you'll be able to spend more time with your smelly boyfriend."

I hadn't told Hunter anything about what Linh and I were up to, nor did I plan to, but who knew what might happen over the coming weeks? If Hunter and I grew closer, how long before I felt the pressure to tell him I was planning to escape? How would he react? He'd tried escaping once on his own, but it seemed he'd changed since then. Now, he was rushing Legacies.

"He smells good, actually," I said to Linh, deflecting my own thoughts.

•

Two weeks crawled by. Whenever he could, Hunter taught me all the magic he'd picked up from his football and wrestling teammates in the Legacies. He'd come over after practice, his skin still smelling like grass, slide his ironwood arms around me, rest his chin on my shoulder, and hold my hands.

"We're going to make a light ball," he said into my ear. I raised my shoulders because his breath tickled my ear. He thought my ticklishness was cute, so he kissed me. "We've got to focus." I cupped my hands and waited for something to happen, but nothing did. "You've got to believe you can do it."

Movies made magic look easy: you just waved your wand around, and *boom*. But in reality, it was complicated and dangerous. There were two methods for casting a spell. The first method: visualize the spell in your mind's eye. This was the method most non-Lineage kids used, and it was superdangerous. I had to imagine the light coalescing in my hands, feel the warmth against my fingertips, see the light rays budding from the ball like the seeds of a dandelion.

"If you gather too much heat," Hunter said, "you could end up with a fireball."

"What then?" I asked, pressing back against his chest.

"Then you got a fireball," he said with a chuckle. "And if you don't know what to do with it, we'll blow up."

I dropped my hands. "Isn't there an easier way to do this?"

The second method created longer-lasting effects, but it was more complicated: reaching into the vivit apparatus and rearranging the machinery itself. Hunter said whenever wizards were waving their hands around in movies and stuff, that was what they were doing: turning cogs and wheels. You couldn't just grab the machinery and make it do whatever you wanted, though. All the machinery was governed by sequences. Simple sequences for simple elements, like water, fire, wind, and earth, and complex sequences for complex things, like people, animals, and Asuras. Air was one little cog you could spin, but my arm was a million little cogs and wheels all interlocked and working together. If you didn't know how the sequence worked, you could turn the cogs and wheels all you wanted, but they'd just reset back to where they were. (When Melchior had warned me that using magic might change something forever, he hadn't bothered to add that it might not. He had just been trying to dissuade me from using magic at all).

Magic circles and other symbols were shortcuts, little pieces of machinery themselves, like triggers that set off their own sequences.

For example, Hunter's healing circle set off sequences that caused cells to rapidly regenerate. Theoretically, wizards could cure all kinds of ailments like this, but new sequences were always emerging in the vivit apparatus, so the best shortcuts were usually pretty simple. Unfortunately, only Legacy kids were trained in using the vivit apparatus.

The heavier and more tangible a thing was, the bigger and clearer its machinery; finer, smaller things had machinery you had to squint to see. "You're not going to blow us up," Hunter said, squeezing me tighter. "Believe in yourself. Imagine the light gathering in your hands."

I cupped my hands again. You could gather the cogs and wheels of simpler elements like air just by imagining it; the pieces would gather in your hand. If you joined enough smaller pieces together, they made bigger pieces. If you wanted, you could gather a bunch of little air cogs, mash them together, and make the air thicker, even shape it into a ball. Breaking things down was more complicated, because once you built something, it changed, and so did the sequences governing its machinery.

I imagined the rays shining in through the window were flowing into my palms. A ball of light bloomed in my hands and floated there. Hunter kissed me on the cheek. "There you go." He drew closer until he was completely pressed up against me. The ball started growing hotter, hotter. Then he spun me around, and the ball dispersed.

"Have you seen Blake lately?" he asked.

I rested a hand on his chest, felt his heart beating. "He had to move into Ares Hall. He's going to keep eating lunch with us, though. But next semester the Institute'll force him to take Legacy classes."

"Lucky guy. What about Alison?"

"She's really sad about everything. She stays in her room all the time, sleeping and going into Everywhen. I think she was hoping we'd have escaped by now."

"I'm glad you haven't," Hunter said before pressing his soft lips against mine.

●

Since Blake left Veles Hall, Linh had tried being a vigilant RA, but she didn't strike me as someone who liked keeping others in line. She'd remind students they weren't supposed to be fooling around, but sometimes I'd see her stomp up to a busy bedroom, bring her fist to the door like she was about to knock, then go completely red and bolt. I wouldn't have knocked either. Talk about awkward.

Occasionally, Smiths walked the halls, making sure students weren't getting frisky, but keeping apart horny teenagers wasn't a top priority for the Institute. Even though we couldn't spend the night together, there was a huge chunk of time between the end of classes and curfew, and enterprising teenagers could get a lot done in fifteen minutes.

Hunter didn't know I was a virgin. Whenever we made out, he'd try to see how far I'd go with him. He'd come over after practice and drag me into his room and throw me on his bed and crawl on top of me and kiss me, kiss me, kiss me, and I loved kissing him, but knowing he wasn't a virgin made me nervous. Our make-out sessions were always accompanied by the fear any minute, he might ask for sex, and I didn't know whether I'd beg for it like a dog, or recoil, scratching and hissing like a cat.

During one particularly heated make-out session, he kept nuzzling his face in my neck. I shrugged him off and giggled. "That tickles." He slipped his hand under my shirt and kept trying to kiss me until I blurted out, "I'm a virgin!" Smooth, I know.

He moved his face away from my neck and smiled at me. "Okay . . ."

"Why're you looking at me like that?"

"We were just kissing."

"I know, I was just saying—"

"Do you want to stay a virgin?" He gave me an exaggerated sexy look, narrowing his eyes and waggling his brows. I smiled, so he pressed up against me and smiled back. He wasn't kidding. I could feel how serious he was. I didn't know whether to laugh or panic.

"I, uh . . . are you worried that . . . because I've never done it before . . . I'll be bad at it?"

"Everyone's got a first time at the rodeo." He crawled between my legs, undid my belt, and whipped it off. This was it. Soon, his mouth would be on me and I would lose my virginity and there'd be no going back.

After I closed my eyes, the greatest feeling rushed over me. It was like landing face-first on a fresh, cold pillow, like finding a five-dollar bill when you were only looking for a quarter, like checking the mail and finally getting that package you'd been waiting for.

Everything started tingling. My hairs stood up like lightning was fixing to strike me. Lightning *was* fixing to strike me—the biggest lightning bolt in all of heaven was zooming down, and I was lying there, helpless.

This was it.

I clenched the covers.

Sucked in a deep breath.

My muscles tensed.

Oh shit.

Oh shit.

Oh. *Shit!*

Boom.

My body twitched and shivered and did all kinds of weird jerky things, like a broken animatron at Disney World. When all the tingling stopped, I exhaled and opened my eyes. My heart was racing like I'd been riding a roller coaster.

Hunter sat back on his heels. "My first time was quick too."

Underwear. I needed my underwear. I reached over and slapped around on the floor until I felt them, then snatched them into bed with me. "So that's it? That was sex?"

"Most people just call it a blow job." He started undoing his belt. "Did you want to do more?"

Holy crap. I squirmed my underwear back on and squeaked, "Huh?"

"I've never gone all the way before."

"Who would . . . who would do what?"

"What do you mean?"

"You know. Who'd be the one doing the . . . *sexing*?"

Hunter laughed. "What're you talking about? Sexing?"

"Who'd be the pitcher and who'd be the . . . catcher?"

"Oh! Do you want to be the . . . catcher?"

"Why? Do I seem like a catcher or something?"

He chuckled. "I don't know. I've never played baseball before. Why don't you just go down on me too?"

"You want me to do that to you?"

"It'd be nice. Unless you don't want to?"

"N-N-No. I want to." I nodded so hard my head almost shook off. I'd never wanted to do anything more in my whole life. I wanted to take off Hunter's pants, get down there, and—well, I didn't really know what I was going to do. I hadn't paid that much attention. Honestly, Hunter could've gone down there and just stared really hard, and everything would've played out the same way. He was in for a disappointing experience. "It's just . . . I've never done it before, so I'm probably going to suck at it."

"That's the point." He laughed and wiggled out of his boxers. Then he put his arms behind his head and waggled his eyebrows again.

Chapter 24

Heading back to my room from Hunter's, I caught Linh lurking outside my door with her back turned to me. "Linh?"

She startled and turned around. *Didn't I tell you to please stop creeping up behind me?* she said with her mind. *We need to talk.* A couple of students walked by down the hall. "Hey, can I borrow your math notes?" Linh said out loud to throw off any suspicion we might be communicating psychically.

What about? I thought, opening my door to let us both in.

Luther finally got us a way into Sanctuary. We're supposed to meet up with Aquila in Misthaven on Saturday. She'll help us get out.

I was so excited, I virtually floated over to my desk, fetched some random notes from my math book, and handed them to her.

"Thanks," she said. "See you later." Just as quickly as she'd swept to give me the good news, she was gone, leaving me to catch my breath. I tried lying down, but after what Linh had told me, I couldn't get to sleep. I went to Alison's room to see if she was awake. She didn't respond to my knock, so instead I went by Hunter's room—I figured he'd still be awake.

He came out and smiled at me. "Maybe I should just start sleeping in your room."

Using my mind, I told him, *Hug me. I need to tell you a few things with my mind.*

Hunter grabbed my hips and pulled me to him, swaying and grinning. *What's up?*

Linh's got a way out of here.

He pulled away. *What're you talking about?* He shut the door. "J, what's going on?"

"Linh's been working with the Defectors and . . . so have I."

"What are you thinking?"

"I had to find a way out of here, Hunt. Alison's mom is really sick. And my dad—"

"Johnny, the Institute erased your old life. They told us that when we arrived."

"How do you know? Have you ever been out there to see for yourself? What if they're just lying so we don't try to escape?"

"If they were lying, this place wouldn't be here. I already told you about Maleeka. If the Institute catches you, they won't just bring you back. They'll drag you under the Heka Building."

"I've got to do this, Hunter."

He was growing irritated. "No, you don't. We could try to rush the Crowns again, do this the right way. Work from inside the Institute."

"I don't want to work from inside the Institute. We want to escape it. Ali and me."

He threw up his arms. "What about us, Johnny?"

"Hunter, I"—I held back the rush of emotions flowing through my head—"I want you to come with me. But I won't ask you to put yourself in danger. I already know too much, Hunt. Staying here would only put me in more danger. This is the only way." With those words, I turned, opened his door, and walked out. Every step away from Hunter's room felt like jamming jagged shards of glass into my chest.

●

The next morning, I went by Alison's room, but when I knocked on the door, just like the night before, there was no answer. Curious, I tried the door. It creaked open. It wasn't like her to leave the door unlocked—she was way too paranoid. I pushed the door open and found her lying in bed, asleep. Figuring I should wake her for school, I walked in and nudged her arm.

"Alison. Alison, wake up. Come on, wake up!"

She didn't move. Alison could be a heavy sleeper, but this was different. I shook her harder. Nothing.

"Alison?" I panicked. Normally, I'd never read someone's thoughts, but I was worried something had happened to her. I closed my eyes, imagined myself wandering into her mind, and hit a black wall. Emptiness. There was nothing in her head. Opening my eyes, sweat broke out on my forehead. "Alison, wake up! Alison!"

Nothing could stir her. It was like she was in a coma.

"What's wrong?" It was Blake. He must've come by for a visit.

"She won't wake up."

Blake reached for her wrist and checked her pulse. "Her pulse seems normal." Then he leaned forward and put his ear near her mouth. "And she's breathing too."

"I tried reading her thoughts. There's nothing in there. What's wrong with her?"

Blake closed his eyes for about a minute, also exploring Alison's mind. "She's in a dream trance. Her body's still alive, but her mind is lost somewhere in Everywhen."

"What do we do?"

"If someone doesn't get her out of there, the Institute'll come and take her."

Hunter and Linh came to the door. "Hey," Hunter said, "we were looking for you."

"What's going on?" Linh asked.

"Close the door." Blake said, his eyes floating over Alison. After Linh shut the door, he said, "Alison's in a dream trance. We've got to help her."

"How do we wake her up?" I said, sitting down next to her on the bed.

"We've got to find where her mind went in Everywhen," Blake said.

"How?"

"The Night Market," he explained. "It's a place in Everywhen. You can trade memories and dreams for information. If anyone knows where Alison's mind is, the creatures there will. We have to do a dream rave."

"What's that?" I asked.

"A union," Linh said. "That's the technical name for it. We join our minds together and go into Everywhen at the same time. We're not really supposed to do them."

Confused, I pressed Blake. "Why not?"

Blake turned to me. "While our minds are joined, we might learn each other's secrets. Sometimes, you see things you really shouldn't."

Linh knitted her eyebrows at me. Blake was in a Legacy now. To Linh, that meant he couldn't be trusted. If he was a spy, we'd all be in big trouble. But I wasn't going into Everywhen without him. "I don't care," I said. "We have to help Alison."

"I'm coming too," Hunter said.

"All right, count me in." Linh sighed. I was a little surprised. "What?" she said, reading my expression. "I'm not leaving her like that. Besides, the more the merrier, right? It is called a *dream rave*."

"Okay, everyone. Lie on the floor, make sure your heads are all touching, and close your eyes," Blake said.

We formed an X with our bodies, each of our heads touching the other three's, then closed our eyes. "Think happy thoughts," Blake said. I couldn't even control myself—I imagined lying on my bed kissing Hunter, his full lips quirking into a smile as he pressed them against mine.

He pulled away, his gentle eyes studying my lips, my face. "I'm sorry . . . about last night."

"You don't have to be."

"I want to go with you."

"I don't want to put you danger, Hunt. I really like you and—"

He hushed me with a tender kiss. I sank into the bed, closing my eyes and feeling the little hairs over his lips tickle me. He rested his hand on my chest, so I laid mine over his. Nothing could shut me up quite like his lips. Gently pulling away, his face only a sigh's breadth from mine, he whispered, "I want to go with you."

"Whenever you two are done," Linh said.

We sat up and found her and Blake standing there, giving us unimpressed looks.

"Are we . . . dreaming?" I asked.

"We're in Everywhen, if that's what you mean," Blake said.

"Can we leave now, or are you two planning to find out if you can get Johnny pregnant?"

"Wait, so you think I'm the catcher too?" I asked.

"What?" Linh gave me a funny look.

"I—never mind."

Blake opened the door, and my senses were overwhelmed in a burst of spiced air: lavender, cinnamon, coriander, cumin. We walked out to an incredible sight: a floating market sat shimmering on black waters, illuminated by string lights dangling over its creaky wooden avenues. Then came the weirdness: Slimy green flesh, violet eyes. Toad men draped in colorful silks, hovering over scales, weighing pounds of eyeballs. A bustling webwork of shaky wooden piers, with people and creatures—some humanoid, some not—going in and out of lavish canal boats, doing business with toad-like vendors who sold their wares from the comfort of lighters, scows, and wherries. Makeshift wooden stands with huge monsters selling cages full of yipping fur balls. Boxing rings with oxlike men circling each other while noisy spectators waved tattered dolls and spit-stained pillows like bets.

"What are all these things?" I whispered to Blake.

"The Institute calls them Maras. They're like Asuras, but they live in Everywhen."

"Will they hurt us?"

"Not here. Fighting is banned in the Night Market. Unless you're in that boxing ring, of course."

Maras took all manner of forms. Some were big towers of fur with glowing yellow eyes, sitting inside shacks crowned with Christmas lights, luring shoppers to their stands with promises of timepieces that could count down the minutes of your life. Others were big clouds of smoke billowing out of brass tea kettles, guaranteeing eternal youth in exchange for your first memory of tasting chamomile. But the strangeness didn't end at the milky-eyed toads hawking snow globes they swore contained childhood memories. I looked up and saw the sky itself was a lightless nothing. Not a black sky sans starlight, but an actual nothing stretching infinitely.

"Why does the sky look like that?" I asked.

"We're close to the Night City," answered Linh, a few steps ahead of me.

"The Night City?"

Blake kept his eyes forward as he slipped between two ogres. "We don't ever go there. It's too dangerous."

"It's the place where dreams meet death," Linh said.

I had no idea what that meant, but when a sweaty bundle of skin slithered past me with a basket of junk dangling on one of its bloated arms, I forgot to even ask. Approaching the pier's edge, I glanced at the black waves splashing below and saw something scaly and long moving around in them. Quickly, I moved to Hunter's side. He smiled and put his arm around me. "Are you scared?"

I looked back into the black water at the scaly tentacle sploshing around. "Nu-uh."

"Don't worry, I'll protect you." He grabbed my hand.

I wondered how old this colorful bazaar was. A place like this, hidden deep in the dreamworld, could've been older than human civilization. "How long has this market been around?" I asked Blake.

"Nobody knows. Not even the Maras."

"Really?"

"Some of them say there're vendors who've been around since they built the place, but the market always changes. It's like a dream: it never stays the same. Vendors come and go all the time."

"What's the longest that you've ever been here?"

"Not long. Like I warned you guys, if you stay in Everywhen for too long, you'll eventually get lost."

We walked past minotaurs swishing glass vials glimmering with sapphire-blue liquid; magpie men offering steaming pies stuffed with maggots, keenly named "mag-pies"; and twisted crones setting out bail jars filled with screaming faces. All this time, Blake had been asking shoppers and vendors alike if they could "lead him to a secret keeper." I didn't know what that was, either, but I didn't want to keep stopping him with questions. A pair of tall, faceless shapes in black robes listened to Blake, then pointed inhumanly long fingers at a skiff with a single lantern dangling from a hanger.

Inside the boat sat an enormous man in a blue velvet blazer. He had several arms poking out of his sides. He took a drag from a hookah and blew smoke rings into the black sky. Linh and Blake exchanged a nervous look.

"He seems pleasant," Linh said.

Blake walked over to the boat, and we followed. On closer inspection, the man was even less human-looking than I'd first thought. His skin was a strange pale blue, and he didn't have legs. In fact, his lower body stretched like a caterpillar's abdomen, coiling around the boat's bottom boards. He wore a monocle and lifted his head high, narrowing his little eyes and peering down his pointy nose at us. "Yes," he said in a voice that drew out like a string of melted cheese.

"Hi," Blake said, "we're looking for a secret keeper. Can you help us?"

The caterpillar man brought the hookah's mouthpiece to his lips and inhaled deeply, his bulging chest bloating up like a balloon. Then he let out a cloud of smoke. "All things come with a price."

"A memory, right? I've got a few I'd like to get rid of."

"Yes, especially painful memories can be burdens to bear." He pointed to a white, wooden door at the end of the pier. "Step through there. I will claim what's rightfully mine, and you will have what's yours in time." Blake nodded, shot the creature an uneasy smile, then eased away.

We walked to the end of the pier and gathered around the door. "Okay, guys," Blake said, "we have no idea where this thing leads, so just remember, our powers are stronger here in Everywhen. If we get separated, we'll search for each other with our minds. Remember, no matter what changes in the dreamscape, our auras will always be the same."

He turned the brass doorknob, pushing the heavy door open. Darkness waited on the other side, a hungry void as empty as the sky looming over us. Blake stepped through. Linh stepped through.

Hunter let go of my head and smiled at me. "Just think of me if you can't find me, okay?" Then he stepped through.

My heart pounded in my chest. My throat was dry. I inched up to the portal, rested my hands on the doorframe, and poked my head in. Nothing on the other side but darkness, infinite darkness. "Can you guys hear me?" I called. My question echoed into the void, unanswered. This was definitely going to get weirder before it got any better. *Okay, Johnny*, I said to myself, *you're a badass wizard. You can do anything.* I didn't feel any more badass after saying that. I felt stupid. But I had to follow them.

I gulped hard and dove head first into eternity. Time and space warped around me, and I found myself standing in the middle of a sunflower field. I took a wobbly step forward. The ground was unsteady, squishy. Under the sunflowers, the ground was made of ears—ears covered in flies, buzzing and running their little legs all over their bodies. Horrified, I froze, then slammed my eyes shut and imagined Hunter's smiling face.

When I opened them again, I was on a beach surrounded by fish the size of people, with human arms and legs. They marched around carrying pig heads mounted on spikes and buckets full of money. One of them turned its fishy head and stared at me. I shut my eyes again. *Hunter, Hunter, Hunter.*

Next, I found myself standing in a mudroom. An empty coat rack hung over a shoe stand holding some boots, a pair of white-and-blue Nikes, and a pair of white Reeboks. A flight of stairs bisected a hallway that led to a dining room, where light poured in through some sheer curtains. It was a nice house, everything pris-tinely white—the cornices, the walls, the balustrade on the stairs. An angry voice from upstairs cracked the silence: "Joe, I think you need to head home. Right now."

Another voice, younger than the first, responded, "Yes, sir." Then footsteps came tromping down the stairs, growing louder, until a boy who looked about fourteen darted past me. He pulled on his Reeboks in the mudroom, then darted out the front door. A gust of hot, smelly farmyard air hit my face before the door closed.

Grabbing the handrail tight, I walked upstairs and found Hunter looking into a room, shaking. I walked up beside him and followed his eyes. A younger Hunter, no older than the boy who'd just left, stood in the dim afternoon sunlight, staring up at his father like an ant watching the movements of a giant foot. "Dad, I—"

"Shut up!" his dad's voice boomed off the walls.

"This is the day my dad caught me with Joe. I don't want you to see this, Johnny," Hunter said.

I grabbed his hand, squeezed it tight.

Outside the window, the sun settled behind black treetops,

darkening the room. His dad stood there in the dying light, glowering at young Hunter. Then he shot forward, grabbed his son, and slammed him against the wall, shaking the window frame and knocking some trophies off a floating shelf. The trophies smashed to the floor, most breaking. Young Hunter cringed.

"Do you know what that was, what you were doing?" Young Hunter kept shaking, but didn't answer. "Do you?" his dad hollered. But young Hunter still kept quiet. "It was sin!" his father said, bringing his seething face even closer. Young Hunter cowered, digging his fingernails into the paint on the wall. His quivering lips parted, but he only whimpered. "It was a vile, dirty sin! Do you want to go to hell, Hunter?" Hunter, still too petrified to answer, couldn't form a single word, so his dad raised his big, meaty hand in the air and drove it down, whopping young Hunter across the head. "Do you want to go to hell, Hunter?"

Young Hunter shut his eyes and clenched his teeth. "No, sir!"

Then his dad grabbed his face and squeezed until young Hunter's lips puckered like a fish. "That's what's going to happen, Hunter!" he shouted. "If you ever do anything like that again, the devil will take your soul straight to hell!" A tear crawled down young Hunter's cheek. Disgusted by this display of emotion, his dad let go and backhanded him across the mouth. "Is that what you want, Hunter?"

"No, sir!"

His dad hurled his open hand across young Hunter's face again. "Is that where you want to end up?"

"No, I'm sorry, I'm sorry!" His dad raised his fist. The boy trembled behind his tiny shaking hands. "No, Dad. Please don't!"

"Stop him," I said.

"What?" Hunter looked at me, a tear rolling down his cheek.

I put my hands on his cheeks and wiped away the tear. "This isn't real, Hunt. You can stop him."

My words sparked something in Hunter's eyes. Now, they shone with courage. He took a step forward. "Hey!" His father turned around, snarling like a rabid dog. "Stop hitting him."

Then his dad's body twisted and warped, his arms growing longer, his nails spearing out into claws, his teeth stretching down into razor-sharp fangs. He huffed out a cloud of smoke through his red snout. He was a monster—a real monster. Hunter backed up and looked back at me, his sweet eyes filled with vulnerability. I grabbed his hand again. "You're awesome, Hunt. You're always awesome."

His monstrous father stomped toward us, his body growing, skin turning red, eyes going yellow. Hunter set his jaw, glowered at the beast, and with newfound bravery, said, "You don't scare me anymore."

The beast spread his massive arms and roared so loud that everything shook. But Hunter was determined; he wouldn't let this terrible moment define him. Not any longer. "No!" he yelled back, now squeezing my hand so tight it hurt. "I'm not scared of you anymore!"

The monster roared again with such ferocity my cells quaked. The room dimmed until everything was suffused in a reddish glow. Then I felt heat, like someone had set the house on fire. His father had transformed into a hellish beast with horns and cloven hooves and a hungry maw filled with jagged teeth. He took a giant step forward, making the floorboards rumble under our feet. Beside me, Hunter blanched.

Clenching his hand, I let my aura fill him with bravery, fed him kindness he'd never known. I didn't want anything to hurt Hunter ever again. I wanted him to be happy, and I wanted that happiness to bring him strength.

He let go of my hand, marched forward, and screamed, "No!" And he kept screaming until he'd chased away the shadows surrounding us, until he'd fought back the flames encircling us, until he'd cowed his horrible father, who stepped back and shrank into a man before exploding into a pile of dust.

When the room was quiet and moonlight drenched everything in a woeful blue, Hunter turned to me, his eyes filled with pain, filled with sadness. I took a few steps forward and reached out to him, so he grabbed my hand and pulled me in close, hugged me so tight I thought we'd break. Then he cried, deep and hard, into my shoulder. I rubbed his soft hair, let him cry until he was hoarse, until his strong legs were weak and trembling, and then, when he couldn't stand anymore, I held him up.

After Hunter had cried out all the pain his father had left him with, we closed our eyes, thought of Blake and Linh, and found ourselves in a room with damask wallpaper and wooden floors. On one side of the room, a single leather armchair rested next to a floor lamp, and on the other side, the wall was covered in big, fat jabbering mouths. Blake walked along the wall, placing his ear to each mouth, listening to the droning nonsense they were spewing. Linh was stretched out on the armchair, swinging her arm over the side. She perked up when she saw us. "You're finally here. Where were you?"

Hunter looked down at his shoes, then up at me. His cheeks were still a little red from crying so hard, the whites of his eyes still pink in the corners, but I wouldn't let anyone know his secrets. I rubbed his back. "We got lost."

"Apparently that's a secret keeper," Linh said, pointing at the mouth wall. "Blake said it hears everything that's happening everywhere in Everywhen—that's a mouthful. And these mouths are supposed to just"—she cocked her head to the side—"spit it out? He's got to figure out which one is talking about Alison."

Blake leaned over and put his ear to one of the mouths. The mouth flapped its lips, slapped its tongue, and covered Blake's cheek in spit as it yammered. Somewhere in the whirling nonsense, Blake heard something that brightened his face. He straightened up. "Found her!"

"Where is she?" I asked.

"Her old house?"

"Yeah, I know where that is," I said.

"Okay, you can take us there. Close your eyes and imagine it, and we'll all go."

We closed our eyes, and I reconstructed Alison's old house in my mind, its shingled mansard roof, its single turret in the attic, and then we heard rushing water, then we *felt* rushing water. When we opened our eyes, we found ourselves in Alison's old living room. Water poured through holes in the ceiling, flooding the room up to our stomachs. Couches, armoires, and fake potted plants bobbed in the water. At the other end of the room, Alison sat cross-legged on top of her mother's '60s record cabinet, staring at all the chaos with a vacant look on her face.

"Okay, you guys," I said, "I'll go talk to her. Just stay here." Alison had come to this place because she wanted to get away from the Institute. The last thing she'd want to see was people who reminded her of that place.

I slogged over to her, wading through the water. A ceiling tile fell and plopped in the water right next to me, then water poured down from the hole and drenched me. Trying to block the torrent with my arm, I kept ploughing forward, scooting aside the TV, a yellow armchair, and a lamp before I reached her.

"You're taking this whole head underwater thing pretty literally, huh?"

Alison did a double take. "Johnny? What the hell are you doing here?"

"We came to get you."

"Where the hell am I?"

"Trapped in Everywhen."

"Oh. Blake said that could happen."

"Yeah."

"Are you mad at me?"

"No. I just don't want anything bad to happen to you."

"I love you, Johnny."

"I love you, too, Alison."

The water was still rising, forcing Blake, Linh, and Hunter to climb onto a soggy upturned couch. I rested my arms on the cabinet and paddled my feet to keep afloat.

"Alison, Linh's working with the Defectors. We finally have a way out."

"Are you serious?"

"That's what I was coming to tell you when I found you in a dream trance."

"But how do you know she's not a spy trying to trick us?" she said in a hushed voice.

"I've been working with her for a while. If she wanted to turn me in, she could've done it long ago."

"Why didn't you tell me?"

"Because she warned me not to, and I was worried that if I didn't do as she asked, I'd mess everything up and we'd never get out of here."

"I guess I can forgive you this once for hiding things from me."

She looked around. "So . . . I don't know how to get out of here."

"Blake can help us." I waved him over.

He splashed into the water, swam over to the cabinet, and grabbed onto the edge. "You know, you still owe me a date."

"You always so corny?"

"Like a bag of tortilla chips."

Alison smiled at him. "Get us out of here, dork."

"Can you make the water go down first? Just close your eyes and imagine it going away."

She closed her eyes. The water vanished. We were standing in her old living room, nothing disturbed, everything back in its proper place. There wasn't a drop of water in sight, and even our clothes were dry.

"That's that," Alison said. "So what's this about the Defectors, Linh?" She never did know when to keep her mouth shut.

Blake looked sharply at Linh.

"Oh, thanks for busting that out, Johnny," Linh said.

"What're they talking about, Linh?" Blake asked.

She wouldn't even look at him, like she was ashamed she'd hidden it from him. "I've been . . . working with the Defectors."

"That could get you locked up in the Heka Building! How long have you been with them?"

"Since a little after Maleeka disappeared."

"Was Maleeka working with the Defectors too?" Linh nodded, and Blake just got angrier. "Why didn't you tell me?"

"I was going to—"

"So why didn't you?"

"Because you joined a Legacy."

Blake looked at the floor. Then he said, "If you're trying to escape, I'm coming with you."

The sound of hissing sand filled the air. We all went silent and looked around for the source of the noise. "Do you guys hear that?" Blake said. I had. Then that familiar feeling came. Dread. Imminent. Deadly. I'd felt that aura before too.

"What's that?" Linh said, scared.

The hairs on my neck stood up. Turning around, I kept my eyes trained on the archway between the living room and the kitchen. Something was coming. I didn't know what, but my wizard senses confirmed it.

A cloud of sand snaked its way into the living room. Then a shambling leg lurched through and landed on the floor with a dull thud. The eerie shape took another step into the room.

Ripped jeans.

Dingy sweater.

Sand pouring from the mouth of a hoodie.

Sandy stumps where fingers should be.

The Sandman.

It was the creature that had tried killing me the night before I was extracted. The hissing sand that stalked me in my sleep, hunted me in my waking hours. The black-haloed nightmare I'd seen in my dreams.

"What the hell is that?" Alison grabbed for my arm, but caught Blake's hand instead.

"Probably just some spooky Mara," he said. "We need to wake up. Alison, I'll help pull you out. Everyone, just close your eyes and imagine yourself waking up."

Alison and Blake closed their eyes and vanished. Linh vanished. Hunter vanished. I closed my eyes. Opened them. Nothing. The Sandman was moving toward me. I closed my eyes again. Opened them. Again, nothing. It was closer now, swaying its shoulders back and forth with every gentle step. Just like the first time I'd seen the Sandman, I couldn't wake up. I was stuck in the dreamworld.

I about-faced and headed for the staircase to the second floor. Hurrying up the steps, I found a door at the top. There hadn't been a door in Alison's real house, but I swung it open anyway, just trying to get away from the monster. I ran through the doorway and found myself charging back into Alison's living room through the front door. The dreamworld had looped me around. And the Sandman was still staggering toward me, its sandy hands raised, reaching for me.

Zooming back upstairs in a panic, I searched for another way out. The Sandman was at the bottom of the stairs, climbing toward me. On the wall beside me hung a small painting of Majere Hall's cafeteria. According to Professor Bigsby, anything was possible in Everywhen. I was about to find out, anyway. I grabbed the picture frame and stretched it wide as a doorway. Then I stepped through the painting and into the empty cafeteria. I looked behind me—the portal was gone.

Taking a minute's respite, I sucked in a quick breath before the familiar hiss of sand slithered into my ears and broke the peace. Not wanting to look, I closed my eyes and prayed I'd wake up back in the room with everyone else. I couldn't believe I wanted to be back at the Institute, but there I'd probably be safe away from this monster. Finally turning to look, I saw the Sandman weaving through the cafeteria toward me, sweeping its sandy fingers across tabletops, leaving dusty trails that vanished into smoke seconds later.

Magic. I had to try magic. I looked at a table and imagined it floating. It did. Using my mind, I flung the table at the Sandman. It merely raised a hand and stopped the table midflight. Then it waved its hand, redirecting the table against a column, shattering it. I closed my eyes, imagined all the tables smashing together to form one giant monster. I opened my eyes and found the table construct standing before me. I imagined our bodies were linked, our movements synchronized. And they were. I swung my fist at the Sandman, and the table monster did the same. But the Sandman held up a hand, pausing the giant's attack, and closed its fist. My construct exploded into a million shards of wood.

What to do, what to do, what to do? I've got to get out of here.

The kitchens behind the restaurants. Maybe I could run back there and hide. With the superspeed of dreams, I ran to the counter, slid over the top, and bolted into the kitchens, rushing past industrial stoves and prep tables in a mad dash to find a hiding place. My eyes caught a counter with a cabinet underneath. The cabinet looked big enough for me to hide inside. I flung the cabinet open and found a wooden tunnel shaped like the hollow inside of a tree.

Once again, the sound of hissing sand was coming closer, growing louder. I didn't have time to ponder how the dream was warping and changing; the Sandman was coming, so I crawled into the tunnel and wormed my way through the knobby crevice . . . until I heard Hunter's voice. "Johnny! Johnny, wake up!"

"Hunter!" I screamed. "Hunter!" I kept squirming through the tunnel until at last I emerged through the hollow of an old oak tree. Grabbing at the mossy cover, I pulled myself out of the tree and got to my feet in the middle of Darkwood Forest.

I brushed dirt and grit off my clothes before remembering I was in a dream. I spun around. The Sandman moved through brush, shrubs, and branches like none of it existed, skulking through reality. The black halo swirling around its body swallowed dream stuff, spit out nothingness. The Sandman's very nature cast aside the physics of the dreamworld. It was a master of dreams, a master of magic. I whirled about looking for an escape route.

Then, Melchior's voice rang out in my head. "Wake up, Johnny." He was standing still as a specter amid some bushes. He didn't part his lips, but his voice emanated again: "Wake up."

But I couldn't. I clenched my eyes shut, opened them, but no matter how hard I tried, I couldn't pull myself out of the dream.

"I can't wake up!"

I charged through the forest, bowing my head against the twisting branches, until I found myself standing in the middle of the Stevenson Expressway, on the broken line between two lanes. Two cars sped by, blasting me with a tarry gust.

"Are you kidding me?" I muttered to myself.

Balling my fists and standing still as a mouse hiding from a circling hawk, I hoped the booming semis wouldn't splatter me into Johnny paste. A truck's blaring horn rattled my eardrums as a barreling semi rumbled right at me. Eyes closed, I imagined myself in Veles Hall. The ground under me trembled. *Veles, Veles, Veles.* The scattered pebbles under my feet hopped up and down as the rumbling increased. The truck's roar jostled my brain. *Veles, Veles, Veles.* The ground started shaking like a giant was jostling it.

A swooshing sound like wind battering a car window filled my ears. When I opened my eyes, I was standing in front of my room in Veles Hall. Seeping sand hissed behind me. I spun around. The Sandman was still shambling after me, its outstretched hands reaching for my throat. I closed my eyes again, imagined the monster being engulfed in a pillar of flame. A blast of fire erupted around the monster and swallowed it, scorching the floor and ceiling black. But the blaze wasn't enough. The Sandman moved right through it.

Balthasar appeared next to me. "Step aside," he said.

Retreating behind him, I watched as Balthasar, with no more than a look, summoned several stone columns that burst through the floor, ceiling, and walls and crushed the Sandman. Still, the Sandman moved through the obstacles like they weren't there. Balthasar's bushy eyebrows quirked up, his skin going pale. Nothing could stop the Sandman's terrifying advance.

Melchior zipped into the dreamworld next to Balthasar. "How did this thing get through the barrier?"

"It may not be a Mara," Balthasar said.

"Then what the hell is it?"

They both reached forward, reshaping the dream with their hands. The hallway crinkled up like a wad of paper around the monster, trapping it and leaving us floating in nothingness. The wad of paper became a ball of sand, then started growing—first into a boulder, then larger and larger, until it was big as the moon. Bursts of sand looped around the ball like solar flares on the surface of the sun. The Sandman's immense aura filled the space. It felt like ancient secrets buried deep in old caves, memories long forgotten by ordinary people but etched into the psyches of wizards. It swallowed all sound and plunged us into an unfeeling vacuum. There, in the cold, soundless nothing, I heard a voice like a serpent hiss, "Cintamani."

Melchior looked at me and, with his mind, said, *Wake up, Johnny!*

Wake up, wake up, wake up.

Chapter 25

I startled awake with Hunter's head floating in my line of sight. His face lit up when he saw my eyes spring open. "Johnny!" he said, scooping me into his arms. "I'm so sorry I left you in there! I didn't know how to get back to you."

I smiled. "At least I'm out now."

I wanted to take a moment to recover, regain my bearings before breaking it to the others that I'd seen Melchior and Balthasar, but before I could, there was a crash at the door—a couple of Smiths had kicked it down. They stormed Alison's room. I heard Linh's voice in my head. *Lock up your thoughts!*

The Smiths peered around the room. "You'll all need to come with us."

Hunter helped me to my feet. The five of us exchanged wary glances. If they searched our thoughts, we were screwed, but we weren't looking for a tussle just yet. Better to go with them now, see what they wanted. One of the Smiths went out into the hallway while the other waited in the room for us to file out. Blake strode out first, then Linh, then the rest of us. We followed the Smiths outside into the quad.

In the sky, dark clouds hid the moon behind their thick folds. Our only sources of light were the lampposts whose sickly orange beams cast rings on the cement walkways. At night, the Institute was weirdly quiet—no chirping crickets, no hooting owls, nothing. The place was a tomb, its towering structures now like barrows hiding the sleeping dead. Just beyond the walls, the billowing fog formed a membrane over Darkwood Forest.

The Heka Building's outline grew in the distance, transposed against the shadows as it reached up for the moon. The black pyramid stood like a nightmarish monolith, a gloomy prison warden making sure no one would ever escape. My run-in with the Sandman had left me shaken, so at that moment, the Heka Building was a welcome sight. After all, it was Melchior and Balthasar who'd saved me.

Hunter held my hand tight, staying as close as our bodies would allow. We'd all sealed our thoughts, but Linh was obviously nervous. If the Institute learned that we knew about a Defector on campus, they would disappear us under the Heka Building forever.

The Smiths guided us through the dead office. Its emptiness— rolling chairs tucked under quiet desks, water coolers burbling lone bubbles—was a grim reminder of how lonely and eerie the Institute really was. Of course, below us, deep underground, the labyrinthine network of labs bustled with bizarre, frightening things. Experiments, monsters—who knew what else?

We reached the elevator, and one of the Smiths grabbed my arm and started pulling me into the elevator with him.

"Where're you taking him?" Alison demanded.

"None of your business. Keep quiet."

She looked back at me, her eyes brimming with fear.

"Let him go," said Hunter. I tried to pull away from the Smith holding me.

Alison grabbed my hand. "Johnny!"

"Let him go!" Hunter shouted again, grabbing my arm and bracing his feet against the floor. "Get off him!" The Smith holding on to me pulled against Alison and Hunter. Linh and Blake's eyes went wide. He jerked me back, and Hunter charged and shoved him. "Get the hell off him!"

Linh froze, caught between wanting to help and being unsure of what to do. Blake balled his hand into a fist, his body tensing like he was about to start throwing punches.

"Let him go!" Alison said, yanking on me even harder.

The Smith behind all of us drew out a canister, shook it, and sprayed Alison in the face. Her fingers slipped through mine, and she fell to her knees, coughing and wheezing. Blake turned to the Smith with the canister and punched him in the mouth. He almost got another shot in, but the Smith sprayed him too. Blake grabbed his throat and spun around coughing then fell unconscious next to Alison.

I bit the Smith holding on to me, so he twirled me around and slung me into the elevator, slamming me so hard against the back wall the whole thing shook. Hunter charged and tackled the Smith, who pressed down on Hunter's shoulders, trying to pry him off. Then Hunter kneed him in the groin and sent him toppling over. When Hunter turned around, he came face to face with the other Smith's knockout spray. As I wobbled out of the elevator I saw the Smith spraying Hunter.

"Hunter!" I cried, leaping onto the Smith's back.

The Smith shook me side to side, hoping I'd fall off, but I clamped down, so he sprayed the canister over his shoulder, at first missing me, but eventually covering my face with the stinking fluid. I fell off, shook my head, sneezed, then started coughing. Linh stood perfectly still the whole time. Hunter hit the floor, and I followed shortly after him.

●

Cold steel under my head—a feeling I'd become strangely familiar with. Like a loose puzzle piece, my mind joggled back into place. Sitting up, I scanned my surroundings: I was in a white cell with a single cot attached to a wall with two plastic ropes and a metal toilet in the corner. After checking that my legs didn't feel like wobbly blobs of Jell-O, I stood up. I walked up to the door, which had a barred hatch, and tugged on the handle. Locked.

I examined every inch of the cell, looking for any kind of crack or small opening. Nothing. It was surprising I could still breathe in such a tightly sealed space. I took a seat on the cot and waited— for what, I didn't know. I waited and waited and waited, until the silence became an unbearable drone.

"Hello?" I said, just to pierce the quiet. Still, nothing. Panic set in. What were they doing to Alison? To Hunter? To Linh and Blake? What were they going to do to me?

Finally, the door shifted. I stood up as Balthasar walked in. There was no way I could protect my mind from a wizard as powerful as him.

"Please, stay calm," he said. "There's no need to worry. Your friends are perfectly fine. We just needed everyone to calm down a bit."

"What're you going to do with me?" I said.

"Nothing, Johnny. We just wanted to make sure you were all right," he continued. "You saw something quite disturbing in Everywhen. When it came after you, for some reason, you had a hard time waking up. Do you have any idea why?"

"No. Do you?"

"We're still trying to figure out what happened, Johnny," Balthasar said. "We don't know what it was. At first, we thought it must be a Mara, but the Institute's magic barrier actively protects us from Mara attacks. Had you seen that creature before?"

"Yes, once. Before I was extracted," I explained. "The night after Alison and I did that spell."

"What can you tell me about the spell you two performed? Where did you learn it?"

"It was a ritual from a book Alison got from some strange lady."

"Did you see the lady yourself?"

"No," I admitted.

"And what happened to the book?"

"It was at Alison's house. Maybe in her basement."

"What happened when you performed the ritual?"

"There was an earthquake."

"And later that night, you dreamt of this creature for the first time?"

"Yes."

He watched me like he was cycling through everything he could say. Was he trying to read my mind? I kept up my mental wall just in case, but I didn't get that weird feeling I was being watched.

"Very well," Balthasar said finally. "You'll be taken back to your dormitory, and your friends will join you shortly, after we've spoken to each of them." Why hadn't he tried reading my mind? Surely, that would've been easier than questioning me. Maybe he wasn't as strong as I thought—or maybe his rift with Melchior was more serious than I'd imagined.

Balthasar left. A minute later, a Smith walked in. "Let's go, kid."

I followed him through the white tunnels under the Heka Building, up the elevator to the office area, and back through the darkened quad to Veles Hall. I kept my thoughts clear, not wanting anyone from the Institute to hop into my head. The Smith left me in the entryway. The nighttime silence filled me with dread. Was this real? Or was I still in a dream?

The shadows on the walls danced, like they were gathering to whisper secrets to one another. Somewhere in that darkness, the Sandman lurked, watching me, waiting for me to drop my guard. I tensed up and swallowed. I didn't want to be here alone.

"Hey." Even though I'd heard Linh's voice, I still pivoted around like the Sandman was standing right behind me. Linh flashed a quick smile, probably amused she'd finally snuck up on me. "Where is everyone?" she asked.

My heart was pounding so hard it took me a second to speak. "I . . . I don't know."

If we were lucky, everyone else had managed to secure their thoughts and their mouths. But there was no guarantee of that, so Linh and I stared nervously at each other, wondering how long we had before our whole plan went up in smoke and we ended up under the Heka Building.

Chapter 26

1 MONTH AND 2 WEEKS AFTER EXTRACTION

We waited for what felt like an ice age. Time ticked by so slowly you could hear the minutes twiddling their thumbs. We waited in the entryway, me standing at the door, staring into the abyss outside, and Linh sitting on the RA's desk, looking down at her own swinging legs. "So," she said, "what'd they ask you about?"

"That sand monster."

"And?"

"I've seen it before."

"You have? When?"

I told Linh all about the weird spell Alison and I had performed—the mysterious book, the woman, the earthquake, and the monster that attacked me in my dreams before I was extracted. Her face was impassive, like she was hiding her true feelings from me. Maybe she didn't trust me. Maybe she didn't trust anyone. I didn't blame her. She was so close to getting out, and now all her plans were in jeopardy. She didn't say anything after I finished. "What about you?" I asked.

"Balthasar asked me the same questions, but I didn't know anything about that monster."

We waited another nerve-wracking thirty minutes, and then I saw a Smith guiding Hunter to the glass doors. His green eyes went wide when he saw me. He hugged me, burying his face between my neck and shoulder. I squeezed him and smelled the ghost of his cologne on his soft cotton shirt.

"Where're Blake and Alison?" Linh asked after the Smith had gone.

"I didn't see them," Hunter said. He didn't let go of me, and I didn't let go of him.

"What did they ask you?" I said.

"Balthasar wanted to know about the monster, but I didn't know anything. Then he said they were going to leave me in the cell to cool down."

"I was so scared that . . . I wouldn't see you again."

"I'm not going anywhere, Johnny. I promise," he said, rubbing my back. We sat together on a bench in the sitting area by the door and waited.

Another painful thirty minutes passed before Blake came in with another Smith. Hunter and I hopped off the bench and joined Linh in greeting him. After the Smith left, we gathered in the sitting area. It'd been a whole hour since I'd last seen Alison, and little men in my brain were playing tennis with my nerves. "What'd they say to you?" I said to Blake.

"Balthasar asked about that monster. I said I didn't know anything about it. Why was it after you, Johnny? Why couldn't you wake up?"

"I don't know."

"Elephant in the room," Linh said. "Did anyone get their mind read?"

"Not me," Hunter said.

Blake shook his head. "Not me either."

"And we all talked to Balthasar," I said. "Does anyone think that's weird?"

"Why wouldn't Balthasar just read our minds?" Linh said. "They've read our minds over less." It didn't make any sense. A strange monster had broken through the school's defenses—the head scientists should've been raring to read our minds to find out our connection to it. But Balthasar had taken our word for it that we knew nothing. Linh eyed all of us. "Do you think Balthasar is with the Defectors?"

"It would explain why he didn't read our minds. Maybe he already knows what we're up to," I said. "Maybe he's the reason Defectors are getting in here so easy. I heard the Smiths say he and Melchior don't trust each other anymore."

"But why?" Blake said. "No doubt this place is messed up, but don't they believe in their mission?"

"What is their mission, anyway?" I asked him.

"To keep us safe. And to keep normal people safe from us."

"If that were the case, then why do Legacies get to sling magic everywhere? The Institute certainly doesn't seem too interested in protecting people from the Legacies," Linh said. Her words gave us pause. "They train the Legacies, but not us. Why is that?"

"And there's that rumor about them experimenting on wizards under the Heka Building," Hunter said.

"Not Lineage wizards, though," Linh said. "Funny how that works."

"What do you think this place is for?" Blake asked Linh.

"It's obviously a prison for non-Legacy wizards," she said. "But maybe two out of the three head scientists don't agree with that mission. So what's really going on? Who're the Administrators, and what do they seek to gain from operating this facility? And what do the Defectors seek to gain by bringing it down?"

There was an awful lot to chew on, but my mind was still on Alison.

Another hour passed. Then another. It was almost one in the morning and Alison still hadn't come back. Hunter was asleep on my shoulder, every now and then teetering forward. I kept a hand on his arm to make sure he wouldn't wake up to a face full of floor. Linh had fallen asleep curled up on the sofa across from us, and was softly snoring. Blake was pacing around the doorway, arms crossed, staring into the quad like a knight keeping watch.

Balthasar had promised that Alison would come back with everyone else. Maybe he'd lied to placate me, keep me from hurling spells I didn't even know. I couldn't figure out why they'd keep her for so long. Dread crept into my mind—what if they never let her go? I couldn't imagine my life without Alison.

Finally, at close to two o'clock in the morning, Alison walked in, pale, with another Smith. I grabbed her and hugged her. She felt limp in my arms, her eyes lost in thought. Over her shoulder, I watched the Smith until he left.

"Ali," I said, "what the hell happened? Why'd they keep you so long?"

The other three gathered around us, maintaining some distance, as though they were worried they'd frighten Alison by coming too close.

"They took me into some room," she said, her eyes still distant. "It had an examination chair and kind of smelled like a hospital.

That Melchior guy said he was going to go into my mind, read my memories. I didn't want to at first, but he said it was the only way to help you." So Ali had been questioned by Melchior. No doubt he'd raided her thoughts.

"Help me?" I asked.

"That's what he said. He thinks that spell we cast has something to do with that monster. I sat in the chair, they gave me a shot of this green stuff, then I fell asleep. He went into my head looking for the day we cast that spell, but he said he couldn't find it, J. He couldn't find the lady or the book. None of it." She focused her frightened eyes on me. "It's like none of it ever happened. Like the whole memory was fake."

"But I was there. We both were. Melchior must be messing with you."

"But why, J? Why would he lie about this? That spell is supposed to be the whole reason we were brought here," Alison said softly.

"He must know more about what's going on and not want to tell us."

"Do you think he found out about our plan?" Linh asked.

"It doesn't matter," I said. "What else would we do, Linh, stay here?"

"He's setting us up," Blake said.

Linh grabbed her elbow. "He's trying to get us to lead him to the Defectors."

"So what do we do now?" Hunter asked.

"We go," I said.

"What do you mean?" Linh asked me. "We can't lead him to the Defectors."

"If he'd found out about that, he would've dragged us back to the Heka Building and searched our thoughts too," I said.

Linh scoffed. "Do you really think Melchior *wouldn't* try to read Alison's thoughts?"

"Johnny's right, Linh," Blake said. "We don't have any other options. Even if we stay here, he'll just get in your head eventually and learn everything you know anyway. Plus, who's to say Melchior couldn't just take control of our minds with his magic and *make* us lead him to the Defectors?"

It was an impossible situation. We knew we were being set up, but there was no turning back. "I don't think standing around here talking is going to help anything," Blake said. "Let's try to get some sleep. We'll figure it out tomorrow."

We all headed for the stairs. Hunter grabbed my hand as we started up the steps. "I'm coming in with you."

"We're not allowed."

He smiled. "What're they going to do? Expel me?"

"I wish we could get expelled."

At Alison's door, she touched my face, like she was afraid to let me go, and glanced over at Hunter. "Will you guys be okay?"

I wasn't sure. But I didn't want everyone to know how scared I was about what had happened. I glanced at the shadows gathering in the corners of the hallway, then swallowed and looked back at her. "I'll be fine." She hugged me, then went into her room.

My heart racing, I walked into my room along with Hunter. I didn't know if I could sleep tonight; I was afraid that the minute I closed my eyes, the Sandman would be right there, slipping its hands around my throat.

Hunter put a hand on my chest and tilted my chin up so he could look into my eyes. "I won't let anything happen to you, Johnny." He backed me onto my bed and kissed me on the lips—a kiss that promised he wouldn't leave my side until I was safe, a kiss that told me he'd die trying to protect me. I looked in his courageous eyes and saw that certainty.

Chapter 27

1 MONTH AND 2 WEEKS AFTER EXTRACTION

My old room. Cheap gray carpet. Band posters splattered on the wall next to my bed. Hunter sat on the floor wearing a backward baseball cap and jeans. I'd never seen him in normal clothes before. It was nice. With his tongue folded up over his lip, he wobbled the PS4 controller in his hands. I lay on my bed, hanging upside down over the edge and watching him play. I smiled at him, so he spun his cap around and kissed me on the forehead. Then we got caught up in smiling at each other. Behind me, Alison and Blake sat watching old episodes of *Teen Wolf* on her laptop, sharing a bowl of popcorn.

"This show is so good," Alison said. "There'll never be another like it."

Blake stuffed a handful of popcorn in his mouth, eyes glued to the screen. "Whatever you say."

"What? You don't think so? This show is totally a metaphor for wizards."

Blake scoffed. "No, it's not."

"Look at Stiles. He's totally a wizard. He even uses his wizard powers to see how everything's connected."

"That boy's only special power is being white."

Hunter died in his game. "Crap." He set the controller aside and sighed through his nose. Then he looked over his shoulder at us. "You guys want to go do something?"

Blake put another handful of popcorn in his mouth. "Like what?"

"Go to a movie?"

Alison folded up her knees and wrapped her arms around them. "What about that movie where the guy cuts the girl's face up with a pizza cutter?"

Blake's eyes lit up. "*Final Slice.* I've been wanting to see that."

We hopped into Blake's Jeep and headed to the mall. Holding a hand out the window, I felt the wind kiss my fingertips, and as music floated out of the car stereo and into my ears, I threw my head back and let the rushing breeze lap at my face. Hunter wrapped his arms around me, hugged me, kissed me.

This was the life I'd always wanted, the closest thing to freedom I'd ever known. We were blazing up and down lives that would burn out in a handful of decades, and these were the memories we'd cherish when the embers settled in our raging souls.

Hunter kissed me all the way to the theater. When we got there, we loaded up at the concession stand before riding an escalator downstairs to where our screen was. I walked into the theater, took a few steps forward, then stopped. There was no one in the theater. It was totally empty. Everyone—Blake, Hunter, and Ali—had disappeared.

"Hello?" I said.

My voice echoed off the soundproof walls. Inching down the ramp, I kept looking around, refusing to believe I was the only person in the theater. But every row was empty; all the sticky seats and armrests were folded up.

A spotlight boomed on. Where a movie screen should've been stood a stage with red curtains. The curtains pulled apart, and the smiling man in white stood in the spotlight with two magician's boxes for disappearing people behind him.

"Who are you?" I yelled at him. "Are you Gaspar? Are you the third head scientist?"

"You already know who I am."

"Did you join the Defectors?"

He didn't answer. Instead, he walked up to the first box and threw it open. A woman with dreads and a red leather jacket stepped outside of the box, her dark-brown skin glistening under the spotlight. Gaspar rubbed his hands together, and a card appeared between them. He held the card high: the queen of hearts. He slipped the card into the woman's breast pocket. "The Red Queen knows where we are," he said.

He flung open the second box. A three-story house stood just beyond the door, as if it were a portal connecting two separate worlds. It was an old gothic, like many houses in Chicago, with fish-scale shingles on its mansard roof and a rounded turret. Two-story brownstones surrounded the house on both sides. Boat horns blared faintly in the distance. Then, Gaspar pointed at the house's front door. "Come find us here," he said. The door creaked open, and a pale woman with raven hair and a black dress stepped out, her eyes shut tight. I squinted, struggling to see her. She opened her eyes, and I gasped. She had big yellow cat's eyes, just like the woman

Alison had described, the one who gave her that spell book. The smiling man joined the woman in front of the house and grabbed her hand. "Only we can help you stop the Sandman."

Hissing. Hissing sand. Panic froze me. The noise grew. Slowly, I turned my head and looked behind me. Nothing. There was nothing there. But I could hear it. The Sandman. The hissing slithered through the air like someone had dropped a sack of snakes into the room.

With a quick turn, I bolted out of the theater, flinging open the doors and stepping into an airplane aisle—I'd just come out of the lavatory. Every passenger turned and faced me, their unmoving, wide-eyed stares unnerving me. Hoping to free myself from the nightmare, I shut my eyes—*Wake up, Johnny. This is a dream. Wake up*—but when I opened them, I was still on the plane. The mysterious trance was impossible to break. At the other end of the aisle, the Sandman stood, watching me. Not a single passenger noticed. It lurched forward with one jerky step, the sandy cloud around its feet spreading over the cabin floor. The lavatory's door handle was stuck, so I couldn't flee back to the theater. With nowhere to run, I inched back into the corner, closed my eyes, and kept trying to wake up.

Without warning, the plane shuddered, and the aisle tilted into a slope. I fell, raking my fingers across the floor until I grabbed onto the bottom of a chair. My stomach flew up into my throat as the plane lost altitude. With my fingers looped around the chair bottom, I pulled myself up. Below me, the Sandman climbed up the aisle toward me even as the plane went vertical. I was going to fall right into its murderous hands.

Kicking my legs, I pulled my torso up over the backrest and looked down. The shifting gravity had no effect on the Sandman.

It continued crawling upward toward me, so I flung up my left leg, straining to climb onto the backrest, but before I could, the Sandman grabbed my right ankle and tugged.

"Johnny!" Hunter's voice echoed through my mind. I sat up screaming, back at the Institute, back in my bed. Hunter threw his arms around me.

"J! J, calm down. I got you. Nothing's going to hurt you. I got you." I clutched at Hunter's arms and buried my face in the crook of his elbow. He held me until my breathing slowed down, until my heart stopped racing. When I was calm, I eased away from him. He looked me in the eyes and kissed me.

It had all been a dream. Or had it? The line between dreams and reality didn't exist for a wizard. Whatever I experienced in a dream, I may as well have experienced in real life. Whether that had been the real Sandman or one that I'd made up, it had been real to me.

•

Snow covered everything, turning Darkwood Forest's black treetops into white spires. It gathered along curbs and roadsides and melted into a big black slush. The usually watchful Smiths were too busy blowing on their hands to pay us any mind when we passed through the north gate's turnstiles. Our plan? We were going to walk right out of the Institute, meet Aquila in Misthaven, and somehow— somehow—she was going to ferry us out of there in broad daylight. No problem.

None of us knew if the half-baked plan would work, but the real problem was the Institute probably knew what we were up to. Maybe those Smiths at the gate had ignored us because Melchior was hoping we'd lead the Institute right to the Defectors. All I knew was I had to find the woman with the Red Queen card. She knew where I could find Gaspar. And only he could help me stop the Sandman.

We gathered around the bus stop and waited fifteen minutes before the bus pulled up with a hiss, a cloud of steam billowing from under it. After clomping our way to the back, we clustered together, Blake next to Alison, me with Hunter, and Linh alone. The rumbling bus stirred, lurched forward, and started for Misthaven.

"The other day," Alison said to Blake, "when they found me in that . . . dream trance, what were you doing there? Shouldn't you have been at Ares Hall?"

"I was coming to see you. You know, to ask about that date that you owe me," Blake said.

"Why do you like me so much?"

"Am I not supposed to?"

"I didn't say that. I just want to know why."

"Because you're a cool girl."

"You don't have to tell me twice."

"Do you . . . like me?"

"We're friends, aren't we?"

"That's not what I mean."

She didn't answer him immediately, but she kept her eyes on him, like she could learn everything about him just by looking. Her pause must've felt like a year to him. Then she said, "I'm still trying to figure out if you're a spy."

We reached Misthaven and dropped our phones into a trash can next to the bus shelter. Linh led us to a wooden sign marked *Natches Walking Trail* and an arrow pointing east. Hunter's teeth chattered as he hopped along, his arms wrapped around himself, his letterman's jacket providing little protection from the frosty wind.

The rest of us were in our Institute-issued blazers, which provided even less reprieve from the biting cold.

The warm, glowing lampposts along main street had been decorated with colorful Christmas lights. Garland dangled over the avenue, suspended roof to roof between buildings. The lonely founder's statue in Explorer Park now had company in the form of a towering pine tree decked out in ornaments. We passed Bayard House, the fancy breakfast place. Inside its glass lanai, a few adults sat enjoying steaming plates of eggs and bacon. The town almost seemed normal, but those watchful eyes didn't stop following us just because they had hot cups of cocoa pressed to their whispering lips.

We hurried over a slushy crosswalk to a park entrance. Once we were on the paved walking trail, Alison kept an eye out over her shoulder.

"If they're watching us," Linh said, "you're making it really obvious that we're up to something."

Alison straightened up—probably a little too straight—and sped up her pace. The walking trail snaked along Lake Misty's perimeter over an embankment. Weeping tree limbs cried drops of snow onto the trail, covering the black pavement in white. Lake Misty was one big milk bath, its shimmering surface reflecting the snowy trees all around it. Linh led us off the path onto the snow. We followed her to a cluster of old, crumbling picnic tables. Aquila was sitting at one of the tables, adjusting a skinny scarf. When she saw Linh, she stood up and prepared to leave.

Linh rushed over to her. "These guys are coming with us, Aquila."

"Luther said you were bringing one other person, not four."

"The Defectors are supposed to help people. Well, they're trapped in there with me, and they want out too."

"You think I'm stupid, Linh?" Aquila waved a hand at Blake. "That one's a Thorn."

"He only joined the Thorns to protect us," Linh said.

This was our only chance. If Aquila turned and left us all behind, we'd never get out of the Institute, and my chances of finding Gaspar would narrow even further. I felt peering eyes brush the back of my neck; Aquila was trying to read our minds. I had nothing to hide from her, though, so I didn't put up a wall. Escaping the Institute was the most important thing.

"Okay. But we do this quickly. We don't have much time," Aquila said.

She led us off the picnic grounds to a parking lot close to the walking trail and popped open the hatchback of her blue crossover SUV. "There's too many of you, so I'm going to need a couple of you to get in here."

I looked at Hunter—he nodded and slipped in, then I slid in after him. Aquila shut the door, and everyone else piled into the car. Hunter put his arm around my shoulder and smiled, trying to act cool even though his palms were sweaty and his heart was pounding like a pile driver. I squeezed his hand and leaned against his shoulder.

Aquila backed out of the parking space and headed off onto some woody back road. Alison and Blake sat side by side, watching the frosty road. We slowed to a halt at a four-way intersection with a black Camry and a blue Chevy truck. Hunter and I peered at them through the windows in the back.

"Do these hicks even know what to do at a four-way stop?" Aquila muttered, waiting for the truck to make a turn. But it didn't move. Its driver, his face a shadow beneath a red trucker hat, just sat there. Maybe he wasn't really a truck driver at all. Maybe it was a disguise. Maybe he was really a Smith, sitting there sending psychic signals to his buddies, telling them we were getting away. A few jumbled escape scenarios played out in my head, but none of them made sense. They were all just images of kicking and screaming and biting and being sprayed in the face with knockout gas before being thrown into the back of a van.

Then the Camry vroomed across the road, its exhaust pipe blowing a cloud of smoke into the cold air. The truck sat there. Everyone went stiff as a new pair of shoes. Finally, the truck lurched forward and took a right. I let out the breath that had tightly coiled itself around my lungs. We all did.

Aquila snaked through one winding path after another, the white corridors in the forest like the ones under the Heka Building, reminding us what we were running away from, but also reminding us how easily our flight could land us in those same white hallways on our way to uncertain fates. Hunter grabbed my hand.

Aquila's careful eyes hovered in the rearview mirror. She didn't say a thing to any of us, hunched over the wheel like a wary cat surveying the road. I could tell she was stressed. Linh, who was sitting next to her, seemed on edge too.

We rattled across a covered bridge—shaking snow off its shingles—and onto a frontage road alongside the interstate. Behind us, a black van emerged seemingly out of nowhere, dreadful as a game of Russian roulette with five bullets in the pistol. In the rearview mirror, Aquila's hawklike eyes watched every little move the vehicle made. Its tinted windows were too dark to see inside. Same as the ones on the van used to kidnap me. There was no doubt in my mind: that was an Institute van.

Aquila sped onto a ramp joining the highway. The black van didn't follow. I watched the roads disappear behind us as we merged, the gnarled trees, suspicious townsfolk, and ominous towers slowly fading from view. But that dark, immovable pyramid was branded into my mind. Those white sterile hallways. Melchior's cold, detached eyes. Canisters of stinking knockout spray tucked inside every jacket. How would I ever forget this? It made me sick just thinking about it.

The little Puerto Rican flag hanging from Aquila's rearview mirror dangled wildly as she barreled down the highway, weaving in and out of traffic like the chilly wind itself. Sheets of snow belted the car, threatening to veil the windows in white. The windshield wipers hurried back and forth, working overtime to keep the window clear. Hunter and I passed the time with hand-slapping games and rock-paper-scissors. "The Little Drummer Boy" came on the radio, but the volume was turned so low you could barely hear the *pa rum pum pum pum*. Linh slumped in the passenger's seat, her knee pressed against the glove compartment.

I couldn't be sure how many hours we were on the road. Halfway through our journey, we took a break at a rest stop, and I pieced together from all the Chicago kitsch in the gas station that we were finally in Illinois. Hunter must've been right about the Institute being somewhere in the Ozarks. Once we were back in the car, we rode for another few hours before green road signs reading *Lakeshore Drive* popped up. We were headed north along Lake Michigan, which meant a little farther on, we'd cross through Lincoln Park, where Alison and I used to live. She looked back at me, her face tight with nerves. I knew she wanted to ask Aquila if we could go to her mom's.

"Are we going through Lincoln Park?" I called up to Aquila.

"Yes," she said over her shoulder.

Alison leaned forward. "Can we make a stop?"

"Do you need to go to the bathroom?"

"No. I want to go see my mother."

"This isn't a joyride."

"It won't take long. Please."

"Didn't they tell you that your family won't remember you? Even if they see you, it just won't click in their heads."

"She's sick. She has cancer. I don't care if she doesn't remember me. I just want to see her."

Aquila looked at Alison in the rearview mirror. "Fine," she said, against her better judgment. Familiar buildings cropped up around us, and a painful shard of nostalgia weaseled deep into my chest. There were people gathered at the bus stop I used to take every morning, steam rising off their coffees. I watched them like a ghost, watched their chattering lips, their laughing faces. Without documentation, without any evidence of our existence, we weren't even memories here.

The old potholes that had once littered these streets had been repaired. I couldn't help but feel like them: paved over. I tapped Alison on the shoulder and passed her my hand, and she grabbed it tight, so tight it went numb.

"Can't you reverse the spell? The one that erases people's memories and stuff?" I asked Aquila.

"That's not how the vivit apparatus works," she said. "Once a spell is cast, new machinery is made; the world changes forever. All you can do is cast a new spell over the old one."

"So can't we cast a new spell to restore everyone's memories?"

"Don't you think we would find a way to reverse it if we knew how?" she said. "I'm going to need directions to your house."

Alison directed Aquila to her mom and grandma's house, and Aquila parked out front on the curb. I followed Alison out into the falling snow and up the cracked walkway to her front door. All the ivy shrouding her house in the summer months had died, becoming a brown wreath. She pressed a hand to her chest and started moving more and more slowly, so I grabbed her other hand.

"I can't do this, J," she muttered a few steps from the door.

"Do you want to go back to the car?"

A cold wind swept past, brushing our cheeks with flecks of ice. I could tell that in Alison's mind, she was standing on a precipice, considering whether or not to jump. "No," she said. "Let's go." She rang the doorbell, and we waited. Her grandma answered, looking at us like she was expecting us to sell her some candy. Alison's face lit up at the sight of her, but then she pushed back the joy and cleared her throat. "I'm looking for Cecilia?"

Her grandma's eyes widened. "Cecilia?" She pulled back, eyes softening, glistening with tears. "Cecilia . . . Cecilia passed away some time ago, young lady."

Alison's lips trembled. No magic on Earth could take her pain away. She'd been holding on at the edge of a cliff for so long, but she couldn't anymore. No matter how badly she wanted to. Her grasp was slipping. She was starting to fall, and I just wanted to say, *It's okay, Ali. I love you. I'm sorry.*

"Do you"—she cleared her throat again—"do you remember me, Gran?" Her voice was so trembly, so weak, the words came out a whisper.

"I'm sorry, young lady?"

Alison turned and ran, and I quickly gave chase. "Alison!" I shouted. She ran past Aquila's SUV, heading down the sidewalk to god knew where. Aquila stepped out of the car, mortified. "I'll get her," I said as I jogged after Ali.

We'd run down these sidewalks so many times before. They were as familiar as the hallways in Cecilia's house. She used to tell us to stop running and settle down, and if we didn't listen, she'd sit us down and read Plato's *Republic*, demand we become good civic members of society. Cecilia always had something wise to say. Back when Alison had first started HRT, her breasts hurt so bad it left her crying, so Cecilia wiped the tears from Alison's big brown eyes and told her, "It only gets worse from here," and they both laughed.

I found Alison on her knees in the dirty snow, crying in an alley between two bungalows not far from her house. Falling to my knees, I hugged her. She cried and cried and cried, and I cried with her. I loved Alison more than life itself, and I felt her pain stabbing into me, felt it work its way through my ribs into my heart. Maybe it was those wizard powers we'd never asked for. The Institute had stolen everything from us. Everything.

Alison's aura was spooky campfire stories, and telling her best friend he'd be the first guy in history to have a best woman instead of a best man at his wedding. It was her grandma's repulsive German food and her mother staying up late to read Alison one more Pablo Neruda poem. And now, it was something else, too: sadness, a deeper sadness than either of us had ever known. A sadness that sank down to the center of the Earth. And it didn't stop there.

"What's the point of any of it?" she cried out. "I never got to say good-bye"—she sucked in a desperate gasp of air, and her voice fell to a whisper—"I never got say good-bye. Why are we even alive? Why didn't Todd and them just kill us that day? I should never have done that spell. This is all my fault. I should be dead, J—I should be dead."

The Institute's crimes against us were many, and they were coming into sharp relief.

Aquila found us a few minutes later. "Hey, you two, I know

there's a lot going on right now, but we need to go. It isn't safe to be outside like this."

Alison pulled herself together as best she could. Clutching hands, we hurried back to Aquila's car. Before we got in, Alison stopped, warm tears still pouring out of her. "I have to go to Graceland."

Aquila paused with her hand on the door handle. "We can't. We don't have any more time."

"But I know where my mother's plot is," Alison said, her words broken up by sobs. "Please. I've just got to see it. I want to say good-bye."

Aquila's face blanched. "I'm sorry. I really am, but I can't take you there." Opening the car door, Aquila slipped inside, and Alison cried even harder. I grabbed her and hugged her, stroked her hair, calmed her down, then we both got back into the car.

Sitting beside her in the back seat, I put my arm around her. Alison wouldn't let herself turn into an emotional mess in front of strangers, so she just rested her head on my shoulder and stared vacantly out the front window. The others—Hunter, Blake, and Linh—stayed quiet. No trite apologies. No empty words of comfort. I knew Alison appreciated that. She'd always said it made her uncomfortable when people said they were sorry her mom was sick.

I thought about seeing Dad, but I knew Aquila would just say we didn't have time, so I closed my eyes and told myself: *He wouldn't remember you, anyway, so what's the point?* It brought me little comfort, but regardless, it would've been impossible to change Aquila's mind; the Institute could show up any minute.

We weren't in the car for much longer. The snow had picked up, blanketing the roads and sidewalks in big downy sheets. Aquila pulled into a parking lot behind a warehouse on North Halsted Street. Just behind the lot, a few boats sat in the harbor, and the sounds of blaring horns and cawing seagulls filled the air. The whole scene seemed familiar, but I couldn't place why. Everyone got out into the biting cold. "Follow me," Aquila said, crunching across the parking lot and up a ramp to a metal shutter. She crouched down to unlock the shutter, then pulled it open.

Inside, polished cement floors gleamed in the sunlight pouring in through high windows. Once we were all in, Aquila closed the shutter and locked it. The ceiling was about thirty feet high, with big cement columns holding up steel beams that supported the whole structure. A huge, open space, it felt just as cold inside as outside, and it smelled like wet paint. At the other end of the warehouse sat a control room on stilts with an L-shaped staircase leading up to its door.

Aquila hurried up the stairs and into the control room, and we followed. Under a dusty control panel, she found a bucket of paint and a brush.

Blake walked up to the control room window and stared out into the empty warehouse. "What is this place?"

"Just one of our safehouses."

"And what's with that?" he asked, watching her unseal the paint bucket.

Aquila dipped the brush in the thick red paint. "You'll see." We stayed quiet as she swiped a big red circle on the wall then started painting symbols around it. She returned the brush to the bucket every few swipes, for fresh paint. When her array was finished, she took a few steps back and set the bucket under the control panel again. Closing her eyes, she clasped her hands in front of her chest and made a series of quick hand gestures. The magic circle briefly glowed blue, and the space within it rippled like water. When it settled, a black woman wearing a red dress, a black leather jacket, and dreadlocks emerged from the circle, followed by two men. My mouth fell open. It was her—the woman from my dream. The woman with the Red Queen card in her breast pocket.

"What's wrong?" Hunter said, watching my face.

"That woman. I saw her in a dream."

"Hey, Nephelie," Aquila said, smiling.

The woman from my dream, Nephelie, was a leader in the Defectors. The Smiths were right: Gaspar had left the Institute to work with the Defectors.

Nephelie studied us with red-brown eyes that shone like murky rubies. "Who're all these children, Aquila?" Her voice was even, like perfectly tempered steel.

Aquila cleared her throat, "They kind of caught me and Linh sneaking around and wanted us to help get them out."

"Luther told me two students were coming."

"Yeah, well, they brought some of their friends too."

Nephelie waved her hand at the circle behind her. "Step through. This portal leads to Sanctuary, our base of operations."

We all looked at each other nervously, no one wanting to be first to step forward. But I had other important things on my mind. I inched toward Nephelie.

"You . . . you know Gaspar," I said.

She looked at me, her impassive expression as intense as when she'd walked in. "Gaspar? Yes."

"I need to find him."

My friends all gave me confused looks. "Johnny, what are you talking about?" Hunter asked.

"Gaspar says he's the only one who can help me deal with the Sandman." My mention of the Sandman gave my friends pause. They knew exactly what I was talking about, even if the

Defectors didn't. "I had a dream last night. In it, Gaspar showed me Nephelie"—I nodded to her—"and said that she knows where he is, and that he's the only one who can help me."

"You believed him?" Blake said. "It could've been a Mara."

"What's a Sandman?" Nephelie asked.

Unsure how to answer, we all paused. "We're not sure," Blake said. "Some kind of monster. It got through the Institute's defenses and attacked Johnny in Everywhen."

Nephelie's brows rose. "It surpassed the Institute's Everywhen barrier?" Blake nodded. "Gaspar parted ways with the Defectors some time ago," Nephelie continued. "We don't agree with his methods, and you shouldn't trust him either."

"But I have to try. If I don't do something, the Sandman's going to kill me. It's okay, you guys can go on without me."

Hunter shook his head. "I'm not leaving you." Then he looked at the others. "You all can go. I'll stay with him."

Alison placed her hand on my back. "I'm not losing anyone else. If Johnny thinks this guy can help, then I'm staying too."

"Okay," Blake said, "count me in too."

"Blake, you can't . . ." Linh said.

"Sorry, Linh. We've made it this far. You go on with the Defectors. I can't leave these guys alone."

"Do you know where Gaspar is?" I asked Nephelie again.

"His hideout isn't far from here. It's in a little neighborhood a few blocks west of North Halsted. Let me show you." She closed her eyes, so I did the same. With her mind, she showed me an image of that same house I'd seen in my dream.

I opened my eyes. "Thanks."

"You can't be serious, Neph," Aquila said. "If we let them go, the Institute'll pick them right back up, and who knows what'll happen. What if they find out about Luther and our operation in Misthaven?"

"Luther's no fool. He knows how to cover his tracks, and he's planned for being discovered."

"So we're just going to let these kids go to Gaspar's?"

"I'm not forcing anyone to go to Sanctuary, Aquila. We aren't the Institute. I'm sure they're well aware of the danger they're facing."

Aquila's frustration with us was clear on her face. The two men who'd come with Nephelie stepped back through the portal. Linh looked at the circle, then back at us, her forehead furrowed.

"Go with them, Linh," Blake said.

"Thanks for everything, Johnny," she said. "I really hope this Gaspar guy can help you. If you guys get caught, I'll come back for you. I promise."

Linh turned and stared at the circle on the wall. She gave Blake one last weary glance, then raised her shoulders, sighed uneasily, and stepped through. Nephelie followed her.

"Anything could happen," Aquila said. "We won't be able to help you."

"Don't worry," I said. "We'll watch out for each other." Hunter grabbed my right hand, while Alison wrapped her hands around my left arm.

Aquila nodded, then walked through the circle. The paint seeped into the wall and vanished without leaving a trace. There was no turning back now.

Chapter 28

As both the night and the snow bore down on us, we trekked about two blocks to the neighborhood I'd seen in my dream, then found the old gothic house Gaspar had shown me. Two five-foot brick pillars sat at the base of the stairs leading up to the front door. "I'm sorry," I said, staring up at the house's wrought-iron cresting and finials. "If we get taken back, it's all my fault."

"We've got to deal with the Sandman," Blake said. "One way or another."

I climbed up to the portico with the others behind me and tapped a brass knocker against the black door. The sound echoed through the neighborhood, dampened only by the howling wind.

A flurry of snow swept past us, wrapping our legs, arms, and waists in cold, so we huddled closer together. The door creaked open, only a slit at first, then wider, until I could see Gaspar standing in the doorway. Instead of wearing white this time, though, he was wearing a beige vest and brown slacks. With a satisfied look on his face, he pushed the door open all the way. "We've been waiting for you," he said, stepping aside and ushering us in.

We walked across herringbone wood floors into the foyer. The house looked barely lived in, like an ornate shell. Dead gaslights hung on the walls over dusty wooden cabinets. The chandelier hanging over us was swathed in so many cobwebs, you could barely make out its brass arms. Gaspar pointed to a pair of mahogany doors. "Please, in the parlor."

Blake pushed open one of the heavy doors before I could say anything. Although it still didn't look very lived in, the parlor was slightly more outfitted than the rest of the house. Densely packed bookshelves lined the walls, and a few Victorian couches faced each other across a Persian rug. On the left side of the room, a pedestal desk stood before a group of tall, black-curtained windows looking onto the street outside.

A pale woman with raven hair was standing in front of a parchment-colored globe in a wooden stand. She gave it a lazy spin before looking up at us with amber cat's eyes. It was her. The pale woman from my dream with Gaspar. She moved away from the globe and flashed us a wicked grin, We stalled in the doorway. "What's with her eyes?" Blake whispered.

"No way," Alison said, walking past us into the parlor. "What're you doing here?" She circled around the pale woman and looked at me. "J, this is the lady who gave me the book. The same lady and the same book that Melchior told me didn't exist in my memory."

Just as I'd thought, the woman from my dream and the woman who'd given Alison the spell book were one and the same. Before I could say anything back to Alison, the pale woman brought a lithe hand to her face and stroked her skin with long black nails. "Yet here I am, and here you are."

"Was he just lying?" Alison asked.

"When men's lips move, they are lying."

I had a million questions I wanted to ask Gaspar—about that day in the arcade, and why I'd been seeing him everywhere—but the first thing that popped out was, "You said you could help me deal with the Sandman."

He walked into the room and leaned against the big wooden desk, arms folded over his chest. "The only thing that can rid you of the Sandman is the cintamani."

"That thing we summoned?" Alison asked.

"No," the pale woman said, "you didn't summon the cintamani. You summoned the weaver. The weaver makes the cintamani."

I remembered seeing the word *weaver* next to the diagram in that spell book. "And what's a weaver?"

The pale woman watched us like a curious cat. "An ancient creature. The only thing that can forge a cintamani. Of course, it's rather elusive and will reveal itself only to its summoner."

"That's us, right?" Alison said.

"The one whose blood was used in the ritual is the weaver's summoner."

Alison looked at me. I was the summoner. I was the one whose blood we'd used to cast the spell. That meant the creature would only appear to me. "Okay, so what do I have to do to find this weaver?"

"You could say the threads of fate are working hard just to keep you and the weaver apart," Gaspar said. "But in Everywhen, one only need look for a thing to find it."

"I have to . . . go back into Everywhen?"

"Yes."

The place where the Sandman was waiting for me. To stop the Sandman, I had to barrel right into its lair, find this weaver, and get it to make a cintamani. No biggie.

Hunter snatched my hand and squeezed it. "Don't worry, Johnny. If you've got to go in there, I'm going with you."

"Me too," Alison said.

"I wouldn't advise that," Gaspar said. "The weaver is shy. The more of you there are, the less likely you'll be to find the creature."

"I'm not letting him go alone," Hunter insisted.

Gaspar rubbed his chin with one hand. "Then, perhaps, take just him. Any more and you're asking for trouble."

Alison looked at me fearfully. "This doesn't feel right, Johnny. This was my idea."

"Don't worry, Ali. Me and Hunt have got this."

"Guys!" Blake muttered through gritted teeth. "We need to huddle up. Now." We gathered around Blake while Gaspar and the pale woman looked on, amused. "I don't like this," Blake said quietly. "I don't trust her—she can't be human. And if she's not human, what is she? And why don't the Defectors trust this Gaspar guy? Why're they helping Johnny?"

"Yeah, I don't trust Gomez and Morticia either. They probably want that magic wishing rock for themselves," Alison said.

"We could just ask them," Hunter said.

"Fine." Alison spun around and smiled awkwardly at the pale woman. "Um, what exactly are you? Or did you just get the eyes at Hot Topic? Because I'm totally into the whole cat-girl thing. You can ask Johnny—I own like fifty pairs of cat ears. Well, I did."

"You call me Mara," the woman said. She was a Mara, like the creatures in the Night Market, but except for her eyes, she looked human.

"And why have you been helping us?" Alison asked.

"Because we're also looking for the cintamani," she said. "It's the only way I can return to the ecstatic Void whence I came. Whence all things come. Once, there was only nothingness, but in that nothingness stirred what you call Asuras, servants of the Void. Some Asuras longed to feel the warmth of love—you call them Devas. They left the darkness and began building a world where they could feel love, but the other Asuras grew jealous and sought to upend their project. The Devas fled into their first creation, Everywhen, and continued working on their next one. The Asuras pursued them, destroyed their dreams and turned them into nightmares, forcing the Devas to flee into the world they were building. A world of limitless potential where they could feel endless love. This world.

"The Asuras chased the Devas here, hunted them down one by one until they were gone. Then the Asuras filled the world with death and suffering. Some Asuras stayed here, became mortal, but many tried returning to the Void, only to become hopelessly lost in Everywhen. Those lost Asuras are what you call Maras. I've been lost for a long time and would like to return to the Void."

"You're saying this world was built off the bones of a dream-world?" Alison asked.

"Those cogs and wheels you see don't exist in Everywhen. That's because they were built there specifically to define the boundaries of this reality. That's why Everywhen and this world behave so differently."

"Then, what are wizards? Why are we able to manipulate the Devas' creation?"

"Perhaps wizards are descendants of the Asuras who became mortals in this world. I don't have answers for all of these questions."

I wondered how much of what she said was Mara nonsense and

how much was true. Were we really all descendants of Asuras? I still
had so many questions. I looked at Gaspar. "And what about you?
Why're you looking for the cintamani?"

He paused, considering his words. "Everything they've told
you about the Institute is a lie. I'm sure you've gathered that. The
Institute's presumption is only a select few are born with the ability
to use magic, and everyone else who manifests the ability is a dangerous outlier, a threat to society. The truth is everyone on Earth is
capable of magic. But if people realized that, it would threaten the
existing power structure."

If everyone in the world could become a wizard, then according
to the Mara's legend, we were all descendants of the Asuras. The
Bandersnatch; the unicorn, Amalthea; the creatures of the Night
Market; the Mara standing before us—we were all the same.

Gaspar continued. "Magic is the dividing line, that which sep-
arates kings and queens, business leaders and their lackeys, from
the masses. The kings enslave us all, convince us we have no magic,
because if we realized that we do, we would no longer serve them. The
Institute may have been established by a cadre of like-minded wizards
a hundred years ago, but its purpose was never to cultivate the powers
of wizards. The Institute's sole purpose is to keep what they consider
the lesser element from overthrowing the existing power structure."

"How?" I asked.

"By killing them. The Institute exists to subjugate and kill
non-Lineage wizards."

Blood drained from my head, leaving me cold.

"New wizards are born every day, threatening the power held
by the ancient Lineage families. The Lineage wizards created the
Marduk Institute to contain those non-Lineage wizards and, when
the time is appropriate, to kill them en masse."

"How does it kill them?"

"A curse. Look into the vivit apparatus." I did as he said. My own aura smelled like my favorite pizza place, and music hummed off me like I was a stereo, but in the background, you could hear my parents arguing. If you listened very closely, you could hear clanging swords and gurgling monsters and all manner of fantasy things. Gaspar made a few hand gestures, and then I sensed something else. Something darker. In my mind's eye, I saw a sea of blood filled with millions of thrashing bodies, their slick skin shining red. Within the bloody mess, I saw Hunter, I saw Alison, I saw every non-Lineage wizard I'd met at the Institute: Suhaila, Linh, Aquila, Nephelie, every Veles Hall kid. Then I saw myself, arms flailing, spitting out gobs of blood even as it filled my mouth and threatened to drown me.

Shaken, I quickly opened my eyes. I looked at my friends and saw from their faces that they'd had the same vision. "What the hell was that?"

"The minute you stepped foot inside the magic circle around the Institute, you were marked by this curse. When the time comes, the Institute will activate the curse, and all of you will die." He turned his attention to Blake. "Except for him."

"Why me?" Blake asked.

"You are in a Legacy now. Your aura is marked with the sigil of the Thorns." I hadn't studied Blake's aura since he joined the Thorns, but Gaspar was right: I could sense thorny vines wrapping themselves around all the *Dragon Ball Z* marathons and kung-fu movies. "The initiation ritual they used to induct you nullified the curse.

"They call this mass killing 'the quelling.' I saw my first quelling thirty years ago, when I was a Legacy at the Institute." Thirty years.

What Suhaila had told us was the longest anyone had been at the Institute. Every wizard before then had been murdered. Except for the Legacy wizards. The Lineage families must have known about this. But they stayed quiet, even kept it from their bloodthirsty children. "Since its inception, the Institute has been conducting quellings."

"I saw the picture of you and Melchior and Balthasar. You and Balthasar have aged, but Melchior looks the same. What is he?" I asked.

"I don't know. I don't imagine he's mortal. He was the Institute's first leader. Perhaps the Administrators created him to keep watch."

"And what about the Legacies? Why are they at the Institute?" Blake asked.

"They are being trained to become the wardens of wizard society. If at any time the non-Lineage wizards should attempt to revolt, the Institute uses its agents and the Legacies to control them."

"Can we get rid of this curse?" I asked.

"To my knowledge, only joining a Legacy and undergoing the initiation ritual can protect you from the curse. Times are changing, and after nearly a century, the Institute is now on the losing side of this war, but lucky for them, they're overdue for another quelling, anyway. The Defectors have long known the true purpose of the Institute, and they seek revolution to destroy it. My plan was to use the cintamani to achieve the same goal."

Alison narrowed her eyes at Gaspar. "Why couldn't you summon the weaver yourselves? Why did she give me the book?"

Gaspar and the Mara exchanged a glance. Then Gaspar pulled a pocket watch out of his vest and clicked it open. "If saving Johnny's life and stopping the Institute are important to you, you'll stop asking so many questions and fetch the cintamani."

Chapter 29

1 MONTH AND 2 WEEKS AFTER EXTRACTION

If Gaspar was telling the truth, thirty years ago the Institute had used a horrible curse to kill hundreds of thousands of non-Lineage wizards. And they were going to do it again. And we were the ones marked for extermination this time. Finding the cintamani wasn't just a matter of helping me deal with the Sandman. Now, the survival of hundreds of wizards rested in our hands.

Hunter and I lay on the tufted red velvet couches in Gaspar's parlor. Closing my eyes, I rubbed the back of my head against the soft cushion. The trickle of liquid being poured into a glass tickled my ears. I opened my eyes and found Alison hovering over me. "If you guys mess this up, we're all going to die"—she popped on a fake smile—"so no pressure or anything."

Gaspar pressed a tumbler of brandy to his lips, and the ice ball inside slid down and jingled. "Be careful about trying to alter

Everywhen with your magic," he said. "Any sudden shift in the dreamworld could frighten away the weaver."

I shut my eyes again and sighed as the whole world went dark. After a few minutes, my skin tingled as a breeze ran its fingers over it. Then I smelled salt. Damp wood. Opening my eyes, I watched a golden butterfly flutter off the tip of my nose and dissolve into sparkling flecks as it rose. Then a white rabbit hopped over my face onto the creaky wooden floor nearby.

Supine on the floor next to me, Hunter opened his eyes. Sounds of the ocean—seagulls cawing and waves crashing—seeped in through a window behind us. We were splayed on the floor of an empty wooden room. Surveying the space, I noticed a doorway leading out to a hallway. I pressed my hands down on the dank floor, and the porous wood squeaked under my fingers as I pushed myself up. The entire room groaned like an old man straining his aging back. The floor tilted slightly to the left.

"Did you feel that?" Hunter said, eyes wide.

As I eased onto my feet, the whole house whined around me. The floor didn't shift this time, though. Hunter rose delicately, his hands low to the ground, so he could catch himself should the room start tottering again. On the floor near the doorway, the white rabbit sat watching us, a brass pocket watch tied around its little neck. It wiggled its nose and sped off down the hallway. The room groaned again, so I spread my arms and tried to steady myself. Hunter and I looked up at the exposed, moldering rafters. Sunlight glinted through holes in the roof's planks. Once the room settled, I crept to the doorway and balanced myself against the frame. Hunter did the same.

"I really wish we could just fly out of here," he said.

"Remember what Gaspar said? If we use too much magic, we might scare away the weaver."

I poked my head out into the hallway, and the room behind me yawned, its achy floors and walls crying out again as the floor continued its leftward tilt. We waited for the wobbling to stop. Like a teeter-totter, the room readjusted to center, and so did our nerves. On my tiptoes, I looked out the window at the other end of the room. Outside, all I saw was ocean—nothing else.

The hallway dead-ended to my right, but to the left, the narrow passage stretched past a few doors into other parts of the house. The floor trilled and squeaked as I nodded for Hunter to follow me. We balanced ourselves against the hallway's dilapidated wood panels. Hunter inched up behind me and grabbed the back of my shirt, and we sidled along the wall. The crumbling wooden house must've been old. There was no electricity—no wall outlets, no electric lights, no switches.

We passed a door on the left side of the passage, and I made the mistake of looking through the opening. It was like the room beyond had been ripped away by a storm. Shattered floorboards reached their splintered fingers out to the sea, and the collapsed roof did the same. Below, sharp rocks sat like teeth in a hungry monster's mouth, foamy waves splashing around them like drool. The whole structure was teetering at the edge of a cliff. I'd had this nightmare a million times. Especially during Mom and Dad's divorce. I pressed myself against the wall, closed my eyes, and tried to calm my raging heart.

"What's wrong?" Hunter said.

"Nothing. Don't look through that door."

He looked. "Holy—"

"I told you not to look." We scurried down the hallway like a couple of scared mice until it opened onto a wider space that looked like a living room. The house pitched forward. We stood still, but clearly the house's grumpy mood was getting worse. It was about ready to fling itself onto the rocks below, with us inside. An archway led into a kitchen and—hopefully—a back door.

Our advance toward the archway was cut short when the house roared and tilted to an impossible angle facing the rocks below.

"Get in the kitchen, Johnny—now!" Hunter yanked my arm and bolted. We made a mad dash for the kitchen as the floor slanted even more. Dropping to his knees, Hunter reached into the floorboards, mashing through the slimy wood to form hand grips. I followed his lead and jammed my fingers into the floor too. Then, wedging our fingers between the mushy floorboards, we crawled toward the archway. The floor lurched again, and we held on tight as the house went completely vertical.

We were almost to the kitchen when half the living room detached with a horrifying crunch and fell to the rocks below. Hunter quickly climbed into the kitchen and rolled onto the wall on the other side of the archway. I tried to follow him, but a moldy plank shattered under my fingers. Half the board broke and swung me to the side. Threads of rotting wood were all that was keeping me from the rocks below. Hunter stretched his upper body through the archway, ignoring any sense of self-preservation to reach down for me. "Johnny!"

My fingers were slipping. Holding on to the cracking plank much longer would be impossible. I looked down. Waves. Rocks. Death. I had to grab his hand. Looking back up, I saw my scared reflection in Hunter's green eyes. "Grab my hand, Johnny!"

I reached my hand up. The fibers holding the plank together were snapping, coming undone like yarn. My fingers brushed against his. Almost there. The board snapped, on the verge of breaking off. I let go as it fell off the rest of the way and swung my hand up into his. He reeled me up onto the wall on the other side of the archway. The whole house was getting ready to topple over into the sea. Above us where we stood on the wall, the back door dangled open, but there was no way we could reach it. Our next decision would either deliver us safely from this nightmare, or into the hungry jaws of the rocks below. Hunter looked around frantically, searching for some sort of solution. Then, behind him, I spotted a refrigerator lying on its side. If we couldn't climb to the door, we'd have to make a new one.

Grabbing Hunter's arm, I rushed him over to the refrigerator with me. "Help me tip it over." We both stood on one side of the refrigerator, Hunter pressed his back against it, and we started to shift it with the full force of our upper bodies. It fell on its back, and its door swung open. At that moment, with a crack, the roof ripped away from the house and fell into the sea. "Get in."

"If we use magic, we could scare the weaver," Hunter said.

"I don't care. Get in!"

We hopped inside and closed the door behind us. In the darkness, everything around us rumbled as the house continued collapsing. *Think, think, think. Somewhere new. Somewhere else.* Hunter grabbed my arm, calmed me. I grabbed him back and imagined the easiest thing for me: a park. Any park. I didn't care which park. *Just get me to a park.* I heard the house groaning, felt gravity tugging on me as the refrigerator went into freefall.

Park, park, park, park, park, park!

Then, silence. Nothing moved around us. Everything perfectly still.

Out of the silence came music. It tickled my ears. But only faintly. Strings—violins, cellos, violas—sighed and lilted like voices. I opened my eyes to lacquered wooden floors with twisting arabesque inlays, shimmering crystals drooping off a golden chandelier, rounded marble pilasters, and elegant long tables draped in white linen. It was a luxurious ballroom like nothing I'd ever seen. Dancers waltzed around me, throwing back their long necks as their partners swayed them from side to side.

It wasn't a park, but at least it wasn't that falling house either. I examined myself. I was wearing a tuxedo, but didn't have a mask, like everyone else did. Overhead, a lustrous canopy bloomed from the ceiling like a silk peony. A woman in an ornate domino mask with a horn on it was standing in front of me. "Please," she said, "dance with me."

"I—I don't know how."

"Of course you do, this is a dream."

She took my hand, and we were off. She took the lead, dragging my graceless body along with hers. I thought, *I know how to dance*, and then I became lithe and supple as a crane's neck. But where was Hunter?

"Listen carefully," she said as she swept across the floor, "you mustn't forge the cintamani."

I stiffened. "What do you mean? It's the only way to stop the Sandman and the Institute."

"You are being misled. The cost of making a cintamani is too great."

I broke free and pushed away, taking a few steps back and almost bumping into some other dancers. "You don't know what you're talking about," I said. "Who are you, even? What do you want?"

Before she could answer, Hunter pushed between a couple and snatched my arm. We ran, shoving other dancers on our way to the door. "Johnny, what're you doing? We're supposed to be looking for that weaver thing."

The woman with the horned mask stared at me as I ran. I could feel sorrow burning in her crystal-blue eyes. She put a hand to her chest and disappeared behind the throng of dancing bodies. I couldn't shake how important she had felt. Her aura had been familiar, nostalgic, but I couldn't place it.

Hunter threw open the heavy doors of the ballroom, and we jumped into the void beyond, dropping face first onto a fuzzy heap of white mold. Jumping up, Hunter slapped mold off his shirt and started spitting like he'd swallowed a mouthful of spores. "Yuck. What the hell's all this?"

Getting to my feet, I studied the white dust on my hands, then looked up. High-rise buildings covered in white mold climbed toward a lightless sky. Stoplights dripped with dry rot, suspended over lanes littered with rusting, mildew-covered cars. We were standing near the Marriott on Michigan Avenue. It looked like a snow of fungus had covered all of Chicago. Great big mushroom stalks loomed over us like trees, and on the underside of their caps, gills filled with spores spewed a mist that smelled like mothballs into the air. Thick, stinking clouds settled over the city, wafting down from the nothingness hanging over us and covering everything in a sheet that rose to our ankles. Everything was long dead, reclaimed by forces of decay.

Hunter cupped his hands around his mouth and shouted, "Hello!" His voice echoed through the valley of decaying buildings, bouncing off the withering cement structures. He turned to me. "You think that weaver thing is here?" I was still thinking about the strange woman in the horned mask. Hunter waved his hand in front of my face. "Johnny?"

"Sorry, I was just thinking about something. That weird lady I was dancing with—she told me we were being misled, and that the price of the cintamani was . . . too great."

"Look, she's probably just some Mara. Let's just find that weaver thing and get the hell out of Everywhen. I hate this place."

We plodded through Michigan Avenue, small buildings crumbling into dust at the sight of us. Passing under traffic lights with stretchy globs of white mold dangling off them, our feet dusted up fledgling clouds of spores with every footfall. If this had been real, all the mold in the air would've choked us by now.

"How are we going to get out of here?" Hunter asked, his arms wide.

I opened my mouth to answer, but the sound of hissing sand cleaved my thoughts. Spinning around, I spotted the Sandman not far behind us, a sandy cloud eddying around its feet. It spread its arms, an angel of death, and summoned winds that cleared a path through the white mold, straight to us. Now, with nothing in its way, it took one graceful step forward. I'd never seen it move so delicately. It was no longer a shambling revenant. It was a limber creature. With its arms spread and its back parallel to the ground, it dashed toward us, sending my heart shooting up into my throat.

"Come on, Johnny." Hunter grabbed my hand and led us into a darkened alley between two office buildings. We were moving so quickly that I didn't even feel my own footsteps. Looking behind us, I didn't see the creature chasing us, which gave me pause. We hurried to the alley's other end—and the Sandman burst out of a pile of white mold, sandy whips spinning around its body. It pointed at us, and its tentacles leaped at us, so we threw up our arms like shields. I imagined a barrier, and the tentacles smashed into an unseen shield around us. The whips spiraled away in all directions, spearing brick walls, aluminum trash cans, even the cement under the white mold. One of us had blocked the creature's powerful magic. But it wouldn't be enough. The Sandman slung its arms at its sides, calling back its whips as it slowly moved toward us.

Again clutching my hand, Hunter led us back out the way we came, to the streets, but we didn't get far before the Sandman appeared in front of us again. Then behind us. Then beside us. Copies. It had duplicated itself, surrounding us with nine doppel-gängers. Hunter tried easing me behind him, but I wouldn't let him. He couldn't take on one Sandman, never mind the nine surrounding us.

"Johnny." He dropped to his knees in front of a manhole cover and wrenched it off. I peeked into the bleak opening and wondered where it might take us, but the sandmen were inching closer, so I didn't have time to fret about it. I grabbed his shoulder, steadying myself against him, and jumped into the hole. Hunter followed.

We splashed into a cold muck that stank like rotting eggs. I grabbed a handful of mud that had enough squirming things in it to make me yank my hand away again. We'd landed in a swamp with towering cypress trees and glowing green waters that rose almost a foot off the ground. Covered in stinking slime, we stood up. Hunter dusted moss off his hands. "It'd be great if this *weaver thing*"—he raised his voice deliberately—"could show up already!" His voice echoed through the dismal marsh.

Even though the necks of the cypress trees extended into the void hanging over us, the ambient green light of the swamp kept us from total darkness. In the distance, I saw flickering orange lights between a copse of trees. I pointed. "Look."

Hunter followed my finger to the soft gleam of lights. "I really, *really* hate Everywhen."

I looked down at my shoes. Even though I knew this wasn't real, freezing-cold water prickled my feet like needles. We entered the copse of trees, and I took only a few steps before Hunter grabbed me and yanked me back. I looked at him, confused. He nodded his chin at something in front of us. I followed his eyes. He'd kept me from walking into a huge spiderweb built between two trees. He wrapped his hand around mine and led me around the giant web. "You going to freak out if a giant frog tries to eat us?"

"I'm not making any promises," I said.

"You city kids are wimps." Emerging from the copse, we came across a rickety old stilt house. The light we'd been following was coming from a few burning torches secured in mounds of mud around its base. Nestled against a wiry wall of vegetation, the structure was impossible to see behind, but a quick search revealed a shaky, winding staircase leading up to a rain porch with an aluminum roof. "I feel like we're going to get *Wrong Turn*-ed or something," Hunter said.

"I'm just glad the Sandman isn't here." We climbed up to the porch to a screen door that was just a storm away from being blown off its hinges. The door behind the screen was wide open. Whoever lived here must have felt safe enough to do that. Then again, anyone brave enough to establish a permanent residence in Everywhen probably didn't worry too much about intruders. I called out a quick greeting. Hunter winced nervously. Then a feeling overcame me that I was supposed to walk inside. I looked through the screen door, then back at Hunter. "I think this is where the weaver is."

He exhaled and stared into the house, still looking disquieted.

"Trust me, Hunt," I said. "I can feel it. I think it's in there."

I opened the screen door. Clutching Hunter's hand to steel myself, I inched inside. A creaky floorboard startled me. I hoped that whatever lived inside hadn't heard us creeping into its lair. We looked at each other with dread written across our faces. Once we were certain some hideous monster wasn't about to come out and chop us into stew meat, I crept another foot over the threshold.

Next to the doorway, a single gas lamp sat on an entryway table lighting a narrow passage piled floor to ceiling with dusty junk. There were glass cases filled with pinned butterflies and stacks of soggy old books too tattered to handle. We followed the curving passage around a bend and down a hallway, until we reached a dining room with a shambling wooden table. Old tea sets and rusty candelabras dressed in cobwebs covered a raggedy white tablecloth. Two humanoid creatures with snakelike lower bodies stood at opposite ends of the table. Alarmed, I stepped back and bumped into Hunter. He grabbed my shoulders and tried easing me out of the room, but instead, I reached down, gripped his hand, and stopped him from moving. I was supposed to be here. I could feel it.

"Hello?" I said to the two snake men.

"*Mo hy*," the one closest to us said. Hunter tried again to pull me out of the room, but I ignored him.

"*Aries vivos whet*," the man at the far end of the table said. They didn't even move their lips to speak. Their low voices just emanated from them.

"*Ardyth mathewson vivie—*"

"*Ecus tinnier*," the one closer to us said.

"What the heck are they saying?" I said.

"I think they're speaking in True Tongue."

The language of dreams. "How come they didn't talk like that in the Night Market?"

"Most Maras are so eager to strike a deal that they've learned human languages. Only really old ones still talk in True Tongue." Hunter scanned them again. "You don't know that you know True

Tongue, but you do. Every wizard does. The next time they say something, just believe you understand them, and you will."

"Could you repeat yourselves?" I asked the snake men.

"Who are you?" the closer one said.

"Johnny. And this is Hunter. We're looking for the weaver."

"I was a weaver in a loom once," the farther one said.

The closer chortled. Then he stretched his long, reptilian arm across the table and grabbed a teapot. As he tipped the contents into a tiny cracked teacup, a spider quickly crawled out of the cup. The snake man poured something thick as blood and just as red into the cup. "Sometimes," he said before the fluid stopped flowing from the spout, "the answers to questions—"

"Are more circuitous—"

"Than one might expect."

"Sometimes, you solve one problem—"

"By starting another."

Their back-and-forth speech rang like a riddle. "Is one of you the weaver?"

"If we were—"

"What would you—"

"Need of us?"

"We're looking for the cintamani." The snake men looked at each other, confused. "The wishing stone?" I clarified.

"The void stone? You're the one—"

"Who called us."

Relieved, I smiled at Hunter. "So one of you guys is the weaver. Or is it both of you?"

"One, two—"

"Three half dozens of the same."

"What is a number?"

"I don't have time for this," I said.

"But you've made it much further—"

"Than any of the others—"

"In a long time."

"We're surprised—"

"That nasty guardian—"

"Didn't kill you."

"You're lucky—"

"It hasn't fully—"

"Recharged all its strength—"

"Because then—"

"You would be dead."

Hunter pinched his eyebrows together.

"Guardian?" I asked.

"Yes. A safety measure—"

"Left behind—"

"So we couldn't have fun anymore."

They leaned forward and curled their dry reptilian lips into crooked smiles. "But now you're here."

So the Sandman was a fail-safe placed on the weaver to keep people from summoning it. That was why Gaspar had rushed us into Everywhen when Alison asked why he didn't just summon the weaver himself: Gaspar and the Mara had tricked us. Regardless, we needed the stone to wish away the Sandman, and to wish away the Institute and its twisted death curse. "Can you make a cintamani?"

"Make?" the closer one said, chuckling.

"We don't make—"

"The void stone—"

"We keep—"

"The void stone."

Hunter and I shared another couple of frustrated looks. "What?"

The farther one pushed his chair back and slithered up, teacup and saucer in hand. The nearer one did the same.

"Please—"

"Follow us."

They slithered through the room into the kitchen. We followed them through a back door onto a lanai. Behind the house, the vegetation rose up into a dome around a circular pond so deep that the water didn't glow. A wooden staircase descended from the lanai to a jetty over the pool's still-as-a-grave black waters. "In there," one said.

"Sh'kar," the other said.

Those brackish waters creeped me out. "Sh'kar?"

"A giant fish—"

"Yes, a giant fish—"

"With a void stone—"

"Growing right—"

"On its head." The snake man took a sip from his teacup.

"How on earth are we supposed to get that?"

They looked at me as if I'd asked them whether it was raining in the middle of a downpour.

"You pluck—"

"It out."

This was ridiculous. "What? You want us to grab a jewel off a fish's head?" I said.

"It shouldn't—"

"Be difficult—"

"Sh'kar is—"

"Quite big."

They weren't kidding. One of us would have to jump into those murky waters, lure out a giant fish, and wrestle a stone off its head.

"All right, let me at him." Hunter rubbed his hands together.

My mouth almost slid off my face. "What're you talking about, Hunt?"

"What? We need the cintamani. I'm going to go get it."

"It should be me. I called it here."

"You ever wrangle something that big before?"

"No."

"Well, I've wrangled pigs, I play football, and I wrestle. I think I'll have a better chance than you."

"This is a dream."

"And because I've done it in the real world, I can imagine it in here better than you can."

"What if that big fish eats you?"

"Johnny, one of us has to go in there and get this jewel, or we're all dead anyway."

He was right. We'd come here to get the cintamani, and we couldn't leave empty-handed. I walked up to him and looked in his eyes. He grinned at me. "What?"

I slid my arms around him. He closed his eyes and hugged me back. "I don't want anything to happen to you," I said.

"I've been wrangling pigs my whole life. How different could a big fish be? Just have some faith in your boy, okay?"

We walked down the shaky steps to the jetty over the black pool. Hunter put his hands on his hips, craned his neck over the edge of the dock, and scanned the motionless black waters. He tittered and shot me a grin as unsteady as the pier we were standing on.

"Can't we just, like, cast a spell or something?" I said. "We've already found the weaver."

"The cintamani is a magical object. No telling what'll happen if we use magic directly on it."

Hunter closed his eyes and, with just a thought, produced a second Hunter, who stepped out of him. A duplicate. Hunter pointed to the lake, and the copy splashed into the water and swam out. Then Hunter held up his hand. Flecks of light gathered around his fingertips and formed into a ball. He grew the light ball a few inches, then sent it skimming over the water until it was hovering over his copy. Then he hopped into the water himself, swam out a few feet, and waved at his copy. "All right, you, start kicking around like you're drowning."

The copy thrashed around in the water, trying to draw attention to itself, while Hunter bobbed nearby and watched. There was no guarantee that another magical creature would fall for the lure, but it was the best plan Hunter had. As I stood on the jetty, a groan welled up from the depths, and little bubbles rose to the surface, but Hunter couldn't make out its source through the black waters. The rising and falling waves around him grew more erratic, and the mire stirred like soup in a cauldron, bouncing Hunter up and down like a buoy. Then the water bulged, and a big circular swell formed under him and his copy. I was leaning so far forward, I almost fell into the lake trying to keep my eyes on him.

Hunter focused on the light ball and made it grow until he could see a giant shadow slithering up from the abyss. He kept his eyes trained on the shape until the light shining over the pool glinted on the creature's silvery scales. Sh'kar had a trunk like an elephant and a head like an alligator, with monstrous, jagged jaws like broken glass. Its body was like that of a fish, but with patches of fur all over and webbed appendages similar to arms and feet. Sitting right in the middle of its hideous head was a glowing red rock pocked like a meteorite.

Hunter shot like a bullet down into the water, using magic to boost himself until he smacked right onto a patch of fur along Sh'kar's back. He latched on and held on tight as Sh'kar erupted through the water, showering me, and swallowed the copy. Sh'kar flopped back into the pool and descended so quickly into the darkness that the upward current almost displaced Hunter. He clamped down onto its fur more tightly.

Once Sh'kar was again gliding through the water at a steady pace, Hunter reached up, grabbed another clump of fur, and pulled himself forward. One hand at a time, he inched up the creature's back, eventually making his way to its head. Sh'kar shifted right, then left, jerking Hunter from side to side, and corkscrewed through the water. Hunter flattened himself against Sh'kar's back and held on tight. After spiraling down a few yards, Sh'kar made another sharp turn. The force jerked Hunter off its back and sent him spiraling in a whirl of bubbles.

Hunter flapped his arms and legs, fighting to steady himself. Sh'kar dove away a few yards, and when it had enough room, it took a sharp turn, opened its jaws, and barreled toward Hunter. Meanwhile, Hunter had finally stabilized himself. His eyes almost popped out of his head when he caught sight of Sh'kar approaching. He tried maneuvering out of the way, but when Sh'kar passed, one of its giant fangs snagged his sleeve, catching Hunter's arm between its bottom teeth. Sh'kar rushed through the water, its mouth ajar, dragging Hunter along like a rag doll. Hunter squirmed and wriggled his arm, but his sleeve was twisted around the tooth, holding him in place like a vice.

Any minute now, Sh'kar would clamp its mouth down on Hunter's arm. Hunter wrapped his other arm around the tooth for leverage and pulled back until the sleeve ripped. Just as Sh'kar brought its teeth crashing down, Hunter tore the sleeve away with one last tug. The monster's mouth slammed shut so hard that the force blasted Hunter away. After he stopped spinning, he paddled and quickly swam up to the surface.

When his head popped up out of the water, I called, "Hunter!" The monster pursued him, once again opening its gigantic maw in hopes of swallowing him. Hunter teleported out of the way, leaving behind blue sparks. Sh'kar snapped its mouth up through the surface of the water, making waves that rocked the pier I was standing on and knocked me back onto my hands.

Hunter reappeared on top of Sh'kar, between the creature's eyes, just inches away from the cintamani. The flesh on the monster's snout was too smooth to hold on to, so Hunter transformed his fingers into claws and dug them into the creature's skin. Sh'kar dove back into the water and began a swift descent, maybe hoping the current would yank Hunter off again. But Hunter held tight and started clawing toward the glowing stone between the creature's eyes. The creature dove so deep that Hunter's light ball was useless. The faint glow of the cintamani was his only guide. He steeled himself. Almost there. Another stab. And another. Then, another. He reached a clawed hand at the glowing rock, touched a pointy nail to its mottled surface. The stone's light grew even brighter, the red glow turning white, then enveloping Hunter, enveloping Sh'kar, enveloping me, and everything.

Chapter 30

1 MONTH AND 2 WEEKS AFTER EXTRACTION

The sound of rain barraging a window woke me up. I opened my eyes. I was still in Gaspar's parlor. Sitting up, I searched the room for Hunter and found him lying on the couch across from me, his eyes fluttering open too. Alison and Blake surrounded me like a couple of worried parents. "You okay, J?" Alison said.

Relieved, I jumped up, darted over to Hunter, and threw my arms around him as he sat up. "Did I get it?" he asked. "How'd I do?"

I pulled away and looked in his eyes. "You're awesome, Hunt. You're always awesome."

Gaspar jiggled the ice ball in his brandy glass, drawing our attention to him. With her hands clasped, the pale woman approached Hunter and me with a pleased look on her face. I checked out Hunter's aura. The Institute's curse was gone—but I was hit by such a powerful force that I almost fell off the couch. Hunter steadied me.

"Whoa, what's wrong?"

I couldn't articulate it. His aura felt heavy, like a wrecking ball, and it hit just as hard. In my mind, I saw an ocean of black, and sitting in the middle of the nothingness, a giant red eye, its massive iris darting around, agitated. Hunter rose, then gritted his teeth and fell backward. Circling rings covered in strange symbols flickered all over his skin.

"Hunt!" I said, quickly propping him up.

He chuckled, playing it off. "Just got a little dizzy."

"You tricked us," I said, turning to Gaspar angrily. "You gave us the spell book so we'd summon the weaver because you knew the Sandman would come after us. You knew the cintamani was cursed."

"Typical," the pale woman said. "Men always get the credit for a woman's hard work."

She slid her ghostly fingers along Hunter's jaw. I pulled him back, out of reach. He grunted again as the strange symbols came stuttering back on like a dying light bulb. Holding on to him tightly, I tried to support him as his knees buckled and wobbled.

"Gaspar came to the Night Market looking for information on the cintamani," she said. "He had written so many notes, but didn't know what to do with any of them. I told him to scour the city for wizards we could use to conjure the weaver. We had planned on fetching you before the Institute came, but things didn't go as planned, so instead he sent out his mind and lured you to us."

That was why he'd been in the arcade that day: he'd been out searching for wizards. And he'd found me. "What's wrong with Hunter?" I asked her.

Gaspar moved behind the desk, opened the top drawer, and drew out a revolver. He pointed it at us and clicked back the safety. "He *is* the cintamani."

Hunter went down on his knees again. The strange symbols blinked all over him. I knelt close to him.

The Mara smiled down at us. "The price for forging a cintamani is a wizard's soul."

"But the weaver didn't forge anything," I said. "Hunter wrestled it off a fish."

"The boy used his soul to wrest the stone free. He performed the weaving. Now *he* is the cintamani."

I stood up, rage blackening my eyes. "What're you going to do?"

Gaspar snaked around the desk, his gun still trained on us. "We've already told you what we're going to use the cintamani for."

"What do you mean, 'use' him?"

"Right now, his powers as the cintamani are latent, but the Mara knows how to activate them. Once his powers are active, we'll use him to send her back to the Void and to destroy the Institute."

My voice dropped to a whisper. "What happens after you've . . . used the cintamani?"

The Mara's yellow eyes glinted with satisfaction. "It returns to the place where all things come from, along with the wizard and his soul."

Alison jerked Blake's arm. "Blake, can't you use magic or something?"

"I can't," he muttered.

Overhearing them, Gaspar addressed Blake and Alison. "I've locked all the apparatus's machinery inside the house, so magic won't work. Now"—he waved the gun at me—"move away from the cintamani."

But I wouldn't. I stepped in front of Hunter and shielded him with my body. "Why Hunter?"

Gaspar's calm exterior cracked. "You have no idea what a quelling looks like!" Settling back down, he lowered his voice. "All those dead bodies. Everywhere. His life for the lives of many. Now, move away." It wasn't indiscriminate rage driving Gaspar to stop the Institute—it was guilt. He was trying to assuage his guilt over the last quelling.

I still couldn't bring myself to take a single step away from Hunter. "There's got to be a better way."

"This is the quickest." Gaspar blasted one of the books on the shelf behind me. The gun's report rang in my ears.

"Johnny," Hunter grunted, his skin still flickering with strange symbols, "get away. I don't want him to hurt you."

"No, Hunt. I won't let him hurt *you*."

He grabbed my shirt and pulled it. "It's going to be fine, Johnny. Just go over there with Blake and Alison. Please."

Gaspar aimed the gun at my head.

Hunter tried to nudge me aside. I took a few steps away. Then, the heavy pattering of the rain outside stopped, and the floors trembled—as did the chandelier, the walls, the desk. At first, the noise was dull, then it grew louder and louder until the whole room was shaking. Gaspar's face tensed. He kept the gun trained on us and inched toward the window, bumping into the desk on his way. Pushing aside a curtain, he peeked outside. His eyes widened. The rain hung in the air like it was frozen, like time had stopped.

With Gaspar distracted, Blake, Alison, and I all ran to the window to look outside. The rumbling grew as a fleet of black sedans and vans rolled down the street and surrounded Gaspar's hideout. Smiths poured out of the vehicles, shielded themselves behind car doors, and cased the house through binoculars. From a cluster of Smiths, Melchior emerged. "The Institute," Gaspar muttered.

"How'd they find us?" Alison turned her dread gaze on Blake.

Blake raised his hands in the air. "Whoa, you still think I'm a spy? This has nothing to do with me, I promise."

"He's no spy," Gaspar said. "They probably followed you to Chicago, lost track of you somewhere, then found us after the boy forged the cintamani. I underestimated how much magical energy the weaving would disperse."

Outside, Melchior grabbed a Smith's binoculars and studied the house. Balthasar got out of a sedan and joined Melchior, his face stricken with concern. Melchior summoned a blond Smith, whispered something into his ear, then pointed to the house. The Smith's mouth went slack, his nervous eyes darting between the house and Melchior's face a few times. Then he rolled his shoulders and popped his neck. Taking a deep breath, the Smith approached the stoop. He put one foot down on the bottom step. Paused. Stood still. Clutched his chest. His eyes went completely bloodshot. He clawed at his shirt, his heart. Foam bubbled from the corners of his mouth, veins bulged all over his face. The other Smiths gaped in horror as the blond one took a heavy step away from the house and collapsed, his eyes rolling into the back of his head. He was dead.

"What the hell just happened?" Alison asked.

"The house is protected with a spell that instantly kills any and all Institute personnel," Gaspar said, walking around the desk back to the middle of the room. "That's how I know your friend isn't a spy."

The Mara yanked Hunter up by his arm, forcing him to stand. "We don't have any more time. You must drop the anti-magic field so that I may begin the ritual."

Gaspar moved toward the doors and reached into the vivit apparatus, his gun still pointed at us. With his free hand, he spun wheels,
turned cogs, and shifted entire pieces of machinery, bringing them
all together in front of him and building his own little towers of
clockwork. The Mara swept her hands through the air, and all the
furniture in the middle of the room scooted across the floor, one
of the couches dragging the Persian rug with it. In the space she'd
opened up, she walked in a ring. Every delicate step she took left
glowing red symbols on the floor. They formed a circle. When she
had finished making the ring, the glyphs sizzled and burned into
the wood. Then she raised her head, closed her eyes, and floated up
into the air. A pale light swallowed Hunter's body, and he went limp
before drifting up into the air with her.

"No!" I screamed, moving forward. Blake and Alison held me
back so Gaspar wouldn't shoot me. With tears in my eyes, I yelled,
"Leave Hunter alone!"

Another tremor drew our attention back outside. A few rumbling vans rolled up to the curb. Smiths popped out of the front and
opened the back doors; personnel in white lab coats rolled out twelve
transport gurneys, each with a white-haired kid strapped to it.

Blake gasped. "No way. Somnambulists." For the first time,
Gaspar's face twisted in horror.

The Smiths lined up the somnambulists' gurneys in front of
Gaspar's hideout. Then they came up behind the white-haired
kids, holding injection guns filled with green fluid. These the
Smiths held to the backs of the somnambulists' necks as they
removed their restraints. The twelve somnambulists stepped forward and opened their eyes. Melchior waved toward the house,
then all twelve white-haired kids reached into the vivit apparatus
and started dismantling clockwork, moving aside machinery and

rearranging cogs, removing the protective spell Gaspar had placed around the house. Unable to maintain his anti-Institute barrier with only one hand, Gaspar quickly tucked his gun into his waistband and reached both hands into the vivit apparatus.

Here was my chance. I ran around the desk toward Hunter, but he and the Mara were too high up for me to reach. Looking around, I spotted one of the couches and decided to drag it back to the middle of the room. If I stood on it, I might be able to reach Hunter. When I dashed to grab it, I heard something behind me. Seeping sand. Impossible.

"Johnny . . ." Alison's voice quaked.

I spun around, and, like in a nightmare, the Sandman was standing in the parlor with us. Somehow, it had manifested in the real world.

Gaspar, still fighting to keep up his barrier, looked over. "The creature can manifest in the real world once its powers are fully recovered."

It didn't matter that we'd already forged the cintamani. The Sandman's mission was to destroy anyone who tried to use it, and in its simple understanding, I was that person. Blake formed a light sword. "Get away from that thing, Johnny!" But I was too afraid to move.

The Sandman grabbed my throat with one hand. Blake charged from around the desk, leaped into the air, and hacked off one of the Sandman's arms with one well-placed slice. The Sandman spun around and swung its remaining arm, but Blake ducked under the punch. A new arm burst through from the stump. Blake clenched his teeth and staggered back as the monster approached. It swung at him again, so he backed up onto a sofa, ran across the couch, and hopped off the armrest, heading back toward the desk.

Blake couldn't fight that thing alone. I had to do something, so I closed my eyes and remembered the monster I'd used to fight in my daydreams back in school. A magic sword would always materialize in my hands whenever I needed it. My mind shifted to Hunter's light spell, to how I could sculpt the light coalescing in my hands into any shape. In my mind's eye, I saw the ball in front of me, glowing, warm, but this time, I reached for it, flattened it, made it into a shining blade. I felt its warmth against my fingers, squeezed, felt its handle in my hands, real as any steel.

"Hey, dirtbag!" Alison ran over to one of the bookshelves, grabbed a book, and launched it into monster's shoulder, to no effect. Blake kept backing away from the Sandman, toward the desk. He rolled over top of the desk so it was a barrier between himself and the Sandman, but the creature put its hand on the desk and pushed it across the room like it was weightless. Alison kept tossing books at it, but her strategy wasn't helping, and now there was nothing keeping the creature away from Blake.

Hearing a hum, I looked down and found a light sword glowing in my hands. I'd done it—I'd made a light sword! But there wasn't time to feel satisfied with myself. Wrapping my hands around the sword, I ran at the Sandman with absolutely no clue what I was doing. I'd never used a sword in my life. My plan was to swing and swing until one of us went down. As the Sandman lunged for Blake's throat, I drove my sword right through its back.

"All right, way to go, Johnny!" Alison said, grabbing another book and throwing it at the Sandman.

Unphased, the monster spun around, clamped its hands around my throat, and lifted me into the air. Flanking the monster, Blake cleaved off its arms and dropped me to the floor. I scuttled a few feet away from the Sandman and stood up, then Blake joined me. Side by side, we stood with our weapons facing the Sandman.

"Hope you know how to use that thing," Blake said.

"I don't."

"Then I hope you're a quick learner."

The Sandman sprouted two new arms. Blake held fast, widening his stance. I glanced at him and followed suit.

Hovering above everyone, Hunter's body shone with golden light. As the pale Mara wrapped her sinewy fingers around his face, the glowing ring on the floor beneath them swirled into a black pool of shadows. "Take me back to the ecstatic void," she said.

Inky tentacles reached up from the black slime and snatched her legs, wrapped around her neck, her waist, pulled her down. She closed her eyes and smiled as the darkness swallowed her in its infinite gullet. Gaspar's eyes perked up when he saw the Mara return to the Void, but he didn't stop fighting to maintain his barrier. When the Mara was gone, the pool of shadows shrank and disappeared, leaving nothing behind, not even the ring. The cintamani's power still surging through him, Hunter stayed afloat over the room.

The Sandman swept its hand at Blake and me. Blake dodged the swing, but it caught me right in the jaw, knocked me off my feet, and sent me sliding across the floor. Alison ran behind the creature and battered her hands against its back. It turned to her, and when she saw its face—no more than a cascade of pouring sand—she blanched. Blake kicked the monster in the back, drawing its attention away from Alison. He raised his sword over his head, ready to chop the monster in two, but the Sandman kicked him in the stomach and flung him across the room. Blake smashed into a bookshelf, shattering the shelves. He crashed to the floor, and a flurry of books rained on top of him, knocking him out.

The Sandman turned its sights back on Alison. She reeled back her fist and gave the Sandman a mean right hook that sent its head off to one side. I sat up, reality whirling around me, my sword gone. The monster grabbed Alison's throat. She grunted and wrapped her fingers around its wrist as it lifted her into the air. Then it flung her against the parlor doors, right by near Gaspar, and she hit the floor, unconscious. Staggering to my feet, I reimagined the sword, formed it, and swung at the monster, instead teetering clumsily past it. I regained my composure, turned, and swept my sword across the monster's midsection. Again, the Sandman was unaffected. It reached for my throat and grabbed me. Without enough calm now to focus on the spell, my light sword dissipated. I threw my hands around the Sandman's wrists and pulled and pulled, but I couldn't break free.

The monster drove its fingers into my throat, and in the cold sand dripping from its cowl, I saw my doom. I kicked my feet as it lifted me into the air. It squeezed. Harder.

Hunter was still glowing above the room. *At least he's safe*, I thought, but this was it for me. Fear clutched my heart like a thorny vine, squeezing as hard as the Sandman's hands, but then, as if summoned by my impending doom, Hunter floated down and grappled with the Sandman in his glowing arms. I dropped to the floor, hacking and wheezing. Swinging futilely, the Sandman jerked and tried to pull away from Hunter, but my boy wouldn't let go. The powers of the cintamani had made him more powerful than any of us could've imagined. A flash of light surrounded them, forming into a great big ball that shone bright as a supernova. I stood up, shielding my eyes as the light ball grew brighter and brighter. Its brilliance eventually forced my eyes shut. In the darkness, a roar filled my ears. The light ball exploded and sent a blast of wind sweeping through the room. Nothing was left. Not the Sandman. Not Hunter.

Gaspar dropped his focus on the vivit apparatus. "No! No! He used the last bit of it!"

Shock overtaking me, I fell to my knees. I searched for Hunter's aura, but all I felt was emptiness. The cold fingers of the void touching my face where Hunter's hands once had. He was gone. He'd used the last bit of the cintamani's power to send both himself and the Sandman to the Void. Dread crept through my veins. My skin tingled. This wasn't happening. *Please, please, please, don't let this be happening.*

"No," I muttered, gritting my teeth as tears slid from my eyes. I wrapped my arms around my stomach, caving into myself.

A crash rang out in the foyer. The Smiths were coming into the house for Gaspar, for us. Gaspar tried reaching into the vivit apparatus, but the cogs and wheels wouldn't appear for him. Somehow, his magic had been locked. With a trembling hand, he fumbled the gun out of his waistband and backed away from the parlor doors. They burst open, and Melchior marched in, flanked by two Smiths. Gaspar held up the shaky gun, aimed at Melchior, and fired. Melchior merely waved his hand, and the bullet redirected, flying away from him in an arc and hurtling through Gaspar's throat. Gaspar clasped his neck and hit the floor.

He dipped his finger in the blood pooling under his head and used it to draw a healing circle. But his magic still wouldn't work. He wheezed and reached out a quaking hand toward Melchior, his bloody fingers tensing as he closed them in front of the stony-eyed wizard's face. Then his body went limp.

Chapter 31

The Institute was the cage I'd been given. Hunter was the cage I'd chosen. My only freedom had been in his arms, and now he was gone. Sitting on Gaspar's parlor floor, my knees folded up to my chest, I was set adrift in a sea of what-ifs. Smiths scurried around me, collecting evidence, overturning furniture, casting various spells in hopes of discovering Gaspar's connection to the Defectors. I waited for it all to stop. Alison and I had lost everything. Now the Institute was going to destroy our hearts and bodies.

One Smith was helping Alison, another tending to Blake. Then a shadow fell over me.

"Hey, kid." Through bleary eyes, I saw a Smith hovering over me. "You need to get out of here. Come on." He held out his hand and yanked me up, he ushered me over to join Alison and Blake.

"Where's Hunter?" Alison asked me, but when she saw my face

ruined with tears, she went pale. She put her arms around me, and I couldn't hold it in anymore. At first, it welled up from the pit of my stomach and bubbled out like a whimper, then as a deep groaning from the center of my soul. I cracked like glass, and dissolved into pitiful sobs.

"Come on, kids," some Smith said, trying to usher us out of the room.

Alison snarled at him. "Get the hell away from us! We can walk on our own."

Nonetheless, two Smiths guided us out of the house. Outside, the Institute's strange time spell had worn off, so the rain pelted us on our way to a black sedan. We slid into the back, and Alison and I cried together. Blake watched shadowy forms pass by through the rain-stained glass, his lips pressed tightly together, like he was holding back his own feelings.

Every now and then, the blue of a flashing police light would shine in through the windows and sweep over us. Tomorrow, surely, the news would tell of some child kidnapping ring that had been busted up. Eventually, two Smiths got into the car with us, turned on the engine, and pulled out the street. Gaspar's hideout disappeared behind us. Everything he'd told us, everything that'd happened, stained the insides of our souls like black-cherry wine.

My head against the window, I watched everything swim past like a daydream. Green exit signs. Fast food restaurants. Other cars. Chicago disappeared behind us, and the open mouth of hell stood in front of us, welcoming us with jagged teeth.

For hours, darkness poured into my heart like an oil spill, blackening everything, sinking me deeper and deeper into the realization Hunter was never coming back. When we got back to the Institute, a few agents walked us back to our dorms. I took a few steps into my cold, hard cell, cast my eyes on its unforgiving mattress, stiff as stone, its rectangular windows peering into the cold symmetry of the quad, its cheap furniture as plain as if it were designed for prison inmates. I reached deep into my soul and tried to stop the dam bursting in my heart, holding fast and bracing against it with my back, hoping to allay the flood—but finally, I couldn't. I wouldn't. Collapsing on my knees, I looked up at the ceiling like I was staring into the heavens.

And I screamed. I screamed into the cold, black heart of the universe. "Give him back to me!"

The darkness shrugged me off.

His face. His smiling face. I saw it, heard his voice, smelled his cologne. I wanted Hunter back, wanted him to hold me, wanted him to touch me. I was empty without him. I needed him, needed to hear his voice, needed to hear him tell me everything was going to be all right. I wanted to kiss him . . .

I just wanted to kiss him.

I cried so hard I lost my breath. With my fingers bearing down on my pillow, I prayed it'd turn into him. But it couldn't, and I didn't have the kind of magic, anyway.

Alison knocked on my door, came in, and we quietly held each other, poured out our pain, crying for her mother, crying for Hunter, crying because we'd come so close to escaping this monstrous place, but failed.

•

In the morning, two Smiths came to take me to the Heka Building. I knew they were going to ask me questions about the cintamani, about Gaspar, about everything. But I didn't feel like talking. They brought me into a white room with a single metal chair and a mirror.

A light flashed on behind the two-way mirror, illuminating Melchior. "I have a few questions for you."

"Why bother asking me anything?" I said. "You can just get in my head, can't you?"

"Of course. But I thought this would be more civil. You left here with Linh. Where did you go?"

There was no use hiding anything from him. "We met up with the Defectors in Chicago. Linh left with them, but we stayed behind because I had to find Gaspar."

"Why did you have to find Gaspar?"

"Because . . . he told me he was the only one who could stop the Sandman."

"When did he tell you that?"

"In a dream. In Everywhen."

"What happened in that house? How did Hunter acquire the cintamani?" Just the mention of Hunter's name was enough to choke me with guilt. Hunter was gone because of me. I gave Melchior a cold stare. Let him drag my thoughts out of my head. Let him throw me under the Heka Building. I couldn't talk anymore.

Melchior stood still, watching me, probably scouring my thoughts and seeing everything we knew, everyone we'd seen. Hopefully, Luther had already escaped, and the Defectors had already abandoned their project in Misthaven, because now Melchior would know everything. The light went off, and a metal screen came down behind the window. Then two Smiths guided me back to Veles Hall, up to my room. After they'd gone, I walked to the window and stared out into the quad. A knock at the door rattled my mind back into reality.

It was Alison. I let her in, and she sat down on my bed.

"Did they interrogate you too?" she asked.

"Yeah."

"So they know we know their whole messed-up plan."

"It's weird. We worked with the Defectors, escaped, and now we know their whole plan, but they haven't even locked us up in the Heka Building or anything."

"Ten bucks says they have something else up their sleeves."

"What if we told people their whole plan, got them to riot or something?"

"What do they care? They have the Legacies and the Smiths to keep us in line. If we start a riot, we're the ones who're going to end up hurt, not them. Either way, I'm not going to sit around and worry about it. I'm more worried about getting rid of kill curse."

"Do you think we should try to escape again?"

She smiled at me and stood up. "Are you kidding me? Of course we're going to try to escape again." She walked over and put her hands on my shoulders. "And next time, we're getting out."

Locked in a hug, we kept quiet, our minds on her mom, on Hunter. It took everything we had not to fall down crying. I didn't want to say *Sorry about your mom*, and I didn't want her saying *Sorry about Hunter*. Those words would've been trite. Each of us was padding down a flood of pain, but we had to come up with a new way to get out of this place.

•

I passed through the north gate, got on the little commuter bus, and rode into Misthaven. Maybe the Institute shouldn't have let me go—after all, I'd already tried escaping once. But they did. Maybe Melchior was hoping I'd lead them straight to Luther, do the leg-work for him, but I didn't.

Once in Misthaven, I followed the same streets Hunter had shown me. At times, my knees got weak. Familiar places brought old memories screeching back. Somehow, I held it together and made it all the way to Ms. Alwina's. I wanted to see Amalthea. Alwina came to her door after I knocked. At first, she had to adjust her spectacles to make out who I was. She smiled when she recognized me. "You're Hunter's friend, aren't you?"

It took everything in me not to start bawling at the sound of his name. "Yes ma'am."

"Come on in." I followed her into the living room, where she sat by the fireplace with her back to me, staring into the dancing flames. "Where is Hunter?"

How was I supposed to answer her? How could I tell her that a boy I had only just met, yet who'd come to mean the world to me in only a handful of weeks—had sacrificed himself to save me? My nose stung as I fought back tears. "He . . . he . . ." But I couldn't say it. I just clamped my mouth shut and let a few tears escape my eyes. I wondered what she was feeling. She was a wizard, so she must've sensed the pain etched deep into my aura. Sniffling, I said, "He's not here anymore." She stayed quiet. "I was hoping to see Amalthea."

"I'm sorry, darling. But she died a few days ago." If hearts could weep, mine would've drowned in an ocean of its own tears. Everything I associated with Hunter was gone. Unable to fully grasp it, I stood there, thinking about what I should say next.

"I find things are often much more simple than they seem," Alwina said. "At first, you see something, and it doesn't strike you as anything special"—I remembered the first time I saw Hunter, in the Veles Hall dining area with his cheesecake—"but as you come to know the thing, it reveals itself in layers, like the petals of a rose"—I remembered Hunter teaching me how to play basketball, making fun of my smelly cologne, kissing me in the field—"and suddenly, without realizing it, the thing has transformed in front of you. What once seemed like nothing special has become immeasurably important." She looked back at me from her chair. I shielded my eyes with my hand so she couldn't see how hard I was crying. "Maybe you should go back to your room and think of something that didn't seem very special at first. It may have exactly what you're looking for in it."

"What do you mean?"

"What's that, sweetie? I can't remember what I was talking about."

Of course. Nothing but senile rambling. "Thank you, Ms. Alwina."

"No problem, sweetie. Tell Hunter hello for me."

I turned and headed for the front door. On the way out, I noticed an old portrait tucked between a desk and another armchair. Alwina was still facing the fire, so I knelt down and removed the picture. My breath fled my lungs when I looked at the image. It was a black-and-white photo that must've been taken in the late nineteenth century. A young woman who looked like Alwina was seated in a chair, smiling at the photographer, while behind her stood a young man with long white hair who looked like Melchior. He didn't stand so much as loom, and his face was as fierce as it was now.

I straightened up and turned to Alwina, but she was gone. Not only that—the house stood empty. All her things had vanished. No dressers brimming with old clothes. No high shelves lined with old pictures. No stacks of newspapers and magazines and academic journals. There was no one, nothing here. I ran outside. The paddock was empty. The stable was empty. The farm was empty. My skin tingled furiously. I ran back into the house and searched for the portrait—I must've dropped it—but it had vanished too.

Shaken, I hurried back to Misthaven and got on the first bus back to the Institute. What had happened to Alwina? Who was she? And why did she have an old picture of herself with Melchior? I had so many questions.

•

For a few days, I just lay in bed thinking about Hunter. With my arm dangling between my bed and the wall, I smothered myself with my tear-stained pillow, closed my eyes and saw Hunter's face in the darkness. My fingers brushed against something, so I peered into the space between my bed and the wall. Gaspar's notebook. I'd forgotten about throwing it back there. I squeezed my arm into the crack and tried to clasp the spine with two fingertips, but it didn't work, so I hopped off the bed, got on all fours, and stretched under the bed frame. Finally, I grabbed the notebook.

Why would Gaspar have written a whole book on building, setting, and fixing old clocks? I lay on my bed, studying the pages. All of a sudden, Alwina's word replayed in my head: "Maybe you should go back to your room and think of something that didn't seem very special at first. It may have exactly what you're looking for in it."

This book about old clocks must contain coded instructions on how to operate the vivit apparatus. I flipped over onto my stomach, revived by my epiphany, and skimmed through the book looking for anything useful. I must've been reading the whole day when I found a spell he'd nicknamed "unwinding." Originally, Gaspar had used it to retrieve things from the Void. Apparently, he'd spent a lot of time at the Institute throwing random things into the Void, then using this spell to fish them back out, just to study the effects.

Hunter had used the last bit of the cintamani's power to banish himself and the Sandman to the Void. That meant he was trapped there now. But that might also mean I could fish him back out using the unwinding spell. I had to tell Alison about my plan, so I tucked the book under my arm and rushed out to the hallway.

When I reached her door, I heard Alison's muffled voice coming through it. "Blake, I'm going through a lot right now. What do you want?"

"I just want to talk." Blake's voice sounded closer to the door.

"About?" Alison sounded like she was moving toward the window.

"Why do you get so defensive around me? Do I scare you? Do you think I'll hurt you?"

"It's not that. I don't trust you."

I probably shouldn't have been so nosy, but I perked up my ears and listened.

"You know I'm not a spy—why don't you trust me?" Blake said.

Silence. The last guy Alison liked had almost killed her. But now, now that her mom was gone, now that pain had seeped so deep into her heart that her walls were crumbling, maybe she was starting to see Blake differently. "I'm lying," she said finally. "It's not that."

"What is it?"

"Some . . . some guys hurt me, Blake," she said, voice cracking. "They tried to kill me."

"Do you want me to go now?"

"No, don't go."

"I'm sorry people have been crappy to you, Alison. I just think we click. I like being around you. I just want a chance."

"A chance for what?"

"To see if there's something here. Something we both feel."

"I guess sometimes I really don't like myself, so I wonder why you do."

"I just do, Alison. It doesn't have to be supercomplicated."

"Call me Ali. Everyone I like just calls me Ali." The floor creaked like Blake was closing the space between them—if I closed my eyes tight, I could almost hear their racing hearts—then, their lips came together.

I could hear the smile in her voice when she muttered, "Wow."

"What?" Blake said.

"We should've done that sooner."

Alison was fine, safe with Blake, so I hurried back to my room. I'd have to reach into the vivit apparatus alone to bring back Hunter. I would defy death and every law of the universe just to hold him again. Nothing would stop me. Consequences be damned.

•

I opened the book and followed the instructions for the unwinding spell. I drew a magic circle on the floor and, around it, jotted down a few strange-looking symbols from Gaspar's notes. I was probably too arrogant, so foolishly convinced I could reverse the laws of the magical universe, but I had to do this. Hunter was the beacon I used to find my way through the darkness. I needed his light again, or I'd be lost forever.

I placed my hands down around the glyph, and it started glowing crimson. The vivit apparatus appeared all around me, shimmering, golden. My lips parted, my eyes widened. I inched back a bit, but kept close to the circle. A glowing red halo appeared above me near the ceiling, and a clockwork engine descended through it. The machine whirred, pulsing with the strangest aura I'd ever felt. I couldn't easily put it into words, but it felt like the beginning of everything, like the first light of dawn stretching its warm fingers over a nascent ocean brimming with life. The weird-looking thing was covered in mysterious symbols I'd never seen. It hovered above the circle I'd drawn on the floor, just in reach of my trembling hands.

When I was certain the thing wasn't going to vanish, I looked back through Gaspar's notes. Getting the machine to work was like solving a puzzle. I had to move every piece in just the right way to get the machine working. So I did exactly as the notes told me. I spun every cog and every wheel. When everything was in place, the machine roared to life and glowed like a dying sun, bathing the room in blood-red light. The color of all things before they're born, when they're still hidden deep within their mother's wombs.

The notes told me to visualize the thing I was looking for, so I closed my eyes and thought of Hunter, imagined myself fishing for him in the endless nothing: his smile, his gentle eyes, his soft hair, his letterman's jacket and his smelly socks, his breath on my skin, his face nuzzled against mine, his arms around me, his lips on mine. Red light swallowed everything, radiant, warm.

The engine's pieces spun faster and faster, shaking everything. The entire room trembled—the floor, the ceiling, the bed. The whole universe boomed alive, and dread crept into my soul, wound its way around my heart—perhaps a warning, but nothing could stop me. I wanted Hunter back. I would stop at nothing until he was in my arms again, holding me, kissing me.

Nothing before Hunter mattered and nothing after Hunter mattered and the Institute didn't matter and Smiths didn't matter and

Defectors didn't matter and Maras didn't matter and Asuras didn't matter and magic didn't matter, because the only magic I'd ever felt was in his arms. When he was looking into my eyes and making me feel like we were two shooting stars scribbling our names across the sky in gold dust.

The engine and all the machinery around it vanished. Everything went perfectly still. No more rumbling. No more noise. I looked around to see if the ritual had worked, but Hunter didn't magically materialize in front of me or anything. I left my room and ran over to his, but he wasn't there either. Back in my room, I looked under the bed, out the window, in the bathroom. Nowhere. Then, I heard a clunking noise coming from inside my wardrobe.

I stared at the shaking cabinet for a few seconds before approaching it. Something inside was struggling to escape. As I reached for the handle, I heard a muffled voice inside, so I swallowed hard, looped my fingers around the grip, and opened the door.

Out tumbled Hunter, naked, crashing into me and sending us both to the floor with a thud. After everything stopped spinning, I opened my eyes, looked up. Saw him. Lost my breath.

His feathery hair.

His dewy green eyes.

His perfect lips.

He was back!

Lying there, I looked up into his wild and frightened eyes, and it hit me: I'd done the impossible. I'd rescued Hunter from the Void. For a whole minute, we stared into each other's eyes, not saying a word, just staring.

"Johnny?" Hunter said, breaking the silence.

"Hunter," I said, tears gathering in my eyes.

Our lips collided, and our auras exploded like a pair of supernovas, a birdsong of football games and rowdy punk songs, parents shouting and bullies fighting, men in black suits in black vans and black pyramids that pierced the sky—and two boys holding hands through it all. We didn't know what the future had in store for us, but we could handle it.

We could handle anything.

Together.

Acknowledgments

I'd like to thank the innovative and inspiring Allen Lau and Ivan Yuen for bringing Wattpad to the world; Ashleigh Gardner for fighting to reshape the industry for writers like me; Samantha Pennington, one of the first people to reach out to me at Wattpad; and Alessandra Ferreri, who found my little story at under half a million reads and believed it could represent Wattpad—I couldn't be more honored to be part of that amazing legacy. I'm grateful for the expert skills of Deanna McFadden, my editor, who did everything in her power to make this dream come true; Monica Pacheco, my talent manager, who helped me every step of the way; Catharine Chen, my copy editor; Gwen Benaway, my sensitivity reader; Amy Wood and Michelle Wong, for my amazing book cover; Rebecca Mills; Sarah Salomon; Taylor Pearce; and every other amazing person at Wattpad who helped bring *I'm a Gay Wizard* to life.

I'd like to thank my poor, poor husband, Zak, who went

through every up and down with me; my wonderful friends Ashley and Adam, who always lent me their ears when I wanted to complain (which I do a lot); my good friend Erica and my amazing sister-in-law Hat, whose lived experiences, light, and love helped me tell this story; Kobey, *Gay Wizard*'s original cover designer and one of *Gay Wizard*'s biggest and earliest supporters; Melissa, for my lovely author portrait; my sister, whom I love without end; and my big diverse group of friends, who inspired these characters. I've always been blessed to have people around me as colorful as the world we live in.

To Miss Ruby, this one's for you, baby, and for every one of my amazing readers on Wattpad, who encouraged me and blessed this book with their kindness and support.

I didn't write *Gay Wizard* alone. We all did. Together.

About the Author

V. S. Santoni is a Latinx, gay, nonbinary guy who spends way too much time daydreaming. When he isn't thinking up queer dream-punk stories and scouring YouTube for retro-anime movies, he's sobbing to sad, old punk songs with his best friend, a Chihuahua named Darla. He lives in Nashville with his husband. *I'm a Gay Wizard* is his first novel.

wattpad

Where stories live.

Discover millions of stories created by diverse writers from around the globe.

Download the app or visit www.wattpad.com today.